She was everything a lady should be... until a pirate stormed her senses and a daring adventure stirred her...

D0456187

Claremont rose from the bed, taller than she remembered, all traces of both mockery and amusement erased from his face. "You don't need to read fiction, Miss Snow. You're living it. Despite your tender and hopelessly romantic fantasies, this fellow Doom is a desperate, ruthless bastard who has nothing left to lose and everything to gain."

"You speak as if you know him."

"I know many like him. It's unavoidable in my profession." For the first time since she'd known him, Claremont's speech was underscored by the harsh cadences of the London streets. "And not one out of the bloody lot of them would let some lonely brat—"

Stung by his unfairness, Lucy cried, "But I'm not—"

His next words robbed her of her defense. "—no matter how breathtakingly beautiful, stand in the way of what they wanted." Claremont caught her chin in an implacable grip. "If your path ever crosses Doom's again, God forbid, don't make the mistake of underestimating him. He might not be such a gentleman."

Lucy blinked back tears. "So you think me a sentimental fool?" she whispered.

His grip softened. His palm wandered up to smooth a wing of damp hair from her cheek. Her breath caught at his scorching tenderness. "On the contrary, my dear Lucy. I think your noble Captain Doom a fool. If I had a woman such as you at my mercy, I'd never let her go. . . ."

THIEF OF HEARTS

♥ ♥ ♥ ♥ ♥ ♥ ♥ ♥ ♥ ♥ ♥ ♥

Bantam Books by Teresa Medeiros

A WHISPER OF ROSES
ONCE AN ANGEL
HEATHER AND VELVET
THIEF OF HEARTS

THIEF OF HEARTS

Teresa Medeiros

BANTAM BOOKS
NEW YORK LONDON TORONTO SYDNEY AUCKLAND

THIEF OF HEARTS

A Bantam Book / October 1994

ISBN 0-553-56332-7

Published simultaneously in the United States and Canada

Bantam Books are published by Bantam Books, a division of Bantam Doubleday Dell Publishing Group, Inc. Its trademark, consisting of the words "Bantam Books" and the portrayal of a rooster, is Registered in U.S. Patent and Trademark Office and in other countries. Marca Registrada. Bantam Books, 1540 Broadway, New York, New York 10036.

PRINTED IN THE UNITED STATES OF AMERICA

RAD   0 9 8 7 6 5 4 3 2 1

For Rebecca Hagan Lee and Elizabeth Bevarly. *Just when I thought I was too old to make friends like you, there you were*

To Tim and Cindy Noel for loving Terri instead of Teresa

To Doris Knight, for being there when it counted most

And for the captain of my own heart, the most uncommon man I know—my husband, Michael

PROLOGUE

London
1780

HIS MOTHER'S SCREAM SLICED THROUGH
the fabric of the night.

Its agonized timbre went unheeded amidst the rattling cart wheels, bawling street vendors, cooing prostitutes, and clamor of voices outside the narrow crib.
The boy crouched beside a pile of quilts and pressed a
rusted dipper against his mother's lips. Brackish water
trickled down her chin.

"There now, Ma. Try to drink a bit," he urged.

As she attempted a feeble swallow, the boy's nervous gaze flicked to her distended abdomen. Its
bloated contours were an obscene contrast to her flac-
cid skin and prominent ribs.

She was too old to be having this baby, he thought
frantically. Nearly a month past twenty-eight. Her fingernails dug into his knuckles as another bout of agony

seized her. The dipper slid from his hand. He clenched his teeth against his own cry of pain and held fast to her hands, fighting the despairing litany that drowned out even her screams. *Too old. Too thin. Too poor.*

Her fingers slowly relaxed as she lapsed into exhausted stupor. Her silence frightened him more than her screams. It was as if she'd surrendered her last pathetic hope of relief. He was reaching to shake her awake when the door behind him burst open.

A man stumbled in, his rumpled uniform marking him as a sailor. "Molly!" he bellowed, his breath reeking of gin. "Where's my pretty girl?"

The boy leaped to his feet. "Out, damn y'! Y've no right to burst in here like y' own the bloody place!"

The boy was shocked by his own virulence. The man might even be the father of this child, he thought, before realizing bitterly that it could be any one of a dozen men.

The sailor blinked stupidly at him, more addled by gin than given to petty cruelty. "Damn your insolence, whelp! I been at sea for ten months without so much as a kiss from a comely chit." He lifted his fist to cuff the boy out of the way. "No need to be jealous, lad. There's ample room 'tween thighs as willin' as Molly's."

Futile rage tinged the boy's vision with scarlet. Without even realizing the gravity of what he was doing, he snatched up the paring knife his mother had laid out to cut the baby's cord. His ears roared with the remembered grunts and groans of all the men his mother had bedded to put bread in his mouth.

He brandished the knife like a sword. "Out of here, mate," he said softly, "before I carve y' a new gullet."

The sailor lowered his fist, sobered by the unflinching light in the boy's eyes. He'd sailed in the Royal Navy for over twenty years as an able seaman, thumbing his nose at the death-spewing cannons of both pirates and Frenchies, but now his nostrils twitched as if he could already scent his own spilled blood.

Before he could retreat, a hoarse whimper, more animal than human, arose from the shadows behind the boy. The lad spun around and dropped to his knees beside the tattered quilts. The sailor peered over his narrow shoulders, catching a glimpse of sunken cheeks, stark eyes, and the tortured contractions of a swollen abdomen.

His stomach rebelled. Most of his mates were eager to spill their seed, but only too happy to be at full sail when it took root. He clapped a hand over his mouth and stumbled out of the hovel, knowing with a sailor's instinct that he had witnessed not only impending birth, but impending death.

"The babe's comin', lad," Molly whispered through cracked lips.

The intruder forgotten, the boy fumbled with the things she had commanded he fetch. A basin of cloudy water. A nest of rags. A length of dirty twine. Swallowing his fear, he drew back the sheet that covered her legs.

She arched off the quilts and bit her bottom lip until it pearled with blood, but she did not make another sound until the tiny creature spilled into her son's waiting hands. A groan of pure relief broke from her throat.

The boy followed her whispered instructions, refusing to look at the cause of her pain, already hating it for what it would cost him. He swaddled it in the rags, then laid it in the crook of her arm.

As she gazed into her baby's face, the echo of a smile trembled on her lips, giving her son a heartbreaking glimpse of the beauty that must have once enchanted his father.

When he would have turned away from the sight, she clutched his arm, searching his fine features as avidly as she had searched the babe's. "Y're a good boy, son. Just like y'r pa. Don't ever forget it."

He closed his eyes against the bittersweet refrain. If his pa was so fine, why had he left them for the sea? Why had he chosen her salty grave over the adoration of a wife who would have waited forever for his return?

A wisp of a sigh rose from the quilt. He lifted his head to find his mother's eyes as barren as his hopes. A burning knot tightened in his throat. He leaned over and kissed her cool brow.

"Night, Ma," he whispered, gently closing her eyes.

The alien creature was beginning to squirm in her limp arm. The boy eyed it with distaste, then reluctantly reached for it as he knew his mother would have wished. *It*. He refused to think of it as anything else. As he drew it toward his chest, his trembling legs folded beneath the weight of responsibility.

He would have to find a girl to nurse it. He should have no trouble there. Births were as common as deaths in this twisting warren of alleys. His disgruntled gaze lingered on the thing's face. He supposed he should wash it. It was dirty, but when had anything clean ever come from this place? It would be coughing up soot like the rest of them soon enough.

He stroked a finger down the babe's cheek, marveling that anything so chubby had emerged from his mother's wasted flesh. Their gazes met, the baby's unfocused, his sullen. Curiosity overcame his disgust and he unwound the rags.

Amazed at the miniature perfection, he felt his lips twitch in bemusement. "Well, lad, it seems y've got all the right equipment."

Lad. Boy. Brother.

His brother. A wave of protectiveness crested in him as his arms tightened around the tiny bundle. The poor creature had no mother. Tears of grief welled in his eyes; he dashed them away. At least he'd had a pa to give him a name. This little bugger had no one. No one but him.

From outside the crib, a roar of drunken laughter mocked his fresh emotions. He couldn't bear another moment trapped with the empty shell that had been his mother. Cradling the baby awkwardly against his chest, he rose and ducked into the chaos of the night.

No one paid him any heed as he rushed down the cobbled alley, blindly seeking the one place where he might wash the stench of birth and death from his nostrils. The graceful spars of the docked ships soared into the night sky, drawing him like a beacon.

Was this what had drawn his father? he wondered, dropping to his knees on the rough planking. The siren song of the waves lapping gently at the pilings?

He knew what he had to do. He had to take his brother away from here. To a place where the scent of the sea wasn't befouled by the oily stench of the river.

He drew back the rags to gaze into the puckish face God had entrusted to his care. "I'll take y' away, lad," he whispered. "I swear I'll find a place where we both can breathe."

His little brother's flailing fist struck him square in the nose. The boy threw back his head and laughed, his misgivings tempered by a fierce surge of joy.

PART ONE

Be thou as chaste as ice, as pure
as snow, thou shalt not escape
calumny.

Beauty provoketh thieves sooner than gold.

WILLIAM SHAKESPEARE

CHAPTER ONE

"AYE, THERE'S SOME THAT SAYS HE'S THE ghost o' Captain Kidd come back from the dead to revenge hisself on those who betrayed him."

Lucy Snow peeked over the top of her book, finding the lure of such torrid gossip more irresistible than the modestly titled, self-published memoirs of *Lord Howell: Nautical Genius of the Century* her father had provided for her journey. The creeping shadows of twilight had made reading nearly impossible anyway.

Unaware of her scrutiny, the sailor leaned against a barrel, his ancient bones creaking in harmony with the deck of the *HMS Tiberius*. His audience consisted of a handful of sailors and a starry-eyed cabin boy. "None's ever seen him and lived to tell of it. Some say only a glance from his evil eye'll skewer you to the deck like a bolt o' lightning. Aye, bold and ruthless is Captain Doom."

Lucy sniffed back a derisive snort. *Captain Doom indeed.* This mythical pirate was beginning to sound like a character in one of the dreadful Gothic novels Lord Howell's flighty daughter Sylvie insisted on reading.

One young sailor was of like mind. Lucy wrinkled her nose as he spat a wad of tobacco on the freshly scrubbed deck of the modest frigate. "Balderdash! I heard the stories, too, but I says it's nothin' but rum talkin'. There ain't been true pirates in these waters for o'er seventy-five years." He tilted his hat to a cocky angle, underscoring the brashness of his youth. "We ain't livin' in lawless times like Captain Kidd. This bloke'd be more likely to get his timbers shivered by the Channel Fleet than not."

Knowing her father would not have approved either her eavesdropping or interrupting what was meant to be a private conversation, Lucy bit back an agreement. The war with France had lapsed into tentative truce with the Peace of Amiens, but the quieter the winds blew from Napoleon's burgeoning empire, the more nervous the Royal Navy became. This Captain Doom would have to be either foolhardy or foolish to put himself in their eager cannon sights.

"Not if he truly is a ghost," the cabin boy whispered, startling Lucy with his precise reply to her musings. "Then he'd have nothin' to lose. Nothin' at all."

Lucy shivered in spite of herself and huddled deeper into her shawl. *Now, Lucinda,* the Admiral admonished from perfect memory, *seafaring men are a superstitious lot, but you're not a girl given to fancy.* For once, his chiding voice brought comfort instead of humiliation.

A sailor in a worn peacoat drew a whalebone pipe

from his pocket. As he struck a match and touched it to the capped bowl, the flame cast wavering shadows over a face leathered by sun and salt spray. "I seen him," he announced curtly, earning all of their attentions, including Lucy's. "I was on lookout in the foretop on an eve much like this one. There weren't nothin' but sea and sky for miles, then suddenly the sea opened up and out she sailed like a demon ship cast from the bowels o' hell."

Lucy suspected her own eyes were now as round as the cabin boy's.

"I couldn't speak. I couldn't move. 'Twas as if the very sight o' her froze me blood. Before I could pry me mouth open to shout a warning, the sea swallowed her without so much as a billow. I never seen nothin' like it in all me born days." He shuddered. "Never hope to again."

A pall of silence enveloped the men, broken only by the eerie creaking of the spars and the lazy flapping of the sails against the wind. Full dusk had fallen as they spoke. Tendrils of mist came creeping out of the darkening sea like the tentacles of some mythical beast. Lucy saw one of the sailors glance over his shoulder and sign an unobtrusive cross on his breast. As if to banish the spell of foreboding, the men all began chattering at once.

"I heard he carves his mark on his victims just like the devil he is."

"Won't tolerate babblin'," they says. "The lass wouldn't stop screamin', so he up and sewed her lips together with sail twine."

"Cleaved the poor bloke in two, he did, with one mighty stroke of his cutlass."

The young sailor who had earlier dared to express scorn for the spectral captain wiggled his eyebrows in a mocking leer. "I'll wager that ain't nothin' compared to the cleavin' he does on his lady captives. One o' my mates swears this Captain Doom ravished ten virgins in one night."

"Ha!" scoffed a grizzled tar. "I done as much after seven months at sea and nary a glimpse o' stocking."

The young sailor elbowed him in the ribs. "Aye, but them weren't hardly virgins, was they?"

The men roared with laughter. Lucy reluctantly decided she'd best make her presence known before she learned more than she ever wanted to know about the romantic foibles of sailors. She extracted herself from her seat of coiled ropes and stepped into full view. The men snapped to flustered attention as if Admiral Sir Lucien Snow himself had marched onto the deck of the ship.

Lucy was not impressed. She'd been receiving such welcomes since she'd been old enough to toddle up the gangplank of a ship. Her father's reputation as one of the most revered admirals in His Majesty's Royal Navy had preceded her every step.

She favored them with a benevolent smile. "Good evening, gentlemen. I do hope I haven't interrupted your charming discourse on the merits of piracy." She nodded toward the young sailor, whose tanned skin had flushed a becoming peach. "Do go on, sir. I believe you were about to treat us to more of your speculations on Captain Doom's romantic exploits."

One of his mates cleared his throat meaningfully and the sailor snatched off his hat, crumpling it into a ball. "M-M-Miss Snow," he stammered. "Didn't know you were about. 'Twas hardly fit talk for a lady's ears."

"Then I suppose we'll have to string you up from the yardarm, won't we?"

The lad's Adam's apple bobbed with obvious distress and Lucy sighed. For some reason, no one could ever tell when she was joking. She knew that most of her acquaintances suspected she'd been born with no sense of humor at all. She was, however, blessed with a finely honed sense of the absurd.

The weathered sailor in the peacoat shoved his way forward as if fearing she might actually weave a noose of her delicate shawl. "Allow me to escort you to your cabin, Miss Snow. 'Tisn't safe for a young lady of quality to be roamin' 'bout the deck after dark."

He gallantly offered her his arm, but the patronizing note in his voice struck the wrong chord with Lucy.

"No, thank you," she said coolly. "I believe I shall take my chances with Captain Doom."

Tilting her nose to a regal angle, she sailed past them, ignoring the discordant murmur that rose behind her. Some perverse seed of rebellion drove her away from the narrow companionway leading to her cabin and toward the deserted stern.

She studied Lord Howell's memoirs for a moment, then tossed them over the aft rail into the churning froth of the ship's wake. The leather-bound book sank without a trace.

"Sorry, Sylvie," she whispered to her absent friend.

Since Lord Howell was an old friend of her father's, she suspected the Admiral had only recommended the book because of its flattering, if somewhat exaggerated, accounts of his own cunning exploits during the Americans' ill-mannered rebellion against England.

She wondered how her father was faring on his overland voyage. Since his untimely leg wound had forced him to retire from His Majesty's service six years ago, the Admiral had never missed a chance for a sea voyage, even one as tame as the journey from their summer home in Cornwall to their modest mansion in Chelsea on the bank of the Thames.

She drew her shawl close around her. True to its fickle nature, London society had spurned all things

French except for their fashions. The brisk wind blowing off the North Atlantic Sea whipped up Lucy's skirt and bit through her thin petticoat. But she could bear that discomfort better than being trapped in the stifling confines of her cabin, her fate decided by the whims of others. If she stayed on deck long enough, perhaps the Captain's half-deaf mother would retire for the evening and Lucy would be spared bellowing at her over the galley dining table.

Lucy usually found a ship by night soothing to her senses, but the peace she sought drifted just out of her reach, her solitude tainted by restlessness. Even the low-pitched music of male voices working in perfect accord seemed muted and distant.

She frowned, licking away the sea salt that flecked her lips. In the rising mist, sound should carry with the clarity of a ringing bell, but the night was draped in silence as if the sea were holding its breath with her. She strained her eyes, seeing nothing but fog swirling up from the inky darkness and the rising moon flirting with tattered patches of clouds.

Chill ribbons of mist coaxed their way through the gauzy muslin of her gown, dampening her bare skin with their greedy touch. The sailors' tales of Captain Doom haunted her. On such a night it took little imagination to envision a phantom ship stalking the seas in search of prey. Lucy could almost hear the chant of its betrayed sailors vowing vengeance, the hollow bong of a bell that would seal their doom.

She shook off a delicious shiver. She could only imagine what the Admiral would say if he caught her indulging in such whimsy.

She was turning away from the rail to seek the more mundane comforts of her cabin when the veil of darkness parted and the ghost ship glided into view.

Lucy's heart slammed into her rib cage, then

seemed to stop beating altogether. She clutched the rail, her shawl falling unheeded to the deck.

A glimmer of moonlight stole through the clouds as the sleek black bow of the phantom schooner crested the waves, its towering spars enshrouded by mist, its rigging glistening like the web of a deadly spider. Ebony sails billowed in the wind, whispering instead of flapping. The vessel sailed in eerie silence with no lanterns, no sign of life, no hint of mercy.

Lucy stood transfixed, mesmerized by a primitive thrill of fear. Although the wind whipped her hair across her face and fed the hungry sails of the phantom ship, she seemed to be standing in a vortex of airlessness. She couldn't think. Couldn't breathe. Couldn't scream.

It was then that she saw the ship's Jolly Roger rippling from the highest spar—a man's hand, ivory against a sable background, squeezing scarlet drops of blood from a captive heart. Her fist flew to her breast as she battled the absurd notion that it was *her* heart, no longer beating of its own will, but thundering in accord with the dark command of the ghost ship's master. If she was the only one to see the ship, then surely its grim message was meant for her.

The phantom ship came about with lethal grace. Remembering the sailor's story, Lucy pressed her eyes shut, knowing the ship would be gone when she opened them. A poignant sense of loss tightened her throat. There was no place in her neatly ordered life for such dark fantasy, yet the ship's unearthly beauty had touched some secret corner of her soul.

Cannonfire blazed against the night sky. Lucy's eyes flew open in shock as the ghost ship fired a very earthly warning shot over their bow in the universal demand for surrender.

CHAPTER
TWO

IN THAT FIRST DAZZLING BURST OF LIGHT, the name carved on the phantom ship's bow was forever emblazoned in Lucy's memory: *Retribution*.

Hoarse cries of alarm and the stampede of running feet shook the deck of the *Tiberius* as the panicked crew wavered between battle and surrender. Lucy was jerked from her openmouthed astonishment by a rough hand on her arm. The young sailor who had earlier jeered the mere existence of Captain Doom pulled her away from the rail with a familiarity he wouldn't have dared only moments before.

"You'd best take shelter in your cabin, miss. This looks to get ugly." His bold demeanor could not hide a complexion chalky with terror.

Lucy found herself dragged through the fray and shoved none too gently toward the main companionway. Obeying without thought, she flew down the narrow passage, thankful for once to be unencumbered by heavy skirts and petticoats. She slammed the door of her cabin behind her and whirled around in the middle of the floor.

A fresh salvo of cannonfire shuddered the hold. Lucy dropped to her knees and clapped her hands over her ears, choking back a frantic scream. As a child, she had once scampered into the garden only to plunge through an enormous spiderweb strung across the path. She had beat at the sticky fibers with her small hands, screaming in terror. She felt again that same helpless fear. She couldn't bear being trapped like an animal with no control over her fate.

She could still remember the Admiral's contemptuous words as he had watched her sniffle into Smythe's crisp waistcoat while the servant patiently plucked the tattered web from her hair. *Silly little chit. Given to hysteria just like her mother. French blood will tell every time.*

Lucy's hands curled into fists and fell away from her ears. Her back straightened. She was Lucinda Snow, daughter of Admiral Sir Lucien Snow, and she'd be damned if she'd let some ridiculous ghost pirate frighten her into hysterics.

Spurred to practical action, she rifled through her tidy valise, searching for anything that might serve as a weapon. An ivory-handled letter opener was her only find. She slipped off her shoes so she could move silently if the need arose and tucked the letter opener into one of her stockings. Then she grabbed the low-burning lantern and crouched down beside her rumpled bunk to wait.

A masculine bellow of terror and the thunder of running footsteps sounded overhead. Lucy gritted her teeth to keep them from chattering. The wire handle of the lantern bit into her palm. She knew the lantern was useless as a weapon. The dangers of fire aboard ship had been too deeply ingrained in her since childhood.

She would die a gruesome death before hurling the lantern at an attacker.

She feared that noble notion was about to be tested when the door to her cabin crashed inward and a hulking shape appeared in its place. Lucy killed the lantern's flame and squeezed her eyes shut in the childish hope that if she couldn't see the intruder, he wouldn't be able to see her either.

But all of her hopes, present and future, were smothered by the gag thrust into her mouth and the dank length of burlap tossed over her head.

♥   ♥   ♥

"Damn it to blasted hell!"

The oath rolled from Captain Doom's lips like the thunder of cannonfire. The deck listed beneath his long, furious strides, but he never stumbled, never faltered, his flawless balance as finely tuned as each of his other senses. Had any of his enemies seen him in that moment, they would have sworn lightning bolts actually could sizzle from his narrowed eyes.

"I can't believe you brought a woman on board." He swung past the dangling rigging with the natural swagger of a born sailor. "You know how superstitious Tam and Pudge are. They're liable to jump ship if they find out."

The ebony-skinned giant marching in his wake appeared unaffected by his captain's ire. Only someone who knew him well could have detected the sarcasm in his melodic bass voice. "Shall I fetch the cat-o'-nine-tails, sir, so you can flog me?"

"Don't tempt me," the Captain growled. "I should have left you to hang in Santo Domingo when I had the chance."

Doom ducked his head at the precise moment it would have struck the foreboom and folded his lean frame into the hold. His companion dropped after him, landing with a cat's lithe grace on the pads of his bare feet.

The Captain rubbed his beard in frustration. "Have you been at sea so long you didn't notice she was a bloody woman?"

"She squirmed more like a rat. She was soft in spots, but since the Admiral has retired, I thought he might have gone soft himself. Like a rotten peach."

"I do believe you've gone soft. In the head."

"The cabin was listed in the ship's log just as you said it would be—L-U-C-period-S-N-O-W."

Doom had never before been so tempted to curse his mate's gift of being both literate and literal. Steering his way through the shadowy hold, he shook his head in disgust. "If she's of any importance, we'll have the whole Channel Fleet down on our heads by dawn. Couldn't you even get a name out of her?"

"Sorry, sir. The iron maiden was occupied. Kevin was sleeping in it. Besides, you're the one with the reputation for terrorizing innocent maidens."

Doom shot him a dark look as they halted before a door bolted from the outside. "She's probably mute with terror already. You're enough to give any proper young English virgin nightmares."

As if in full agreement, his mate flashed his teeth in a dazzling smile, emphasizing the raven purity of his skin. His bald head had been polished to a sheen so bright the captain caught a glimpse of his own scowling reflection. There was no man Doom would rather have at his side during battle, but his composure in the face of such disaster made Doom want to choke him.

The Captain turned toward the door. With a gesture from another lifetime, long gone and best forgotten, he ran his fingers through his shaggy hair and smoothed his cambric shirt.

"Are you going to interrogate her or court her?" his companion rumbled.

"I haven't decided. Maybe neither. Maybe both." All traces of humor fled his face. The grim twist of his lips would have given even those most skeptical of his legend pause for reflection. "I'll do whatever it takes to find out why the morally upstanding Admiral Snow had a woman sequestered in his cabin."

With that vow, Doom lifted the makeshift bolt, unlocked the door, and slipped into the sumptuous confines of his own quarters.

♥ ♥ ♥

A child, was Doom's first horrified thought. His mate had stolen a little girl.

A rapid blink proved his perception flawed. Oddly enough, it wasn't his captive's size, but her stern demeanor that made her look no more than twelve years of age. She sat rigidly straight in the spartan chair as if having her ankles bound to its legs and her hands tied behind her were mere inconveniences to be tolerated like a pair of too-tight boots.

He had been dreading her hysteria, but the pale cheeks below the sable silk of the blindfold were free of tearstains. Her lips were pursed in a faintly bored expression as if she wished someone would happen by and offer her tea. Her transparent determination to ignore his presence both irritated and amused him.

His gaze raked her in blunt appraisal. His mate had taken no chances. The only thing unbound about her was her hair. It streamed down her back in a fall of ash-blond silk, unmarred by a single frivolous curl.

Doom scowled. The silly garment she wore troubled him. Had his mate dragged her out of her bunk? Surely fashions hadn't changed *that* much in six years. He remembered only too well when he'd been intimately acquainted with every lace, hook, and button of a woman's elaborate toilette.

His captive's high-waisted gown was shamelessly devoid of such restraints. The skirt of the gossamer sheath clung to her parted legs, the sheer petticoat beneath more enticement than hindrance. Silk stockings, the delicate blue of a robin's egg, enveloped her slender feet. The angle of her bound arms thrust her small breasts upward to strain against the thin fabric of her bodice. Doom's gaze lingered there of its own volition. His mate had been wrong. Her softness was not that of rotten peaches, but of fresh peaches. Ripe, tender peaches.

His too-long-deprived body surged at the image with a violence that made him ache. His captive might have the deceptive appearance of a child, but his response to her was definitely that of a man. Alarmed by the rapacious slant of his thoughts, Doom strode to the teakwood sideboard bolted to the cabin wall and attempted to douse the passions she'd ignited with a slug of brandy.

He wiped his mouth with the back of his hand, nursing the childish urge to punish her for his weakness. But the vulnerability of her posture gutted his anger, tinging it with contempt for what he was about to become.

He put the brandy glass aside, steeling himself to be as dispassionate and remorseless as his task required. There was no room for passion or pity in the black heart of Captain Doom. Especially if he was dealing with Lucien Snow's whore.

He moved to stand directly in front of her, hands locked at the small of his back and feet splayed, his silence a blatant challenge. He watched, secretly amused, as a flush of pink crept into the hollows beneath her elegant cheekbones. He would have almost sworn it was caused not by fear, but anger.

Lucy had known she was in trouble the moment this man entered the cabin. She had recognized in the space of a skipping heartbeat that he was not the same man who had abducted her, the man whose hands had been almost gentle as he apologized for frightening her, his voice melodious and soothing.

There was nothing soothing about this man. The very air around him crackled with threat. Lucy feared she was in the presence of Captain Doom himself, no phantom but flesh and blood—solid, disturbing, and only inches from her face.

Being deprived of vision had heightened her other senses. Her ears were tuned to the harsh whisper of air from his lungs. Her nostrils flared at the scent of him —an alluring brew of salt spray, brandy, and the pure spice of male musk. He smelled like the predator he was and she knew instinctively that if she allowed him to scent her fear, she was done for.

She was thankful her initial panic had been swallowed by outrage at being trussed up like a Christmas goose. When he had first entered the cabin, she had refrained from speaking for fear she would gibber in terror. Now she was simply too obstinate to be the first to break the taut silence.

Back straight, Lucinda, the Admiral snapped from memory. *Feet together like a little lady.*

But Lucy could not bring her feet together. They were bound to opposite chair legs, making her feel exposed, vulnerable, and in the wake of the Admiral's imaginary rebuke, deeply ashamed.

The stranger's gaze seared her cheeks, but she refused to avert her face from his scrutiny. Her jaw was beginning to ache from being clamped so hard. She could almost envision him standing arrogantly before her, his legs braced against the faint swell and dip of the cabin floor.

"Your name."

Lucy flinched as if he had struck her. His husky words were a demand, not a request. Had he claimed her soul with such merciless authority, she would have been equally as powerless to resist him.

"Lucinda Snow," she replied, her only defense the shards of ice dripping from her voice. "My friends call me Lucy, but I think under the circumstances, you'd do well to address me as Miss Snow."

Her captor was silent for several heartbeats, but his excitement was palpable. Gone was the barely repressed violence, replaced by a ferocious satisfaction she sensed might be even more dangerous to her.

"*Miss* Snow?" he finally said. "May I assume there's no Mr. Snow fretting over your untimely disappearance?"

His voice was both rough and smooth, like well-aged whiskey steeped in smoke. She suspected its raspy timbre was designed for disguise, but it still sent a shiver of raw reaction down her spine. She prayed he did not see it.

"*Admiral Sir* Snow is my father and I can assure you that when he finds out I've been abducted by brigands, he'll be a man given to action, not fretting."

"Ah, a worthy opponent." The contempt in his words chilled her.

His boot heels clicked in muted rhythm as he began to pace in a maddening circle around her chair. Not knowing exactly where he stood was even more disconcerting than having him glare at her. She couldn't shake the sensation that he was only biding his time, seeking her most vulnerable spot before he pounced for the kill.

Fear made her reckless. "I've heard enough about

your cowardly tactics, Captain Doom, to know your favored opponents are innocent children afraid of ghosts and helpless women."

A loose plank creaked behind her, startling her. If he had touched her then, she feared she would have burst into tears.

But it was only the mocking whisper of his breath that stirred her hair. "And which are you, Miss Snow? Innocent? Helpless? Or both?" When his provocative question met with stony silence, he resumed his pacing. " 'Tis customary to scream and weep when one is abducted by brigands, yet you've done neither. Why is that?"

Lucy didn't care to admit that she was afraid he'd embroider a skull and crossbones on her lips. "If I might have gained anything by screaming, you'd have left me gagged, wouldn't you? It's obvious by the motion of the deck that the ship is at full sail, precluding immediate rescue. And I've never found tears to be of any practical use."

"How rare." The note in his voice might have been one of mockery or genuine admiration. "Logic and intelligence wrapped up in such a pretty package. Tell me, is your father in the habit of allowing you to journey alone on a navy frigate? Young ladies of quality do not travel such a distance unchaperoned. Does he care so little for your reputation?"

Lucy almost blurted out that her father cared for nothing *but* her reputation, but to reveal such a painful truth to this probing stranger would have been like laying an old wound bare.

"The Captain's mother was traveling with us." Fat lot of good that had done her, Lucy thought. The senile old woman had probably slept through the attack. "The Captain of the *Tiberius* is a dear friend of my father's. He's known me since I was a child. I can promise you that should any of the men under his command so much as smile at me in what might be deemed an improper manner, he'd have them flogged."

"Purely for your entertainment, I'm sure."

Lucy winced at the unfair cut. "I fear my tastes in amusement don't run to torture as yours are rumored to," she replied sweetly.

"Touché, Miss Snow. Perhaps you're not so helpless after all. If we could only ascertain your innocence with such flair . . ."

He let the unspoken threat dangle and Lucy swallowed a retort. She couldn't seem to stop her tart tongue from running rampant. She'd do well to remember that this man held both her life and her virtue captive in his fickle hands.

His brisk footsteps circled her, weaving a dizzying spell as she struggled to follow his voice. "Perhaps you'd care to explain why your noble papa deprived himself of your charming wit for the duration of your voyage."

"Father took ill before we could leave Cornwall. A stomach grippe. He saw no logic in my forfeiting my passage, but feared travel by sea would only worsen his condition."

"How perceptive of him. It might have even proved fatal." He circled her again. "What provoked this timely bout of indigestion? Too much tea? A bad bit of kipper?"

Lucy shook her head. "I couldn't say. He was reading the *Times* over breakfast as he always does when he suddenly went white and excused himself. He told me later that he'd decided to travel by carriage."

Doom's clipped tones softened. His footsteps ceased just behind her. "So he sent you in his stead. Poor, sweet Lucy."

Lucy wasn't sure what jarred her most—the rueful note of empathy in his voice or hearing her Christian name caressed by his devilish tongue. "If you're going to murder me, do get on with it," she snapped. "You can eulogize me *after* I'm gone."

The chair vibrated as he closed his hands over its back. Lucy started as if he'd curled them around her bare throat. "Is that what they say about me, Miss Snow? That I'm a murderer?"

She pressed her eyes shut beneath the blindfold, beset by a curious mix of dread and anticipation. "Among other things."

"Such as?"

"A ghost," she whispered.

He leaned over her shoulder from behind and pressed his cheek to hers. The prickly softness of his beard chafed her tender skin. His masculine scent permeated her senses. "What say you, Lucy Snow? Am I spirit or man?"

There was nothing spectral about his touch. Its blatant virility set Lucy's raw nerves humming. She'd never been touched with such matter-of-fact intimacy by anyone. Smythe prided himself on maintaining the reserve of a servant and the Admiral found physical displays of fondness distasteful.

The odd little catch in her breath ruined her prim reply. "I sense very little of the spiritual about you, sir."

"And much of the carnal, no doubt."

His hand threaded through the fragile shield of her hair to find her neck. His warm fingers gently rubbed her nape as if to soothe away all of her fears and melt her defenses, leaving her totally vulnerable to him. Lucy shuddered, shaken by his tenderness, intrigued by his boldness, intoxicated by his brandy-heated breath against her ear.

"Tell me more of the nefarious doings of Captain Doom," he coaxed.

She drew in a shaky breath, fighting for any semblance of the steely poise she had always prided herself on. "They say you can skewer your enemies with a single glance."

"Quite flattering, but I fear I have to use more conventional means." His probing fingertips cut a tingling swath through the sensitive skin behind her ears. "Do go on."

Lucy's honesty betrayed her. "They say you've been known to ravish ten virgins in one night." As soon as the words were out, she cringed, wondering what had possessed her to confess such a shocking thing.

Instead of laughing as she expected, he framed her delicate jaw in his splayed fingers and tilted her head back.

His voice was both tender and solemn, mocking them both. "Ah, but then one scrawny virgin such as yourself would only whet my appetite."

"They also swear you won't abide babbling," Lucy blurted out, knowing she was doing just that. "That you'll sew up the lips of anyone who dares to defy you."

His breath grazed her lips. "What a waste that would be in your case. Especially when I can think of far more pleasurable ways to silence them."

Doom was treading dangerous waters. He'd known it from the moment he'd buried his fingers in the flaxen silk of the girl's hair, the moment he'd inhaled the lemon-scented purity of her skin. He'd clenched the chair back to keep from touching her, but his hands had acted with a stubborn will of their own. Now he could feel the warm waters of temptation closing over his head, making it impossible to breathe anything but her scent. Her mouth maddened him, its generous contours at odds with the chaste angles of her features.

It had been so long. Too long. He had sacrificed desire on the altar of his revenge as he had all other pleasures and emotions that might distract him from its consummation. How ironic that his first flush of victory should free that desire, render it more potent and enticing than the sweet assurance of vengeance trembling beneath his fingertips.

When the girl had confessed her identity, he'd been unable to believe his good fortune. His initial euphoria had been dampened by suspicion. It was simply too delicious to have the girl delivered so neatly into his hands. Did he run the risk of being ensnared by his own trap? he wondered. His intense scrutiny of Snow's past had failed to reveal information about a wife or a child. Was his captive truly Lucien Snow's daughter or only a clever decoy? Had Snow intended her as bait to flush him out of hiding or as some sort of sacrificial lamb? He knew of only one way to find out.

His thumbs caressed the fleecy velvet of her ear-lobes. Her skin was as soft as a lamb's, making him wonder if she would be that malleable everywhere he touched. She made him ache with need, tempted him to live up to his reputation for sensual ruthlessness. The teak and mahogany splendor of his stolen bed seemed to beckon him as he faced the dilemma of every man who has ever had a woman completely at his mercy.

He wouldn't have to hurt her, he assured himself. He could be gentle, persuasive. He would leave her with no bruises, no marks on her pretty skin, only haunting memories of a phantom lover who had possessed her in darkness and vanished at dawn.

"Please," she whispered as if she could divine the dangerous direction of his thoughts.

"Such charming manners," he murmured, thankful he could not see her eyes. He feared a sheen of tears in them might ruin all of his wicked intentions. "Tell me, Lucy, what do you plead so prettily for? Your life?" He wove his fingers through her hair, making her captivity absolute. "Or your soul?"

Her soft words surprised him. "Perhaps *your* soul, sir. It will be the one at stake if you commit some grievous sin."

His bitter laugh made her flinch and he immediately gentled his grip, stroking his fingertips across her brow. "Have you forgotten? I'm a dead man already, untroubled by qualms of conscience or soul."

"The soul is eternal, Captain. And I suspect yours isn't as black as you'd like me to believe. Yet."

Doom's gaze lingered on her lips. Generous, treacherous, tormenting him with the memory of a time when he had craved justice more than revenge. A time when he could still tell the difference.

If he bedded this girl against her will, he'd be no better than his father, who had won his mother's love, then sailed away forever, taking the light in her eyes with him. No better than the nameless man who had gotten her with child and left her to die in squalor.

Frustration made his voice crisp. "Your concern for my soul is touching, Miss Snow, but if I'd have wanted a sermon, I'd have abducted a priest. I should have skipped the blindfold and gagged you instead."

Doom suspected her eyes might prove to be as great a hazard to his dormant conscience as her lips. Those lips were parted now, gone slack beneath the probing ministrations of his fingertips. She was as responsive as a kitten to his practiced touch, making him wonder how she would respond if he pressed his suit, how she might move beneath him, what sort of soft, broken sounds she would make.

He swore under his breath. He might deny himself the bounty of her body, but he'd be damned if he was going to forfeit a taste of her luscious mouth. He leaned over and gently rubbed his lips against hers, feeling their sensitive contours ignite like dry tinder beneath an unquenchable flame. His tongue traced their tantalizing softness, priming them for his tender invasion.

A fist pounded the door. "Seventy-four-gunner approaching from the north, Captain." The imperturbable calmness of his mate's voice only underscored the terrible urgency of his message. "Channel Fleet, sir. Flagship *Argonaut*."

CHAPTER THREE

DOOM STRAIGHTENED, BITING OFF AN oath. He gazed down at the girl's treacherous lips, still parted and glazed with the mist of his folly. He regretted keenly that there was no time to find out if she was half as skilled a whore as she was an actress.

He cursed himself for nibbling at the succulent bait, giving Lucien Snow all the time he needed to hook him with the Channel Fleet. For one black moment he was tempted to surrender his last shred of decency and swallow her whole so he'd at least have a shuddering spasm of ecstasy to compensate him for his trouble. But as he gazed down at her trembling lips, one question nagged at him.

What if he was wrong?

What if the *Retribution* had simply blundered into the *Argonaut*'s course? What if the girl had never been intended as bait?

What if she were innocent?

Either way, he could hardly afford to indulge his ravenous appetites while his ship waged open warfare on one of the Royal Navy's seventy-four-gun flagships. The *Tiberius,* primarily an escort vessel, had been easy prey, surrendering without a fight. The *Argonaut* would not succumb so readily to his forced seduction.

"Shorten the sails and heave to," he commanded.

His mate had never before questioned an order. There was puzzled silence from the other side of the door, then a hesitant "Aye, sir," before his stealthy footsteps moved away.

Counting on the elements of mist and mystery to buy him time, Doom drew a knife from his pocket and knelt to saw at the girl's bonds.

Lucy flinched, jerked out of her sensual daze by the burn of cold steel against her skin. Her lips still tingled from their brief, tantalizing brush with sweet disaster.

Doom wielded the knife with expert skill. The muscular breadth of his shoulders brushed her inner thighs as he squatted between her knees. His warm fingers encircled her ankle, bracing it so he could slice away the ropes.

He paused briefly to rub circulation back into her chafed wrists. "It seems we're about to entertain uninvited guests. Friends of yours?"

She snatched in a shaky breath. "No, but I suspect them to be enemies of yours."

"Who isn't?" The weary resignation in his voice disturbed Lucy more than she would have cared to admit.

He jerked her up, but her numb feet refused to support her. She collided clumsily with his chest and he was forced to catch her around the waist to keep her from falling. They hung suspended in time, lips almost touching, breath mingling, bodies meshed in a dangerous harmony that rocked Lucy's staid world to its foundations.

Possessed by a compulsion beyond the restraints of

caution, her hand crept blindly upward to explore the forbidden planes of his face. He drew in a sharp breath, but did not stop her. Her fingertips brushed the rough silk of his beard.

The ship lurched as it came about, throwing her away from him.

Flung back to sanity by the creaking protestations of his vessel, Doom caught her by the arm, more roughly this time, and jerked her toward the cabin door.

Lucy had no choice but to stumble after him, her fate sealed by his unyielding grip. They raced through the belly of the hold, the walls brushing her shoulders at each tortuous twist and turn.

She gasped in surprise when Doom's strong hands closed around her waist and lifted. "Duck," he commanded, shoving her up and through a narrow opening.

She obeyed, having no way of knowing if she'd just avoided rapping her head or losing it. As she was cast from the shelter of the hold, wind gusted around her, plastering her gown to her body and making her teeth chatter. When Doom emerged behind her, she could not resist pressing herself against his solid warmth, thankful for once that he was more substance than spirit.

Fresh shivers raked her as his arms enfolded her from behind. "Silly chit," he muttered into her hair. "Girl as smart as you should know better than to get kidnapped in your nightdress."

Puzzled, Lucy opened her mouth to ask him what he meant calling her perfectly respectable gown a nightdress, but he had already grabbed her hand and was dragging her toward another part of the ship. A strange exhilaration seized her. She felt as if she might race blindly at this man's side forever, into danger, into darkness, into the buffeting wind that snatched away her breath and whipped her hair across her cheeks.

Was this the wicked legacy of her mother, she wondered, the sinful weakness of the flesh the Admiral had always warned against? Or was it simply the surge of primitive excitement all sailors felt before storming into battle?

She tuned her ears to hear the *Retribution*'s crew preparing for conflict. She heard nothing but the ghostly wail of the wind and Doom's boots pounding along the deck.

"Your crew?" she dared to shout over the wind. "Where are they? I can't hear them."

"I fear you've caught us making do with a skeleton crew."

"Rather appropriate for a demon captain, is it not?"

Doom's sure steps faltered and Lucy stumbled into his back. Catching both of her hands, he dragged her beneath some sort of shelter where the wind whistled instead of roared, and collapsed against something solid. She realized with a shock that he was laughing.

His hand cupped her cheek with more tenderness than she would have believed possible. "Ah, Lucy, I do believe I'm going to miss you when you're gone."

A muffled shout carried across the water. Doom stiffened. Reversing positions, he shoved her to a crouch.

"Stay here," he commanded. "Don't move or make a sound. Not one step. Not one whisper." Then he was gone, leaving her shivering against the damp wood.

He was obviously a man accustomed to being obeyed. Such was his authority that Lucy cowered there for several minutes, head spinning and heart aching from his abrupt swings between tenderness and threat. Then his ominous words began to sink in.

I'm going to miss you when you're gone.

Her voice of logic, which sounded suspiciously like the Admiral's, whispered, *You've been abducted by a ruthless pirate, Lucy. Where might you be going?*

Cornwall? Chelsea? Heaven?

It made no difference how nice he smelled or how rich the timbre of his laughter. The man was going to murder her. And there she squatted, blind and passive, like a dull-witted mouse waiting patiently for the return of the tomcat who would devour her.

Stiffening with anger at her own stupidity, she reached up and dragged off the blindfold. The sea air stung her raw eyes. For a moment all she could see was more darkness, wavering through a veil of tears. She blinked them away to find herself tucked into the shadows beneath the foreboom.

A man stood less than three yards away, gripping the starboard rail, his broad back beneath its ivory shirt presented to her. Black breeches hugged his lean flanks, tapering into knee-high jackboots of polished leather. At the sight of him, Lucy's heart thundered so loudly she was afraid he might hear it.

Hidden from view by the billowing shadow of a sail, he was watching the *Argonaut* inch along beside them to investigate what must appear to be an abandoned vessel. The mighty cannons of the navy flagship dwarfed the graceful schooner, yet Doom held his ground with no sign of fear, his patience more dangerous than a lesser man's actions.

Lucy knew what she must do to save herself. Easing her fingers into her stocking, she drew out the letter opener, clenching the handle to keep it from sliding in her damp palm.

He was a murderer, she reminded herself. A thief. A merciless cutthroat. He'd been on the verge of ravishing her when the other ship had appeared, of proving her as weak and sensual a creature as her French mother had been. Doom turned away from the rail. A ray of moonlight pierced the racing clouds.

Lucy bit her lower lip, knowing if she caught even a glimpse of his face, she would be lost. But the fickle moon was her salvation and his downfall. It dipped behind a cloud, dimming until he was no more than a bearded shadow, striding boldly into her trap.

Gripping the letter opener in both hands, Lucy plunged it toward his heart.

She could not bear it. In that whisper of silence between one of his unsuspecting breaths and the next, she slammed her eyes shut, deflecting the blade to his shoulder.

Doom sucked in a breath through clenched teeth. Her hands empty, Lucy dared to open her eyes, but she could see nothing more than the steely gleam of his eyes as he glared down at her in disbelief.

"Why, you treacherous little witch! You stabbed me!"

He ripped the weapon from his flesh, then wrapped his other hand around her throat and drove her back against the foremast, pinning her there by flexing one powerful knee between her legs. His artful fingertips tasted every frantic beat of her pulse. He towered over her, the darkness flooded with the harsh rasp of his breathing and the heat of his fury.

Lucy had been wrong. This man wasn't going to send her to heaven; he was going to personally escort her to hell. The bloodstained blade in his hand caught an errant beam of moonlight.

I heard he carves his mark on his victims just like the devil he is.

Although dreading the bite of the blade into her tender cheek, she swallowed her terror and turned her face away.

Doom tangled his hand in the hair at her nape and

turned it back, his voice a strangled growl. "Why, I ought to—"

Without warning, his lips seized hers, his tongue ravishing her virgin mouth in a kiss so dark and full of power that her legs buckled beneath the force of it. Her hands fisted in his shirtfront, clinging as she melted against him in helpless surrender. Her world narrowed to the forbidden taste of his tongue plundering her mouth, the spicy musk of his scent flaring her nostrils, the unyielding press of his knee between her legs, making her ache and tingle in places she'd never even named. His warm blood soaked the flimsy bodice of her gown.

A disembodied voice floated down from the heavens. "*Argonaut*'s comin' about, Cap'n. We ain't got much time."

Doom tore himself away from her with a grunt of pain. Before Lucy could regain any semblance of reason, he had untangled her hands from his shirt and thrust her into the harsh arena of the open deck.

He advanced on her, swaying like a drunkard, letter opener in hand.

She backed away, feeling naked, exposed.

His shaggy hair whipped in the wind. The shadows of the rigging crisscrossed his bearded face, weaving a tantalizing latticework of truth and illusion.

"Give your father a message for me, Miss Snow," he shouted over the roar of the wind. "Tell him Captain Doom is coming to collect his debt."

He stalked her; she took another step backward.

"What do you want from me?" she screamed, her throat raw with fear.

"Surely you've heard of pirates making their victims walk the plank."

She nodded mutely. Her back came up against the

starboard rail. He leaned forward until their noses touched. "Well, I haven't any plank."

The letter opener clattered to the deck as he snatched her up by the shoulders and kissed her again —briefly, savagely—before shoving her over the rail and into the sea.

♥　♥　♥

Doom sank to his knees at the rail, losing the will to battle the strain of shock and pain now that the girl was gone.

"Cap'n!" Tam called from his lookout position at foretop. He lacked the seasoning of Doom's mate. His voice cracked with near hysteria. "Two ships comin' in battle formation at port. We'll be surrounded!"

Where the hell was Kevin? Doom wondered wildly. Still napping in the iron maiden? Sleeping off last night's debauchery, no doubt.

"Hold our position," he bellowed, peering down into the murky water.

Loss of blood must be making him mad. He couldn't believe he was risking the lives and freedom of his crew just to make sure the chit could swim. Kevin was supposed to be the gambler in the family.

"Cap'n!"

Doom ignored Tam's plaintive wail.

The girl was splashing around in feeble circles like a wounded turtle. Christ, he thought, was he going to have to rescue her himself? As he was hauling himself to his feet to do just that, she found her bearings and struck out with tidy strokes toward the nearest ship.

Doom narrowed his eyes, his last doubt that she was indeed Lucien Snow's daughter banished by her unfaltering instinct for self-preservation.

Tam's pleas had degenerated to mumbled Hail Marys, but still Doom waited. Garbed in that ridiculous wisp of white, the girl should be impossible to miss.

A cry penetrated the wind from the direction of the *Argonaut.* "Man overboard!"

"Now!" Doom shouted. "Get us the hell out of here!"

The trapdoors at the aft of the ship flew open, releasing clouds of billowing steam. The artificial mist shrouded the *Retribution,* disguising her intentions as the ebony silk of her sails unfurled to catch the brisk tail winds. She cut through the water toward the horizon, as sleek as a satin ribbon gliding through a woman's hair. Tam's whoop of joy heralded their success.

One of the *Argonaut's* sister ships fired a half-hearted shot, but was still too far away to give chase. The *Argonaut* herself had better things to do than pursue ghosts. Such as rescuing that charming little piece of flotsam he'd tossed into her path.

Grunting with exertion, Doom crawled to the capstan and collapsed on a pile of discarded rigging. He closed his eyes, wanting nothing more than to slink into the nearest darkened hole and lick his wounds, diverse though they might be. He'd survived five years in hell only to be nearly murdered by a prim young miss wielding a letter opener. Going light-headed with blood loss, he laughed, his head lolling back against the ropes.

"Hell, Captain, are you going to let Pudge sew you up or are you just going to sit here and bleed to death?"

Doom's head snapped up at his mate's approach. "You might wish I had when I'm through with you," he growled. "What sort of pirate are you? I can't believe you didn't search her for weapons."

The man squatted beside him, his huge hands surprisingly gentle as he pressed a cotton kerchief to the wound. "She looked harmless enough." Supporting Doom's wounded shoulder, his mate helped him to his feet.

Doom gazed off at the rapidly fading lanterns of the *Argonaut,* haunted by his brief glimpse of huge gray eyes fringed by charcoal lashes.

He pressed a hand flat over his chest. "Your mistake, man," he said softly. "The little wench damn near got my heart."

CHAPTER FOUR

London

"THE ABOMINABLE WRETCH!"

Lucy flinched as the Admiral's fist crashed down on the newspaper spread open on his writing desk.

"Captain Doom again, Father?" she murmured, resting her paintbrush on the rim of the water jar to hide the sudden trembling of her hands.

"Who else? Just listen to what the scoundrel's done now." Ignoring his brass-handled cane as he often did when incensed, the Admiral rose to pace the drawing room, crumpling the hapless *Gazette* between his fists. " 'After bringing the *HMS Lothario* sharply to heel,' " he read, " 'the cunning captain not only stripped the ship of her booty, but her crew of their uniforms as well.' Cunning captain indeed! The man may be cunning, but he's no captain. He's a pirate! A pox on decent seafaring men! How dare the press try to paint him as some sort of colorful scoundrel!"

Lucy smiled behind her easel to envision those bastions of nautical dignity reduced to shivering in their flannel drawers. "That is what the newspapers pay them for."

He tossed down the paper in disgust. "I can assure you it costs far more to keep them quiet. If I hadn't lined their pockets with gold, they would have turned your own encounter with the brigand into some sort of romantic escapade. You would have been ruined."

Lucy's smile faded. Her father of all people should know she hadn't been "ruined." As if believing her too harebrained to understand his tactless questions after her fortuitous rescue by the Channel patrol, he had insisted on having her examined by his personal physician. Over a month had passed since then, but the memory of those cool, impersonal hands on her still made Lucy shudder.

Her father mistook her shiver for one of fear. "No need for hysterics, girl," he barked, startling her into dropping her paintbrush. "That rapscallion will never lay his hands on you again."

Lucy rescued the brush and swirled misty fingers of blue through the crystalline water, remembering that dark interval when her fate had rested entirely in Doom's implacable hands. They were all she had really known of him. Ruthless. Tender. Mocking. Stroking her nape. Cupping her cheek. Threading through her hair to hold her captive to his will.

Jerking herself out of her reverie, she tapped the paintbrush on the side of the jar, making the glass ring. "I have nothing to fear from Captain Doom, Father. He swore he was coming to collect his debts from you, not me."

He grunted skeptically. "So you say."

Avoiding his eyes, Lucy dabbed fluffy whitecaps on another of the seascapes her father adored, hoping he'd be pleased with the results. She'd never been able to hide anything from him. Even as a little girl, she'd often confessed her rare moments of mischief before they'd been discovered rather than risk even a hint of his reproach.

Yet she'd hoarded stolen moments of her encounter with Doom, fearing her father's scrutiny would twist them into something monstrous and shameful.

Even now, his sharp eyes were assessing her as if it were she, and not Doom, who was the criminal. "You're absolutely certain the wretch gave you no reason for his personal grudge against me? Spewed forth no accusations? Cast no slur upon my good name?"

Sighing, Lucy packed up her easel, resigning herself to yet another grueling interrogation where she would be forced to repeat every word and nuance culled from her encounter with the pirate. Almost.

She was saved by the appearance of Smythe in the vaulted archway. Her father disdained the gentry's habit of adorning their servants in livery, preferring the military simplicity of cropped blue naval jacket and starched white knee breeches. Since Smythe had spent his youth as the Admiral's chief petty officer before retiring to household service, the ensemble suited him. It was impossible to determine the butler's age from his appearance. His dark hair was thickly salted with silver, yet his form was as trim and dapper as a much younger man's.

He clicked his booted heels and gave her father a smart salute. "A Mr. Benson to see you, sir."

The Admiral drew a compass and an astrolabe from his waistcoat pocket before finally locating his trusty chronometer, missing the amused wink Smythe shot Lucy before he exited.

"Twelve hundred hours on the dot," the Admiral proclaimed. "Excellent! If there's anything I can't abide in a solicitor, it's tardiness. The applicants should be fast on his heels."

"Applicants?" Lucy echoed.

This time her father swept up the *Gazette* with triumph instead of disgust. He tossed it into her lap, stabbing his ruddy finger at the open page.

" 'Wanted,' " she read. " 'Reputable male skilled in art of protection. Military experience preferred. All inquiries to be directed to Heronius Benson, Esquire.' "

Before she could absorb the words, Mr. Heronius Benson himself strode into the drawing room and pumped her father's extended hand. "Such a pleasure, Admiral. It's not every day a man has the privilege of meeting a living legend."

"I should say not," the Admiral agreed jovially.

Lucy frowned at the newspaper as the men exchanged jocular small talk. Doom's threat must have spooked her father more than she realized. She'd never known Lucien Snow to hide behind any man.

Declining the glass of sherry the Admiral offered, Mr. Benson settled into a wing chair of burgundy leather. He nervously smoothed his few remaining tufts of hair over his shiny pate. "My associate has spent the past week interviewing prospects. He's promised to send over only the best of the lot."

Rapid footsteps thudded toward the archway. Smythe's clipped voice rang out. "I say, young man, get back here this instant!"

Astonished, Lucy dropped the paper. She'd never heard Smythe's voice raised above its beautifully modulated baritone. Even more shocking was the sight of the staid butler sliding around the corner, his boots vainly seeking purchase on the polished parquet. His knuckles were curled in the collar of a young man straining against his grip.

The Admiral rose, his rigid posture making him tower over the low-slung writing desk. He despised a hubbub of any sort unless he was the direct cause of it.

Smythe avoided his icy glare. "Sorry, sir. He got past me."

The Admiral's contemptuous gaze raked the flailing pup. "If you've come to make a delivery, lad, I suggest you use the servant's entrance."

Smythe's captive renewed his struggles, wiggling so fiercely that the butler was forced to free him or risk unraveling the remaining shreds of his dignity.

Shooting Smythe a triumphant look, the lad snatched off his battered cap. His freckled face had been scrubbed clean, but Lucy wagered she could have guessed his age by counting the layers of dirt around his neck.

"I ain't no servant, sir. At least not yet. I come about the position."

Lucy cringed with empathy at the boy's crude brogue. The only thing her father hated worse than a Frenchman was an Irishman. The overgrown urchin favored her with such a beguiling grin that she could not help smiling shyly back.

"Lucinda!" her father snapped. "Don't encourage the whelp!"

"I'm sorry, Father." Cheeks flaming, she gazed at the half-finished seascape, wishing she could dive into the cool blues and grays and disappear.

The Admiral sank into his chair, cracking his bulbous knuckles. "Very well. You're dismissed."

Grateful for the reprieve, Lucy rose to go.

"Not you," he snapped. She hastily sat as he jerked his head toward the young Irishman. "Him."

The boy lunged forward, but Smythe already had him collared. "Don't be so hasty, sir," the boy pleaded. "I can scrap with the best of 'em. I'm small, but wiry."

"As am I, lad," Smythe said, plainly savoring the taste of victory as he dragged the interloper from the room.

The creak of the main door opening was followed by the muffled thumps of a body rolling down the front stairs. Lucy could almost see Smythe dusting off his immaculate hands.

Benson squirmed in his chair, but the Admiral pinned him into stillness with nothing more than an arch of one snowy eyebrow. Lucy busied herself with capping her paints, thankful that for once she wasn't the recipient of that withering glare.

Even the sparse tufts of the solicitor's hair seemed to wilt beneath its chill as the Admiral echoed ominously, "The best of the lot, eh?"

♥　♥　♥

The Admiral's words were to prove prophetic as the long afternoon wore on. The brash Irish youth, if not the most qualified, was without a doubt the cleanest of the lot. Lucy had never seen such a motley collection of men. None of them could have borne more than a passing acquaintance with soap or water.

An Oriental gentleman, who insisted on favoring them with a demonstration of his fighting skills, earned her father's blistering dismissal by accidentally shattering the Admiral's favorite bust of Captain Cook. A towering fellow, who shyly confessed his only experience with the criminal element lay in his many years as a pickpocket, was forcibly ejected by two footmen after Smythe caught him pilfering silver spoons from the tea tray.

After the footpad's abrupt departure, Mr. Benson sank lower and lower into his chair until it seemed he might vanish altogether. His damp hair clung to his pate in defeated strands. The chronometer ticked away the minutes with ruthless efficiency as the Admiral lit a pipe and hunched behind the writing desk, puffing out billows of smoke like an angry dragon.

Lulled into near stupor by the potent combination of the fragrant smoke and the warmth of the autumn sun beating through the bay windows, Lucy was nodding over her cold tea when Smythe once again appeared in the doorway. His voice seemed to come from a great distance.

"A Mr. Claremont to see you, sir."

Lucy frowned without opening her eyes. Was it her imagination or had Smythe lingered over the name as if it left a taste of foreboding in his mouth?

The Admiral's voice dripped resigned contempt. "Send him in. He's probably an escaped murderer or Captain Doom himself come to kill us all and put an end to this ridiculous farce."

She heard Mr. Benson shift as if preparing to bolt. Spurred more by boredom than genuine curiosity, Lucy opened her eyes to lazy slits and peered through the haze of smoke to find a man standing beneath the archway.

A rather ordinary man, she thought sleepily. Her leisurely gaze drifted downward from his brown cloth cutaway tailcoat to the clinging doeskin pantaloons tucked into short leather boots. His garments were simple, but clean and neatly pressed. Even Smythe, who hovered in the doorway, eavesdropping shamelessly, would be loath to find fault with the crease in his trousers. His boots, though unfashionably scuffed, showed evidence of a recent buffing.

At the appearance of this model of presentability, Mr. Benson perked up, sniffing at the air like a hound on the scent of a fox.

The man was lean of hip and long of leg, but the

breadth of his shoulders lent him an imposing air. He moved past Lucy's corner with casual grace to approach the writing desk. A whiff of bayberry shaving soap made her nose tingle.

Oddly relieved that she'd escaped his notice, Lucy continued to study him. A pair of steel-framed temple spectacles perched on his nose. He drew off his hat. His neatly clipped hair just brushed his nape. Ordinary hair, she echoed. The shadows had painted it an innocuous shade of brown, but a persistent ray of sunlight sought and found in its depths a ripe hint of ginger.

He offered the Admiral a tentative hand. "Gerard Claremont, sir, at your service. Or at least I hope to be."

There was nothing ordinary about that voice. Its drawled cadences poured over Lucy, stirring her dormant senses like a forbidden swallow of Jamaican rum —rich, dark, and sparkling.

"So you've come about the position, have you?" The Admiral ignored the man's outstretched hand.

Mr. Claremont tactfully withdrew it, using it instead to shape the wide brim of his tan-crowned hat. Lucy's gaze was drawn to his hands. Their backs, too, were sprinkled with crisp ginger. "I have."

"Speak up, lad. I've no tolerance for mumblers."

Claremont met his gaze squarely. "I have," he repeated, his voice ringing with clarity. "And I've brought references."

The Admiral grunted skeptically and held out his hand. Ignoring it, Claremont drew a brown envelope from his coat and tossed it on the desk. Lucy held her breath, waiting for her father to dress the man down for his deliberate insolence.

The Admiral studied Claremont from crown to boots, lips pursed, before shaking his head. Lucy was surprised to see an admiring gleam burnish his eyes.

Claremont waited patiently as the Admiral pawed through his desk drawers, muttering loudly beneath his breath. "Damned careless girl. Lost my favorite letter opener. Ivory-handled. Shot the elephant myself during my last African jaunt."

Lucy sank deeper into the corner. She'd neglected to tell her father that she'd used his precious letter opener to stab Captain Doom. Not even his forgiveness would have been worth reliving that grim moment.

She gasped as an object appeared in Claremont's hand. Not a letter opener, but a knife, its lethal blade glinting in the sunlight only inches from her father's face. Mr. Benson beamed openly at the man's bold display of dexterity.

Claremont wryly lifted an eyebrow, toeing the line between respect and mockery with a dancer's uncanny grace. "May I, sir?"

The Admiral raised both hands in surrender. "Be my guest."

Claremont slit open the envelope. The knife disappeared back where it had come from while Lucy's father perused his references.

He shot Claremont an approving look. "Former Bow Street Runner, eh? Admirable calling. Done a lot to make the streets of London safer. Don't suppose you've had any military experience? Army perhaps?" Then more hopefully. "Merchant marines? Royal Navy?"

Claremont threw back his head and laughed. Dazzled by the warm, rich sound, Lucy tried to remember if she'd ever heard anyone laugh in that room before. If she'd ever heard anyone laugh at all before.

"I'm afraid not, sir," he confessed, the very picture of sheepish charm. "I fear I'm prone to seasickness." He flattened his palms on the desk and favored her father with a conspiratorial whisper audible throughout the drawing room. "Why, just walking into this house almost made me ill."

Lucy could see why. Her father had christened the house Ionia after the infamous sea where Rome's naval supremacy over the world had first been established. He'd proceeded to decorate nearly every inch of it in the nautical style. Even after living here for most of her nineteen years, Lucy still expected the polished wood flooring to list beneath her feet.

The steering wheel from the Admiral's first command, the *HMS Evangeline,* hung proudly over the mantel. Every piece of furniture was dark and heavy, polished oak or mahogany chosen for its utilitarian nature rather than for its beauty. There were no Oriental rugs, no vases of fresh cut flowers, no frivolous knickknacks to mar the overwhelmingly masculine effect. Instead there were globes, compasses, maps, sextants, Lucy's own watercolor seascapes, and glowering busts of her father's seafaring heroes.

The gloom of the furnishings was offset by the airiness of the spacious rooms and the sunlight that poured through the generous bay windows. Their lead-glazed panes overlooked a sea of clipped lawn that had begun to trade its billows of summer green for the golds and russets of autumn.

At Claremont's confession, Benson's smile deflated. Fighting her own inbred flare of disdain, Lucy braced herself for her father's scathing denouncement. She did not relish the idea of this bold soul being reduced to scampering away with his coattails between his legs.

The Admiral sighed. "Just as well, I suppose. I've no plans of taking to the sea until that rogue Doom is caught and hanged. You're hired."

This time the Admiral took the hand Claremont offered him. "You shan't regret it, sir. I'll do everything in my power to keep you safe. Even if it costs me my own life."

"Such sacrifices won't be required, Mr. Claremont. It won't be my life you're responsible for, only my daughter's."

Lucy was still reeling from her father's matter-of-fact announcement when Claremont pivoted on his heel, his gaze finding her with such unerring accuracy that she realized he'd been conscious of her presence from the moment he entered the room.

She stiffened to find his hazel eyes narrowed in flagrant dislike.

CHAPTER FIVE

DISLIKE WAS TOO MILD A WORD. GERARD Claremont loathed her.

Lucy knew she wasn't particularly likable. She didn't possess Sylvie Howell's dimpled charm or even her father's jovial bluster, but she couldn't fathom what she'd done to earn this man's contempt. As he approached through the lingering haze of sunlight and smoke, she was jarred by a disturbing sense of recognition.

The sun glinted off his spectacles, hiding his eyes and making her wonder if she hadn't been cursed with her mother's vivid imagination after all. She hadn't thought him a very large man, but he seemed to tower over her. He reached down and captured her hand. For a disconcerting instant, she thought he was going to bring it to his lips. But he simply enfolded it in his palm in a perfectly respectable gesture of greeting.

"Forgive my negligence," he murmured. "I had no idea my charge was to be such a charming one."

Nor was he pleased by the discovery, Lucy deduced, unnerved by the possessive warmth of his fingers. Her sluggish mouth refused to so much as stammer a response.

"Lucinda!" her father snapped. Lucy shot to attention as if someone had lit a charge beneath her chair. The familiar volley rumbled off the Admiral's tongue. "Have you forgotten your manners, girl? Back straight. Head up. Knees together." He rolled his eyes in one of his droll asides to the ear of God. "Heaven knows if your mother had done the same, it would have spared us all a great deal of scandal."

Drawing the frosty veil of her dignity around her, she inclined her head. "How do you do, Mr. Claremont. Lucinda Snow. My—"

"Why, I'll wager your friends call you Lucy," he cheerfully interrupted. He cocked his head to one side and his eyes reappeared behind his spectacles, twinkling with humor.

Lucy coolly withdrew her hand. "Some do. You, sir, however, may address me as Miss Snow."

"I'd be honored." His crisp bow implied the opposite. His bold gaze mocked her, offering none of the deference she had come to expect from both servants and her father's subordinates.

The mannerless clod hadn't even the decency to excuse himself before presenting his broad back to her. Lucy glared at it, silently seething. How could her father have hired such an odious man?

He waited, hat in hand, while the Admiral cut Mr. Benson a banker's draft of considerable worth before dismissing the delighted solicitor. At her father's gruff invitation, Claremont commandeered Benson's chair, stretching out his lean legs and crossing his booted feet at the ankle. The Admiral poured two glasses of sherry from the mahogany sideboard.

Claremont took a glass from her father's hand.

"Your solicitor tells me you've made quite an enemy of this Doom fellow. Have you any idea why he bears you such animosity?"

"A man of my rank who has served his country so long and so faithfully is bound to have trod upon a few criminal toes." The Admiral took a grudging sip of his own sherry. " 'Tis my theory the scoundrel is French. God knows I've been fighting the French for half my life. When I wasn't fighting those ungrateful Colonials, that is."

"But, Father, I told you the man hadn't even a trace of accent—"

"Hush, Lucinda. If I'd have wanted your opinion, I'd have solicited it." He waved an impatient hand in her direction, relegating her to the same importance as the potted fern in the opposite corner.

Lucy subsided, knowing further argument would be futile. If she didn't curb her tongue, he wouldn't hesitate to remind her of the French blood lurking in her own veins.

Claremont tossed back his sherry in one swallow. "You'll have to forgive my confusion, sir, but your solicitor led me to believe I was to serve as *your* bodyguard. Have you any reason to suspect Doom or one of his minions might make an attempt on Miss Snow's life?"

"He's already abducted her once, hasn't he? That proves him to be the sort of scoundrel who would prey on an innocent young girl to achieve his own sinister ends. Lucy has also been privy to many covert military strategies while helping me gather material for my memoirs. Should she fall into Doom's hands again, it could bode ill for His Majesty's navy. I've found it necessary to prepare her for all eventualities. Lucinda, come."

Lucy sprang out of her seat to stand before the

desk, feeling the same helpless rush of love she always felt when the Admiral displayed her as his daughter.

"Explain to Mr. Claremont what you're to do should that nasty brigand kidnap you again."

She studied her kid slippers in a vain attempt to dodge Claremont's piercing gaze. "Resist giving him any information under torture and throw myself overboard at the nearest opportunity."

The Admiral reached across the desk and gave her hands a benevolent squeeze. "That's my girl."

Flushed with pride at the rare tribute, she returned to her seat as her father and Mr. Claremont began to discuss terms.

"Your monthly wages, of course, will include board and lodging," her father explained. "There's ample room in the servants' quarters belowstairs—"

"Won't do," Claremont said. Apparently the man had no qualms about interrupting her father either.

The Admiral's left eyebrow shot up a notch. "Do tell?"

"Of what use will I be to your daughter if I'm buried in the cellar? I'll require lodgings with an unhampered view of her window."

Lucy made a mental note to keep her drapes drawn at all times.

The Admiral grumbled beneath his breath for a moment before surrendering. "Suppose that can be arranged. There is the gatehouse. Though Fenster won't take kindly to being evicted."

"Unless this Fenster wants my job, I'm afraid I'll have to insist."

Lucy smothered a smile at a vision of the ancient coachman charging to her rescue.

"Very well," her father said. "You may begin your duties tomorrow. Smythe can provide you with a written copy of Lucinda's schedule. I've simplified it for her convenience. She is expected to rise promptly at oh six hundred and attend breakfast at oh eight hundred. She spends from oh nine hundred to eleven hundred hours in the library transcribing my memoirs."

"A fascinating endeavor, I'm sure."

Lucy frowned. Had that been a hint of sarcasm in Mr. Claremont's expressive voice? If it had, her father remained blissfully oblivious to it.

"Quite so. From eleven hundred thirty to thirteen hundred, she partakes of luncheon and is free to prepare for any social calls she is obligated to make that afternoon."

Was it Mr. Claremont's eyes or his spectacles that were beginning to glaze over? Lucy wondered.

"Barring any calls," her father droned on, "she takes tea at fifteen hundred and may dabble in her watercolors from sixteen hundred to seventeen hundred. She then dresses for dinner, which is served promptly at nineteen hundred hours. I am frequently absent in the evenings, advising the Admiralty Court on strategies and such, but if I happen to be entertaining, Lucy is expected to act as hostess for a late supper at precisely twenty two hundred. Of course, all of her activities are interspersed with the social obligations appropriate to a girl of her age and position such as afternoon teas, balls, routs, theater parties, et cetera, et cetera." The Admiral relaxed enough to smile at his captive audience. "I have found that a productive life is a happy life. Don't you agree?"

"Indubitably." Claremont's smile lacked its former verve.

The brass skeleton clock on the mantel chimed the hour. Lucy rose, bobbing a flawless curtsy. "May I be dismissed, Father? It's time to dress for dinner."

The Admiral checked his chronometer, then nodded his permission. Before Lucy could escape, Claremont stood, stepping neatly into her path. She was forced to tilt her head back to meet his gaze or risk being thought as rude as he was. His warm fingers curled around hers, bringing her tightly fisted hand not to his lips, but to his heart. She could only glare at him, too shocked by his familiarity to jerk back her hand as she should have.

"Have no fear, Miss Snow," he drawled, his voice laced with mockery. "I promise to hold your life as dear as I hold my own."

♥   ♥   ♥

Answer correspondence—0700
Organize calling cards by rank and alphabet—1230

Gerard Claremont glared down at the schedule in his hand. It had come slithering beneath the gatehouse door earlier that evening, outlined with military precision in the butler's neat script. It seemed his bombastic employer had omitted several colorful and thrilling tasks from his verbal itinerary of his daughter's life, such as reviewing the daily papers for mentions of him and polishing the brass buttons on his uniforms. Gerard was surprised the man hadn't allotted her specific minutes in which to make use of the chamber pot.

"A productive life is a happy life," he mimicked savagely, crushing the elegant sheet of vellum and tossing it into the fire he had lit to burn off the chill of the autumn night.

He watched with satisfaction as it shriveled to ash. There had been little of happiness in the girl's shadowed eyes.

Absently rubbing his clean-shaven jaw, he paced the gatehouse. Decorated with the same spartan practicality as the main house, the long, narrow room was an excellent one for pacing. There were no overstuffed ottomans to stumble over, no porcelain figurines to bump with his elbows. There was only a wooden bed-stead, overlaid with a weary feather tick and a worn but serviceable quilt, a tall wardrobe, a round table, a bedside stand, and four nicked and scarred Hepple-white chairs doubtlessly cast from the family dining room after overstaying their welcome. The grumbling coachman Gerard had inadvertently ousted hadn't left so much as a trace of his own thirty-year occupancy.

The rough-planked floor creaked beneath Gerard's angry footsteps. It seemed that all of his hard-won plans had been laid for naught. He had expected his position to entail guarding a pompous military hero far past his prime. How was he to accomplish what he'd come for when forced to play nursemaid to some imperious young miss whose every thought and feeling was regimented by her father? The Admiral had claimed to be protecting his daughter from Doom, but Gerard suspected he was protecting himself from what Doom might reveal to her should she once again fall into his hands.

He'd been able to learn that Lucy was the only female Lucien Snow tolerated in his domain. Even his household staff had been culled from retired seaman who had served under him and were willing to award him the adulation and unquestioning obedience he considered his due. Just as his daughter had proved herself only too willing to do.

As his contempt raged higher, the walls of the gate-house seemed to shrink around him. The high-raftered lodgings were spacious, even luxurious, compared to most of his former dwellings, but Gerard's sense of confinement mounted until the flames of the fire wavered before his eyes, cloaked by a billowing blackness that threatened to smother him.

Flinging open the door, he escaped into the moon-light, drinking in hungry gulps of crisp night air redolent with the tang of autumn. He flexed his shaking fingers as if to assure himself they were no longer skeletal ruins. Despising himself for his weakness, he drew a cheroot from his pocket and lit it, hoping its savory smoke would steady both his hands and his nerves.

A dog barked in the distance, the sound both mournful and oddly comforting. Withdrawing into the shadows of the brick wall that surrounded the modest estate, he tilted his head back to study the stars. The familiar constellations danced like flecks of crystal before his restless eyes. They'd steered him many places in the past—some exotic, some dangerous, some breathtakingly beautiful, but he'd never dreamed they'd bring him to a place such as this.

His gaze lifted reluctantly to the second-story window that belonged to the Admiral's daughter. It was the only room on the front of the yellow-bricked manor hung with curtains—lace and damask confections drawn back to reveal the lamplit panes of the sash window. He'd requested residence in the gatehouse to escape the prying eyes of the other servants. He ought to be plotting how to turn this bitter twist of fate to his advantage, not glaring up at Lucy Snow's window, haunted by a pair of enormous gray eyes and a lush mouth set incongruously in a pinched little face.

He remembered the cool feel of her hand in his, the cultured bite of her voice, the stormy spark of defiance in her eyes whenever she turned them on him.

He had held his breath in anticipation, waiting for that spark to ignite beneath the flame of her father's bullying. But it had remained banked as she sprang up like a well-trained terrier to stand before the Admiral. She had dutifully described her impending death at the hands of Captain Doom as if she were reciting her multiplication tables. He could almost see her jotting it onto her schedule: *0800—Resist torture. 0830—Throw self overboard. 0900—Be eaten by sharks.* No sacrifice too great for the noble Admiral and His Majesty's Royal Navy!

Acrid smoke burned Gerard's throat. His pleasure spoiled, he snuffed out the cheroot and hurled it into the darkness, quenching it as ruthlessly as Lucien Snow quenched all traces of his daughter's spirit whenever she was in his exalted presence.

Gerard exhaled sharply as a figure appeared in the window, silhouetted against the lamplight. He scowled. The girl was as slight as a wraith, yet the gentle curves outlined beneath the fabric of her demure nightdress were unmistakably those of a woman. Her pale hair, caught in two long plaits, gleamed like braided silver in the moonlight.

She was angled toward the gatehouse and he wondered if she might be searching the night for him. Impossible though it was, he would have almost sworn their gazes met and mingled through the darkness before she reached up and snatched the drapes shut, her outrage a palpable thing.

Gerard might have been amused had he not been so consumed by his thwarted plans. While he could afford no distractions, he also couldn't allow himself to forget that the Admiral's daughter wasn't dry tinder, but a damp fuse on a keg of gunpowder—slow burning, unpredictable, and dangerous.

CHAPTER
SIX

AT PRECISELY 0600 THE FOLLOWING MORN-
ing, Smythe came tapping at the gatehouse door. Believing there was little need to guard Miss Snow's
precious life while she dressed and coiffed herself, Gerard dragged the quilt over his head and ignored the
butler's polite queries as to his state of wakefulness
until he finally went away. Gerard crawled out of bed
after nine o'clock, his head pounding from too little
sleep and too many misgivings.

After giving himself a meticulous shave, polishing
his spectacles, and breakfasting on a stale torte, he reported to the great house for duty only to discover that
instead of exploring Ionia as he'd hoped to do, he was
to accompany Miss Snow on some trivial errand.

From what he could gather from the frantic menser-
vants, their negligent young mistress had misplaced a
valuable resource—the recently published memoirs of
Admiral Lord Howell. As penance, she was to be sent
to Lord Howell's country estate to secure another
copy. Her father had determined she could make the

most efficient use of her time by letting the visit double as a social call to Lord Howell's daughter Sylvie.

Gerard was waiting in the entrance hall, tapping his hat impatiently against his thigh, when Lucy came tripping down the stairs in a pair of delicate sandals. The white muslin of her simply cut dress was gathered in tiny pleats beneath her breasts and complimented by a pastel pink stole. Her straw bonnet sported matching satin ribbons. She painted such a portrait of girlish charm that Gerard could not help smiling.

Until he saw her eyes. Her gaze was a blast of early winter that might have withered a lesser man. Taking a wary step out of her path, he donned his hat and swept a mocking hand toward the front door.

Without missing a step, she slapped a brass spyglass into his palm. "Perhaps in the future, Mr. Claremont, you'd care to use this for your nocturnal spying."

If a footman hadn't scampered to open the door, Gerard was convinced she would have walked right through it.

Watching her pert rump twitch beneath the clinging muslin, he muttered "And a good morning to you, too, Miss Snow," before plunking the spyglass down on a pier table and following.

♥ ♥ ♥

The morning dazzled Gerard's eyes as they waited for the carriage to be brought around from the stables. Sunlight poured down like manna from a heavenly vault of azure blue, blistering the crowns of the maples to fiery peach. Gerard breathed deeply, savoring the crisp fragrance of autumn. Not even being forced to dance attendance on the Admiral's brat could spoil his ravenous appetite for fresh air and sunshine.

A mischievous breeze wafted off the river to sift the treetops, sending leaves cascading down in showers of crimson and gold. Gardeners were scattered across the

grounds, their rakes poised to capture the daring inter-
lopers before they marred the pristine carpet of the
lawn. Gerard fought a wicked urge to kick his way
through their captive piles, scattering them to freedom.
Instead, he threw back his arms and stretched, ex-
ulting in the flex of his restless muscles.

Beside him, a delicate throat was cleared. Gerard
glanced down to find Miss Snow's generous lips
pressed to a disapproving pucker. If it hadn't been
physically impossible, he would have sworn she was
gazing down her slender little nose at him.

"I'm terribly sorry I missed breakfast," he said,
sniffing the air for her tart perfume. "The lemons must
have been delicious."

He was rescued from her retort by the clatter of
carriage wheels on the cobbled drive. What a shame,
Gerard thought, to be traveling in a closed conveyance
on such a flawless day! He had hoped for a curricle or
even a sporty perch phaeton that he might drive. But
Fenster, the aged coachman, crouched on the driver's
bench like a squat, shriveled spider, his countenance
even more sour than his mistress's.

Which should have warned Gerard when Lucy laid
a gloved hand on his arm and smiled sweetly up at
him. "I do hope the motion of the vehicle won't aggra-
vate your . . ." She glanced around as if to ensure no
one would inadvertently mock his shame, before whispering, *"Unfortunate condition."*

Refusing to be disarmed by her smile, he tipped his
hat back with one finger. "Your concern touches me,
Miss Snow, but I don't generally get seasick on carriage rides." He proffered her the carriage door.

She climbed into the vehicle with the assistance of
an underfootman and tried to tug the door shut in
Gerard's face. Elbowing the hapless servant out of the

way, Gerard clambered in after her, settling into the opposite seat.

Infuriated by his gall, Lucy drew herself into a sullen knot to keep their knees from touching. She'd always prided herself on her independence and loathed the thought of relinquishing her privacy to a man who was little more than a mercenary.

As the coach rolled into motion, she blurted out, "Wouldn't you be better able to protect me if you rode *outside* the carriage with the coachman? What if we were set upon by highwaymen? Or pirates? Or . . . or . . . Indians?"

He lifted an eyebrow. "I wasn't aware there'd been a rash of Indian attacks in Chelsea." He eyed the silky sheafs of hair streaming from beneath her hat. "Although I must confess your scalp would be a trophy even the most civilized of savages would be hard put to resist."

Lucy tingled beneath his sleepy-lidded perusal. "All the more reason for you to ride with Fenster."

He sighed as if possessed by a patience too great for her comprehension. "Your father can assign outriders to protect the outside of the carriage if he deems it prudent. As your personal bodyguard, it is my duty to remain by your side." A faint wince of distaste crossed his features. "Every hour of the day."

Lucy found the notion almost as insufferable as the man. Oblivious to her horror, Mr. Claremont drew a calf-bound book from the inside pocket of his coat and began to read. Pretending to straighten her gloves, Lucy studied him from beneath the scooped brim of her hat.

With his mild expression and those homely spectacles perched on the bridge of his well-defined nose, he resembled a schoolmaster more than a soldier of fortune. What would he do if they were set upon by highwaymen? Lucy wondered. Cane them? Whack them over the knuckles with his book?

Her disdain was tempered by the memory of him stretching in the drive as they had awaited the carriage. He had flexed his muscles beneath the brown cloth of his coat like a dangerous beast that had been caged too long. Lucy had found his sensual pleasure in the boorish act most disturbing.

She narrowed her eyes, trying to deduce why she had taken such an instant dislike to the man. Perhaps it was his disarming size. He seemed to grow larger at each of their meetings. Even now she was huddled against the leather squabs to escape the muscular length of his thighs, outlined all too clearly beneath the clinging doeskin of his pantaloons. Each time the carriage struck a rut in the dirt road, their knees brushed. His very presence crowded her, made her breath come short and fast as if there weren't enough air in the carriage for both of them to breathe.

Perhaps it was his manners she abhorred—his delicate juggling of insolence and deference. She reminded herself that he was a man of the working class. He was no gentleman and it was unsporting of her to judge him by the standards of her peers. Her innate sense of fairness demanded she offer him a chance to redeem himself.

When her polite sniff failed to draw his attention, she pasted on a stiff smile and asked, "May I inquire what you are reading, sir?"

His gaze remained fastened on the page. "*Robinson Crusoe* by Mr. Daniel Defoe. Have you read it?"

Lucy shook her head violently. "Oh, no. Father doesn't approve of the reading of fiction. He thinks it weakens the mind."

Claremont slanted her an inscrutable glance over the spine of the book. "And what do you think?"

Having never had her opinion solicited before, Lucy could only stare at him blankly.

He quirked one eyebrow in blatant amusement. "Are you sure you haven't been reading novels on the sly, Miss Snow?"

Knowing it might take several minutes before she realized he'd insulted her, Gerard buried his nose back in the book. He was only too aware that the conventional Miss Snow would never have been allowed to venture out unchaperoned with a man of her own class. But his servant's status effectively emasculated him in the eyes of her father. Probably in her eyes as well. The irony failed to amuse him as it should have.

When Mr. Claremont remained immersed in his book, Lucy resolved to shock him out of his mocking complacency.

"I may very well be the first person abducted by Captain Doom to live to tell of it," she announced.

Claremont responded with a noncommittal grunt.

"The rogue is utterly ruthless. 'Tis fortunate I was blindfolded, for one look from his evil eye will turn you to stone. His ship comes out of the mist like Satan's chariot fleeing the gates of hell. Some say he's the ghost of Captain Kidd haunting the seas to seek revenge against the investors who betrayed him."

Claremont slowly lowered the book. Lucy knew she was babbling, but now that she had his attention, she was loath to surrender it. She raced on, shamelessly embellishing the tales she'd heard from the sailors on the *Tiberius*. "He wears a hideous necklace of human ears. He plucks the hearts from his victims barehanded and feeds them to the sharks while they're still thumping. He drinks human blood for breakfast and he's been known to carve the entire text of the pirate articles on the chests of his captives."

Claremont's gaze dropped to the snowy expanse of

skin revealed by the fashionable décolletage of her bodice. "You seem to have remained relatively unscathed. Not even a freckle."

Unsettled by his scrutiny, Lucy demurely drew her stole around her shoulders. "I was very fortunate." She gazed into her lap, completely unaware of the dreamy cast that overtook her features or of its jarring effect on her companion. "Doom is utterly merciless when it comes to the pursuit of his own pleasures. 'Tis rumored he can ravish ten innocents in a single night. Before midnight," she added, inspired.

Gerard was mesmerized by the haze of pink blooming in Lucy's cheeks, the voluptuous slackness of a mouth that begged kissing. He realized that it wasn't her features that had been pinched, but her expression. He'd never thought himself the sort of man to envy a ghost, yet his fingers bit into the cover of the book as he lifted it to hide his expression.

"You have to admire the man's stamina," he said coolly. "Virgins are such a bother."

Lucy was silent for several revolutions of the carriage wheels, as if trying to digest such a crude observation. "I fear I was in danger of being ravished myself."

Her thoughtful confession did not improve Gerard's temper. He snapped the book shut, raking her slender figure with such a scathing glance of appraisal that she would have had every right to slap him had she been so inclined. "I think not, Miss Snow. I've heard Doom's tastes run to women with a little more meat on their bones."

Lucy paled, her gray eyes dominating her gamin features. She turned her face to the window as if captivated by the elm-lined drive streaming past.

Halfway regretting his deliberate cruelty, Gerard laid the book aside. "Forgive my lapse of manners,

Miss Snow. I'm a professional man and this position isn't quite what I expected it to be."

Gerard was startled to realize that honesty had become so foreign to his nature that even the truth had the discordant ring of a lie.

♥　♥　♥

Lord Howell's country estate presented a startling contrast to the regimented existence at Ionia. Here the falling leaves whirled in a merry dance only to be caught by pudgy little hands and scattered gleefully to the wind or gathered into crispy amber mountains for disheveled children to romp and tumble through.

Gerard drank in the sight with a thirst that parched his throat with bitterness. He'd once envisioned such a future for himself only to have it snatched from his fingertips like a leaf before a harsh winter wind. He was reminded of how quickly seasons passed and opportunities were lost.

More eager than ever to escape this farce and be about his business, he swept open the carriage door. As Lucy alighted, a pair of spaniels and a lanky greyhound loped out to greet them. A dusky-haired young woman flew across the grass, her lavender hat ribbons streaming behind her. Her squeal of delight drowned out even the excited yipping of the spaniels.

"Lucy! Dear, dear Lucy! I've never known you to make a morning call. What's the occasion? Did the Admiral get his chronometer crossed with his barometer again?"

Gerard ducked his head to hide a smile, already liking Miss Howell immensely.

"Good morning, Sylvie. I do hope our unexpected visit won't cause you any undue inconvenience." Lucy stood stiffly in her friend's embrace, deigning only to press her pale cheek to Sylvie's rosy one.

Gerard cynically supposed that given Miss Snow's

frigid temperament, the affected gesture was tantamount to an undying declaration of love.

Sylvie's blue eyes twinkled as they peered over Lucy's shoulder to discover Gerard lounging against the carriage door. "Oh, my God!" she said in a stage whisper loud enough to be heard at the Theater Royal on Drury Lane. "Where did you find such a handsome creature? That hair! Those shoulders! Why, he's sumptuous! Incomparable! Have you a beau?"

Lucy could feel Claremont's mocking amusement warming her shoulder blades like a palpable thing. After unwittingly exposing him to Sylvie's shameless adulation, she felt compelled to deflate him.

"I should say not. He's no one," she explained. "A mere servant."

Sylvie's artfully plucked eyebrows shot up. "Do tell."

"Oh, very well, if you insist. Father hired him to be my bodyguard."

Sylvie erupted into musical trills of laughter. She cupped her hand around Lucy's ear to whisper something. Claremont's smug expression warned Lucy that he had deduced every scandalous syllable.

His smirk melted to wariness as Sylvie turned the full force of her dimpled charm on him. When he politely declined her invitation to accompany them, she caught his hand and tried to forcibly drag him away from the carriage.

"Oh, no, Miss Howell. I really should stay here. My job, you know. I must keep an eye out for cutthroats and brigands."

"And Indians," Lucy interjected. Relishing his discomfiture, she said, "Come now, Mr. Claremont. Wasn't it you who told me that outriders should be hired to look after the carriage? 'Tis your duty to look after me."

Gerard glared at her over Sylvie's head, warning her that he'd love to *look after her*. Later. In private.

She'd left him no choice but to follow Sylvie's chattering path up the leaf-strewn slope. They were forced to dodge several scampering children before arriving at a blanket spread on the poorly trimmed grass. An enormous baby sat in the middle of it, his countenance as placid as that of a well-fed Buddha.

A uniformed man and gaily dressed woman waved cheerily from the bowling green at the foot of the hill. Gerard supposed them to be the parents of all these remarkable progeny.

" 'Twas Mama's idea to breakfast alfresco while the weather was still warm," Sylvie explained as she filled a china plate from a tea cart laden with food.

She thrust the plate into Lucy's hand. Lucy stared down at the buttered eggs, salted ham, and marmalade-slathered hunks of freshly baked bread with undisguised longing before stealing a surreptitious glance at the silver watch pinned to her bodice. Gerard couldn't bear it.

He snatched the plate from her hand. "Now, now, Miss Snow," he chided. "You know you're not to eat again until eleven-thirty. What would the Admiral say?"

Just as he'd anticipated, Lucy snatched the plate back. Her gray eyes blazed with defiance. "You'd do well not to forget your place, sir. My eating habits are none of your concern."

Sylvie was openly gaping at them, making Gerard wonder if this was her first glimpse of the mouse's fangs. It seemed she only bared them in her father's absence. From the amusement sparkling in Sylvie's eyes, he gathered the sight hadn't entirely displeased her. His regard for the girl shot up another notch.

While their hostess prepared a plate for him, Lucy

claimed the farthest corner of the blanket and drew off her gloves. She snapped tiny bites from her ham as if afraid he might have another change of heart and take it away from her. Gerard dove into the feast with relish, the torte he'd breakfasted upon nothing more than a vague memory.

"There are twelve of us in all," Sylvie began with no prompting whatsoever. "I'm the eldest and Gilligan here is the youngest. Mama always said that every time Papa went to sea, he left her something to remember him by."

While Sylvie regaled Gerard with her unabridged family history, Lucy tried to ignore a pang of guilt as she imagined what the Admiral would say if he could see her eating ham with her fingers. At ten hundred hours no less.

Sylvie was shaking her head sadly. "No one's heard Gilligan speak a word, but we think he'll be like Christopher. Christopher was almost four before he started talking."

Probably because he couldn't get a word in edgewise, Lucy thought unkindly. It never mattered if she didn't have anything clever to say around Sylvie because Sylvie did all the talking. All that was required of her was an occasional nod or sympathetic murmur.

Her friend's fashionably cropped curls bobbed as she described her brother Philip's bloodcurdling tumble down the garret stairs. Lucy had never told anyone, but she fancied her mother had been much like Sylvie Howell. Possessed of irrepressible good humor. Somewhat flighty. And pretty. Dazzlingly pretty.

She stole a glance at her bodyguard, expecting to find him already besotted. But he was occupied with feeding ham to the spaniels and bits of bread to the baby, his concentration focused on not getting his hands mixed up.

She studied him with a newly critical eye—Sylvie's eye. Unlike most men, the uncompromising sunlight showed him off to his best advantage. It accentuated the tiny crinkles at the corners of his eyes and warmed his unfashionable tan to honeyed bronze. His age was difficult to gauge; he'd obviously spent a great deal of time outdoors.

His was a compelling face, wide of cheekbone, strong of brow, a face that might have remained too boyish had it not been honed by time and experience. She was loath to admit that it was the very traits she found so annoying that made her reluctant to look away. The irresistible glint of humor in his hazel eyes. The amused slant of his lips. He always seemed to be on the verge of smiling, as if he were privy to some wonderful joke that had escaped the rest of the world.

As he tilted a goblet of water to those expressive lips, she generously decided that there were some who might even call him handsome.

"Avast, ye lowly scoundrel. I'll hang yer severed head from the yardarm or me name ain't Cap'n Doom!"

Claremont choked and sloshed water over the rim of his goblet, drenching both baby and spaniels, as two small boys exploded through a nearby fortress of fallen leaves, tree branches clacking in a mock cutlass fight.

"Sorry," he murmured, dabbing at the baby's bald head with his handkerchief. "They startled me."

Sylvie waved away his apology. "They're only playing Cap'n Doom. It's been one of their favorite games ever since Lucy's thrilling adventure." She clapped a hand over her mouth. "Oh, dear, I forgot it was a secret. You see, the Admiral confided in Papa who confided in Mama who confided in me—oh, what a galloping ninny I am!"

Lucy was tempted to agree. "Mr. Claremont is not a

spy from the *Times,* Sylvie. He is well aware of the incident. It's the reason my father hired him."

Sylvie's eyes shone with admiration. "Who would have ever thought Lucy could be so brave? Why, she was far more intrepid than those spineless ninnies in Mrs. Edgeworth's *Castle Rackrent!*" She plucked a cricket from the baby's fingers before he could eat it and shot Lucy a sly look. "I suspect our Lucy was rather taken with the villain. She colors quite prettily every time his name is mentioned."

"I do not!" Lucy felt a rush of heat in her cheeks even as she protested. Keenly aware of Claremont's eyes on her, she inclined her head, hoping the fall of her hair would hide the betrayal of her fair complexion.

A merrily unrepentant Sylvie trotted off to put the baby down for a nap and fetch a new copy of her papa's memoirs, abandoning Lucy to her bodyguard's company.

The jibes she dreaded did not materialize. Instead, Claremont drew a cheroot from his pocket and clamped it between lips that bore no trace of a smile. His eyes narrowed to brilliant slits behind his spectacles as he watched Sylvie's brothers play at pirates. The sun had lost its warmth and the temperature around the blanket seemed to have dropped by several degrees.

Lucy sensed that once again she'd done something inexplicable to annoy him. Let him fume, she thought, retreating into her own stony silence. He'd get no satisfaction from her. She'd lived with the Admiral for nineteen years. There was no one better versed in tolerating the punishment of aloof indifference.

Without asking her permission as was the custom, he lit the slender cigar and inhaled deeply before pursing his lips and blowing a flawless smoke ring.

Lucy found something profane about a man taking blatant delight in such a carnal and wicked pleasure. Perhaps that was what she found so unsettling about him. He did everything as if it were both his first and last time. She smothered a delicate cough into her hand.

A handkerchief appeared, dangling like a Jolly Roger before her eyes.

Lucy stared at the challenging scrap of linen, offended by its unsullied purity. A new emotion stirred in her breast, dangerous and exotic. Anger, sweet and hot, washing away her passive melancholy with its unfamiliar fire.

For years she had allowed her father to dismiss her, to treat her with the same casual disregard as he did his subordinates. Dreading his bullying almost as much as she craved his affection, she had learned to render herself so invisible that sometimes she feared she might disappear altogether.

Mr. Claremont's mocking indifference had the opposite effect. She could feel her spirit sputter to life in her breast, winking, flickering, then igniting in a furious blaze.

She ignored the handkerchief. If the rascal thought he could goad her into a response, he'd be a long time waiting.

The handkerchief disappeared. The next smoke ring floated straight at her, neatly hooping her nose.

"Mr. Claremont!" His name shot from her lips in an explosion of pure wrath. She scrambled to her feet, slapping her gloves against her thigh. "It has been obvious from the first that our association is a fool's endeavor. We are utterly incompatible in both temperament and moral character."

He lounged back on one elbow, the very image of a rumpled reprobate. That infuriating quirk had reappeared at the corner of his mouth. "Then it's fortunate the Admiral hired me to guard you, not marry you."

Lucy sucked in a furious breath. It seemed the wretch was stealing all the air from outdoors as well. A very unladylike trickle of sweat eased between her breasts. "It is the Admiral who made an enemy of Captain Doom, sir, not I, and there is no reason I should continue to be punished for his folly." She snapped on her gloves. "I'm perfectly capable of looking after myself and I shall endeavor to convince my father of that at the nearest opportunity."

She marched up the slope toward the carriage, spoiling her dignified exit by stumbling over the hem of her gown.

Gerard rose to his feet, flicking the cheroot into the grass. So little Miss Mouse thought she would have him dismissed, did she? Thought she could look after herself without the bumbling assistance of an ill-mannered commoner?

His eyes narrowed as he ground out the cheroot's flame with his boot heel. He wasn't about to let the Admiral's brat spoil all of his carefully laid plans by having him dismissed. She'd left him no choice. To keep his position, he would have to show the haughty miss just how badly she needed a man like him.

CHAPTER SEVEN

SMYTHE'S ATTACK ON THE GATEHOUSE door the following morning at 0600 was executed with far less discretion and far more volume. The pounding continued until Gerard was forced to stumble blindly out of bed. Tripping over the quilt he'd anchored around his naked form, he threw open the door and glared at the butler through tufts of disheveled hair.

Smythe blinked at him with such maddening serenity that Gerard would have sworn the man knew about the trip he'd made into London the previous night after Lucy's lamp had been extinguished, the four ales he'd consumed at a Whitechapel tavern, and the fact that he'd stumbled into bed shortly before dawn with the grim satisfaction of knowing Miss Snow would soon be begging him to stay on in his position to protect her.

"Admiral Snow extends his invitation to breakfast with him and Miss Lucy this morning."

Invitation, hell! Gerard thought. He knew a royal summons when he heard one. He suspected it was simply the Admiral's sly way of nudging him out of bed before ten o'clock.

"It will be my bloody pleasure," he growled before slamming the door in the butler's unruffled face.

♥　♥　♥

Lucy and her father sat at opposite ends of the dining room table, separated by a lustrous sea of oak. The Admiral was surrounded by scattered newspapers, his only concession to untidiness in the immaculate room. The only thing visible of him over the *Times* was his lush pompadour of white hair. His hair was the Admiral's keenest vanity. Even when wigs had been fashionable, he'd refused to wear one.

Lucy cleared her throat and added a dollop of fresh cream to her tea. Her father looked positively regal in his dark blue broadcloth coat with its gleaming brass buttons and gold-braided hem. In nineteen years, she'd never once seen him out of uniform. She always felt somewhat smaller in his presence, dwarfed by the grandeur of his rank and authority. She tapped her foot nervously, halfway surprised it would still reach the floor.

She'd been searching for just this opportunity since returning from the Howells' yesterday, but as she stole another glance at her father, her tongue was seized by that same painful mingling of adoration and guilt that had plagued her since childhood. Guilt for so frequently failing to live up to his expectations. Guilt for constantly having to battle her inherited moral flaws. Guilt for being born to a woman who had been fool enough to scorn such an exceptional man.

He made her feel five years old again, as if she were standing on the dock, gripping Smythe's hand and watching him disembark from some heroic voyage to the approving roar of the crowd. She had always wanted to yell "That's my papa!" but never dared.

She drew in a steadying breath. "Father, there's something I really must—"

The newspaper crackled disapprovingly. "Speak up, girl. You know I can't tolerate mumbling."

She took a sip of the tea, silently damning Claremont for goading her into making the foolish boast that she would be rid of him. "Father, it's imperative that I—"

The words lodged in her throat as the cause of her discomfiture strolled into the room, inclining his head graciously in her direction. "Miss Snow."

She coolly returned his nod. "Mr. Claremont."

Ignoring the expressionless footman standing at attention at the Admiral's elbow, Claremont captured a plate for himself and stood frowning down at the marble-topped sideboard. Lucy could almost see him mentally comparing the spartan fare to the sumptuous spread at the Howells'. Her father forgotten, she nibbled her dry toast, riveted by details she'd never noticed before—the worn seams on Claremont's tailcoat, the scars on his boots that no amount of buffing would smooth. Just how badly did he need this position?

He sank into a chair and began to slather a miniature mountain of butter on his toast beneath the reproving eyes of the footman.

Lucy frowned, beset by a reluctant pang of conscience. Mr. Claremont certainly liked to eat. Would he go hungry if she forced her father to send him packing?

"Well, what is it, girl?" The Admiral slammed his fist on the table, rattling the silver. Lucy jumped, sloshing her tea over the cup's gilt-edged rim. "If it's so damned imperative that you have to interrupt my breakfast, spit it out, won't you?"

Why did her father have to choose that moment to emerge from his cocoon of newsprint? she wondered despairingly. "I thought . . . well, it's just that I . . ."

Claremont fixed his gaze on her face, his expression so pleasantly mild that only Lucy suspected he would have liked to gag her with her napkin.

"I need some money for paints," she blurted out. "I've used the last of the cerulean and I can't finish my Cornwall seascape without it."

The Admiral's smile was rife with such patronizing affection that Lucy wanted to duck beneath the table-cloth to avoid the coming salvo. "Ah, my darling Lucinda. I can always count on you to dramatize the trivial." He disappeared behind a sheaf of the *Times* with a hunk of dry toast. "It was a special talent of your mother's."

Lucy pushed her plate away. She dared a sullen glance at her bodyguard, expecting to find his eyes twinkling with amusement at her expense.

Claremont had vanished. In his place sat a danger-ous stranger, watching her father with pure murder in his eyes. A frisson of fear shot down Lucy's spine, a premonition of disaster not for the Admiral, but for herself. Before she could convince herself she wasn't simply giving in to fancy as her mother would have done, her father choked and Claremont's affable ex-pression slipped into place like a mask.

Lucy stared in horror as her father dropped the newspaper, his florid complexion deepening to scarlet, then bruised purple. For one irrational moment, she believed Claremont had done something terrible to him with nothing more than the power of that murder-ous stare.

Her bodyguard leaped to his feet and hastened around the table, shoving the panicked footman out of the way. Locking his hands together, he gave the Ad-miral one sharp blow between the shoulder blades.

The Admiral sucked in a tortured gasp of air, his eyes watering with relief. Lucy snapped out of her daze and rushed to her father's side, pressing a water goblet into his hand.

Claremont pounded the Admiral's back with more relish than Lucy deemed necessary. "You might try some butter next time, sir. It makes the toast go down more smoothly."

Lucy scowled at him, but her father was in no condition to chide Claremont for his insolence. "Not the bread," he wheezed, stabbing his forefinger at the fallen newspaper. "*Him!* The bastard's going to be the death of me yet!"

Claremont reached for the paper, but Lucy swept it out from under his hand, immediately finding the words scripted in bold letters beneath the paper's banner.

" '*Captain Doom*'," she read softly, the name an unwitting entreaty on her lips.

Gerard was thankful her father was still occupied with fighting to breathe. One glimpse of his daughter's unguarded face in that moment and Gerard had little doubt that the Admiral would lock her away and toss out the key. Her color had heightened to creamy peach and her taut lips had softened to a tantalizing pout. With a distinctly unpleasant shock, Gerard realized that he would have liked to touch them, nibble them, plunge his tongue between their delectable curves.

The unbidden notion opened up a realm of disturbing possibilities. Dangerous regrets.

" 'After forcing the frigate into surrender off the coast of Dover,' " Lucy read, " 'the masked pirate invited (at pistol point) the blindfolded captain and his officers to join him and his crew for a gentlemanly game of faro aboard their ship. Although it is rumored Captain MacGower of the *HMS Guenevere* won back over one thousand pounds of the Royal Treasury gold confiscated by the brigands, he was not amused by the pirate's antics.' "

Neither was Gerard.

Lucy lifted her gaze from the paper to stare right through him, her eyes softened to the misty gray of the sea at dawn. The tender yearning in their depths struck him high in the gut, dangerously near to his heart.

He was beginning to hate Captain Doom almost as much as the Admiral did.

"How dare he? Have you ever heard of such boldness? Such unmitigated gall?" The Admiral slammed the goblet down.

Unsure of whether he was saving Lucy from her father or himself, Gerard snatched the paper out of her hands, jarring her face back to its haughty cast.

He scanned the rest of the article, his temper growing grimmer with each word he read. "Rascal's getting damned reckless, if you ask me. He's liable to get his fool neck stretched if he pulls any more stunts like this one."

"I'll drink to that!" The Admiral hefted the goblet.

Lucy shot Gerard a triumphant glance. "But don't you see, Father? If Doom is on the high seas, then there's really no reason to—"

"—relax our guard," Gerard finished neatly, ignoring Lucy's murderous glare. "A rogue like Doom probably has minions scattered all over England. What better time to execute an abduction than when blessed with an alibi provided by the entire crew of a Royal Navy frigate?"

"Quite right, sir," the Admiral concurred. "We must be more vigilant than ever."

Lucy snatched up a napkin, wringing it between her hands as if she wished it were his neck. But as her father polished off his water, his hands trembling visibly, her sullen expression melted to one of tender concern. Gerard knew he wouldn't be finishing his own breakfast. Lucy's groveling for her father's favor had robbed him of his appetite.

She dabbed at the Admiral's damp brow with the napkin. "There now, Father. Shall I fetch you some more water?"

He shoved her hand away. "You know I can't abide being fussed over. Why don't you take yourself off somewhere? Go buy those paints you need. That scoundrel has upset me far too much to work on my memoirs this morning."

Gerard bit back an oath. Another opportunity lost.

"As you wish, Father," Lucy replied dutifully.

As she crept from the dining room, her posture was submissive, but the glance she shot him was anything but. Gerard's eyes narrowed in speculation. It would only be a matter of time before she screwed up the courage to approach her father about his dismissal. Perhaps his day wasn't to be wasted after all. A shopping expedition might provide the perfect opportunity to spring the trap he'd set for his tart-tongued mouse.

As Gerard started after her, the Admiral cleared his throat as if he were choking on more than just dry toast. As soon as he spoke, Gerard knew it was his pride. "Thank you, lad. You saved my life."

Gerard gave him a crisp bow and an enigmatic smile. "Just doing my job, sir. Just doing my job."

♥ ♥ ♥

As their carriage clattered toward Oxford Street later that morning, Gerard wondered if Miss Snow owned any gowns that weren't white. The chaste hue was beginning to tell on his patience as well as his eyes.

Against his will, his gaze lingered on the creamy shoulders and fluted collarbone bared by the severe lines of her Grecian-styled gown. He hated to admit it, but the absence of color suited her almost as well as her name. Her skin was like fresh snow—soft, virgin, alluring. Too bad she'd been cursed with an icy temperament to match.

Jarred by his dangerous musings, he craned his neck toward the rear window, heartened by the sight of a single rider trailing far enough behind the carriage to keep from arousing the footman's suspicion. After today, Lucy would probably entreat her father to raise his wages.

The vehicle halted before a shining expanse of shop windows, behind which a dizzying array of perfumes, fabrics, liquors, jewels, pastries, and books were displayed for the pleasure of the genteel shoppers milling along the flagstone pavement.

"What shall it be?" Gerard asked as he handed Lucy down from the carriage, holding her gloved hand a heartbeat longer than was necessary. "The stationers? I should so hate for you to be deprived of the fulfillment of completing your Cornwall seascape."

She popped open her pagoda-style parasol to shade her face from the sun. Bells of warning jangled in Gerard's head as her lips tilted in a deliberate smile. "I'm off to the silk mercer this morning for some . . ." She trailed off, studying the stocking toes peeping out from her sandals as if too shy to continue.

"Purchases you'd rather not discuss in public," he gently provided.

"Quite so. You needn't accompany me. I'm afraid you'd find it quite dull."

Au contraire, ma chérie, Gerard thought. He was tempted to trail along just to prove to her that he knew more about those gossamer scraps of silk and lace than she could hope to learn in a lifetime.

She plainly believed she'd found a way to rid herself

of his company, not realizing that she was playing right into his devilish hands.

He escorted her to the doorway of an elegant shop with tall windows draped in folds of Italian silk, Brussels lace, patterned chintzes, and muslins even more translucent than the one she was wearing. "I'll wait right outside for you. Take all the time you need," he graciously assured her.

She blinked up at him, clearly thrown off balance by his amiable surrender. He gave her a gentle shove through the door.

Gerard could not resist sneaking a peek into the gilded salon. One of the proprietors rushed toward Lucy to press a swath of silk into her hand, crooning in heavily accented English, "Our finest Italian, miss, so diverting, so cool."

Lucy fondled the sleek fabric, utterly unaware of the sensual languor that stole over her features. Diverting indeed, but hardly cool, Gerard thought as his mind transposed heated images with torturous clarity. Her fingers on the silk. His fingers on her.

Fists clenched, he swung away from the door, knowing he'd best escape before the trap snapped shut on his own tail.

♥ ♥ ♥

Lucy emerged from the tasteful gloom of the mercer's salon over an hour later, blinking against the bright sunlight. She was still congratulating herself on her cleverness. Not only had she shed herself of her bodyguard's vexing company to enjoy a brief interlude of privacy, she had also bid ten shillings a yard on a bolt of Italian silk for which the mercer had been asking fifteen. When the fabric was delivered, the Admiral would undoubtedly praise her for her economy.

Jostled by the crowds, she shaded her eyes with her parasol and peered around uncertainly. There was no sign of Claremont or the carriage. A row of unfamiliar vehicles lined the roadside, their horses drowsing in the noonday sun. Perhaps Fenster had been forced to park farther down the street and her bodyguard had sought shelter from the unseasonal heat in the shaded confines of the carriage.

She ought to be relieved that Claremont wasn't lurking about, she told herself, just waiting to pounce on her with that infuriating smirk of his. She was obviously going to have to devise a more subtle plan of attack. Warning him of her intentions had only given him time to plot his defense.

Tilting her parasol to a jaunty angle, she decided to stroll to the stationers alone. She hurried past the bawling street vendors, trying to ignore the mouthwatering aromas of Banbury cakes and roasted apples. An uncontrollable passion for sweets was yet another of the carnal frailties bequeathed to her by her mother.

She smiled to imagine Mr. Claremont's chagrin when he returned to the mercer's shop only to discover his golden goose had flown the nest.

She was still savoring her satisfaction when a grubby hand shot out, grabbed the braided cord of her reticule, and jerked her into a deserted alley.

CHAPTER EIGHT

GERARD LEANED AGAINST A WROUGHT-iron lamppost, his thumbs tucked into the pockets of his waistcoat, and slowly counted to ten. He braced himself for the shrill woman's scream that should follow.

Ominous silence drifted from the mouth of the alley where Lucy had disappeared.

He drew out his watch and frowned at it, then straightened, beset by a sense of foreboding. He'd wanted to rid himself of the Admiral's brat as an obstacle to his employment, but he'd never intended for her to be hurt. What if she'd swooned? Or fallen and struck her head? An image of Lucy lying crumpled on the cobblestones, her hair spilled around her pallid face, sent him stalking toward the alley.

He marched around the corner, then froze, his jaw dropping in shock at the sight that greeted him.

A masked man lay flat on his back on the cobblestones, cowering beneath the sharp point of the parasol pressed to his throat. Gripping the parasol's ivory handle in her gloved hand, Lucy stood over him, looking as cool and composed as if she'd just come from a garden party. Gerard's abrupt appearance drew no more response from her than a delicately arched eyebrow.

"Please, miss, don't hurt me!" the thief was whining, his brogue so thick the words were almost unintelligible. "I didn't mean no harm, honest I didn't." His voice rose to a relieved squeak as he saw Gerard glaring down at him in disgust. "Help me, mister, won't ye? Don't let her hurt me! It was bloody awful. She beat me about the head, tripped me, then damn near skewered me with that umbreller thing. Why I thought ye'd never—"

Gerard stilled the thief's dangerous babbling by fixing a hand around his scrawny throat and lifting him to his feet. "If you'll excuse me, Miss Snow, I must dispose of this rubbish."

She dusted off her gloved hands. "The wretch tried to steal my reticule. Shouldn't you turn him over to a constable?"

Gerard tightened his grip. The lad's feet kicked vainly at the air. "When I'm through with him, he'll wish I had," he promised grimly.

Gerard returned a few moments later to find Lucy admiring the sweetmeats and comfits in the window of a confectionery shop.

He stopped directly behind her, aware that he was standing far too close for propriety, but too furious to give a bloody damn. The source of his anger galled him even more than its intensity. He wasn't angry at her for thwarting his scheme. He was angry at himself for that brief instant when he'd actually cared about her welfare. God knows he'd already wasted enough of his mercy on her.

Studying her unruffled reflection in the shop window, he demanded, "Why the bloody hell didn't you scream? If I hadn't been following at a distance, anything could have happened to you."

She faced him, showing no sign of being intimidated by his bullying nearness. "It takes more than one incompetent thief to make me scream. Besides, I had the situation well in hand. I do believe I've proved my point, Mr. Claremont." She ducked out from beneath his shadow and snapped open her lethal parasol as if he might well be its next victim.

"What point might that be?"

"That I'm perfectly capable of looking after myself. I've really no need of your services." She shot him a look from beneath the dancing fringe of the parasol that might have been flirtatious coming from any woman other than the Admiral's daughter. "But I've decided that I've no right to deprive you of your position. Therefore, all you must do to assure your future at Ionia is please me."

On that magnanimous note, she flounced away, her parasol twirling at full sail. Gerard refused to give her the satisfaction of trotting obediently at her sandaled heels.

He pulled off his hat and slapped it against his thigh, thinking it a pity that he had neither the time nor the inclination to show his employer's daughter just how much he could please her.

♥   ♥   ♥

Gerard strode away from the great house as if pursued by the demons of hell, lengthening his strides as he heard the telltale creak of a sash window on the second floor.

"Oh, Mr. Claremont! Excuse me, Mr. Claremont!"

He flinched at the familiar dulcet tones and briefly considered not slowing his pace. Considered marching past the gatehouse, out the gate, and all the way to

London to find the quickest horse, coach, or ship that would carry him beyond earshot of that musical voice.

He had fully expected the Admiral to be a tyrant, but the man's imperious daughter was proving Genghis Khan to be nothing more than mildly petulant.

"*Mr. Claremont! There* you are!" she exclaimed, as if they hadn't parted company less than fifteen minutes ago when she'd ordered him to sharpen each of her charcoal pencils with a dull kitchen knife. He felt fortunate she hadn't demanded he lick them to a point.

Blinking rapidly to clear the murder from his eyes, Gerard swung around and marched back to the house until he stood beneath his young mistress's window like some lovestruck swain of yore.

"Yes, miss?" he gritted out dutifully between clenched teeth.

"Could you meet me in the green salon, please? I have need of your services."

As Gerard stomped his way around to the servants' entrance, he muttered beneath his breath the services he'd like to perform for her, one of which he was certain would at least shut her up for a few minutes.

None of them involved the trivial tasks he'd been forced to undertake in the past week: balancing her embroidery frame on his knees at an afternoon tea while she'd proceeded to poke him with her needle whenever the dull conversation tempted him to nap, picking up her gloves each time she dropped them on a shopping excursion, turning the pages of Lord Howell's incredibly dry memoirs for her, as if she were too frail or addlepated to do it herself.

He might have been better able to tolerate her bullying had it been delivered with even a hint of malice, but each command was delivered in a tone of irreproachable sweetness, each coaxing smile accompanied by the beguiling flash of a dimple he'd never noticed before. She'd plainly abandoned her campaign to have him dismissed in the hopes of driving him to resign. Or to strangle her. Her transparency amused him almost as much as it infuriated him.

Her constant demands on his time left him with only the black hours of night to invest in his own stakes. Exhaustion was preying on his already frazzled temper, but he was only too aware that every minute lost to sleep was another minute to be endured in her company.

The drawing room door was ajar, just as he'd expected it to be. His armor of professional indifference nearly cracked to find Lucy bent over the settee, peering intently at something on the opposite side. He eyed her muslin-molded derriere in a mercenary light, the temptation to plant his boot in the middle of it surpassed by a far more disturbing and primal urge.

He snapped off a crisp bow. "At your service, miss."

Her outstretched finger quivered convincingly as she pointed at something on the far side of the settee. "Do hurry, please. It gave me the most awful fright."

Snorting beneath his breath, Gerard went around the settee and peered at the place she indicated. "I don't see a damn"—he cleared his throat—"I don't see anything, miss." Her title escaped with an unintended hiss.

"Of course you do. He's horrible. He almost gave me a fit of the vapors and I can assure you I'm not a woman given to vapors."

Sighing, Gerard drew off his spectacles and took a second look. A tiny spider, nearly invisible to the naked eye, was inching his way valiantly down a gossamer thread. Gerard felt nothing but pity for the little fellow. He reminded him of himself—kept dangling over a hazardous precipice, dancing to Lucy's tune.

He slid his spectacles back on and gave Lucy a look of biting patience. "What would you have me do, Miss Muffet—er, Miss Snow?"

She fanned her fingers at her throat. "You *are* my bodyguard. You're supposed to protect me from things that might do me harm."

A devilish sense of peace washed over him. "Very well, miss." He reached inside his coat to draw out a pistol and fixed the hapless creature in his sights.

Lucy's gasp of alarm was genuine. Her gray eyes widened as she ogled the shiny weapon. He knew she'd had no inkling that he possessed a pistol, much less that he never left the gatehouse without it.

"Mr. Claremont, whatever are you doing?"

He lowered the weapon. "Protecting you, of course. Wasn't that what you wished?"

"Surely you don't intend to shoot the poor creature."

"What do you suggest? Shall I flog it? Deport it to Australia? Capture it and deliver it into your father's hands?"

She sank down on the settee. Her hair shielded her face as she mumbled, "You might remove it to the garden."

To the garden, Gerard thought. Where she'd undoubtedly found it to begin with.

Her unexpected mercy disturbed him more than her duplicity. To counteract its jarring effect, he slid the pistol back into his coat and gave her a sinister leer. "Wouldn't you rather I crush it into the rug with the heel of my boot?" He lifted his foot a menacing inch.

She flung her hair from her eyes. "Oh, no! You

mustn't. He is one of God's creatures after all and I'm sure he had no intention of causing such a row."

She rushed to the hearth to retrieve a brass snuff-box whose immaculate surface suggested it had never known use. She scooped the spider into it without even a shred of squeamishness and handed it to him.

He gazed at the poor creature skittering in circles at the bottom of the snuffbox, wondering if it felt half as trapped as he did.

"There," she said, waving an imperious hand. "Now you can see that he comes to no harm and finds a pleasant home."

"I shall consider it my sacred charge." He swept out one arm in a full court bow, mocking them both. "Anything for you, my lady."

♥　♥　♥

" 'Twas the Battle of Chesapeake Bay in March of '81 when those damned Frenchies threw up a block-ade to stop us from delivering supplies to the British forces at Yorktown. Thomas Graves was rear admiral then and I tried to warn him he'd best not waste time lining up all those ships in perfect formation. 'Tommy, old chap,' I said quite frankly . . ."

The Admiral droned on and on like an enormous bumblebee. Gerard would have sworn the sand in the gleaming brass hourglass perched on the edge of the library desk had frozen to a halt hours ago.

By listening to Lucien Snow dictate his memoirs, Gerard had discovered only that it was the Admiral's keenest regret that after a lifetime of petty skirmishing with the French, he'd been robbed by his injury of commanding the English fleet in some of her greatest victories. He believed it should have been he who de-feated the French fleet in the Battle of the Nile. He who should have been offered a barony, been given a generous pension by Parliament, and earned the fame and fortune awarded instead to an inexperienced whelp of a rear admiral named Horatio Nelson.

The Admiral's daughter sat at a sturdy writing desk, her hair sleeked away from her face and bound at her nape with a blue velvet bow. Sunlight streamed through the bay windows, edging her delicate profile in gilt. Her pen never ceased its scratching as she transcribed her father's memories in her tidy script.

How did she remain so bright-eyed, Gerard wondered, when she must have heard these musty stories a thousand times? Of course, given her worship of her father, she probably considered them more compelling than gospel. It was difficult to believe the docile little mouse was the same despot who had had him summoned from the gatehouse at dawn to retrieve a hairpin that had slipped into a crack in the parquet floor. He lifted the bone-china cup to his lips to hide his simmering resentment.

"More coffee, sir?"

Gerard was startled by Smythe's appearance at his elbow. The butler's fleet-footed stealth never failed to unnerve him. He'd come dangerously close to gutting the man with his soup spoon more than once in the past week.

That would have been a crime he regretted keenly, for upon discovering that Gerard despised the insipid blend that passed for tea in the Snow household, Smythe had taken to brewing a pot of rich, dark Colombian coffee each morning just for his pleasure.

"Please?" Gerard shot the butler a grateful look as Smythe filled the cup to its rim. He warmed his hands on the porcelain bowl, hoping its fragrant steam would revive his waning attention.

". . . that would have been the year old George finally swallowed his pride and knighted me," the Admiral was saying. "It galled him to distraction to admit the son of a common tanner had saved his royal neck. Eighty, wasn't it? Or was it eighty-one?"

"Eighty-two, sir," Smythe interjected. "After your noble sacrifice at the Battle of Sadras."

"Ah, yes. Sadras!" The Admiral's eyes misted over with memories of past glories. Gerard clenched his teeth against a snarl.

Her pen flying, Lucy cast him a reproving look, reminding him that he was neglecting his own duties. He'd gallantly volunteered to sort through a moldy stack of the Admiral's personal correspondence for pertinent dates and names. All he'd managed to learn so far was that most of the Admiral's friends were as pompous and overbearing as he was.

". . . so when the mist cleared at dawn, I found myself staring down the hungry mouths of eighty-six French cannons. There was nothing for me to do but give the order for 'General Chase' and—"

"Seventeen ninety-six," Gerard blurted out before his employer could embroil them in yet another interminable battle. "Would that have been the year of your unfortunate injury, sir?" He blinked owlishly behind his spectacles, using the innocent demeanor they afforded him to his best advantage.

The Admiral's pendulous eyebrows inched together. Lucy's pen stilled. Smythe bent to dust a spotless globe, studiously avoiding Gerard's eyes.

Interrupting the Admiral's dictation was simply not done.

Wagering his dubious future that the man would be unable to resist the flattery of sincere interest, Gerard rose and paced around Lucy's writing desk as if unable to contain his excitement. "One account of the battle claimed that even after the splinter of lead pierced your calf, you refused to relinquish command. That despite your agony, you ordered them to strap you to the mainmast where you continued to shout the orders that won the battle."

"The box, Smythe," the Admiral snapped.

Smythe bustled over to a towering secretary and drew out an ornate brass coffer. Gerard rested his hip on the edge of Lucy's desk, forcing himself to ignore the lemony scent of her hair and the suspicious glint in her eyes.

With great ceremony, the butler presented the coffer to the Admiral, who drew a key from a ribbon he wore around his neck and unlocked it. Gerard half expected a pair of dueling pistols to emerge. Was he going to be shot for his impertinence?

"State secrets of the Admiralty," Lucy whispered to his elbow, her reverent tone chafing his raw temper. "Not even Smythe is allowed a key."

Instead of a weapon, the Admiral drew out a newspaper, yellowed and frayed with age. A nostalgic smile played around his lips. "This would be the piece you referred to. I fear my gallantry was greatly exaggerated," he admitted modestly. "I would never have been able to direct the battle had it not been for the unwavering support of my commanding officers."

Lucy began scribbling madly as without further prompting, the Admiral launched into a tediously detailed accounting of the Mediterranean battle that had ended his naval career.

No one would have guessed from Gerard's enthralled expression and admiring murmurs that he wasn't hearing a single word of it. All of his attention was focused on the gleaming coffer lying open on the Admiral's desk.

♥　♥　♥

Late that night, Lucy sat at her dressing table, drawing a silver brush that had belonged to her mother through her hair in crackling strokes. Her scalp tingled with pleasure at the sensual coddling. The Admiral was out for the evening, attending another interminable strategy session in the Admiralty Court. Lucy longed to savor each minute that she could call her own, but deprived of her father's strict accounting of her time, she felt a trifle lost. And alone.

Perhaps her bodyguard's restless energy was contagious. In the past week, Lucy had found herself both irritated and bemused by the man's habits. He never snapped to attention when the Admiral spoke, never checked his watch for the time, never consulted the daily schedule Smythe persisted in supplying him with.

Henceforth, he was consistently late, always knotted his cravat at the breakfast table, and frequently misplaced his schedule. Lucy had found it in such diverse places as beneath the potted fern in the drawing room, stuffed between the antlers of the moose's head mounted in the library, and draped like a tricorne hat over the terra-cotta bust in the entrance hall that the Admiral had recently commissioned of himself. The only thing her bodyguard did in an efficient manner was eat, shoveling in amazing quantities of food as if afraid it might be snatched away before he could finish.

Lucy had no way of knowing if her cheerful despotism was succeeding or failing. Mr. Claremont ruthlessly quenched his every spark of rebellion before she could take triumph in it. As his apathy toward her mounted, she'd had no choice but to escalate her irrational demands. She supposed she was being childish, but schooled as she had been to unquestioning obedience, this harmless bit of mischief was proving to be irresistible.

She winced as the brush snagged in an invisible tangle. She'd always hated her pale, fine hair. It tended to escape all but the most relentless combs and resisted any semblance of curl. If she had dared to trim it in a fashionable bob as Sylvie had done, she would look like a boyish elf.

Shoving aside the crystal bottles and snarled ribbons cluttering the dressing table, she studied her reflection as if it belonged to a stranger. Since the Admiral wasn't there to chide her for her vanity, she gathered the slick fall of hair at her nape and tilted her head to study her features. High cheekbones, a sharply defined nose, and a mouth too wide for her pointy chin, all dominated by a pair of enormous eyes that would have been better suited to a puppy. Or a courtesan.

Sighing, she let her hair fall in a defeated web around her shoulders, thinking it a pity that while she was cursed with so many of her mother's flaws, she had inherited none of her notorious beauty.

She pulled a crystal stopper from a bottle of lemon verbena and drew it down her neck until it nestled in the hollow of her throat. The smooth hardness against her tender flesh ignited a strange marriage of indolence and restlessness that made her breath come shallow and her heart beat fast. She became achingly aware of the blush of her breasts beneath the silk of her chemise, the painful cling of the sheer lace against their budding peaks.

She'd been seized by this inexplicable fever more than once since her encounter with Doom. She would awaken tangled in her sheets, shivering with yearning for some bittersweet fulfillment that drifted just out of her reach. Just as the *Retribution* and its mysterious captain had drifted out of her life.

Trailing her fingertips across the heated skin between her breasts, she imagined a lover's hands in their place. Doom's masterful hands. Her eyes fluttered shut, but instead of rendezvousing with her phantom lover in the clandestine shelter of darkness, she saw a man's hands tempered with autumn sunshine. Strong, blunt-fingered hands, their tanned backs sprinkled with ginger hair, gently cupping the fulsome weight of her breasts in their palms.

Lucy's eyes flew open. Her expression might have been comical had she not been so horrified. She snatched a hare's foot from a dish of rice powder to smother the flames in her cheeks, then rose to pace to the window. Her unsettled gaze was drawn against its will to the gatehouse. Although it was well after midnight, a lamp still burned bright within the humble lodgings. Didn't the man ever sleep? she wondered peevishly.

A peculiar hollowness had settled in the region of her heart. She feared she would never sleep either. Since wasting time was tantamount to mutiny in the Admiral's eyes, she decided to surprise him by dabbing the finishing touches on her Cornwall seascape. A frustrated perusal of the room reminded her that she had left her easel in the library.

She belted a modest dressing gown over her chemise and slipped from the room, stepping over the sandals she'd abandoned in the corridor. Trailing her fingers along the banister, she tiptoed down the stairs, holding her breath without realizing it. She always felt slightly guilty when emerging from her bedroom after her scheduled bedtime.

She skirted the cavernous entrance hall, darting past the closed doors that veered off the hall like the spokes of a giant ship's wheel. The bust of the Admiral glowered at her from its pedestal. Giving the squares of moonlight streaming through the bay window a wide berth, she hastened her steps as she approached the forbidding door of the library, wishing only to retrieve her easel before her father returned home to chastise her for invading his sacred domain.

Her trembling hand reached for the doorknob, expecting to feel the cool reassurance of smooth brass. Instead, her fingers closed over something warm, rough, and decidedly human. She heard a muffled oath and an ominous click. Before she could draw breath to scream, the hand beneath hers had clamped over her mouth. It drove her back until her shoulder blades pressed against the wainscoting.

A revealing shaft of moonlight penetrated the shadows and Lucy found herself being held at gunpoint by the very object of her wicked fantasies.

CHAPTER NINE

"I WAS WONDERING WHAT IT TOOK TO make you scream."

Lucy glared up at her bodyguard. Claremont seemed in no hurry to remove his hand from her mouth or the muzzle of his pistol from the hollow of her throat. She could feel the pulse there throbbing wildly beneath its steely caress. Mr. Claremont was obviously not a man accustomed to firing warning shots over anyone's bow. Behind the veil of his spectacles, she caught a flicker of annoyance in his narrowed eyes, a distant flash of lightning warning of a coming storm.

She began to squirm. His callused palm lingered briefly against her lips before he lowered it.

She stole a glance at the pistol, remembering with brutal clarity the various indignities she'd inflicted on him in the past week. The muzzle bobbed as she swallowed. "My father may very well lower your wages if you shoot me."

With chilling skill, he disarmed the weapon and slipped it into his coat. "I should hate to be demoted to gardener. Being your humble vassal is so much more fulfilling."

He wore no cravat or waistcoat and his rumpled coat hung open over his shirt in a scandalous disregard for propriety. Lucy was thankful her father hadn't returned yet. He would have undoubtedly given Claremont a scathing dressing-down for his slovenly attire. But, she thought with uncharacteristic whimsy, if the man were dressed down any further, he'd be ambling around the house naked.

Shocked by the wayward thought, Lucy steeled herself to project an aura of abject indifference. It was more of a challenge than she cared to admit, especially with her disturbing vision so fresh in her mind and the moonlight sifting through the burnished chestnut of her bodyguard's hair.

She clutched her dressing gown closed at the throat. What had seemed modest only minutes before now seemed the worst sort of enticement beneath his penetrating gaze. "May I inquire, Mr. Claremont, as to why you were sneaking about the house in such a nefarious manner?"

"It's my job," he replied coolly. "I check the security of the house every night. Doors. Windows."

She arched a skeptical eyebrow. "The library?"

"You've caught me, Miss Snow. I confess." She leaned backward as he leaned forward and said in a sinister whisper, "I like to read."

Lucy sniffed. "You won't find any *novels* in my father's library. He collects only works of consequence."

"Then if you'll excuse me, miss, I need to check the grounds before I retire."

As he gave her a curt nod and turned to go, Lucy lifted her head, surprised by how much his dismissal stung. Suddenly, she didn't want to be left alone in the darkened entrance hall. Didn't want to traverse the deserted corridor to her room by herself. The empty feeling in her midsection had intensified to a longing ache.

"Mr. Claremont?"

It was the tentative note in her voice that stopped Gerard. He bit back an oath. Was this infernal child-woman destined to thwart his every objective? He could still feel the shock of her cool, silky fingers closing over his. When he'd dragged her into the moonlight to find her wrapped in that delicious concoction of lace and silk, he'd felt the blood drain from his roaring head and rush to other, even less rational, areas. Gerard reminded himself savagely that he'd been so long without a woman, he'd probably be equally affected by the sight of Smythe in a dress.

He swung around, his muscles coiled with tension, fully expecting her to tilt her chin in that imperious manner of hers and command him to fetch her slippers in his teeth or empty her chamber pot.

Her chin was set at a regal angle, but he would have almost sworn it quivered just a bit as she opened the library door and beckoned him inside. "I came to fetch my easel. Would you please carry it upstairs for me?" Her smile lacked its usual brittle confidence. "You always seem to be around when I need you."

Gerard steeled himself against a dangerous surge of empathy. "That *is* what your father hired me for."

Lucy was not spared his implication: no man would tolerate her company without being paid for it.

Her most recent artistic effort sat in a bright puddle of moonlight beneath the window. As she packed up her scattered watercolors, Gerard dared do no more than cast the secretary towering over her father's desk a hungry glance.

Lucy was gathering her brushes when Mr. Claremont came to stand behind her, too close as always.

His physical presence was like an invading touch. It made her skin tingle.

Trying to divert herself from the disturbing spice of his bayberry shaving soap, she plunged a stiff paintbrush into a water pot. "Don't be shy, Mr. Claremont. What do you think of my latest effort? Many of my father's associates have told me that I might have enjoyed a career in the arts had I not been born a mere woman." She wiped the paintbrush on a rag, modestly awaiting his praise.

Claremont rocked back on his heels and squinted at the watercolor. "It makes me wonder if you've ever seen the sea."

Lucy pinned him with a disbelieving gaze. There was no trace of teasing or mockery in his face. For once, he looked utterly serious. Lucy didn't want to admit that his opinion mattered one whit to her, but she couldn't quite hide her mild hurt.

She tilted her head, examining the watercolor from all angles. "You don't care for it?"

He shook his head and she knew a brief moment of relief as she waited for him to soothe her wounded ego.

"I loathe it." His opinion was offered with such blunt candor that Lucy found it almost impossible to take offense. He leaned over her shoulder, pointing as he spoke. "Oh, it's technically proficient. You've got the light right and most of the colors." His voice deepened and softened, so close to her ear that his warm breath stirred the tiny hairs at her temple. "But there's not a shred of life in it. Not an ounce of passion."

Unable to resist the seductive timbre of his voice, Lucy's gaze was drawn from the painting to his profile. The moonlight silvered its rugged planes. His eyes shifted from amber to jade in the capricious light. If

Lucy could have sketched him in that moment, he would have never dared to call her passionless.

His hand arched in the air, painting her a vision more vivid than any rendered from paint and water. "The sea at dawn is a cathedral, Lucy."

Her breath caught at the unexpected music of her name on his lips.

"It's where darkness is conquered by light in a battle that's been waging for all eternity. To watch the sun weave that first gleaming thread on the horizon is an invitation to worship, a call to fall on your knees, renounce your cynicism, and embrace the belief that a world as corrupt as ours can be washed clean with nothing more than the spill of the waves against the sand."

Lucy couldn't breathe. She'd long ago resigned herself to being unworthy of love, but the aching knot had moved to her throat—a knot of yearning tainted by agonizing jealousy of something a man could adore so much. She had hoped Claremont's company might ease her loneliness, but instead he had sharpened it, made its edges more jagged.

The lamps of the Admiral's carriage appeared through the bay window, winking in and out among the trees as the vehicle negotiated the curving drive. Panicked more by the foreign emotion than her father's approach, Lucy tore herself free from Claremont's spell and snatched up her paints and brushes.

She tore the offending watercolor from the easel and tucked it under her arm, beyond caring that she was crumpling it. "For a man who's made physically ill by the very suggestion of the sea, Mr. Claremont, you seem to have developed a certain poetic affinity for it."

He folded his arms over his chest. "A common phenomenon, Miss Snow. Don't we all secretly find irresistible that which is most dangerous to us?"

His lips tilted with the mockery she'd come to expect from him, but it was the somber challenge in his eyes that sent her fleeing from the library, easel forgotten, to the tranquil haven of her bedroom.

♥ ♥ ♥

The following evening Gerard learned to his immense frustration that he was to accompany Miss Snow to a Lady Cavendish's supper party. He awaited her in the entrance hall, watching the rain dance down the beveled panes of the bay window. Its plaintive melody made him crave a smoke. The footmen had lit fires in the drawing room and library to burn off the damp, but the entrance hall was already touched by the chill of approaching winter.

Gerard could feel it coming in his bones. Days too short. Nights too long. The inescapable darkness. He wanted to be far from England when it arrived, safe in a place where it was always warm and the misty rain nourished the trees instead of stripping them bare with remorseless fingers.

A light footstep drew him back to chill reality. He turned to discover Lucy descending the stairs. If not for her wretched interference, he thought, he might be on his way to that place even now. Yet a treacherous warmth surged through him at the sight of her.

Her customary white muslin had been replaced by cream silk so sheer he could see the blush of her pink stockings through the graceful folds of her skirt. A wide belt woven from gold filigree girded her waist just below her breasts, accentuating their gentle curves. Her hair had been caught in a loose Greek chignon, artfully arranged to appear disheveled by a lover's hand. Gerard cursed himself to realize just how badly he wished it had been his.

The classical fashions suited her slim form. She glided down the stairs, Persephone freed from the Underworld, bearing the seeds of spring in her lace-gloved fingers.

Gerard couldn't resist the familiar impulse. As she stepped off the last stair, he brought her hand to his lips and pressed a gentleman's kiss to her palm, his lips lingering against the perfumed mesh of lace and skin.

Their eyes met over her upturned hand—hers wide with surprise, his narrowed in challenge. If this were another place, another time, Gerard thought. If he were another man . . .

Realizing how ludicrous they must look, she in her finery and pearls, he in his crudely tailored tailcoat and a hat that had been unfashionable two seasons ago, he dropped her hand.

Smythe emerged from nowhere to drape a cashmere shawl around her shoulders. Gerard scowled, thinking the garment too fragile to protect her from the cold rain.

"My father?" she queried.

"I'm afraid the weather has aggravated his wound, Miss Lucy," Smythe explained. "He won't be attending. He asks that you deliver his regrets to Lady Cavendish."

Gerard hastened Lucy into the waiting carriage. He suspected her father's indisposition had more to do with the fresh exploits of Captain Doom off the coast of the Admiral's own beloved Cornwall. They had been splashed across the front pages of both the *Times* and the *Observer* that morning.

Rain pattered on the carriage roof as Fenster deftly maneuvered them into the congested traffic of the Strand. Its cozy rhythm only served to underscore their awkward silence. Both Lucy's tyranny and the fleeting camaraderie they'd enjoyed in the library seemed to have dissipated in the chill. She gazed out the rain-beaded window, her profile pensive in the hazy glow of the carriage lamp.

Probably fretting over her precious father's conveniently fickle health, Gerard thought unkindly. Or mooning over Captain Doom, nursing her childish infatuation with a phantom.

His irritation increased with every revolution of the carriage's wheels. If the Admiral had wanted a man to squire his spoiled daughter all over town, why hadn't he just hired her a bloody beau? Or a husband? Ionia's library stood unguarded, yet Gerard was to spend the evening banished to some servants' hall, relegated to pressing his nose against an invisible window, separated from everything he'd ever wanted by a mocking twist of fate.

The carriage lurched to a halt. A footman wrapped in an oilcloth cloak appeared at the door. "There's been an accident. Hackney coach overturned in the road."

Gerard opened his mouth to snap a command, but Lucy's cultured tones thwarted him. "Tell Fenster to turn around and take whatever route the other carriages seem to be taking."

Gerard settled back in his seat. He'd do well to remember his place. After all, he was only a servant.

It took the elderly coachman several minutes to untangle them from the snarl of vehicles, but they were soon rumbling after a carriage with an elaborate coat of arms consisting of an eagle with outspread wings emblazoned on its door.

Leaving behind the broad paved lanes haloed by rows of street lamps, the carriages wended their way down an unfamiliar street. Unfamiliar to Lucy, but not to Gerard. He knew every cracked cobblestone, every ramshackle hovel, every smudgepot of an alley. The tainted smell of the river flooded his mind with childhood memories, more bitter than sweet. There was nothing left of the boy who'd been born and raised there. Not even his name.

Some nobleman with a perverse sense of humor had christened the teeming wharf district the Garden. His aristocratic nostrils had obviously never inhaled its hellish stench of rotting fish, stale gin, and overflowing sewage, all layered by centuries of poverty. The river was the pulsing vein of its existence, yet there was never enough water to wash with, never enough water to drink. Was it any wonder Gerard found the lemon-and soap-scented purity of Lucy's skin so unbearably erotic?

Crowds thronged the narrow street, blithely ignoring the rain for most had nowhere to go to escape it. Beggars, whores, and street vendors rushed toward the shiny carriages, hoping their dismal luck was about to change. The clamor of their voices pierced the thin glass of the carriage windows, their cries as timeless as their emaciated faces.

"Spare a farthin' fer a cripple, mate?"

"Come 'ave a glass with me, guv'nor. Ye'll not regret it. Me name's Angel and I can take ye straight to 'eaven!"

"Cat meat! Get yer fresh cat meat!"

Gerard searched Lucy's face for a sign of disdain, not understanding himself why her reaction to this place was so vitally important to him. She was staring straight ahead, her delicately chiseled features as cold and impassive as the Greek statuary she resembled, as cold as the lump of marble she dared to call a heart. Savage disappointment wrenched his gut. He turned his face to the window, knowing he should be relieved that he could no longer bear to look at her.

The ducal carriage had drawn far ahead of them, its occupants eager to escape the seething mass of poverty. The massive vehicle raced toward the deserted corner, its rate of speed increasing as its driver lashed the handsome grays into a dangerous gallop.

Gerard saw Lucy's head jerk toward the window, heard her horrified gasp an instant before he saw the ragged child step into the road, arms outstretched as if to steal just a touch of the splendor thundering past. Then the child was lying crumpled in the road and the carriage was gone, rocking wildly as it disappeared over the horizon.

Gerard bellowed for Fenster to stop, but before their own carriage could lurch to a halt, Lucy had thrown open the door and spilled into the pouring rain.

CHAPTER TEN

GERARD FLUNG HIMSELF OUT OF THE CARriage to find Lucy already kneeling in the street, the fallen child cradled across her lap.

She lifted her face to him. Tears streamed down her pale cheeks, blending with the rain. Pain and fury ravaged her voice. "Were they blind? Couldn't they see her? They didn't even stop! For God's sake, they didn't even slow down!"

"They probably didn't want to risk losing their places at supper," Gerard replied grimly, squatting beside her to check the child's heartbeat and examine her scrawny limbs.

The little girl stirred beneath his probing hands. Her eyes fluttered open, huge in her gaunt face. She gazed up at Lucy in unabashed awe. "'Ave I died, miss? Are you an angel?"

Lucy laughed then, a joyous ripple of sound that arrowed straight to Gerard's heart. He realized that he'd never heard her laugh before.

"I'm afraid I'm no angel, dear. My father would be only too eager to assure you of that."

Gerard smoothed lank strands of hair from the child's grimy brow. "She was only stunned. A few scrapes and bruises, that's all."

A woman came rushing toward them, her sham finery marking her as a whore more plainly than her half-unbuttoned bodice and bare feet. Although she'd clearly tumbled from her most recent customer in a blind panic, she'd taken the time to pin on her bonnet. Gerard was not surprised. He'd had long acquaintance with such displays of pathetic bravado in those with little to wear but their pride. The hat's moth-eaten plume drooped in the rain.

The woman snatched the shaken child from Lucy's arms. "Get yer bloody 'ands off 'er!"

The little girl clung to her mother's neck like an albino monkey, but her adoring gaze remained riveted on Lucy.

Lucy rose to face them, clutching her soiled reticule. "She doesn't seem to have any broken bones, ma'am. We think she'll be fine."

"No thanks t' the likes o' you," the woman snarled.

Gerard held his breath without realizing it, waiting for Lucy to reprove the woman for allowing her child to run wild in the streets. But she endured the setdown with such stoic dignity that the woman launched into a profane tirade, flaying Lucy with the caustic edges of her tongue.

Gerard could not stand idly by as she accepted a rebuke not rightly hers. When the woman paused for breath, he stepped into her line of fire. "Pardon me, madame. Perhaps you misunderstood the situation. It was not Miss Snow's carriage that struck your child. However, she did possess the grace to stop and see to your daughter's well-being."

Something in Gerard's bearing made the woman take a step backward. Her sodden bonnet plume collapsed over one eye. "It don't matter what one run 'er down. Ye're all alike. Bloody selfish bastards, the lot o' you!"

Lucy was fumbling with her reticule. Before Gerard could stop her, she drew forth a wad of pound notes and held them out to the woman. "Please," she said. "Take these for your trouble. Have the child seen by a physician. Buy her something warm to eat." Gerard realized it was more money than her father was paying him in a month.

The woman's gaze lingered hungrily on the modest fortune in the gloved hand before she snatched it and tossed it back in Lucy's face. Lucy blanched, but did not flinch. One crisp note caught in her hair while another fluttered down to sink into a puddle.

"Ye can keep yer bloody charity. I works for my money and proud of it I am." Dismissing Lucy, she raked a bold glance over Gerard, still clutching her daughter to her ample breasts. "If ye'd like t' ditch the duchess and come back later, gent, I'd be more than 'appy t' earn my coin with the talents the good Lord gave me."

Gerard felt his lips harden into a pitiless line as he tipped his hat to her. "Take your child home, madame. Where she belongs."

None of Lucy's clumsy attempts to make reparations infuriated the woman as Gerard's gentle reproof did. With an inarticulate sound of rage, she swiped the hat plume out of her eyes and marched away. The little girl gazed over her mother's rigid shoulder. Her forlorn eyes haunted Gerard. He knew only too well that in a few years she'd probably be selling her own precious body on the street for pennies.

He returned his attention to Lucy, desperate to escape this place and its memories.

She stood staring after the child, her expression desolate, her hair plastered to her head, her beautiful gown soiled and torn. The wet silk clung to her slender curves as if she were Venus freshly risen from the sea. She'd lost both her cashmere shawl and one slipper to a muddy puddle. Her bare toes peeked out from a jagged tear in her left stocking.

Gerard knew then that he'd made a terrible error in judgment. He could have walked away from the woman he had believed her to be without a backward glance. But this was a different woman. One whose lips trembled with vulnerability. One whose sooty lashes were spiked with tears. One whom he could not resist.

He drew off his coat and wrapped it gently around her shoulders. "Come, Lucy. The carriage is waiting."

He guided her toward the vehicle, stepping over the scattered pound notes. Lucy's largesse would not go to waste. Shadows were already creeping out of the alleys and darkened doorways to claim it.

"I've never been so ashamed," she confessed when they were once again settled among the leather squabs of the carriage.

"You weren't the one to run her down."

She toyed with the tattered lace of her gloves. Gerard had to strain to hear her subdued words. "Not then. Before. When I saw those people." She lifted her somber gray eyes to his face. "Why should I have so much when they have so very little?"

He had no answer for that. He'd been wrestling with the same question for most of his life. "Did allowing that woman to berate you and offering her money ease your troubled conscience?"

"I felt sorry for her."

"You saw what she thought of your pity."

Lucy's eyes widened with dawning realization. "She didn't want my kindness, did she? She wanted an excuse to stay angry. She *needed* to be angry. So she could hold on to her pride. How did you know that?"

"Simple. My mother was a whore."

He lounged back in the seat, eyeing her with unbridled arrogance, and awaited the flicker of distaste his crude confession would kindle in her eyes, the politely masked repugnance and veiled pity that would kill his burgeoning regard for her.

Her wistful smile was the last response he'd expected. "So was mine. Only I'm told she accepted no coin for her favors."

Gerard's heart was still struggling to absorb the blow when a footman appeared at the carriage door, poorly hiding his impatience at their delay. "Shall we proceed, my lady?"

Lucy wrung out a fold of her sodden skirt, her broken little laugh sounding more like a hiccup. "Lady Cavendish would have the vapors if I appeared on her doorstep in such a sorry state. There's nothing left for us to do but return home."

Inspired by her feeble attempt at cheer, Gerard held up a hand, stilling both Lucy and the footman. "Stay here," he commanded. "I'll be back in a trice."

Her bodyguard had ducked into the rain before Lucy could remind him that she still had his coat. She snuggled deeper into its depths, both warmed and comforted by the masculine fragrance of bayberry trapped in the coarse fibers.

♥   ♥   ♥

Mr. Claremont returned over twenty minutes later, his arms laden with parcels. Sinking into the opposite seat, he undid his cravat and tossed his hat away with a careless flick of his wrist. His sodden shirt clung to his shoulders. Droplets of rain glistened in the crisp chest hairs curling from the open collar.

He cleared his throat pointedly and Lucy jerked her gaze up, mortified that he'd caught her staring. His familiar smirk of amusement had returned.

To hide her chagrin, she peered out the window at the rainy vista. "The carriage is moving. Where are we going?"

"Why, to supper, of course. I'm your bodyguard, aren't I? 'Tis my duty to see you well nourished."

Lucy sniffed the air; it was fragrant with a potpourri of delicious aromas. An inadvertent moan of anticipation escaped her. "What wicked thing have you done now, Mr. Claremont?"

"Since we've been forced to deprive Lady Cavendish of our charming company, I thought we'd stage our own little supper party."

He spread open his parcels on the seat beside him. Lucy's mouth watered as each new treasure was revealed: roasted apples, a string of sausages, crumbling Banbury cakes, crumpets, a jug of ale, a steaming loaf of bread, and a variety of sweetmeats that made her throat tighten with longing.

"Oh, my!" she whispered. "It's quite splendid."

"The riverbanks aren't completely devoid of charm. They can still provide a feast fit for a beggar king"—he drew a penny-bunch of sweet lavender from his waistcoat with a flourish—"and flowers for his lady."

His humor melted to something more perilous as he leaned forward and gently tucked the sprig of lavender behind her ear. Lucy shivered at his touch. He was doing it again, she thought frantically. Stealing all the air. Shrinking the carriage until their knees touched, their breath mingled, her eyes fluttered shut in foolish invitation.

"I really shouldn't," she murmured.

"Nonsense."

At his crisp reply, her eyes flew open. He was pawing through her reticule. "Ah!" he exclaimed, drawing out a silver object. "I knew there'd be a watch in here somewhere. Probably a barometer and a sextant, too, to measure the precise latitude of the carriage." He dangled the watch in front of her face. "Just as I suspected. Precisely twenty-two hundred hours." The watch disappeared back into the reticule. "And what is scheduled to take place at twenty-two hundred hours, Miss Snow?"

His good humor was irresistible. Lucy tried to swallow a smile, but failed. "Supper?" she ventured.

The carriage rolled to a gentle halt. Lucy lowered the window to find them surrounded by glistening tree trunks. Overhead, a dense canopy of branches melted the rain to a fine mist. Had she been a woman given to fancy, she might have imagined it lent the forested landscape an enchanted air.

"Where are we?" she whispered, hesitant to profane the sylvan hush.

"Berkley Wood. Do you know it?"

"Indeed I do. So does every footpad in London. What are you trying to do? Invite a robbery?"

Claremont crossed his well-muscled arms over the broad expanse of his chest and gave her a dour look. "Why, Miss Snow, your faith in my abilities is touching."

She averted her eyes, disturbed by the masculine display. "What about the servants?"

"They're probably huddled under Fenster's oilcloth sharing their own ale."

Lucy suspected he'd deliberately misunderstood her question. She'd meant, Wouldn't the servants be scandalized by their behavior? But she realized with a shock that for the first time in her life, she didn't care.

She was ravenous and Mr. Claremont's generous feast was simply too tantalizing to resist.

She eyed the string of sausages longingly. "Those aren't cat meat by any chance?"

"Of course not," he promised, breaking off one and handing it to her. She bit into it, savoring its succulent flavor. He grinned. "Only the finest spaniel for Admiral Snow's daughter."

Lucy choked. Claremont handed her his handkerchief and thumped her on the back. "I was only joking. Did it put you in mind of a childhood pet?"

She dabbed her watering eyes. "Oh, no. Father doesn't approve of pets."

"Not even for supper?"

Lucy choked again, this time with laughter. Claremont offered her the jug of ale.

She waved it away, struggling to catch her breath. "I do not indulge in spirits, sir. They only weaken one's moral character."

Leering devilishly, he lifted the jug in a toast before bringing it to his lips. "Precisely."

Lucy covertly admired the flex and ripple of Claremont's tanned throat. She wet her parched lips with her tongue. "Perhaps one tiny sip . . . ?"

He handed her the jug and she wiped its mouth with meticulous care before bringing it to her lips. Realizing too late what she'd done, she reluctantly lifted her eyes to find Claremont studying her with wry amusement.

"Don't worry, dear. You can't get the diseases I've got simply by drinking after me."

Feeling her cheeks flush with chagrin, Lucy took a sip of the ale, then grimaced. Its sour taste was tempered by the thread of warmth that tingled into her belly as she handed the jug back. Claremont cocked an eyebrow in challenge and brought it to his mouth, drinking deeply from the precise spot warmed by the kiss of her own lips. His tongue darted out to catch a stray drop.

Dazed by the deliberate intimacy of the gesture, Lucy reached absently for one of the Banbury cakes.

His hand caught her wrist. "Oh, no, you don't. As your bodyguard, I'd best taste first. After all, it could be"—he lowered his voice to a dramatic pitch—"poisoned."

He bit into the cake, then held it out to her. She reached for it, but he drew it back. The tantalizing treat reappeared just inches from her lips. Lucy glared at him. No one had ever dared to tease her before. It would serve him right if she bit him instead of the cake.

With a woman's instinct she hadn't even realized she possessed, she decided on a more subtle revenge. Ignoring the pristine side of the cake he offered, she turned her head to find the very place his own mouth had touched. Her teeth sank into the crumbly confection. Her eyes closed in rapture and she moaned softly at the forbidden sweetness of the sugar melting on her tongue.

Her eyes fluttered open at the voluptuous shock of his little finger tracing her lower lip, brushing off a faerie dusting of cinnamon.

"Why, Mr. Claremont," she breathed, "your spectacles are fogging up."

"Must be the damp," he said gruffly, jerking back his hand.

Before he could retreat completely, Lucy reached up and gently drew his spectacles off, intending to polish them on her skirt.

But all of her plans, past, present, and future, were forgotten as she gazed, mesmerized, into his unguarded eyes.

How could she ever have thought him mild of manner? Harmless? Innocent? She'd always prided herself on her sensible judgment and the depth of her own folly struck her sharply, shattering the last of her defenses. The shifting hazel of his eyes was wickedness itself, the lush decadence of his lashes temptation incarnate. She'd never seen such lashes on a man. She longed to brush her fingertips across them, suspecting they might shed cinnamon as extravagantly as the Banbury cake.

But the wary vulnerability in his eyes stopped her from touching him and rendered him most dangerous of all.

Depriving him of his spectacles only seemed to sharpen his vision. Lucy was accustomed to being stared through as if she were transparent; she was not accustomed to being stared into. His probing gaze pierced her cool façade as if he could see straight into the lonely soul of the woman beneath.

Her own senses leaped to life with painful keenness. She became achingly aware of the clinging transparency of their garments, the spicy scent of his damp skin, their isolation in the rainy glade, the inches that separated their lips. The Admiral must have been right about her inherited moral shortcomings all along, she thought despairingly. She'd put herself in a position worse than compromising. If this man chose to take advantage of her rashness, she feared she wouldn't have the fortitude to resist him.

"Lucy?"

She swallowed hard, prepared to give him whatever he asked for, including her soul. "Yes, Mr. Claremont?"

"Might I have my spectacles back? I fear I'm blind as a bat without them."

Lucy blinked, doubting her own senses. In the

pause between one breath and the next, Claremont's penetrating gaze had gone vacant. He groped the air between them, rescuing his spectacles from her bloodless fingers.

Before she could question his dizzying transformation, he launched into a flawless imitation of the Admiral, puffing on one of the crumpets as if it were a pipe. Lucy knew she should chastise him for his disrespect, but couldn't seem to squeeze a single reproving word past her muffled shrieks of laughter.

The air outside was chill, but as time lost its edges and melted to a pleasant blur, the carriage was warmed by their teasing accord and the cozy drip of the rain on its roof. They'd polished off the roasted apples and bread and were sampling each sweetmeat in turn when the carriage door flew open.

Lucy gasped in shock. It was not one of the footmen, but Fenster who stood there, weaving like a squat bowling pin.

"Where to, master?" he roared, totally ignoring her. "We've run out of ale. Shall we make a run to the Boar's Head for a fresh keg?"

Claremont shot Lucy a bemused glance. "I think we've sufficiently weakened Fenster's moral character. I'd best drive us home."

Lucy caught his sleeve as he slid past her to climb out of the carriage. "Thank you, Mr. Claremont."

"For what?"

Being kind. Teasing me. Making me laugh.

"Supper," she simply replied.

He covered her hand briefly with his own. "The pleasure was all mine, mouse."

♥   ♥   ♥

Before Gerard could intercept him, Fenster had scrambled into the driver's box with more agility than he'd displayed in decades only to tumble off the other side and lie gurgling happily in the mud. The footmen were of no help at all. They were draped across the back of the carriage, arguing loudly over the chorus to "That Banbury Strumpet, As Sweet As a Crumpet."

Gerard was forced to enlist Lucy's help, and by the time they had gotten Fenster up and strapped to the seat with his own belt, they were both soaked to the skin and weak with fresh laughter.

Shivering, Lucy took refuge in the carriage while Gerard drove them through the deserted streets. He was forced to stop only once, when the footmen came to blows over the disputed lyrics. He interceded, guiding them to a harmony of spirit, if not of song. The words of the ditty were fortunately too slurred for Lucy to understand, but she caught herself humming the catchy melody beneath her breath as they turned into Ionia's cobbled drive. The rich timbre of Mr. Claremont's baritone eased her shivers. She hated to admit it, but she was growing accustomed to the reassuring breadth of his shoulders. His stolid presence suffused her with an unfamiliar warmth.

Had she ever experienced it before, she might have identified it as happiness. As it was, she only knew her belly was full, her toes were tapping, and she was looking forward to rising in the morning for the first time in her memory.

The vehicle rolled to a halt. The swell of voices outside the carriage faded to dread silence. Lucy's toes stilled. Her spirits dampened by a pall of foreboding, she rubbed away a patch of condensation on the carriage's window to find every uncurtained pane of the mansion ablaze with light.

CHAPTER ELEVEN

GERARD WANTED TO HOWL WITH LOSS when the pale oval of Lucy's face emerged from the shadowy interior of the carriage. The warm, enchanting woman he'd glimpsed during their impromptu supper was gone, imprisoned once again beneath an unbreachable veneer of ice. She'd gone whiter than snow, her skin so translucent he could trace the delicate web of veins at her temples. She stepped down from the carriage, ignoring his outstretched hand as if she might crack at his touch.

Sobered by the ominous threat of the lamplight pouring across the lawn, the footmen fled for the servants' entrance, balancing Fenster's tottering form between them. Gerard knew the wise thing to do would be to murmur his own excuses and retreat to the gatehouse, but he found he could not abandon Lucy to face that glaring light alone. He escorted her to the door, his fingers hovering inches from her elbow lest she show any sign of faltering.

Smythe and the Admiral awaited them. Smythe

stood at attention by the bay window, his robe and nightcap so unwrinkled that Gerard wondered if he slept standing, like a horse. The Admiral was resplendent in a dressing gown of royal purple, his hair a gleaming crown of frost. His cane thumped out an irate rhythm as he paced the parquet tiles.

Gerard knew that he had recklessly jeopardized his position, but he wasn't sure he would have traded the stolen interlude, not even if it resulted in his immediate dismissal. The rippling notes of Lucy's laughter had been a song beyond price.

She faced her father, her head bowed like a deposed young queen offering her nape to the guillotine. The mantle of Gerard's coat was still draped across her slender shoulders.

"Why, Lucinda, darling," the Admiral boomed, malice dripping from every syllable. "So glad you decided to join us. You can imagine my distress when I recovered enough to join you at Lady Cavendish's only to discover you'd never arrived. I was quite beside myself with worry."

Lucy gathered her breath to speak, but Gerard spoke first, blinking mildly behind his spectacles. "There was an accident, sir. Two accidents, actually—"

"Silence, Mr. Claremont!" Lucy's voice cut like steel. "If my father had wanted your opinion, he'd have paid you for it."

Gerard had braced himself for the Admiral's rebuke, but Lucy's threw him dangerously off balance. He narrowed his eyes, but she refused to meet his gaze. Who was she protecting? he wondered. Herself? Or him?

"You, sir, are only a servant," the Admiral intoned, implying his status was little better than that of a savage. "I can hardly expect you to honor any measure of decorum. My daughter, however . . ." He trailed off, circling Lucy, the train of his robe swishing like the tail of a hungry lion crouching to pounce on a lamb.

Gerard shoved his clenched fists into his pockets. If Snow so much as rapped Lucy's knuckles, Gerard wouldn't be searching for a new position in the morning. He'd be in the gaol, imprisoned for the murder of his employer.

He should have known Lucien Snow was too cultured to use his fists for weapons. Why should he risk bruising his precious knuckles when he had a weapon as caustic as the contempt he brandished like a cat-o'-nine-tails? Lucy stared at the floor as his arctic gaze surveyed her from the sodden tendrils of her crooked chignon to the soiled and tattered hem of her gown.

When his silence swelled into a punishment all its own, she drew in a shaky breath. "Father, please, I—"

"Hold your tongue, girl. I've no use for your lame excuses or pretty fables. God knows I heard enough of those from your mother after I'd paced the floor all night waiting in vain for her return. She'd stumble in at dawn . . ."—his patrician nose sniffed the air. His cold smile spread as he found what he sought—"reeking of spirits." He smoothed his daughter's tousled hair, his mock tenderness an obscenity Gerard could hardly bear to watch. "Her lovely hair tousled . . . her gown rumpled . . . her lips swollen from her lover's kisses."

Lucy's nape flushed a guilty pink and Gerard cursed himself, knowing she was remembering that innocent brush of his fingertip against her lips. Smythe shot him a glance, the butler's pewter-tinted gaze unreadable. It was growing nearly impossible for Gerard to keep his mask of indifference in place over his seething emotions.

"The only thing that amazes me," the Admiral continued, rocking back on his slippered heels, "is that I am still capable of being disillusioned by the fair sex. Disappointed by the irresponsible and wanton behavior they've exhibited ever since Eve took the apple the serpent offered her and caused the fall of mankind. Have you anything to say for yourself, Lucinda?"

Don't do it, Gerard silently begged. *Damn it to bloody hell, Lucy, don't do it.*

She lifted her head to meet her father's gaze, her gray eyes dominating her chalky face. "I'm sorry, Father."

Smythe bowed his head, looking every minute of his age.

"Very well," the Admiral said, restored to benevolence by his daughter's meek surrender. "I shall search my heart to find forgiveness."

Leaning heavily on his cane, he marched up the stairs, the train of his dressing gown rippling in his wake. Lucy stared after him, her bedraggled appearance making her look like a little girl swallowed by her mother's clothes.

Gerard moved to touch her shoulder, beyond caring what Smythe heard or thought. "He has no right."

Her chin came up, its defiant tilt making his heart contract. Her soft voice was edged with bitterness. "He has every right. He's perfect, you see. I'm the only mistake he ever made."

Shrugging away his hand, Lucy mounted the stairs after her father, her shoulders rigid beneath Gerard's coat. As he turned away, blinded by rage and frustration, his booted foot came down on something spongy.

He bent to discover the penny-bunch of lavender. He picked it up and brought it to his nostrils. The fragile bouquet was crushed almost beyond recognition, but a hint of its elusive fragrance clung stubbornly to the battered blooms. He remembered Lucy's shy smile as he had tucked it behind her ear.

A feast fit for a beggar king . . . and flowers for his lady.

He crumpled the trophy in his fist as Smythe padded around the entrance hall, killing each of the lamps with an efficient flick of his wrist before disappearing into the drawing room to do the same. For once, Gerard welcomed the darkness. It suited his mood.

He narrowed his eyes as he felt someone watching him, savoring his impotent rage. His vision slowly adjusted to find the bust of Admiral Sir Lucien Snow smirking down at him from its oaken pedestal.

He lashed out a fist, toppling it. It crashed to the parquet floor in a satisfying explosion of terra-cotta. Someone behind him politely cleared their throat.

Smythe, Gerard thought, his temper briefly sated by the reckless offering. Of course it would be the Admiral's loyal henchman, the all-knowing, all-seeing Smythe.

He swung around, his unrepentant posture daring the man to challenge him. "Terribly sorry. I must have bumped it in the dark."

Smythe's mild tone held no hint of reproof. "Understood, sir. It might have happened to anyone. I'll fetch a broom."

Gerard scowled as he watched the butler's nightcap bob back into the shadows, wondering if he had an ally or an enemy in the Admiral's enigmatic servant.

♥   ♥   ♥

No one came banging on Gerard's door the following morning. After spending half the night gazing into the dying embers of his fire and the other half tormented by dreams, he slept until ten, waking to discover a slim envelope had been slipped beneath the gatehouse door. Torn between relief and regret, he ripped it open, fully expecting to find his dismissal.

Instead, he discovered a note from Smythe informing him that his services as bodyguard would not be required for several days as Miss Snow would not be venturing out. However, the Admiral would appreciate his continued assistance in organizing his memoirs. A terse postscript in his employer's own handwriting notified him that the price of the bust he'd so clumsily shattered would be extracted from his wages each month in modest increments.

Gerard would have smiled at the last had his eyes not drifted back to *Miss Snow will not be venturing out* . . .

Was the Admiral's daughter to be imprisoned in her room like a medieval princess in disgrace? he wondered, crumpling the note in his fist. If so, why should he give a damn? Lucinda Snow was not his concern. If she chose to spend her life writhing beneath her father's tyrannical thumb, who was he to interfere? Yet he was haunted by his glimpse of another woman—a spirited, laughing woman who had stuffed sweetmeats in her pockets like a mischievous child.

His desperation to be free of Ionia and its young mistress grew as the next few days drifted by in a monotonous stream. He'd never been a man given to loneliness, having long ago learned to tolerate the bleak solitude of his own company, but now a yawning emptiness gnawed at his gut. As the last stubborn leaves surrendered to the ravages of impending winter, he began to wear thin on his own nerves. Each day it grew harder to be civil to the Admiral just for the opportunity to rifle through his personal correspondence or spend a few unguarded moments in the library. His deferential replies hung in his throat, stymied by self-contempt.

He slept poorly, rising before dawn each morning with no prompting to stalk aimlessly across the grounds. He'd forgotten how merciless London's late autumn could be, but he preferred its frigid cold to the familiar chill seeping through his soul. A chill caught in a twisting warren of alleys along the river and nursed beneath layers of damp stone a world away.

Although he kept reminding himself that the Admiral's daughter was a distraction he could ill afford, his ambling journey always led him to the sprawling old oak that stood like a battered sentinel beneath her window. He would lean his shoulder against its grizzled trunk, turn his collar up against the wind whipping off the river, and search the shrouded window for a flutter of curtains or a flash of white.

♥   ♥   ♥

Lucy huddled in the velvet cushions of her window seat, her icy feet tucked beneath a quilt. She peered through the crack separating the lace and damask draperies, watching her bodyguard watch her window. She couldn't pinpoint the moment when his presence had become a comfort instead of an annoyance. She only knew that whenever she crawled out of her cozy bed to find him there, she felt safe, protected from harm by the glowing talisman of his cheroot.

The wind whipped his hair and tore at his coat. Lucy shivered in empathy. As he thrust his hands deep in his coat pockets and turned to trudge toward the kitchens, Lucy pressed her palm to the cold glass and whispered, "Good morning, Mr. Claremont."

♥   ♥   ♥

Five grueling days had passed since Lucy's banishment from polite society when Gerard arrived in the library one morning to discover the spacious room deserted. Seizing the rare moment of privacy, he captured the Admiral's chair and began to rifle through a yellowed stack of ship's logs. He started guiltily when Smythe appeared in the doorway.

Shoving the logs beneath a sheaf of perfumed letters from a married countess who had once believed herself enamored of the Admiral, Gerard said, "If you could learn to do that in a puff of smoke, I do believe we could get you a job on the stage."

"I've always fancied the circus myself, sir. The elephants, you know." Smythe continued to stand there, humming tunelessly beneath his breath.

Eager to continue his search before his employer trundled in, Gerard drew on the rapidly failing reserves of his patience to gently inquire, "May I help you, Smythe?"

The butler snapped to attention, clicking his heels. "I came to inform you that Admiral Snow has stepped out for the morning."

"The morning?" Gerard echoed cautiously. "As in the *entire* morning?"

"The entire morning, sir. He requested that we not wait lunch for him."

Gerard eyed Smythe suspiciously. Why had the butler taken such pains to inform him of Snow's extended absence? Was this some sort of trap? Was the Admiral going to spring out of the chimney and yell "Ah ha!" to catch him at some perfidy, real or imagined? His grim fantasies were only fueled when Smythe made it a point to draw the carved teak doors shut behind him, enclosing Gerard in the hazy gloom of Lucien Snow's sanctuary. The distinctive fragrance of the Admiral's pipe smoke lingered on the air.

Stroking his freshly shaven chin, Gerard paced like a cat left to guard the cream, too skeptical to believe his good fortune. The immaculate surface of the Admiral's desk beckoned to him, the polished brass of the hourglass winking a naughty temptation. The secretary towered over him, its shadowy cubbyholes begging to unfold their secrets. He might never have another opportunity such as this.

Drawing off his boots, he eased open the library doors, edged his way through the deserted entrance hall, and bounded up the curving staircase to the second floor.

♥   ♥   ♥

Gerard's knuckles hung poised in the air, an inch from Lucy's door. He slowly lowered his hand to the brass knob. Why give her an opportunity to refuse him? He'd already concocted a lame fable about a suspicious character lurking about the lawn beneath her window. He had no intention of telling her the suspicious character was him.

He turned the knob, prepared to tactfully, if grudgingly, withdraw if he caught her in some alluring state of dishabille. But as the door swung open, granting him entrée to the deserted room beyond, he wasn't sure he could have retreated had someone held a gun to his temple.

His weighted steps lured him in like a man who had wandered in a barren desert for decades only to stumble upon an abandoned harem, a perfumed bower ripe with the memories and promises of sensual pleasures. His starved senses reeled beneath the subtle assault.

Lucy's refuge was the antithesis of the spartan masculinity that pervaded the rest of the house. A welcoming fire crackled on the brick hearth. Swags of ivory lace draped the testered bed, enveloping the rumpled bedclothes in a gauzy veil. The furniture was inlaid with satinwood, its delicate lines curved and embellished with fanciful curlicues. Plush rugs of dizzying varieties overlapped the floor as if every rug that had ever dared to mar the Admiral's polished planking had found its way here, rescued by Lucy's generous hand.

Gerard grinned as he circled the room, delighted by
his discovery—the flawlessly groomed, impeccably
coiffed, never-a-ribbon-out-of-place Miss Snow was an
abject slob! Captivated by the room's untidy charm,
Gerard ran his palm over the unmade bed, tweaked
the toe of a pink stocking slung brazenly over the canopy, buried his fingers in the seductive waterfall of silk
and lace spilling from the half-opened drawers of the
wardrobe.

An abject slob with decidedly decadent taste in undergarments, he mused, caressing the creamy silk of a
champagne blond chemise between his forefinger and
thumb. He surrendered it with lazy reluctance. It
would hardly do for Lucy to return to find him fon-
dling her intimate apparel.

Pausing at the cluttered dressing table, he brought
the unstoppered mouth of a cut-crystal bottle to his
nostrils, dizzied by the clean, lemony fragrance that
was so distinctly Lucy. A wheeled tea cart, tarnished
with age, crouched near the window seat, its surface
littered with miniature clay pots overflowing with a
profusion of blooming gloxinia.

Gerard stroked one of the fuzzy, veined leaves,
thinking how like their mistress they were, prickly in
appearance, but sheer velvet to the touch. A patchwork quilt lay abandoned in the window seat. He fingered its frayed hem, smiling to imagine Lucy engulfed
in its cozy depths. As he let the edge of the quilt fall, a
fat sketchbook tumbled to the floor.

Gerard squatted to examine it. He shuffled through
page after page, the shame he should have felt at such
blatant prying suppressed by pure amazement.

No insipid watercolors these, but charcoal sketches,
etched in bold, passionate strokes. He'd never
dreamed the delicate blooms of a gloxinia could be

reproduced with such sensual violence. He laughed aloud to discover tucked among the floral sketches a crude caricature of a Royal Navy officer worthy of Hogarth in his heyday. Lucy would undoubtedly deny it if he pointed out how much the bloated prig resembled the Admiral.

His laughter faded as he flipped the page to find a young woman, little more than a girl, with the same bell-shaped flowers twined in her dark hair. Her mischievous smile was marred by an aura of indefinable sadness.

The sketchbook was snatched from his hands. "Mr. Claremont! What in blazes do you think you're doing?"

Lucy stood over him, her hair damp, her silk negligee clinging to her body in all the wrong places. She hugged the sketchbook to her chest as if to shield both it and herself from his hungry gaze. Gerard's excuses failed him, driven from his mind by that haunting sketch and the lemon-scented musk of Lucy's freshly washed skin.

"Who was she?" he asked, rising slowly to his feet.

Lucy didn't have to take a second look at the sketchbook. "My mother."

"You remember her?"

"Of course not." Lucy's voice was brisk with disdain. "She had the grace to die of childbed fever a week after my birth, sparing my father any further embarrassment from her scandalous behavior."

Bravo, Lucy! Gerard thought. He wished nothing less for the Admiral than a taste of that magnificent sarcasm. "It appears to be a remarkable likeness. Was there a portrait? A miniature?"

She dodged his relentless pursuit, seeking refuge in the forest of potted blooms. "Smythe described her for me." Lucy's free hand drifted over the plants almost absently, correcting the angle of a crooked pot so its leaves could drink in the meager light. "Gloxinia were her hobby. All of these came from clippings rooted from her flowers. Smythe cared for them until I grew old enough to tend them."

Gerard's jaw tensed. Any man who would fight for twenty years to keep a woman's spirit alive, both in these frail blooms and in the even more fragile memory of her daughter, was not a man to be underestimated.

"I don't know why she chose gloxinia," Lucy went on, plucking away a dead leaf. "They're the fussiest flowers in the world. They have to be watered from the bottom. They only favor the morning light."

Gerard could barely conceive of what it must have been like to be the Admiral's bride. "Perhaps she needed something to nurture."

Lucy rewarded him with a flash of silver in her gray eyes. "That's rubbish! She wasn't the nurturing sort. She was a woman of weak moral fiber who cared for nothing but parties, champagne, and her latest lover, whoever he might have been that particular week."

Gerard knew Lucy was too bitter to recognize the inconsistencies in her own behavior. Even as she denounced her mother, she tenderly nursed her sole link to the woman and struggled to resurrect her, if only as a ghost sketched in charcoal.

Gerard realized then that the Admiral had not banished Lucy to this cozy haven. She had retreated here of her own accord to punish herself for her mother's sins, be they genuine or existing only in the Admiral's twisted memory. He suspected this wasn't the first time she had willfully shut herself away from her father's unfounded accusations, his bullying, his rigid tyranny of her time.

Gerard advanced on her, hand extended, more determined than ever to goad to life the vibrant spirit he'd glimpsed in her art. "I want to see more of your work."

Both the gloxinia and her mother were forgotten as Lucy clutched the sketchbook with both arms. "I think not, sir. Your position may give you license to spy on me, but not to snoop through my personal belongings."

"Come now, Lucy," he coaxed, favoring her with a shameless smile that had melted wills much sterner than hers. "Don't hide your light under a bushel. Those sketches are quite impressive."

She backed against the tea cart, rattling her precious pots. "And you, sir, are quite impertinent."

"So I've been told."

He reached for the sketchbook, but she ducked beneath his arm to make for the open door. Gerard's reflexes had been honed on fleeter prey than she. He slowed her flight by pressing a stocking foot to the hem of her negligee, then caught her around the waist, fully intending to tickle her into submission if necessary.

But he had not wagered on the lush feel of her in his arms, her trembling acquiescence to his playful embrace. His body betrayed him without remorse, damning him to hell and back for his own rash folly. He touched his lips to her hair, breathing in its soapy scent, drinking in its silken texture.

"Don't!" Her piteous whisper seized his heart. "I don't like to be touched."

He rubbed his cheek to the velvety softness of her temple, groaning hoarsely as her body melted against his in helpless response. "On the contrary, Lucy. I think you'd like very much to be touched."

His splayed fingers were recklessly parting the folds

of her negligee to prove his point when the forgotten sketchbook slid from her arms, spilling at their feet a flawless drawing of a majestic schooner drifting out of the mist, a single stark word etched on its bow.

Retribution.

CHAPTER TWELVE

LUCY FROZE IN CLAREMONT'S ARMS AS they both stared down at the fallen sketch. His embrace underwent a subtle shift, the arm beneath her breasts tightening to imprison her without mercy against the muscled wall of his chest. His breathing resounded in her ear like the threat of distant thunder.

Lucy shivered, overwhelmed by his intensity, his palpable strength, the potent masculinity of his stance. She was shamed by her own yearning to turn in his arms, mold her body to his, and offer her parted lips up like a sacrifice to a pagan god. Not even a lifetime spent in the Admiral's shadow had prepared her to feel so vulnerable, so fearful of being consumed by another's will. She pressed her eyes shut, dizzied by the nagging sensation that she'd danced this dangerous dance before, in another time, another place.

"Stop it! You're hurting me!" she lied, desperate to escape his assault on her bewildered senses.

His arms fell away so abruptly that Lucy felt a pang of guilt, as if it were she who had hurt him. Still unsteady on her feet, she reached for the scattered drawings. Gerard snatched them from beneath her hand with a ruthlessness that warned her they were no longer playing some harmless game of cat and mouse.

"What the bloody hell is this?" His eyes narrowed behind his spectacles as he thumbed through the sketches, taking care even in his haste not to crumple or smear them.

Lucy held her silence, already knowing what he would find. Sketch after sketch of the phantom ship that had haunted her since it had first come drifting out of the mists of her imagination. The *Retribution* sailing across a bloated pumpkin of an autumn moon, cresting a mountain range of stormy billows, teetering on the edge of a churning whirlpool. The *Retribution,* her delicately etched rigging frosted silver by an unearthly web of lightning.

Claremont's taut voice radiated anger. "Quite a departure from your milksop seascapes, aren't they? Positively brimming with passion and majesty."

He went abruptly silent, his stillness more frightening than his frenzied search had been. An alarmed squeak escaped Lucy as he pivoted on his heel to face her. He was beyond furious. The grim sparkle in his eyes made her father's frequent rages appear nothing more than infantile tantrums. He took a step toward her; Lucy took a step away from him.

The wall blocked further flight. Lucy shrank against it and was just contemplating screaming for Smythe when Claremont gently drawled, "Tell me, Miss Snow, does lunacy run in your family?"

She clutched her negligee shut at the throat. "I can't pretend to know what you mean. They're just drawings. They're of no import whatsoever."

He thrust a sketch in her face—a man, more phantom than reality, shrouded in mist, ghostly shadows of rigging crisscrossing his bearded face. "This is him, isn't it? Your precious Captain Doom."

She tilted her head, examining the sketch from all angles as if she'd never seen it before. "I don't remember. It could be anyone."

His skeptical gaze was sharp enough to flay the thin silk of the negligee from her skin. "Have you any idea what you've done?" he asked softly. "How you've endangered yourself? If Doom knew these existed, do you really think he could afford to let you live?" His voice rose to a shout. "Do you?"

Lucy flinched. Claremont swore and whirled to pace the cluttered room, running a hand through his hair. "You seem determined to make the job of protecting you a challenge, Miss Snow. I can only surmise how grateful the Royal Navy was to receive sketches this detailed. Once they start circulating, your pathetic little life won't be worth a trice to Doom." He swung back around to confront her. "I'm sure the Admiral was delighted for you to turn your talents to such a noble cause."

Lucy slumped against the wall, shooting him a sheepish glance before quietly confessing, "My father's never seen the sketches. No one has. Except for you."

Claremont sank down on the edge of the bed and gaped at her as if she'd suddenly begun to gibber in a foreign tongue. Lucy thought it might be ill-timed and rather belated to chide him for his impropriety.

"I don't suppose you'd care to tell me why?"

Reassured by his rational tone, she glided to the bed and rescued her sketches from his limp fingers. She held the drawing of Doom to the light, gently passing her fingertips over his charcoal-shaded beard. She was too engrossed in her memories to see the strange shudder that passed through Claremont.

She said softly, "It might shock you to know that

I've searched this portrait for hours only to discover a thread of honor in this man's countenance, a strain of nobility, if you will."

"Excuse me, but are we referring to the same fellow who adorns his neck with human ears and cheerfully rips the hearts from his victims while they're still thumping?"

Lucy winced. "A blatant exaggeration, I fear. Just one of the many grave injustices I've done the man."

Claremont's eyes hardened to shards of jade. "What of the injustices he did you? Abducting you? Throwing you overboard like so much shark bait?"

Lucy's cheeks heated with the painful fire that had plagued them since her encounter with the pirate. "It's not what he did to me, Mr. Claremont. It's what he *didn't* do."

Her impassioned words hung in the perfumed air between them. A gentleman would have pretended to understand. Claremont was no gentleman.

He lounged back on his elbows, looking shockingly at home in the rumpled folds of her counterpane. "Do go on."

Her hands twisted together, unwittingly crumpling the edges of the sketch. "You know as well as I that given the circumstances, he might easily have . . . could have . . ." She searched for a delicate phrase.

"Raped you?" Claremont offered coolly. "Stolen your virtue and left you for dead?" Lucy should have been mortified by his blunt candor. Instead she was mesmerized by the unholy mischief in his eyes, the black humor that twisted his mouth into a travesty of a smile. He indicated the sketches. "So all this time, because of his dubious restraint, you've fancied yourself protecting the man."

She nodded. "It was the least I could do after misjudging him so harshly."

Claremont rose from the bed, taller than she remembered, all traces of both mockery and amusement erased from his face. "You don't need to read fiction, Miss Snow. You're living it. Despite your tender and hopelessly romantic fantasies, this fellow Doom is not some misunderstood hero. He's a desperate, ruthless bastard who has nothing left to lose and everything to gain."

"You speak as if you know him."

"I know many like him. It's unavoidable in my profession." He advanced on her, but this time Lucy stood her ground. For the first time, her bodyguard's speech was underscored by the harsh cadences of the London streets. "And not one out of the bloody lot of them would let some spoiled, lonely brat—"

Stung by his unfairness, Lucy cried, "But I'm not—"

His next words robbed her of her defense. "—no matter how breathtakingly beautiful, stand in the way of what they wanted." Claremont caught her chin in an implacable grip. "If your path ever crosses Doom's again, God forbid, don't make the mistake of underestimating him. He might not be such a gentleman."

Lucy blinked back tears as he tumbled her idol, trying desperately to hide how deeply his words wounded her. "So you think me a sentimental fool?" she whispered.

His grip softened. His palm wandered up to smooth a wing of damp hair from her cheek. Her breath caught at his scorching tenderness. "On the contrary, my dear Lucy. I think your noble Captain Doom a fool. If I had a woman such as you at my mercy, I'd never let her go."

But Claremont did just that, striding from the room without so much as a backward glance.

♥   ♥   ♥

When Lucy slipped into the library the next morning at exactly 0900, she found her father pacing in front of his desk, Smythe polishing a brass sextant as if his very existence depended upon it, and her bodyguard nowhere in sight.

She had waged a restless battle with her bedclothes most of the night, trying to determine whether she'd been complimented or insulted, cautioned or threatened, protected or compromised. She only knew that every time she closed her eyes, she saw not the charcoal rendering of Captain Doom, but hazel eyes sparkling with raw emotion.

She slid into her chair, hoping to find some peace by throwing herself back into the soothing rhythm of her daily routine, where thought was neither necessary nor desirable.

Her father's cane thumped a staccato warning as he limped around to glower at her. His eyebrows gathered over his aquiline nose like snow-laden clouds. It was the same look he'd leveled at her after her rescue from the *Retribution*. The same look he'd given her as a child when she'd thought to please him by blacking his uniform boots with India ink.

She devoted her attention to organizing her pens and paper, resisting the overpowering urge to start blathering, confessing her guilt for lurid sins and passionate crimes she'd contemplated only in her most feverish imaginings.

Instead, she forced herself to say "Good morning, Father. I trust you slept well," as if she hadn't deliberately avoided his presence for the past five days.

He snorted in disgust. "Not as well as your Mr. Claremont, it appears." He drew out his chronometer and glared at it. His ruddy color heightened. "I'd like to know what in thunder is going on around here. Has the entire discipline of this household gone to rot?

What's next, Smythe? Will you start languishing in *your* bed until noon?"

"I should say not, sir." The butler appeared dutifully horrified at the suggestion. The Admiral considered sloth as number two on his own personal list of the seven deadly sins. Right after adultery and before patricide.

Mr. Claremont appeared in the doorway, his head inclined toward the book in his hands. The sight of his unyielding shoulders tied all of Lucy's sensible intentions into a hopeless tangle. The Admiral stared pointedly at the mantel clock and cleared his throat with the force of a cannon shot.

Claremont looked up then, riveting Lucy with the guileless blink of his cinnamon lashes behind the polished lenses of his spectacles. "My apologies, sir. I became so engrossed in Lord Howell's account of your triumph at Sadras that I lost all sense of the time."

Her bodyguard's bland innocence was so convincing that even Lucy was tempted to believe him. The man was a consummate liar. A trait her treacherous heart would do well to remember.

Claremont slouched in his chair and began to thumb through a sheaf of yellowed letters, missing the piercing gaze the Admiral leveled at him. Lucy could almost see the cogs of suspicion jerking to life in her father's head.

A splinter of foreboding twisted in her stomach. She knew better than anyone that the Admiral's trust, once lost, could never be regained.

♥ ♥ ♥

Lucy huddled alone in a corner of the carriage, thinking how immense its interior seemed to have grown with Mr. Claremont riding atop with Fenster. Not even the threat of freezing rain from the bruised charcoal of the sky could drive him to seek her company.

They were off to the Theater Royal in Drury Lane to watch the great Sarah Siddons portray Lady MacBeth. Lucy thought direly that the tragedy was an appropriate counterpart to her mood. She tried to hum the melody of "That Banbury Strumpet, As Sweet As A Crumpet," but found the hollow sound an unbearable reminder of how empty her life had been before Mr. Claremont had elbowed his way into it.

Since discovering her sketches of Captain Doom, her bodyguard had retreated behind a demeanor of cool professionalism. The man who had taken such wicked delight in teasing and cajoling her the night of their impromptu picnic had vanished, replaced by a punctual, neatly garbed stranger who treated her with the respectful deference of a servant.

There was nothing in Claremont's performance to complain of to her father. He tipped his hat and bowed graciously to her every wish. At social functions, he remained with the carriage or stood at rigid attention in the corner, his aloof glower making the guests fidget. Even Sylvie remarked upon his uncommon devotion to duty.

But when Lucy stumbled out of bed each morning at dawn, the gnarled oak tree beneath her window stood sentinel alone, its naked branches shivering against the bleak sky.

His deliberate distance punished her in ways she hadn't anticipated. She realized for the first time how much she had secretly enjoyed his impertinent scowls, his mocking smiles, his exaggerated yawns at her father's ramblings. His expressive face was now closed and unreadable.

She toyed fitfully with her gloves. Claremont's defection had left her no choice but to resume her lady-of-the-manor posturing, but her spirit was no longer in the game.

The carriage drew to a halt. Catherine Street teemed with the bustle of Saturday night—the chatter of the crowds, the cries and curses of the drivers, the stamping and whinnying of the restless horses.

When the door to the carriage failed to open, Lucy tapped on the front window with the ivory handle of her fan.

Fenster's homely face appeared, screwed into a jack-o'-lantern's grimace. "Sorry, miss. The traffic's in a devil of a snarl. We'll have to wait it out."

Lucy gathered her gloves and reticule. "Sylvie will never forgive me if we miss the opening curtain. It's only a few blocks. We shall walk."

Claremont spoke without turning around. "That would hardly be advisable, Miss Snow."

All the more reason to attempt it, she thought wickedly. "John," she called out. "Please help me down."

Instead of the freckled footman, it was Claremont who opened the carriage door, wrenching it with such force that Lucy was surprised it didn't topple off its hinges. She was unprepared for the quizzical warmth melting inside of her. The hint of a sulk around her bodyguard's mouth only made his face more compelling. She was beset by a terrible urge to touch him, to trace his expressive lips with her fingertips until the lines of tension around them thawed.

"I cannot recommend this," he said. "It will be very difficult to protect you in this crowd."

"Nonsense, Mr. Claremont. I have the greatest confidence in your abilities."

He didn't budge or offer her a hand so she was forced to brush past him to climb out of the carriage. The brief contact dizzied her. Ignoring the brisk wind biting through her thin cape, she swept ahead of him, giving him no choice but to follow. The glow of the scattered street lamps barely pierced the evening gloom.

After they'd traveled a block, she dropped her fan, then hesitated. "Would you be so kind as to retrieve my fan?"

He did, slapping it into her palm.

A few more feet and her satin reticule slid off her arm. "How clumsy of me." She cast him an entreating look. "Could you . . . ?"

His breath escaped in rhythmic puffs of steam. Scenting victory, she marched ahead as he bent to retrieve the reticule, ducking into the darkened doorway of a bookseller's shop. She was too engrossed in her game to notice the three dark shapes who darted into an adjacent doorway.

She peeped around the corner just as Claremont straightened. His eyes scanned the crowd, searching for her. The raw concern on his face shamed her until she reminded herself that he was probably more worried about his monthly wages than her well-being. She was gathering her cape to flee to another hiding place when a hand clamped down on her arm, a hand lightly sprinkled with ginger and smelling of spice.

Claremont's face was as resolute as she had ever seen it as he marched her back toward the carriage.

She stumbled along in front of him, painfully aware of the curious stares of the crowd. "Where are we going? The theater is that way."

"I'm not taking you to the theater. I'm taking you home. I've a job to do and if you persist in behaving like a wayward child, you give me no choice but to treat you like one."

"You're my bodyguard, not my nursemaid." Lucy tried to plant her feet on the pavement to no avail.

"Stop it this instant! You're making a public spectacle of us. Do you want to cause a scandal?"

With no warning, he shoved her into a deserted alleyway, carrying their spectacle into the realm of the private. The comforting chatter of the crowd suddenly seemed very far away.

As he drew her around to face him, his hand still clamped like a vise on her arm, she realized she'd finally succeeded in what she had set out to do. All traces of indifference had been wiped from his eyes, vanquished by glittering fury. He loomed over her, his familiar features obscured by shadow, his big, warm body no longer a refuge, but a threat.

This was no phantom to fuel her midnight fantasies who could be safely banished by the morning light. This was a man—six feet of pure masculine animal tempered by years of experience.

The taste of Lucy's triumph was bittersweet. She could only gaze up at him and try not to tremble.

"We wouldn't wish to damage your father's precious reputation, now would we, Miss Snow?" he bit off between clenched teeth. "So walk with me or, as God is my witness, I shall carry you."

Lucy stuck out her lip a mutinous inch, but the Admiral had taught her since birth that there was no shame in surrendering if you were outgunned and out-manned. Mr. Claremont accomplished both with negligent effort.

"Very well," she said.

He wheeled around and took a few steps toward the mouth of the alley, obviously expecting her to follow.

Defeat made Lucy reckless. Her glove fluttered to the cobblestones. "But not until you retrieve my glove."

He pivoted slowly, staring at the dainty scrap of silk she'd tossed down like a gauntlet between them. A disbelieving smile slanted across his face. More alarmed by his ferocious good humor than she'd been by his anger, Lucy took a step backward. Her shoulder blades came up against a sooty brick wall.

He pointed a finger at her. "You, my dear, can retrieve your own bloody glove. You can also balance your own embroidery frame and sharpen your own damn pencils. I'm tired of being led on a merry chase by the likes of you. I'm not your nursemaid *or* your lady's maid. For all I care, you can run sniveling back to your father because the two of you deserve each other." He tossed her reticule at her. She reacted just quickly enough to keep it from falling. "I quit!"

Panic seized Lucy as he turned to go, his broad shoulders silhouetted against the feeble lamplight. What if this were to be her last glimpse of him? What if he melted into the teeming crowd, disappearing from her life as abruptly as he'd come into it? A blade of pain knifed her heart.

Her gaze darted around the deserted alley, searching wildly for any excuse to make him stay. "You can't just abandon me," she wailed. "What if Captain Doom should abduct me?"

He waved a derisive arm in her direction. "He's welcome to you as far as I'm concerned. And God pity the man!"

At that fresh insult, Lucy drew herself up, swallowed her panic, and gathered her pride. "Your resignation is not accepted, Mr. Claremont. You're dismissed!"

He disappeared around the corner.

Lucy's triumph at winning the last word faded as quickly as her show of spirit. She slumped at the back of the alley, utterly alone. She hadn't felt so miserable since she'd embedded her father's favorite letter opener in Captain Doom's unsuspecting shoulder. It was as if she'd not only done another person injury, but mortally wounded herself.

She ought to be celebrating, she told herself fiercely, blinking back tears. Wasn't this what she had wanted all along? To be rid of Claremont. To drive him into resigning from his position so she could regain her precious independence. Her privacy. Her solitude.

She turned her face to the wall, discovering too late that Mr. Claremont's apathy was far more tolerable than his absence.

The brooding sky chose that inopportune moment to dump a bucket of frozen rain on her head. Its icy teeth chewed through her thin cape, soaking her finery without mercy. She was so enveloped in her haze of misery that she never saw the menacing shapes come creeping out of the shadows.

"Lost yer fine gent, did ye, lass?"

Lucy jerked her head up to find a mouthful of blackened and broken teeth only inches from hers. She recoiled from the stench of the speaker's breath and blinked the rain from her eyes to discover two grimy, rag-swathed men.

The second of them, whose long, lank hair looked no worse for the wetting, clucked at her in sympathy. "Come now, girl, don't be sad. We may not 'ave as much coin as that fine fellow, but we knows 'ow to show a lady a good time."

Only seconds before, Lucy had been certain she had reached the very nadir of her existence. Now she discovered that she had dedicated her entire life to maintaining the appearance of propriety only to end up being mistaken for a prostitute in some dreary London back alley. Mr. Claremont's perverse sense of humor must have corrupted her, for she found herself choked with helpless laughter instead of tears.

She swiped rain from her eyes, confounded by the

odd mixture of despair and hilarity. "I'm afraid there's been a dreadful misunderstanding, gentlemen."

"We ain't no gents," came another voice, low and threatening. "And you ain't no lady."

Lucy's amused chagrin faded as a third figure emerged from the shadows. His narrow face had the sharpness and cunning of a fox's.

His rabid gaze snaked to her reticule. Its satin skin was swollen with her handkerchief and everpresent watch. "Seein' as we ain't got no coin and you do, mayhap you could pay us for our services. We're worth it, ain't we, mates? All the wenches says so."

Their harsh laughter grated across Lucy's nerves. Her heart began to thud dully in her ears. She inched toward the mouth of the alley only to discover her path blocked by the men. She had no parasol with which to defend herself, no tender, teasing bodyguard to protect her.

Fighting the paralysis of terror, she forced a coy smile and dangled the reticule in front of Mr. Fox-Face's greedy eyes. His ragged whiskers twitched in anticipation.

"I doubt even the three of you together are worth this much gold," she said.

He snatched at the bait. Thankful for the solid weight of her watch, she swung the tiny purse in a wide arc, smashing him in the ear. Before she could flee, the other two were on her, dragging her to the cobblestones in a flurry of straining limbs and rending silk.

♥   ♥   ♥

Gerard lounged against the wall next to the alley and waited for Lucy to emerge. He supposed she was sulking, expecting him to soften and return to retrieve both her and her precious glove. His self-contempt mounted as he realized he was doing it again—playing his role as bodyguard with such flair and conviction that even he was coming to believe it. How could he hope to protect Lucy when the most dangerous threat to her was him?

He tilted his head back, letting the icy darts of rain stab his face. They did nothing to cool his rage. The time had come to bring this ridiculous charade to an end. He'd known it the instant he'd seen Lucy's damning sketches and listened to her tender defense of Captain Doom. It was a pity, he thought, that the jaded pirate would never fully appreciate the loyalty, however misguided, of his enemy's daughter.

He shoved himself away from the wall. He had thought to see his young mistress home for the last time, but surely even the disaster-prone Miss Snow could make it one block to the security of the carriage without his protection.

He ought to be thankful to be free of this farce, he told himself as he slipped the spectacles into his coat and started down the pavement. But unbidden memories pelted him with every step: wrapping Lucy in his coat to shield her from the rain, feeding her sugary comfits from his fingertips, drawing her so tightly against his body that she'd felt like a part of him that had been missing since birth. A phantom limb that now ached all the more because of its fleeting restoration.

With no effort at all, Gerard could feel her melting against him through her thin negligee as she'd done in that moment when he had enfolded her in his arms. Could feel the tickle of her damp hair against his cheek. Smell the lingering scent of soap warmed by the secret hollows of her flesh until it incited his body like an aphrodisiac. His loins pounded an exquisite protest, torturing him as he deserved.

He hastened his steps. He might have removed himself from Miss Snow's service, but he still had unfinished business with her father. The rigid contours of his pistol prodded his ribs.

A muffled yelp sounded behind him. He stopped. The crowds streamed around him, recoiling from his fierce expression.

"Her bloody Highness probably wants me to step on a cockroach for her so she doesn't soil her dainty little slipper," he muttered. "Sorry, Princess, not this time."

Ignoring the hollow clench of his gut, he resumed walking, his long strides surer than before. He was done playing knight in tarnished armor to Lucy Snow's lady bountiful.

He froze in his tracks. For over the raucous clamor of the crowd had flown a sound he'd never thought to hear. A single name couched in a terrified scream that chilled his blood to ice.

Gerard.

CHAPTER THIRTEEN

THE IMPACT OF GERARD'S FIRST STRIKE against her attackers rattled Lucy like a broadside from a seventy-four-gunner.

There was no time to feel relief, no time to do anything but crawl through the confused tangle of arms and legs to cower against the wall. Helpless to stop shivering, she drew the tatters of her cape around her, deafened to everything but the uncontrollable chattering of her own teeth.

Her bodyguard dispatched the hooligans with ruthless efficiency. He grabbed the one by his long, stringy hair and smashed his face into the bricks. The man collapsed in a groaning heap upon the cobblestones.

Another rushed at Gerard's back. Lucy tried to scream a warning, but her swollen throat refused to cooperate. Her hoarse squeak proved to be superfluous, for with the well-honed instincts of a born street brawler, Gerard wheeled around and drove his fist into the man's face with enough force to dislodge the remainder of his rotting teeth. The enraged thief was fool enough to draw a knife and charge him again. Gerard grabbed the man's wrist before the jagged blade could pierce his cheek and twisted.

Lucy slammed her eyes shut at the resulting crunch.

Her eyes flew open at another sound, even more damning than the last.

Gerard stood with his feet braced wide on the damp cobblestones, deadly mastery etched in his stance. Even more deadly was the gleaming pistol cocked in his hand. Lucy stopped shivering. A primitive thrill shot through her as she realized for the first time what a dangerous man her protector truly was. Primitive, for instead of cringing in repugnance, her heart swelled with pride.

The object of Gerard's lethal attention was the bewhiskered leader, who had taken advantage of his compatriots' recklessness to slink toward the crumbling wall at the back of the alley.

The man lifted his shaking hands in a plea. " 'Ave mercy, gent," he whined. "There ain't no call to shoot me. We meant no 'arm t' the little lady. We thought ye'd had yer fill of 'er and wouldn't mind us takin' a turn."

Gerard's expressive mouth curled in a sneer of contempt. "That's where you made your mistake, chap. I never let another man touch what belongs to me."

His arrogant assertion, however much of a bluff, should have outraged Lucy. Instead, it sent another peculiar thrill tingling through her.

Gerard's gun arm tensed, and for one terrible moment, Lucy thought he was going to shoot her assailant down cold. Then he slowly lowered the pistol and the man fled, scampering over the wall like a terrified rodent.

The cold, heavy weight of the pistol dangled from Gerard's hand. An icy ball of fury had lodged in his chest, slowing his heartbeats until each one of them rang in his ears like a ship's bell tolling disaster. He could scent blood, taste the heady promise of violence on his tongue. Through the roaring in his ears, he heard laughing taunts in French and Spanish, the dull thud of a boot slamming into his rib cage, the impotent rattle of chains. A hand gave his sleeve a tentative tug.

He swung around, his chest heaving with fury.

"Are you all right?" Lucy whispered.

A wave of self-loathing washed over him. He was supposed to be this woman's bodyguard, yet she stood gazing up at him, her fingers entangled in his sleeve, her eyes luminous with tender concern.

She was shaking so hard that the rattle of her teeth was audible. Disheveled strands of hair tumbled over her face. Shadows bruised the delicate skin beneath her eyes, making them look even more enormous against the stark pallor of her skin. She had valiantly tried to arrange the soot-stained tatters of her cape around her, as if they could ward off more than just the chill.

As she blinked back tears with a stubborn bravery that shamed him, the ball of ice in Gerard's chest began to melt. He felt something he'd only felt once before. A searing heat. A fierce tenderness. A raw desire to protect and cherish. A dangerous vulnerability.

He shoved the pistol into his coat and reached for her, but the ugly stains on his hands stopped him. Bloodstains. Not his own, but the blood of others.

Perhaps it was for the best. Better for her to see his true nature as only those dark, damning stains could reveal it. He waited for her to recoil in horrified disgust for the sort of man he had proved himself to be.

He was stunned when, instead, she threw herself past his hands and into his open arms, burying her face in his cravat and twisting his coat in her balled fists as if she would never let it go.

Caught unprepared by the grace of her trust, he wrapped his arms around her. The crude stains on his hands forgotten, he smoothed her damp hair and whispered hoarse, soothing words, some coherent, some not. When his ministrations failed to ease her violent trembling, he scooped her up in his arms and drew the torn cape over her hair to shield her from the fitful rain.

Undaunted by the weather, a rapt crowd had gathered at the mouth of the alley, their appetites for excitement whetted by the rumor of an ugly brawl. Refusing to expose Lucy to their leers and speculations, Gerard bounded over the back wall. There would be ample time later for remorse, time to lash himself for his sins, not the least of which was leaving Lucy to fend for herself on the hazardous London streets.

For now, all he wanted to do was take her somewhere warm, dry, and private. Home was out of the question since her father's suspicions and censure would render it a prison, not a refuge. He veered away from the carriage and strode toward the welcoming lights of a modest inn.

As Gerard burst through the door in a flurry of wind and rain, the balding innkeeper paused at polishing the bar. A handful of patrons scattered at tables around the hearth glanced up eagerly from their drinking and gaming to see what fresh sport was to be had.

At the sight of the inert, but plainly feminine, bundle in Gerard's arms, the innkeeper slammed down his rag. "Come now, gent! This is a respectable establishment. We'll have none of that here!"

Lucy peeped out from her cozy nest, flinching at the rumble of the hostile male voice. Without a word, Gerard drew a heavy leather purse from his coat and tossed it toward the innkeeper. It landed on the bar with a promising clunk. Even in her muddled state, Lucy thought to wonder how Gerard could have amassed such a relative fortune. The Admiral was not known for his generosity to his staff.

To the innkeeper's credit, he didn't pounce on the purse as he obviously longed to do. Instead, he blinked away his moral indignation, seized by a mercenary spirit of amiability. "There's fresh sheets on the bed, sir. Will you be requiring any ale?"

"Warm water and hot coffee," Gerard snapped with the confidence of a man accustomed to having his orders obeyed. "And see that we're not disturbed."

"Aye, sir, whatever you wish."

As her bodyguard carried her up the narrow stairs, Lucy buried her nose in the worn folds of his badly knotted cravat, breathing in the clean masculine scent of spice and tobacco to wash away the gin-tainted stench of the men who had thought to brutalize her.

The third room they came to was unoccupied. Gerard deposited her on the plain wooden bed and gently pried her hands from his coat so he could draw it off and drape it over her shoulders. Lucy's hungry gaze never wavered from him as he lit a stubby tallow candle and dragged a faded quilt over her lap.

Beads of frozen rain tapped against the windowpane, dissolving like fluid diamonds as they struck the glass. The fireless room was chill, but after enduring the bitter bite of the wind outside, Lucy found it almost cozy. She dabbed at her nose with the back of her hand, admitting ruefully to herself that it was not the shelter that made her feel safe, but the man who shared it.

Minutes later, the innkeeper's wife came banging on the door with the water and coffee Gerard had demanded. She craned her neck to catch a glimpse of the bed, but Gerard nudged the door shut in her ruddy face.

As he poured the steaming water from a ewer into a chipped ceramic basin, Lucy tugged at a damp strand of her hair, knowing she must look a fright. Gerard hadn't spared her so much as a glance since their arrival in the room.

Instead of offering her the water, he dipped his own hands in its depths, scrubbing them with a fervor that made her wince. Only after drying them, taking a bracing gulp of the coffee, and donning his spectacles did he face her, the flickering shadows rendering his expression unreadable. He looked reluctant to come anywhere near her.

Unbeknownst to him, his unselfish ministrations had shaken Lucy more than the attack. Her father had never carried her in his arms, never tucked her tenderly into bed, never smoothed her hair or brushed his lips against her brow when he thought her asleep. She still cherished the memory of her tenth birthday when Smythe had bestowed a shy kiss upon her cheek.

Her heart throbbed painfully. She twisted the empty sleeves of Gerard's coat in her hands, feeling vulnerable, raw, aching with a hunger to be touched and petted and stroked by loving hands. His hands.

A single tear dripped off her nose. It embarrassed her beyond measure to succumb to such worthless emblems of hysteria. *Stop sniveling, Lucinda. He's only doing his job. And don't slump.* Lucy unconsciously sat up straighter, pressing her spine to the wooden headboard.

"You've never called me by my first name before," he said, breaking the awkward silence with the light touch of a professional. "I wasn't sure you knew what it was."

Thinking of the many times she'd doodled his name in her margins when she was supposed to be taking dictation, Lucy swallowed past the lump in her throat and forced a watery smile. "To be honest, I knew it started with a *G,* but I hadn't quite settled on Gaston or Gomer or . . ."

Their eyes met. Her voice faltered. His forbidding image blurred. An uneven hiccup escaped her. Then another. Before she could cup a hand over her mouth to stifle them, a torrent of sobs burst from her throat.

Gerard was across the room in two strides. He sank to a sitting position on the bed and gathered her into his arms like a child. "It's all right, mouse. I won't let anyone hurt you."

Mouse. The casual endearment made Lucy want to melt into him. Was this how her mother had felt when confronted by a temptation too sweet to resist?

As Lucy's lithe body convulsed with the force of the emotional storm, Gerard pressed her to the answering thunder of his heart and rubbed his cheek against her hair. He understood better than anyone the cost of her tears. She was not a woman to weep lightly or without cause. She cried as if to rid herself of all the tears she'd swallowed since birth, beginning with her mother's blameless abandonment.

When her sobs had subsided to fitful shudders, she tried to squirm out of his arms. His iron grip permitted her to do no more than wiggle to a more dignified position. He drew off his cravat and dabbed at her cheeks.

"You must think me a shameless ninny," she gulped out between sniffles. He held the cravat to her nose and she absently blew it. "These hysterics are quite inexcusable. Those men didn't even hurt me. They only frightened me. I'm afraid you've found me out."

sual languor. The rough warmth of his tongue stroked the sensitive contours of her mouth with a tender artistry that blunted all of her inhibitions and entreated her own tongue to respond in kind.

Gerard reveled in the melting sweetness of Lucy's mouth, unable to stop himself from wondering if all of her could be coaxed to receive him so generously. His reckless visions stoked the embers burning low and hot in his belly to a roaring conflagration. Cursing the very imagination that had kept him sane through an eternity of deprivation, he contented himself with her kiss, knowing instinctively that if he pressed her back among the pillows as he ached to do, she would bolt.

He was the one to break the kiss, unable to bear another shy flick of her tongue for fear the delicious torture might snap his tenuous control.

She leaned away from him, still gripping his forearms, and studied his unguarded eyes with quizzical earnestness. A chill of foreboding shot through him as he realized too late that he might have just made a fatal error. But fatal for whom?

"What is it?" he asked, keeping his tone deliberately light.

"I was just thinking," she replied, the husky note in her voice enchanting him, "that you kiss nothing at all like Captain Doom."

A reluctant chuckle escaped him. He ought to take offense, but he was too bloody relieved. Her bottom lip was still moist and swollen from his kiss. He stroked the pad of his thumb over it, marveling at its trembling response. "Didn't the Admiral ever teach you it was bad form to compare kisses? And all this time you led me to believe Doom had played the gentleman with you. I'm quite disillusioned with the rogue."

The urge to wipe Doom from both their minds was

overpowering. So when Lucy opened her mouth to retort "But Captain Doom might have—", he snatched her up by the back of the neck and seized his prize anew in a dark and devilish kiss that took no prisoners and granted no mercy.

"Now what were you saying about Captain Doom?" he asked silkily when her gasps had subsided to tiny pants. His fingers stroked her sensitive nape, eliciting a fresh shudder of delight.

"Captain who?" she echoed dreamily, rubbing her cheek against his forearm.

Gerard's gut clenched. The yearning mist in Lucy's eyes no longer shimmered for her phantom pirate, but for him. He wanted to feel triumph, longed for that heady rush of elation that marked a fresh conquest. But all he felt was burgeoning panic.

Where in God's name was he going to find the strength to turn and walk away from those eyes? From the tender adoration in their depths? His protective feelings toward her had been a warning he'd ignored at his own peril. And hers as well.

He'd entered the Admiral's service to do a job, he reminded himself ruthlessly. A job that would brook no interference. Suffer no distractions. Not even one as tempting as seducing his employer's delectable daughter.

Battling bitter regret, he rescued his spectacles from the quilt and slipped them on. Lucy's eyes darkened as if she sensed the invisible barrier he'd erected between them. He only hoped it wasn't as transparent as it was invisible.

"The theater should be over soon," he said gruffly, avoiding her eyes as he stuffed her arms into his coat. "We'd best get you home before we're forced to endure another of the Admiral's lectures."

"Aren't you forgetting something?"

The challenging tilt of her jaw made him wary. He cocked an eyebrow. "Your gloves? Your reticule perhaps?"

"*Your* position. You no longer have one. You resigned." She folded her arms over her chest. The excess flop of his coat sleeves narrowly missed spoiling her haughty demeanor. "I, sir, am no longer your concern."

Using every ounce of menace at his present disposal, he braced his hands on the headboard behind her, imprisoning her between his muscular arms. She quailed dutifully, but not before her luscious little tongue had darted out to wet her lips. Gerard ached with the need to kiss her again and damn the consequences.

Instead, he leaned forward until his nose nearly touched hers and growled, "You, God help us both, are very much my concern."

CHAPTER FOURTEEN

LUCY STABBED A STOPPER INTO A CRYSTAL decanter of lemon verbena, wishing she could bottle up her feelings with such ease. Since her bodyguard had escorted her home from the inn, leaving her at the front door with nothing but a terse bow, she'd had no luck subduing her rioting emotions enough to let her sleep. For the first time in her memory, she wished she had a mother to confide in. Someone older and wiser who could help her sift through her maelstrom of conflicting feelings.

She wiped a thin coating of rice powder from the marble surface of the dressing table, then began compulsively plucking individual hairs from her silver hairbrush. At least she could bring some badly needed order to the chaos of her bedroom. When the brush was clean, she moved to the bed to snatch a lone stocking from the canopy.

Her fingers snagged the fragile silk as if it were a lifeline. Perhaps her father was right, she thought desperately. Perhaps she'd inherited her mother's tendency toward hysteria after all. Why else would her mood be veering so wildly between despair and exultation?

She closed her eyes, shivering at the memory of Gerard's jaw, roughened by the tantalizing shadow of a day's growth of beard, grazing her cheek. The stocking slipped from her limp fingers to the floor. The unyielding bedpost pressed against her spine, making her acutely aware of the rumpled decadence of the bed behind her.

Her eyes flew open. She wasn't her mother. She was made of much sterner stuff. She couldn't afford to succumb to dangerous, sensual impulses. They had cost her mother the Admiral's love and eventually her life.

Lucy rushed to the wardrobe and began cramming scattered undergarments back into the safe confines of their drawers. The rebellious tangle of silk and lace resisted her bullying. She slammed an overflowing drawer three times before admitting defeat and crossing to the window to sink into the window seat.

A light still burned in the gatehouse, just as she had known it would.

Bits of sleet tapped fitfully against the windowpane. Lucy felt like some helpless creature imprisoned in an hourglass. It was as if Gerard's kiss had turned her world upside down and shaken it with careless abandon, leaving the pieces to settle in unfamiliar patterns around her in glittering shards, as dangerous as they were beautiful.

You're in love with him, aren't you?

The accusing words were so real that the ice glazing the window melted and reformed into the glowering face of her father. She pressed her eyes shut to make it go away.

In the past she'd always had innocence as her defense against the Admiral's spoken and unspoken accusations. She'd bitten back her anger at his unfairness, swallowed her hoarse cries of denial, and hugged the knowledge of her virtue close to her heart.

Now she had no defense at all. She was guilty as charged. Condemned for loving the wrong man.

She rested her brow against the cold glass. Captain Doom might have stolen her soul, but she was in grave danger of bestowing it freely upon Gerard Claremont.

♥   ♥   ♥

Dawn found Lucy huddled on the far side of the ancient oak, watching her nervous puffs of breath drift off like so much flotsam in the frigid air.

She had already determined that subterfuge was a poor weapon against Mr. Claremont, given his tendency to see right through it. He was far more likely to be swayed by a rational, adult discussion of their awkward situation. Surely even a sophisticated man such as Gerard would find her logic irresistible.

From the other side of the tree came the brittle crunch of footsteps approaching across the sleet-glazed grass. Lucy pressed her back to the gnarled trunk and squeezed her eyes shut in miserable anticipation. A curl of cheroot smoke wafted by. She sucked it into her lungs as if it were magical incense burned to give her courage.

Fighting to separate the threads of her intellect from the tangle of her raging emotions as the Admiral had taught her, she swept her woolen mantle in a graceful bell and stepped out from behind the tree.

Gerard halted as if his feet had shot down roots. His eyes reflected only mild surprise and an alarming wariness, as if he had sensed this confrontation was inevitable, but still hoped to avoid it.

Lucy's words were stymied by the presence of her heart in her throat. Her bodyguard's open coat was rumpled, his shirt halfway unbuttoned. A smoking cheroot hung from the corner of his mouth. His hair was tousled as if he had rolled out of bed without combing it, its rich hue gilded cinnamon by the winter sunshine burning through the morning mist.

But it was his face, that boyish face shadowed by the weary cynicism of manhood, that devastated her hard-won composure.

He jammed his hands in his trouser pockets and rocked back on his heels, giving her a quizzical look from beneath his striking brows.

Now was the time, she mentally nudged herself. Time to calmly present the well-rehearsed dissection of their feelings and realistic prospects for the future that she had spent a sleepless night formulating.

She opened her mouth. "I love you" tumbled out.

Gerard felt as if he'd been struck both deaf and dumb. He couldn't trust himself to maintain his mask of indifference beneath Lucy's imploring gaze. He couldn't trust himself to speak without revealing how badly he wanted her. He couldn't even grant her freedom from her father's tyranny. All he had to offer her was another sort of bondage, sensual and brief, that she would regret long after he was gone.

The cheroot hung limp on his bottom lip for what seemed like an eternity before tumbling end over end to the grass. It fizzled in the frost like Lucy's dreams as he turned without a word and marched back toward the gatehouse.

"Was it something I said?" she whispered.

Lucy laid her cheek against the rough bark of the oak, seeking solace from its ancient and uncompromised dignity. A warm fog of tears blinded her to the brittle glint of sunlight reflected from a third-story window of the house.

♥ ♥ ♥

The Admiral snatched the spyglass from his eye as Smythe entered his private sitting room, balancing a breakfast tray and various newspapers with the skill of a professional juggler.

"Dammit, man," the Admiral snapped. "How many times have I told you never to enter a room without knocking?"

"Sorry, sir. My hands were occupied."

"They'll be occupied with seeking a new position if you come barging in here again in that deplorable manner."

Smythe deposited his burdens on an oak pedestal table while the Admiral resumed his unabashed spying. Under the pretense of arranging the papers for his employer's perusal, Smythe sidled past an adjacent window to find Lucy drifting like a wraith across the lawn toward the house, dejection weighting her every step. He frowned.

"Damn chit'll be the ruin of me just like her blasted mother was," the Admiral grumbled, snapping the telescopic neck of the spyglass shut. "Should have never hired that Claremont fellow. Thought he was made of sterner stuff. Man enough to resist all that feminine cunning."

"I've found his performance to be acceptable, sir. I've observed no impropriety in his behavior toward Miss Lucy." Smythe prayed he wouldn't have cause to regret his defense of Claremont.

"Ah, but your standards aren't as exacting as mine, are they?" The Admiral settled his bulk into a wing chair and drew the silver lid off a chafing dish, unveiling the steaming feast of buttered eggs and fresh kippers he always indulged in before joining Lucy in the dining room for dry toast and tea. He gestured toward the newspapers. "Any mention of Doom?"

"None at all, sir. Perhaps he realized it was futile to engage a man of your skill and bravery in open battle."

Fortunately for Smythe, his employer's colossal ego precluded any appreciation of sarcasm at his own expense.

The Admiral speared a kipper with his fork. "I should have crushed the worm beneath my boot heel when I had the chance." He paused, the fork halfway to his mouth. "Has Lucy an engagement tonight?"

"Aye, sir. The winter masque at the Howell estate."

"Excellent!" He chewed with relish, grinding the fish between his blunt teeth. "See that my uniform is pressed. I shall put in an early appearance, then be off to my own pursuits."

"Aye, sir. I'll see to it." Smythe turned to go.

"Oh, and Smythe?"

"Sir?"

"Tomorrow morning, before oh nine hundred, I'd like you to contact Mr. Benson about a replacement for Mr. Claremont. I don't care for the man's attitude."

Smythe kept his face a careful blank. "What reason shall I give Mr. Claremont for his dismissal, sir?"

The Admiral waved his fork, spattering undercooked egg yolk across the newspapers. "Just tell him we appreciated his services keenly and will be pleased to provide the appropriate references, et cetera, et cetera."

"Very well, sir."

Smythe clicked his heels and snapped off a smart salute, thinking it a bloody shame for England that a man of Lucien Snow's innate military skills had been cursed with the fatal flaw of underestimating his enemies.

♥ ♥ ♥

The Howells' winter masque was a cherished annual tradition. It had been conceived by Lady Howell over a decade ago to brighten the long, barren months when the city pleasure gardens were closed and many of the *ton* had retreated to their country estates. To those remaining, the masque was anticipated more eagerly than Christmas.

As they descended the shallow marble steps to the ballroom, Lucy tucked her gloved hand into the rigid crook of her father's arm, expecting to feel the familiar surge of love and pride. Instead, she felt curiously empty, as if the hours of weeping she had done in her bedroom that afternoon had washed away her precious childhood illusions, stripping her heart bare.

Longing to recapture even a shadow of emotion, she slanted a gaze up at her father's face through the eye slits of her silk loo. His own mask of gold tissue was a mere formality, designed to complement the cluster of freshly polished medals that starred his chest. There was no one in this stellar crowd of the military elite who could fail to recognize him. He exuded all the majesty and romance of the Royal Navy itself in his full-dress uniform, fringed epaulettes, and shiny boots. She should be honored that he had chosen to lean on her this night instead of his cane.

His thick mane gleamed like hoarfrost beneath the radiance of the chandeliers. For a fleeting instant, as he angled his head to receive the homage that was his due, that old adoration squeezed at Lucy's heart. He was once again the most handsome man in the world to her.

She seemed to be shrinking, clinging not to his elbow, but to the starched tails of his uniform, tugging, always tugging, in a wordless plea for him to stop and notice her.

Christ, Smythe, why isn't she in bed? If there's anything I cannot bear, it's a clinging brat.

Lucy's fingernails clenched involuntarily, digging into her father's arm. He shot her a disapproving look and disengaged his coat sleeve from her grip to smooth the unsightly wrinkle she'd caused. As their host and hostess approached, he pasted on a jovial smile of greeting.

Lord and Lady Howell's warm welcome did nothing to dispel Lucy's chill. It emanated from the empty place where her heart had been before she'd been fool enough to offer it to Gerard Claremont. What must he think of her after her ridiculous divulgence? That she was a light-skirted hussy? A lovestruck child? She had studiously avoided his eyes as he'd assisted them into the carriage earlier, afraid she'd find amusement, condescension, or worse yet, patronizing pity in their hazel depths.

"Why, Lucy dear, your hands are like ice!" Lady Howell exclaimed, chafing them between her own.

Her face was a well-worn version of Sylvie's, blurred by time like a tissue paper mask that had been left in the rain.

The twinkling of her blue eyes dimmed as Lucy coolly withdrew her hands, afraid she would crumble beneath the burden of the woman's compassion. "Forgive me. It's quite cold outside."

As Lady Howell excused herself, gracefully accepting the rebuff, Lucy found it even colder inside. The plastered walls of the ballroom had been draped in layers of white chiffon. Genuine frost sparkled along the panes of the floor-to-ceiling French windows. The marble fireplaces flanking the far ends of the cavernous room shed little warmth, and in keeping with the theme, many of the guests had retained their mantles and hooded cloaks, adding to their air of disguise.

A galaxy of tiny crystal chips suspended from gold threads dangled from the vaulted ceiling in a dazzling imitation of snowflakes. Their reflected light hurt Lucy's eyes. She couldn't imagine why anyone would want to re-create winter indoors when the entire universe seemed to be trapped in its frigid grip.

Lord Howell and her father wandered off to discuss Napoleon's scandalous appointment of himself as lifetime First Consul of France, leaving her standing alone on the stairs. The masked dancers whirled across the Venetian tiles, the invisible notes of the quadrille jerking them to and fro like winged marionettes.

An inaudible groan of dismay escaped Lucy as she saw Sylvie weaving her way through the dancers, her baby brother propped on her hip. Unlike her mother, Sylvie had not yet learned to be politely daunted by rejection.

The Howells held the uncommon belief that children should not only be seen and heard, but fussed and cooed over at great length. The placid Gilligan had been garbed in the hemp-belted robes of a medieval monk. One of his older brothers had pasted a ragged tonsure of horse's hair around his bald pate. A reluctant smile quivered on Lucy's lips as the enormous baby reached out without his sister's knowledge, plucked a fistful of boiled shrimp from a footman's tray, and ate them, tails and all.

Sylvie's first words erased her amusement. "There you are! I was beginning to wonder if you'd ever arrive. And where is that handsome Mr. Claremont of yours?"

Humiliation curled in the pit of Lucy's stomach. She extracted herself from Sylvie's peppermint-scented embrace, terrified she might burst into tears and make a public spectacle of herself. "He's not *my* Mr. Claremont. I assume he's with the other servants where he belongs. It would hardly do to have him lurking behind the potted palms, frightening your mother's guests."

Sylvie shifted Gilligan's considerable weight to her other hip where he proceeded to yank a handful of pink feathers from her mask. "Isn't he supposed to look after you?"

Sylvie's innocent question conjured up a myriad of images: Gerard bundling her against the warmth of his body, carrying her through the icy rain, tucking a faded quilt around her trembling legs. Pressing his lips to the bruise on her throat as if his kiss alone held the power to heal it.

"Champagne, ladies?" The underfootman's voice interrupted her dangerous reverie.

"Not now, David," Sylvie said, knowing of Lucy's aversion to spirits. "Perhaps later when—"

"Why, thank you. I'd be delighted." Sylvie stared and even Gilligan looked nonplussed as Lucy snatched a fluted glass and downed its sparkling contents in a single swallow.

The tart bubbles made her nose tingle. Infectious warmth spread through her belly although it couldn't quite smooth the razor's edge off her yearning.

"You see, Sylvie, I don't need Mr. Claremont to look after me," she said brightly, depositing the glass back on the tray. "Tonight I have my father to protect me. And when we're together, neither of us needs anyone else."

Sylvie watched as her friend made her way boldly through the dancers to the uniformed crowd slavering over the Admiral's every word. It was impossible to miss the annoyance that flickered over his face as his daughter tugged his sleeve. But Lucy stood her ground until he was forced to gallantly offer her his arm for a dance or appear the worst sort of lout before his staunchest admirers.

Sylvie absently peeled a soggy feather from Gilligan's tongue, wondering if it was the unfamiliar sting of the champagne or genuine tears she saw glittering in Lucy's eyes as she went into the Admiral's arms.

♥ ♥ ♥

Gerard resisted the urge to beat his fist against the frosted glass of the terrace door. Lucinda Snow was back where she belonged. In her father's arms.

Even knowing better, he caught himself falling prey to their spell as they danced. The Admiral's uneven gait added an aura of tragic dignity to his regal bearing. With his immaculate uniform and the cluster of medals gleaming on his barreled chest, he resembled an aged king returned from some noble crusade. Once Gerard had idolized such men and would have sacrificed everything he possessed to walk among them.

As if cursed with the same foolish longing, Lucy reached up and gently corrected the angle of one of the Admiral's medals.

Gerard's heroic illusions shattered, mercifully, swiftly, as beneath the guise of a clumsy stumble, Lucien Snow harshly thrust his daughter from him. He left her standing alone in the middle of the floor as he swept from the ballroom, pausing only to make the curtest of apologies to Lord and Lady Howell. Not even the brave tilt of Lucy's chin could completely disguise the naked hurt in her eyes as her father fled her company.

Gerard was tempted to follow, but he'd been at Ionia long enough to know where the bastard was going.

His gaze was drawn back to the Admiral's daughter. She had wisely eschewed elaborate costumes and feathered headdresses, choosing to adorn herself in a classical Grecian gown with a half-mask cut from the same white silk. Her hair had been drawn back from her face with a gold fillet. An air of ineffable sadness clung to her, as poignant and irresistible as the lemon verbena that lingered in his nostrils even when she was separated from him by an impenetrable wall of glass.

She drifted in a sea of glittering lights and laughing people. As a child, Gerard had only dreamed such places existed. They were as distant to him as the tantalizing glimpse of a single star flung high above soot-laden clouds. As fantastical as the vast expanses of ocean that billowed in his imagination. As out of his reach as heaven itself or the love of a woman like Lucy Snow.

Lucy's courageous confession echoed through his heart like a bittersweet melody. He curled his hands into hungry fists, flooded with the same blind ambition that had once before cost him both his freedom and his name. He'd been deprived of too many nights such as this in his life. He wanted tonight. One stolen night, its memory sweet enough to last a lifetime.

His gaze dropped in disgust to his worn trousers, his scuffed boots. What the hell was he supposed to be masquerading as? The basest of menials? Lucy's inferior?

"I say there, chap, can you help me?"

A man garbed in impeccable evening clothes came limping toward him.

"I seem to have stepped in a bit of unpleasantness," he said with such irritating intonation that Gerard suspected his black half-mask was pinching off his nose. "I've warned Lord Howell about those blasted spaniels. Breed some mastiffs, I said! Those dainty dogs haven't any manners a'tall. I say, have you a rag on you to clean my heel? I'm already appallingly late."

The man had obviously mistaken him for one of

Lord Howell's servants, a groundskeeper perhaps or a poorly outfitted footman. Gerard opened his mouth to suggest the arrogant dandy lick his boots clean, then snapped it shut. He raked a calculating gaze from the blinding white of the stranger's flawlessly knotted cravat to the tapered seams of his trousers, then shot a quizzical glance heavenward, knowing he wasn't deserving of such good fortune.

"Come now, I haven't all night," the man snapped, straightening his ruffled shirt cuffs. "Your handkerchief should do. Will you help me or not?"

Gerard blinked behind his spectacles and gave him a feline smile. "Step right over here to the bushes, sir. I'm just the man you've been looking for."

♥   ♥   ♥

Lucy winced as Sophie's eleven-year-old brother trod hard upon her toe.

"Sorry," he mumbled, his ears flushing crimson. "I hope my dancing master didn't see that. He'll box my ears tomorrow for sure."

"Tell him it was my fault," Lucy whispered to the dusky curls that just reached her chin.

"I couldn't do that, Miss Lucy." His adoring eyes devoured her face. "You're the very best, you know. Brave enough to stand up to the likes of Captain Doom himself."

He suppressed an impolite "oomph" as Lucy did step on his foot. How could she explain to this earnest child that the kiss of a real man had banished Captain Doom to the realm of fantasy where he belonged?

At a loss, she gently excused herself and went in search of another glass of champagne. She ducked behind a chattering flock of guests at the sight of Lord Howell anxiously searching the crowd for her. As if to blunt the impact of the Admiral's defection, Sylvie and her mother had sicced each of the Howell males on her in turn until she feared she would have to toddle around the floor with Gilligan before the night was over.

She wanted nothing more than to escape the maddening babble and tinny music, but her only refuge was the carriage and that meant facing Claremont again, this time without the Admiral's dubious protection.

Fresh mortification heated her cheeks at the prospect. After checking guiltily to make sure no one was watching, she filched a brimming glass of champagne from an abandoned tray and downed it in one greedy gulp. As she lowered the glass, she realized she had made yet another grave error in judgment.

Someone was watching her.

A stranger, leaning against the marble mantel with lazy grace, his beautifully tailored evening clothes and black mask making him look both elegant and dangerous. Droll amusement quirked his lips as he lifted his own champagne glass to her in a mocking salute.

Dismayed to find herself the victim of such a shameless flirtation, Lucy ducked between the dancers, hoping to lose herself in their twirling gaiety. But when she dared a glance over her shoulder, the stranger was still there.

Watching her. His heated gaze caressed her bare shoulders.

Inexplicable panic swept through her. She felt trapped, innocent prey cornered by a master hunter. Desperate for escape, she snatched Sylvie's pudgy eight-year-old brother Christopher from a cluster of his friends.

"Dance with me," she hissed. "Or I'll tell your dancing master to box your ears."

"I d-don't have a dancing master, Miss Lucy," he stammered.

"Then I shall box them myself."

He swallowed his protest, fearful any girl stout enough to best Captain Doom would pack a mighty wallop. They shuffled awkwardly around the floor, Lucy taking mincing steps to match his abbreviated gait. She peeped over his head at the mantel only to discover the man was gone.

His absence taunted her more than his presence had done. She scanned the crowd, searching for any hint of him. Her heart leaped to discover a similarly garbed man across the room only to plummet as she saw the vapid blue eyes behind his ebony mask. Twice, three times, she thought she caught a glimpse of the stranger, but then he was gone again. Elusive. Mysterious. Provocative.

"Miss Lucy?"

"Yes, Chris?" she replied absently, teetering on her tiptoes to gain a better view of the room.

"The music has stopped. May I be dismissed?"

Lucy quit shuffling her feet and dropped her gaze to his cherubic face. "Of course. And thank you, Chris. For being so gallant."

He swept her a clumsy bow that made his apple-cheeks redden. As he scampered back to his snickering friends, Lucy sighed. Now that she had succeeded in dodging the unwanted attentions of her covert admirer, she felt more bereft than before. She resolved to escape the farce her evening had become only to find a broad expanse of chest blocking her path. A crystal globe of golden bubbles floated before her eyes.

"Champagne?" At the caress of the rich baritone, every pulse in her body throbbed.

Determined to give the insolent rake the setdown he deserved, she presented her back to him, preferring to ignore the fact that he'd just witnessed her gulping champagne with all the finesse of a habitual drunkard. "No, thank you, sir. I don't drink."

His voice came again, silky, seductive, so near to her ear that his warm breath stirred the infinitesimal hairs along its lobe. "That's just as well, I suppose. We wouldn't want to weaken your moral character, now would we, Miss Snow?"

Lucy spun around, mesmerized by the wicked glitter of the hazel eyes beneath the mask. Hope and fury warred in her heart. Her mouth widened to an accusing circle, but before she could let fly a string of recriminations, her bodyguard gently pressed the rim of the wineglass to her lower lip. Their gazes melded as she drank deeply and without hesitation.

Gerard didn't need champagne. He was intoxicated by the graceful motion of Lucy's throat as she swallowed, the tantalizing dart of her pink tongue as she licked an errant drop from the corner of her mouth.

He twirled the fragile stem of the wineglass between his fingers. A bemused smile curved his lips. "I knew I had to shut you up before you denounced me, but I feared kissing you might cause a scandal."

"So might plying me with champagne." Lucy's airy tone belied the treacherous thunder of her heart. "A weakened moral character can be a very dangerous thing."

"Ah, but dangerous for whom? You? Or me?"

He opened his arms, inviting her to share the risk. As Lucy went into them, the barriers of class that separated them dissolved. He swept her into the waltz with a natural grace that defied convention.

The marble-tiled floor rolled beneath their feet like the deck of some majestic ship. Lucy was caught up in Gerard's masterful rhythm and the miracle of being enfolded in the warmth of his arms.

"How did you learn to dance so beautifully?" she asked over the swell of the music.

He gave her one of those enigmatic smiles that drove her to distraction. "In my profession, a man must learn to be the master of many talents."

It was as if Lucy had spent her entire life with her senses wrapped in cotton batting only to have them tingle to awareness in that moment with an acuity that was almost painful. Every sensation was heightened, deepened. The notes of the Viennese waltz reverberated through her soul, rich and shaded with secret layers of meaning. She gloried in the sweet burn of the champagne through her veins, the shift of their muscles beneath their finery, the hard press of Gerard's thighs as he guided her through an intricate turn, splaying his powerful hand at the small of her back.

She tossed her head back, answering the smoldering challenge in his eyes with a reckless smile of invitation.

From the corner of her eye, Lucy saw the crowd melting before the inevitability of their twirling flight. Many, like her father, still considered the waltz the height of depravity and sought to have it banned. She knew they were making a public spectacle of themselves. Knew society must have stared at her rebellious mother in just such shocked fascination. But for once she didn't care what anyone thought of her but the man who held her in his arms.

It was as if she and Gerard were floating in one of the champagne bubbles, the only two people suspended in an arctic wonderland. The faux snowflakes glittered above them like stars over the indigo expanse of the ocean at midnight.

Every head in the ballroom turned to follow the path of the handsome couple, struggling to fathom that the vivacious creature whirling in the stranger's arms with such abandon was truly Admiral Snow's sallow, cheerless daughter.

Lucy's cheeks were hectic with color, her gray eyes sparkling with emotion. As she tilted her head toward her partner, her cheek dimpled in a provocative smile. Unable to tear their gazes away, several of the eligible young men nudged each other. They had never even suspected Lucinda Snow of being pretty. Now they realized her looks defied the shallow precepts of prettiness. Her beauty was of the classical variety, as timeless as her transparent adoration for the man who held her so scandalously close.

"Oh, my," Sylvie breathed, studying Lucy's partner from the gleaming crown of his head to his polished slippers. "Who is that glorious creature?"

"I haven't the foggiest." Her mother lowered her lorgnette from her eye, her brow crumpled in a perplexed frown. "Shouldn't you step in, Eustace? With her father called away in such haste, you should stand in his stead."

Lord Howell shook his head sadly. "I hate to spoil it for her. God knows the poor girl's had little enough happiness in her life with Lucien so devoted to serving His Majesty."

From his vantage point on the floor, where he'd been quietly sucking his fingers until he could scavenge something more tasty, Gilligan tugged at the hem of his sister's gown. Her imagination had been so thoroughly captured by the vision of romance gliding past them that she paid him no heed.

Young Christopher came rushing up, his plump hands curled into fists. "Shall I call him out, Papa? I won't stand for anyone accosting Miss Lucy."

The waltz hurtled to a magnificent finish, its last majestic note ringing in the air. Gilligan tugged at Sylvie's skirt again. She absently waved him away, holding her breath along with the rest of them as they waited to see if the mysterious stranger would dare to break the enchanted tableau with a kiss.

Gilligan cared nothing for kisses. His own rapt attention had been caught by the figure sneaking silently down the stairs. Spotting the wide-eyed baby, the man laid a finger to his lips in an exaggerated plea for discretion.

Gilligan pried his fist from his mouth, pointed at the new arrival, and squealed the first intelligible words anyone had ever heard him utter.

" 'Ook, Syllie! Cap'n Doom!"

CHAPTER FIFTEEN

GILLIGAN'S CROW OF DELIGHT WAS FOL-
lowed by yet another sound Lord Howell's guests had
never thought to hear—the bright, merry peals of Lucinda Snow's laughter. The figure on the stairs froze,
trapped in the relentless beacon of the crowd's attention.

He might have strode straight out of a Royal Circus
playbill for a pirate melodrama. From his forbidding
eyepatch to the fuzzy strands of his plaited beard to
the six pistols strapped across his chest, he sported
every pirate cliché known to man with such a haphazard lack of taste that even Lady Howell cringed in
sympathy.

All he needed to complete his ensemble was a cutlass between his soot-blackened teeth and some slow-
burning hemp fuses tucked beneath his misshapen hat.
Had he meandered in with his own severed head
tucked beneath his arm, he might have passed for the
ghost of the dastardly Blackbeard himself.

He bore as little resemblance to the sleek and ruthless predator Lucy had unwittingly engaged on board the *Retribution* as she did to one of Mrs. Edgeworth's intrepid Gothic heroines.

She clutched Gerard's arm, gasping for breath. "Oh, I'm sorry, but it's simply too much. That . . . b-b-buffoon is *not* Captain Doom."

His muscled forearm had gone rigid beneath her hand. "I should say not."

A fresh paroxysm of laughter seized her. "Oh, if only the Admiral had stayed. Can you imagine what he would have thought?"

"Only too well."

Lucy realized that Gerard was no more amused than her father would have been. Beneath the mask, his eyes had narrowed to dangerous slits. It was so refreshing to see him angry at someone besides herself that Lucy failed to feel even a shred of alarm.

A polite smattering of applause went up from the guests to reward the originality of the newcomer's costume. The musicians launched into a rousing navy hymn as the Howell boys rushed to examine the mock pirate.

"Excuse me." Gerard disengaged his arm from her hand. "I'd best see if our host needs any assistance in routing the villain."

Lucy sauntered after him, surprised to find herself a trifle unsteady on her feet. Although the waltz had stopped, it was as if the ballroom were still spinning. Or maybe it was her head. She cupped a hand over her mouth to smother a belated fit of giggles.

"Aaargh, mates," the pirate was growling as they approached. "Shiver me timbers, if this ain't the finest crop o' lads this side o' Madagascar. Which one'll be the first to run away and cast his lot with me crew?"

Christopher Howell shyly lifted his hand. "Me, sir, if you please."

Sylvie hung back behind her brothers, but that didn't stop Gilligan from reaching out from her arms to tuck a frayed plait of the pirate's beard in his mouth.

The brigand dug a finger into the baby's doughy belly. "Can't abide children. Except for supper, that is." He blew Sylvie an insolent kiss. "Comely wenches I saves for dessert."

Sylvie blushed while her brothers howled with laughter.

Their father was trying to peer beneath the ragged eyepatch. "Confess, Georgie, is that you? A simple mask would have been sufficient. There was no need to go to such expense just to entertain my children. God knows they're spoiled enough as it is."

Slender, fourteen-year-old Layne was gazing down the barrel of one of the ancient flintlocks. "Quite impressive, Father. You'd almost think it was genuine." He fixed his approaching mother in its rusted sights.

Gerard's hand shot out to snatch the gun away. Lucy was the only one not fooled by the deceptive façade of his smile. "Of course it's genuine. How else would this scurvy sea dog make war on His Majesty's mighty navy?"

He slapped the pistol against the interloper's breastbone. A grunt of pain escaped the pirate.

Lord Howell's good-natured smile faded as he recognized Gerard. He shot Lucy a concerned glance. She grinned stupidly at him, thinking what a handsome man he must have been in his youth. But not nearly so handsome as her bodyguard.

"Claremont?" Lord Howell confirmed, stiffly drawing himself up. "My, this night is simply rife with intrigue, isn't it?"

"You don't know the half of it, sir." Gerard gave him a curt bow. "Forgive my intrusion, but I found

mingling as one of your guests the most effective way
to look after Miss Snow."

"Is that really necessary? This is a social occasion.
It's difficult to imagine our Lucy indulging in anything
more hazardous than tripping over one of the spaniels."

"You might be surprised, sir, at the hazards *our*
Lucy is capable of embroiling herself in."

Lord Howell's skeptical reply was cut off by the
pirate. "Aye, ye must protect 'er agin rogues like me.
I'm always on the prowl for pretty young lasses to
carry off to me ship." He shot a convincing leer at
Sylvie, his exposed green eye sparkling with mischief.

Sylvie giggled and even Lady Howell tittered nervously.

Caught up in the spirit of the game, Lucy bumped
her way past Gerard, tweaked the gold hoop in the
pirate's ear, and gave him a devilish wink. "And just
what do you do with 'em once you've got 'em there,
mate?"

The pirate looked almost as astounded by her boldness as the Howells did. Gerard caught her elbow in a
viselike grip. "Some things are better left to the imagination, aren't they, Miss Snow? Tales of such gruesome
atrocities aren't fit for your tender ears. You should
leave the interrogation to a professional such as myself."

He thrust Lucy behind him, then yanked the pirate
from the stairs and dragged him toward an unoccupied
alcove.

"Are you going to give him forty stripes? Torture
his secrets out of him?" Christopher called hopefully
after them.

Gerard bared his teeth in a grimace of a smile.
"Only if he resists."

"Intriguing chap, don't you think?" Lord Howell

murmured. "I thought it was Georgie, but now I'm not so certain. Could it be Sir Marcel's son? I've heard he dearly loves a good prank."

Lady Howell lifted her lorgnette to her eye and shook her head sadly. "Whoever he is, he has execrable taste in fashion. I've never seen a villain quite so . . . overdressed."

As the others drifted away, Lucy watched the terse exchange between Gerard and the stranger. She was having trouble focusing her attention on anything of import. Insignificant details pelted her—the strand of sandy gold escaping the pirate's ratty wig, that single green eye, his lanky height. He was taller than Gerard by a good two inches, but his shoulders lacked her bodyguard's imposing breadth.

The pirate's mouth had appeared to be twisted into a smirk of perpetual amusement, but it hardened into a grim line as Gerard marched back to her side.

"Friend of yours?" she asked.

"Old acquaintance," he replied shortly.

"I'm surprised a Bow Street Runner would have such impressive social connections," she said, her earnest tone spoiled by an undignified hiccup.

"There's a lot about me that might surprise you." He caught her by the shoulders, his eyes searching her face as if to memorize it. The desperation of his grip sobered her.

The spell between them was broken by a commotion near the stairs. A troop of abashed-looking gardeners rushed in, their charge led by a man wearing nothing but a pair of flannel underdrawers and a black eye. Shocked gasps went up throughout the ballroom.

The man's nasal braying made Lucy wince. "Threw me in the bushes, he did! Just like so much rubbish. I'm the Duke of Mannington, by God! A peer of the realm! I'll have the villain tossed in Newgate before this night is done." His finger quivered with righteous indignation as he pointed. "There he is! That mask cost me a pretty shilling. I'd recognize it anywhere. Seize him!"

With exaggerated patience, Lord Howell removed his mask just in time to keep his own gardeners from carrying him off to the jail.

His accuser's countenance darkened with dismay as he surveyed the sea of masked faces, then brightened as he flung out his arm again. "There! Cowering behind the column! I'd know the rascal anywhere!"

Lucy snickered. "He's gone and fingered the curate this time."

Outraged chaos erupted as the irate duke began accusing each male guest in turn. From the corner of her eye, Lucy saw the garish pirate beat a hasty retreat through a curtained alcove.

Gerard drew Lucy toward the terrace doors. "I believe that's our cue to exit as well."

She dragged her feet, savoring a rare fit of petulance. "But I wanted to dance some more. I wanted to dance all night long!"

Gerard flung open the terrace doors. Lucy's cheerful wail was snatched by a blast of frigid air as the night engulfed them. She tripped on an uneven flagstone and would have fallen had he not caught her. Their masked faces, his hard and unrelenting, hers soft with shy uncertainty, were separated by mere inches. The air between them seemed to sparkle, glittering with motes of faerie dust. Lucy's gaze shifted upward, her eyes widening with fresh wonder.

She flung herself away from him to dance across the lawn. "Oh, look at it, Gerard! I can't remember the last time it snowed in London! Isn't it magnificent?"

Gerard barely saw the feathery flakes drifting down from the sooty sky. All he saw was Lucy, throwing her bare arms out as if to embrace the world, catching snowflakes on her tongue like the child she was never allowed to be.

"You're magnificent."

At the gravity of Gerard's tone, Lucy lowered her arms to wrap them around herself. It wasn't her sudden awareness of the cold that made her shiver, but the strange heat emanating from his eyes. A magnetic heat that drew her across the grass to him.

Snowflakes dusted his shoulders and hair. To reassure herself that he was truly her genial bodyguard and not some dangerous stranger, Lucy reached up to unmask him.

A quizzical smile touched her lips. "Why, Mr. Claremont, I thought you were blind as a bat without your spectacles?"

His eyes darkened, devoid of the sparkling humor she had come to expect from them. "I am. Blind to everything but you."

Gerard reached down and drew off Lucy's mask, stripping her exquisite face of its only defense. He knew it was an unfair blow, worthy of the street fighter he'd had to be to survive, but somewhere along the way, winning the game had become more important than playing by the rules.

At his first glimpse of the tender yearning in her eyes, Gerard knew he had to get her home. Out of his reach.

He captured her hand and pulled her into a run. They pelted across the frosty grass, braving the night and the wind hand in hand.

Lucy laughed aloud, exhilarated by the challenge. A thread of memory spun through her brain, but in her state of delightful befuddlement, she couldn't seem to weave it into a recognizable pattern.

They stumbled to a halt in the cobbled drive to find the Snow carriage nowhere in sight.

"The Admiral must have taken it," Lucy said, rubbing away a stitch in her side. "He was probably planning to send it back for me later." At Gerard's scowl, she added, "You didn't expect him to walk, did you?"

"Only on water," he bit off.

He dragged her toward a deserted carriage parked on the opposite side of the drive. The evening was still early and the driver was probably off gambling away his monthly wages with the rest of the servants. The flawlessly matched bays nickered nervously at their approach. Steam puffed from their aristocratic nostrils.

"This will have to do." Gerard framed Lucy's slender waist in his hands and swung her into the opulent interior, shooting a glance over his shoulder to make sure they weren't being followed.

Before he could close the door, she wagged a pink-tipped finger under his nose. "Confess, you wicked man. Were you the one to divest that unfortunate nobleman of his clothes?"

He splayed a hand over his heart as if she had struck him a mortal wound. "You're accusing me? A man who's devoted his life to the preservation of law and order?"

"A man who's not above stealing a carriage if it suits his needs," she pointed out with a hint of her tart logic.

"Borrowing," he corrected her.

Her eyes sparkled with mischief. "I'm not sure I should accompany you, sir. What if you should try to divest me of my clothes?"

Gerard's loins hardened with the decadent urge to press her back into the plush squabs of the carriage and do just that. With a lecherous growl that would have put the faux pirate to shame, he caught her nape in his palm and drew her face down until her succulent mouth was only a breath away from his own.

"Don't tempt me."

He gave her a harmless push. She fell back among the cushions, giggling and kicking her slippered feet, giving him a dazzling view of her lace petticoat and pink stockings.

Groaning, he slammed the carriage door. He rested his fevered brow against its cool shell, wondering what madness had possessed him to feed the staid Miss Snow that last glass of champagne.

As he waited for his breathing to steady, he became aware that an eagle was embossed on the gilded door, its outspread wings entwined with an elaborately scrolled name: *Mannington.* The same ducal crest he had seen that chill autumn night when this very carriage had heedlessly struck a child and left her crumpled in the rain.

Gerard threw back his head with a harsh bark of laughter. He seemed fated to mete out justice to others and damned to never winning even a scrap of it for himself.

♥ ♥ ♥

On the ride to Ionia, Lucy kept Gerard entertained with several inventive, if somewhat obscure, verses of "That Banbury Strumpet, As Sweet As a Crumpet." Truth be told, he rather suspected her of making them up as she went along. He rolled his eyes at a particularly ribald turn of phrase, knowing she hadn't the faintest idea what she was implying or the effect her throaty contralto was having on his ravenous body. He slapped the reins on the horses' backs, driving them to a brisk trot.

He brought the carriage to a halt at the far end of the drive, hoping to avoid attracting attention to his *borrowed* vehicle and his inebriated young charge. No groom ran out to greet them. As he'd intended, their early return from an event that traditionally lasted until dawn had caught the household staff off guard.

He yanked open the carriage door, not sure himself whether he should spank Lucy for her naughtiness or kiss her even more insensible than she already was.

He staggered as she tumbled face first over his shoulder, putting her in an ideal position for the former. He gave her bottom a sharp whack, keeping his palm molded over her delectable curves. She kicked her feet in protest, setting up a flurry of silk.

"Dammit, Lucy, stop wiggling," he commanded, more out of self-preservation than genuine annoyance.

His hands seemed to have a life of their own. He could feel the right one creeping up her stocking beneath her skirt, intent on some devilish mischief beyond his control.

"How dare you!" she gasped out as he started across the lawn, bouncing her unceremoniously with each step. "My father never spanked me."

"He should have. Daily. With great vigor."

Her injured sniff was ruined by a giggle. "I gave him no excuse. I was a good girl. Don't you find me a good girl, Mr. Claremont?"

"Delicious," he replied as his questing fingertips came into contact with the smooth, bare skin above her garter.

"Sylvie's oldest brother taught me a new song while we were dancing. Would you care to hear it?"

"No."

Undaunted, she threw back her head and roared:

Across the midnight sea sails Cap'n Doom.
Yer noble birth he'll make ye rue.

> He'll snatch yer lady's heart right from her
>   bosom
> Then rob her of her virtue.

Gerard winced and gritted his teeth. Christ, he hated that bloody pirate! He only regretted that Lucy's position made it impossible to put his hand over her mouth and under her skirt at the same time. That enticing vision made his palms sweat so profusely that he almost dropped her.

The front door swung open as they approached. Gerard hesitated, fearful of exposing Lucy's undignified state to a smirking footman. He sighed with relief when Smythe stepped to the fore, the candle in his hand casting wavering shadows over his bland face and flowing dressing gown.

Without so much as blinking an eye at Lucy's unusual mode of transit, the butler said, "Good evening, Mr. Claremont, Miss Lucy. I trust it was an enjoyable one."

"Tolerable," Gerard replied. "We had to end it a bit prematurely."

Smythe addressed Lucy's squirming bottom. "A prudent idea, it seems, sir."

Lucy twisted around to see him. Gerard obliged her by turning sideways.

"I learned a new song tonight, Smythe. Would you care to hear it?" she asked earnestly.

The butler laid a finger against her lips. "Perhaps in the morning, Miss Lucy. I'm suffering from a dreadful megrim."

The man did look pale, Gerard noted. Lines were etched around his eyes like the shading in one of Lucy's drawings. He couldn't help but wonder if Smythe was suffering from an ailment more severe than a simple headache.

"Poor Smythe," Lucy crooned, adjusting the tassel on his nightcap. "Poor, dear Smythe."

The butler rested his candlestick on a pier table and held out his arms. "May I, sir?"

Gerard's arms tightened around the limp bundle draped over his shoulder in primitive reflex. He hadn't realized how unprepared he was to let her go.

As if sensing how little it would take to make him bolt into the night with Lucy in tow, Smythe offered him a smile that was both kind and weary. "I'll look after her, sir. I always have."

Gerard lowered Lucy into the cradle of the butler's arms. Smythe wasn't a large man, but he bore her weight as if it were no burden at all. She snuggled against his chest, already half asleep.

Gerard's arms ached with emptiness.

As Smythe started toward the stairs, Lucy peered over his shoulder, blinking drowsily.

" 'Night, G'rard."

" 'Night, mouse."

Her wistful little wave tore at his heart. He touched his fingers to his lips in one final salute. Then there was nothing left for him to do but melt back into the darkness where he belonged.

♥   ♥   ♥

Lucy kicked off her slippers just outside the door to her room. "I've been a very wicked girl, Smythe. I had three glasses of champagne. Are you shocked?"

"Scandalized." Smythe's dry tone implied the opposite.

Without bothering to undress her, he tucked her beneath the counterpane with his usual matter-of-fact efficiency, then moved to add a fresh log to the bedroom fire.

Lucy was caught off guard by the sudden plunge of

her mood into dejection. "It doesn't truly matter, does it?"

Smythe lowered the poker and straightened. "What, Miss Lucy?"

"Whether I'm wicked. Or good. Or even perfect. The Admiral's never going to love me, is he?"

Smythe gazed into the dancing flames, his profile pensive. "I don't think he's capable of it, miss. It's really not your fault."

Defiance and pride swelled in her heart. "Mr. Claremont said I was magnificent."

Smythe came over to sit on the edge of her bed. He'd been her nanny, her governess, her cherished friend for as long as she could remember. Her earliest memory was of his sober face bending over her cradle. She knew only too well when he was about to do something he dreaded.

"You're rather fond of your Mr. Claremont, aren't you?"

The champagne had robbed Lucy of any eloquence she might have possessed. She could only nod. Her head felt loose, as if it might topple off her neck if she didn't take care.

"Would it make you terribly sad if he went away?"

An icy fear seized her. She gripped Smythe's arm. "What is it, Smythe? Are you afraid the Admiral will dismiss him if he discovers what a goose I've made of myself tonight? You won't tell him, will you? I'll swear off champagne for the rest of my days, but please don't tell him."

He eased her back to the pillow. "Your secrets are safe with me, dear. Just go to sleep. Everything will be better in the morning."

His hand was on the doorknob when Lucy softly said, "You're a poor liar, Smythe."

He gave her a sad little smile. "I'm afraid I'm a much better liar than you'd ever suspect."

♥   ♥   ♥

Lucy lay flat on her back, watching the reflection of the fire flicker across the tester. Smythe's enigmatic words had deflated her golden champagne bubble, leaving only its bitter aftertaste in her mouth. Her mellow glow faded to bleak gloom as she contemplated a future without Gerard.

There was really nothing new to contemplate. Her life would revert to its former orderly state. She, Smythe, and the Admiral would grow old together in this house, their daily habits carved from her father's indomitable will. The regimented minutes stretched into eternity, the sand in her father's treasured hourglass trickling through one agonizing grain at a time.

Lucy moaned and turned her face into the pillow, haunted by a ghostly melody—the vibrant notes of a Viennese waltz. Tonight she had danced in the arms of the man she loved and felt young and carefree for the first time in her life.

Now she felt ancient. She could almost feel her skin drawing, her bones stiffening, her heart crumbling to dust from both past and future neglect. She lay there, steeped in misery, until she heard her father's uneven step on the stairs.

She held her breath as he approached her room just as she had always done. Beneath his exacting tutelage, she had clipped the wings from most of her flights of fancy, but her stubborn heart had clung to one childhood dream, nurturing it in the secret hours between midnight and dawn.

If she kept her eyes shut very tightly and feigned sleep, her father might ease open the door and tiptoe over to the bed. He might bend down to touch her hair, kiss her brow, and tell her what a good girl she was, how proud he was to have her for a daughter. Then she would open her eyes and fly into his arms. They would laugh and cry at the same time, finally free to confess their love.

Lucy's hands curled in the bedclothes. If he came tonight, she vowed to herself, she would promise to forget Gerard. She would strive even harder to be the dutiful daughter he'd always wanted.

Her entire body started violently as something crashed to the floor outside her bedroom.

"Goddammit!" came the Admiral's voice, harsh and ugly, faintly slurred. "How many times have I told that stupid girl not to scatter things about on the floor? Won't be satisfied till I break my bloody neck."

Lucy kept her eyes closed until his lumbering steps had faded. From somewhere high in the house came the hollow slam of a door.

Once, Lucy would have curled into a miserable ball and cried herself to sleep.

Now, she rose, dry-eyed, and slipped silently from the room.

CHAPTER SIXTEEN

LUCY'S RESOLVE WAVERED JUST OUTSIDE the cozy square of light cast from the gatehouse window. She wished for another glass of champagne to help her recapture her reckless euphoria.

A gust of wind tossed icy needles of snow in her face, making her flinch. How many nights had Gerard stood watch beneath these very eaves, gazing up at the darkened, impassive panes of her window? Tonight it was her turn to shiver like a beggar in the cold and wonder at her welcome.

Wiggling her stocking toes in a vain attempt to relieve their numbness, she lifted her hand to knock. Her curled fingers hung an inch from the door, paralyzed more by terror than the biting cold.

Don't shilly-shally, girl. Chart your course and stay it or you'll soon find yourself sailing in circles.

"Thank you, Father," Lucy whispered to the echo of the Admiral's voice, smiling faintly at the irony.

She drew back her hand and gave the gatehouse door two sharp raps. The haste with which the crisp footsteps approached reassured her that she hadn't dragged Gerard from his bed. He was already speaking as he opened the door.

"It's hardly oh six hundred yet, Smythe. It's too blasted dark out . . . side."

He'd been shrugging on a rumpled shirt as he walked and, upon discovering it wasn't the Snow butler on his doorstep, he jerked it the rest of the way over his shoulders. Lucy was left staring at the sculpted muscles of his bare chest beneath their sprinkling of auburn hair.

Her breath caught with longing. She wanted to touch him with the unbridled curiosity of a child. Wanted to rake her fingers through those crisp hairs and see if his skin was as warm as its honeyed hue. She slowly lifted her gaze to his face.

He wasn't wearing his spectacles so there was nothing to shield her from his scowl. "It's well past your bedtime, Miss Snow. I thought Smythe tucked you in."

"I untucked myself."

When he offered her no sign of welcome, grudging or otherwise, she brushed past him to invade his inner sanctum. The rough-planked floor snagged her expensive stockings, but she hardly noticed. She was too captivated by the masculine ambience of the room. Its inviting warmth was completely unlike the forbidding chill of her father's house.

A lamp burned on the bedside table, wreathing the gatehouse's modest furnishings in a flattering glow that disguised their nicks and scars and hinted at their former grandeur. Several books were scattered across the table. A fire waned on the brick hearth at the far end of the long room, as if she'd come too late and the time to spend its cheer was done.

The faded quilt draped over the humble bedstead struck a wistful chord in Lucy. It pleasured her to imagine Gerard protected from the cold and the dark by its worn folds, his face smoothed free of wariness, his hair tousled like a boy's. A breath of icy air fanned her nape, warning her that he still hadn't closed the door.

"I've never been in here before," she confessed, desperate to distract him from tossing her out on her ear.

"I doubt that Fenster did much entertaining. He doesn't strike me as the gregarious sort. Nor am I at the moment."

When she made no move to leave, he turned his back to her, bracing his hands against each side of the doorframe as if he had every intention of bolting into the night himself if she refused his pointed invitation to depart. The lamplight sought the loose folds of his shirt, outlining his bunched muscles. Lucy longed to touch him, to ease his tension with a caress. She glided toward him, her stockings whispering against the planks.

She reached beneath the tail of his shirt, her trembling fingertips finally making contact with warm skin. Her touch had the opposite effect. His muscles tensed, leaping as if from a blaze of unexpected lightning.

"Don't!"

He slammed the door and spun around to face her, his features robbed of their geniality by desperation. Lucy took an involuntary step backward.

"I'm not one of your girlish fantasies, Lucy. I'm not your tragic and noble Captain Doom. I'm a man. Flesh and blood. Cut me and I bleed. Provoke me and I strike back. I'm fully capable of taking what's offered me for my own selfish satisfaction. Fully capable of compromising a foolish girl who's had too much champagne to consider the consequences of her actions." Lucy would have almost sworn she heard a hint of a plea in his harsh words. "Trust me. You'd be better off passing your lonely nights with your precious shadow of a ghost than with me."

Lucy refused to shrink before his rebuff. "I've spent my entire life with the shadow of a father and the ghost of a mother. I need someone I can touch. Someone warm. Someone real."

"Oh, that's bloody rich!"

Gerard clenched his teeth against a despairing laugh. Before he'd met Lucy, he'd felt as ephemeral as her Captain Doom, nothing more than a murky shade of the man he'd once been. But with this woman standing so boldly before him, her delicate jaw set with determination, her silky hair tumbling from its gold fillet, he felt every inch a man. Rushing blood and straining flesh, fraught with all of its mortal perils. His pulse roared in his ears, pounded a temptation in his aching groin.

He might have been able to resist its siren throb had Lucy not chosen that moment to forsake her stubborn pride. She lowered her smoky eyes and whispered, "I'm not asking for any promises."

He caught her to him with reckless ferocity, knowing this might be his last chance to extract one or both of them from a silken snare of disaster. "What *are* you asking for? This?"

He collapsed against the door, legs splayed, and pinned her between his thighs, lowering his head to tangle his tongue with hers. He thrust roughly into the warm, wet recesses of her mouth in a crude imitation guaranteed to challenge her innocence. She whimpered against his lips and grasped his forearms as if to deny the sensation of falling.

His mouth plundered a ruthless path from her lips to her ear. His voice dropped to a ragged whisper.

"Was that what you came here for, my sweet little mouse? Or was it this?"

Sinking his teeth gently into her earlobe, he filled his palms with her backside and rubbed his hips against the softness of her belly. She gasped as he forced her to acknowledge the full measure of his desire and the high stakes of her surrender.

Still cupping her bottom, he leaned his head back against the door and surveyed her through his lashes, raking his gaze down her shuddering breasts with deliberate insolence.

Gerard expected her to slap him as he so richly deserved. Expected her to gather her icy composure and coolly denounce him for the vulgar commoner he was. Expected her to burst into tears and run screaming for Smythe.

What he did not expect was for her to cup his face in her cool hands and press her lips to his with a loving fervency that crumbled the last of his defenses.

Shamed by her selfless tenderness, Gerard gentled his grip, running his hands up her slender back.

"You're drunk," he muttered against her lips, hating himself for reminding her.

"I'm tipsy," she whispered.

"I'll take advantage of you," he warned.

"Promise?"

She looked so hopeful that a choked laugh escaped him. He smoothed her hair away from her face, held captive by the earnestness in those incredible eyes. She had only tonight to love him, he thought. She would have a lifetime in which to hate him.

Driven by that realization, he backed her toward the bed in a dance as old as time itself. Once learned, its steps were never forgotten.

Lucy felt herself tumbling headlong into some sweet abyss, as dangerous as it was seductive, her fall broken only by Gerard's arms and the scratchy softness of the quilt beneath her knees. They knelt on the bed, face-to-face. The intensity of his gaze sobered her.

Afraid she would start quaking with fear, she reached to extinguish the lamp.

Gerard stilled her hand. "No. I like the light."

It was then that Lucy saw the tarnished candlestick and neat row of candles kept next to the lamp, insurance against the shadows of night. The sight inexplicably touched her. She suspected Gerard didn't like the light nearly as much as he hated the darkness.

Gerard drew the fillet from Lucy's hair. As the silky mass cascaded around her shoulders, the lamp flame seemed to flicker and pale as if she had absorbed its incandescence. Light filtered through her hair, burnished her skin to opalescent pearl, sifted the white of her dress to ethereal gauze. Gerard realized that the lamp flame was but a paltry imitation. Lucy was the embodiment of light. Shimmering. Quicksilver. Elusive.

Gerard buried his hands in her hair. The ashen skein slipped through his fingers like moonbeams.

His hands tightened into fists as he gazed into her misty eyes. He'd been a creature of the darkness for too long. The light he craved was now his enemy. It was too harsh, too revealing. He couldn't bear for her brightness to illuminate his vulnerability, the rawness of his need.

Breathing an oath, he killed the lamp himself, then leaned against the headboard and drew Lucy into the cradle of his thighs until her back was wedged against his chest. It seemed fitting that he should come to her this way—a faceless lover in the dying firelight. His arms circled her from behind, holding her steady when she squirmed in protest.

"But, Gerard, I don't under—"

"Hush." He rubbed his cheek against her temple, soothing her like a child. "Let me take care of you. It's my job. Remember?"

As she ceased her wiggling, the softness of her backside molded itself to his aching flesh. He rolled his eyes and sucked in a shallow breath. He had thought he knew all there was to know of torture, but this mingling of delight and deprivation was a taste of heaven and a blast of hell, a torment beyond any he had known before.

Until he began to touch her.

Lucy had spent almost twenty years building her prickly shell of reserve, yet Gerard cracked it with nothing more than a few artful strokes of his fingertips. They probed her temples, skated down the column of her throat, caressed the fluted valleys above her collarbone.

"I told you once," she said breathlessly, "that I don't like to be touched."

"And I told you," he replied, tasting the sensitive whorl of her ear with the tip of his tongue, "that you were lying."

He proved his accusation with another foray of his magical hands. A man's hands, roughened and callused from a lifetime of hard work. Lucy was hypnotized by their downward glide as he lowered the bodice of her gown, dragged down the delicate puffed sleeves of her chemise, exposing her small, pink-tipped breasts.

Her first instinct was to moan with shame and cover her breasts with her hands. But Gerard, her bodyguard, her protector, did it for her, shielding them from the flickering firelight with his sun-darkened fingers. Lucy shivered with mingled delight and mortification as she realized he was watching over her shoulder, sharing the provocative sight of their mingled flesh.

Her breasts fit the nest of his palms as if they had been made for him. They flushed, fevered by his touch. He teased her nipples to aching buds, circling, stroking, then gently tugging until Lucy felt a kindred tingling between her thighs. Pleasure and need rippled through her. A helpless whimper escaped her. She arched against him, pressing her yearning softness instinctively to the unyielding ridge of flesh beneath her.

Fearing he might reach the limits of his endurance long before she did, Gerard growled deep in his throat and kissed the corner of her mouth. "Shall I stop touching you now? Is it too much for you to bear?"

She shook her head, then nodded, then shook her head again. He took advantage of her haze of confusion to gather the gossamer fabric of her skirt and petticoat beneath his palm. He eased them up, past the blush of her stockings, past the frivolous rosebuds embroidered on her garters, finally revealing the silken folds of her drawers.

"Vive la révolution," he murmured hoarsely, blessing the French for the decadent fashions they'd foisted on proper young English ladies like Lucy Snow. At this juncture of his life he doubted even an iron chastity belt would have kept him from her.

The contrast between the prim purity of Lucy's thighs and the lace-edged carnality of her undergarments maddened him, made his hands shake with hunger. He steadied them on her knees and felt a tiny shudder of panic rip through her muscles.

He nuzzled the pulse beating frantically at the side of her throat. "Don't be afraid, Lucy. I'll stop whenever you like. I swear I won't touch you anywhere you don't want me to."

Gerard's vow failed to ease Lucy's terror. Because

she wanted him to touch her everywhere. All of those sweet, forbidden places she'd never dared to touch herself, not even when in the throes of her darkest, hungriest fantasies. Not even when they ached and melted with anticipation. She wasn't afraid of his touch. She was afraid she would humble herself beyond redemption by begging for it.

"Please . . . ?"

At first she thought the hoarse plea had tumbled from her own lips, giving substance to her fears, but as Gerard's powerful hands used all the gentleness at their disposal to coax her knees apart, she realized the entreaty was his own, offered without a trace of apology.

She watched her legs part for him as if they belonged to someone else, mesmerized by the wanton grace of her own surrender. His splayed fingers stroked the virgin cream of her inner thighs, each tantalizing foray edging his blunt thumbs nearer to the damp silk molded against her like a second skin.

A shudder rocked her to her very soul as his warm fingers unerringly found the thin slit in the expensive fabric and slipped beneath to cup her throbbing flesh.

After a lifetime of being denied intimacy, being touched there was the most exquisite and terrifying sensation Lucy had ever endured. She turned her face away and closed her eyes, no longer able to bear watching. Tears slipped silently down her cheeks to dampen the hairs of Gerard's chest.

With infinite tenderness, his deft fingers parted her, stroked her, explored all but the most vulnerable of her satiny hollows. All the while, his thumb rubbed the sensitive nub buried in her nether curls, striking sparks of fiery pleasure that threatened to incinerate her.

Every nerve in her body began to hum like a piece of Waterford crystal poised to shatter beneath the wild, piercing climax of an aria. Her heels dug into the feather tick. Her hands kneaded his muscular thighs in mute plea. She turned her head from side to side, blindly seeking fulfillment, ease for the void she feared would swallow her whole if she could not soon appease it.

When she would have clenched her thighs together in desperation, Gerard hooked his ankles around hers to pin them open, baring her body, heart, and soul to his tender mastery.

Once when he'd been a younger and more foolish man, Gerard would have sought only his own pleasure. Now he sought only hers. He clenched his teeth, torn between anguish and ecstasy. He wanted to comfort Lucy, reassure her that he would be there to pick up the pieces when she splintered into a thousand glimmering fragments.

But what did he have to offer her? A passel of lies? Promises he could never keep? Vows that would be broken before dawn? He didn't dare speak for fear of what might spill out. So he kept them both imprisoned in a world without words. Without truth. A world of darkness. A world of devastating pleasure and bittersweet denial.

She sprawled against him in wanton abandon, melting into his hand as he had always dreamed she would do. When her murmured litany escalated into piteous cries, he slipped one finger into the honeyed cocoon of her body, never ceasing the provocative ministrations of his thumb. She was softer than silk, hotter than fire. Her husky moan coaxed him to dare more. Two fingers. Her untried body received him with such unabashed generosity that he groaned and arched against her, tempted almost beyond the bounds of sanity to ease open the straining buttons of his trousers and bury more than his fingers in her. Much more.

Then he felt the tiny convulsions ripple out from her womb, gloving his fingers in searing heat. Gerard lost all conscious thought except for the presence of mind to lay his other hand over her mouth to capture the first of her breathless, broken cries in the cup of his palm.

Lucy shuddered again and again as Gerard's hands, his clever, magnificent hands, held her hostage to delight. Rivers of pleasure poured through her in an unending torrent, sweeping the last of her inhibitions away. Her hips moved of their own accord, wildly seeking the mate of the spasms that raked her with such exquisite rhythm. Just when they began to abate, his thumb worked its dark magic again. Her scream would have awakened the entire household had Gerard not had the foresight to tighten his hand over her mouth.

She collapsed against his chest in a shivering heap, her hands groping for the sustenance of his warm skin.

Gerard wrapped his arms around Lucy and cradled her in his lap, his desire to protect never so strong as in that moment when she was at her most vulnerable. That moment when she gave him the gift of her trust although she'd never been more at risk.

He smoothed damp strands of hair from her flushed cheeks, realizing in an instant of ruthless clarity that he held in his arms the perfect tool to achieve all of his goals. He'd sown the seeds for scandal by dancing with her publicly at the winter masque. All that remained was to reap them by ruining her and abandoning her to face the Admiral's wrath and the consequences of their folly alone. Consequences that might very well include his bastard.

The ease of it taunted him. The Admiral's haughty daughter seduced by a servant. Her father's worst expectations of her fulfilled. It would be a scandal of epic proportions to be savored by every gossipmonger in London.

Lucy emerged from her drowsy haze of satisfaction as Gerard's arms tightened painfully around her. She could feel his arousal nudging her rump, unabated and unassuaged. A small, guilt-stricken sound escaped her. He had given everything, but asked nothing for himself. She turned in his arms, no longer content to be held as a child. She wanted him to make her a woman. His woman.

Her lips flowered against his chest, tasting the salty spice of his skin as she had longed to do for so long. Her hands crept through crisp hairs still damp from her tears, drifted upward to ease his shirt over the muscled breadth of his shoulders.

He caught her wrists in his hands. "No!"

Lucy recoiled from the harsh warning, gazing up at him in bewilderment. Conflicting emotions warred in his eyes, as if he wrestled with some dark demon visible only to him. An all too familiar feeling of dread blossomed in her belly. No matter the outcome of the battle, she feared she would be the loser.

His tormented gaze raked her face, then dropped to flirt voraciously with her bare breasts. There was something different about his eyes, some mercenary flicker that made Lucy painfully conscious of the gown bunched around her waist, her crooked garter, the stocking collapsed at her ankle. Something that made her cheeks burn with shame at her disheveled nudity. A tendril of panic wove through her desire.

"What is it, Gerard? What did I do?"

His grip on her wrists softened. His eyes darkened with a bleak regret that made her heart quail. "Nothing. You've done nothing. Which is exactly why you should go now. Before it's too bloody late."

His fingertips grazed her cheek in the ghost of a

caress before he stood, dumping her from his lap to the rumpled quilt. He tugged his shirt closed, his profile implacable in the dim light. Only moments before his hands had been adept enough to melt her trepidation to pleasure, skilled enough to keep that pleasure from becoming pain. Now they fumbled clumsily with the buttons of his shirt as if they'd turned to chunks of ice, devoid of all grace and feeling.

Gerard couldn't afford to be gentle with her. He had no comfort left to offer either of them. He was too frustrated. Too near to the edge. One tender touch from her would push him right over the precipice and he wanted her badly enough to take her along for the fall without a qualm of conscience.

"We can discuss this in the morning," he said, his voice gruff with unspent passion. "When we've got all our wits about us."

For the first time, Lucy allowed her gaze to linger on the gaping door of the wardrobe. On the yawning leather valise that had confirmed her worst fears the moment she'd stepped into the gatehouse.

She tugged the sleeves of her chemise over her shoulders and pushed her skirt down to shield her nakedness, possessed by a calm as fragile as the glassy surface of the sea after a raging storm. "You won't be here in the morning, will you? Smythe as much as told me you'd been dismissed."

"Dismissed?" Confusion touched his features, elusive in the dying firelight, then he shrugged carelessly. "Being dismissed is a hazard of my profession. If you do your job well enough, eventually you're no longer needed."

I need you.

The words hung unspoken between them, as tangible as the knot of longing wedged in Lucy's chest.

As if to escape her challenging gaze, Gerard moved

to the wardrobe and began dragging out his meager collection of well-worn garments, cramming them into the valise with no more care than Lucy would have taken in organizing her dressing table.

Smoothing her skirt, she rose to stand beside the bed. "Take me with you."

Gerard's hands faltered in the motion of wadding a cravat into an untidy ball. Lucy was willing to sacrifice everything for him—her reputation, her wealth, even the improbable but irresistible chance that her father might someday come to love her. The sharpened blade of irony twisted in his heart, giving him the unholy strength to do what had to be done.

"You should go, Miss Snow," he said without turning around, knowing only too well that each cold word was like the jab of an icicle through her tender pride. "I'd hate for your presence here to cost me my references."

He heard the padded sigh of her feet across the rough planks, felt a blast of wintry air against his nape. He rushed to the still swinging door to watch her running figure dissolve like a phantom into the swirling curtain of white.

He slammed his fist into the doorframe. Lucy had been right. He wouldn't be there in the morning. He wouldn't be there in an hour. No matter the cost of his haste, he couldn't spend a minute longer than necessary within sight of Ionia's gabled roof. If he dared, he knew he would find himself slipping into that decadent bower Lucy called a bedroom, smothering her sobs with his lips, and soothing her stricken pride beneath the hard, hungry thrusts of his body.

He rested his mouth against his clenched fist, breathing deeply of the lemon and musk that still clung to his fingers like an aphrodisiac. The Admiral's beautiful daughter would never know how narrow her escape or how devastating the cost of his mercy. He'd come to Ionia believing himself a man with nothing to lose only to lose the one thing he hadn't even known he still possessed.

His heart.

CHAPTER SEVENTEEN

LUCY STUMBLED ACROSS THE LAWN, EACH clumsy thud of her feet breaking the powdery crust of snow. Her heart hammered in her ears as if to drown out the echo of Gerard's crass dismissal. Icy flakes battered her face, melting as they encountered the warm tears coursing down her cheeks.

She didn't know where she was going until she saw the homely old oak, its harsh silhouette blurred by a dusting of snow. She sank to her knees beneath the shelter of its branches, hugging herself as the cold seeped into her naked limbs.

The night whispered its mournful secrets in the creak of the withered branches. Lucy bleakly surveyed the snowswept vista, wishing for the bitterness to pronounce it ugly. But she would be lying if she did. The hills rolling down to the river still sparkled with a heavenly iridescence. The snowflakes still waltzed and twirled to the silent music of the icy gusts. Lucy shivered. It was all so beautiful. So treacherous. Like love itself.

She buried her face in her hands. Gerard didn't want her any more than her father ever had. He might lust after her as all those men had lusted after her mother, but he would never love her. Her body, still tingly and slightly tender from his loving attentions, throbbed in contradiction.

What terrible flaw did she possess that made it so impossible for anyone to love her?

After tonight, there wouldn't even be anyone to watch after her. No one to keep the light in the gatehouse burning after midnight. No one to stand beneath the old oak at dawn. No one to blow smoke rings at her nose or tease her until she sputtered with indignation. After tonight, Gerard's rich laughter would be nothing more than a memory, a haunting echo of a brief interlude in her colorless life.

Lucy's fingernails dug into her elbows as she doubled over, bracing herself for a fresh torrent of tears. But her pain ran beyond tears into a soundless cry of agony. When she finally lifted her face to the murky sky, it was as dry and barren as the winter wind whisking through her soul.

A flicker of light in the darkened windowpane of the library caught her eye. An acrid bitterness burned her throat. Her father couldn't spare the time to wish his only daughter good night, but he could work until the wee hours of the morning. He was probably reviewing his memoirs, gloating over his feats of derring-do transcribed in her own tidy hand.

Lucy climbed to her feet, her spine rigid. The wind molded her thin gown to her legs, reminding her of the night she'd stood on the deck of the *Tiberius* and watched the *Retribution* melt out of the mist. Gerard had been right about one thing. She would have been better off clinging to her fantasies of a dashing pirate than risking her heart to the fickle affections of flesh-and-blood men.

She started for the house, her strides brisk with purpose. Gerard might leave of his own choosing in the morning, but she would not have him driven off by her father's bullying or her own pathetic infatuation. She had no idea how she would broach the subject when she stormed the Admiral's hallowed retreat, but she was done with being dismissed. Never again would she meet rejection by crawling off into a corner to lick her wounds.

She slipped through a side door and made her way to the entrance hall. Shadows draped the cavernous room, swallowing the whisper of her footsteps across the polished parquet. Lucy's confidence waned as she approached the massive library door. How many times had the beautifully carved teak barricaded her from her father's life? It would have taken so little to make a lonely child happy—an adjustment to her ribbon, a welcoming smile, even a well-intentioned scold instead of the glacial scorn that had withered her tender feelings before they could bloom.

Lucy could feel herself shrinking again, remembering all the times she'd stood on tiptoe to reach the brass knob. Her hand betrayed her with a slight tremble as she inched the door open.

The only sound in the fireless room was the ghostly tapping of snowflakes against the windows. A host of dizzying impressions assaulted Lucy: a menacing shadow by the secretary, a harshly indrawn breath, a flicker of matchlight quickly extinguished.

She crept forward. "Father?" she whispered, then more tentatively, "Smythe?"

She was beginning to wonder if one of the servants hadn't slipped in to filch some sherry when a dark shape separated itself from the shadows, closing the

distance between them with the lethal grace of a charging predator.

Claws of terror raked down Lucy's spine. Even as
the Admiral's voice chided her . . .

*He doesn't give a farthing about you, you silly chit.
He won't come.*

. . . she opened her mouth to scream for the one
man who had offered her refuge, however brief, in the
shelter of his arms.

Gerard.

A merciless hand stifled her cry, clamping hard over
her mouth. She found herself imprisoned against a
man's unyielding chest, dragged away from the door
toward her father's desk. Desolation threatened to rob
her of her will to resist. It washed over her in bleak
waves, sharpening the sense of abandonment she'd
fought since a child.

Gerard wasn't coming. He wasn't going to stage a
daring rescue. He wasn't going to defeat this faceless
demon in the dark or dry her frightened tears.

She was truly, completely alone.

That grim realization gave her the strength she
needed to fight. It infused her veins with the reckless
courage of someone who has nothing left to lose. She
twisted wildly in her attacker's arms, flailing out with
her fists and feet. A muffled grunt escaped him as her
heel connected soundly with his shin, giving her an all
too brief rush of satisfaction.

His back collided with the unmoving mahogany of
the Admiral's desk, jarring every bone in their meshed
bodies. Lucy took advantage of the impact to sink her
teeth into his unyielding palm until she tasted blood,
salty and metallic, against her tongue.

With a vicious oath, he jerked his palm away, but
before she could draw breath to scream, something
damp and bitter-smelling was pressed over her face.

For one dark moment, Lucy believed he meant to smother her as punishment for her rebellion.

Sickly sweet fumes stung her eyes, flooded her lungs. The rigidity of terror drained from her limbs, leaving them too weak to support her. Consciousness wavered before her eyes like a watercolor seascape. Realizing in some tiny corner of her brain that her attacker's grip had softened, she turned in his arms, desperate to cling to something solid in a world gone liquid.

Her hand clutched his nape, then slid to his collar in a mocking travesty of a lover's caress. She clawed for substance, parting his shirt over the heated skin of his shoulder. Her curled fingers went lax, unfolding over a slash of puckered scar tissue.

The precise sort of scar that might have been carved by an ivory-handled letter opener.

"Doom," she breathed. His alias. Her fate.

She flung out an arm in one last desperate grasp for reality, sending her father's precious hourglass tumbling end over end off the edge of the desk.

Time crashed to a halt in a cool spill of sand over her feet as Doom's powerful arms broke her fall into oblivion.

♥   ♥   ♥

"Smythe!"

The crisp bellow fractured the well-ordered serenity of Ionia's morning. The servants who had served under the Admiral prior to his retirement flinched and scurried for cover, already tasting the bite of the cat-o'-nine-tails into their flesh.

Lucien Snow ploughed down the stairs, gripping his cane as if more inclined to break it over someone's head than use it for support. He was too enraged to humor his own frailties.

"What the devil has gotten into that man?" he muttered. "Must be going dotty in his dotage. Smythe!" he shouted to the deserted entrance hall. "Where the bloody hell is my breakfast?"

There were no carpets or tapestries to absorb the sound. The hall threw back a barren echo, giving him the unsettled impression that something more important than breakfast had gone missing from his routine. The Admiral despised feeling unsettled. When every mundane detail of his daily existence wasn't carefully under his control, he suffered from the same jittery sensation he used to get while dodging his father's drunken blows and shouted jeers that he would never amount to anything.

He strode toward the gaping door of the library, cheered by the prospect of verbally castigating whoever had dared to profane his sanctuary with their unworthy presence.

He froze in the doorway, paralyzed into inaction by the odd sight that greeted him.

Smythe sat cross-legged on the floor in front of the desk, surrounded by scattered sand and fragments of broken glass. His uniform was rumpled and soiled.

"Oh, bloody Christ, Smythe, not the hourglass! First that rapscallion Claremont breaks my favorite bust and now this. I warn you, man, this is coming out of your wages and don't think it's not. Why I've had that hourglass since my first command on the *HMS* . . ."

The Admiral trailed off, disturbed by the vague, but repetitive, motions of the man's hands. Smythe was scooping up fistfuls of sand, but no matter how tightly he cupped his fingers, the fine-grained sand trickled through the gaps until he was forced to begin again. Tiny cuts crisscrossed his knuckles.

"Smythe?" the Admiral whispered, battling a formless dread.

Smythe had seemed oblivious to his bellows, but the tentative whisper brought his head upright. His face was haggard, his skin a pasty gray.

He blinked once, twice, like a child awakening from a bad dream. "She's gone sir. He's taken her."

As the butler's hand closed in a bloodless fist, squeezing the last of the sand from his fingers, the Admiral staggered backward, forced to lean on his cane or fall.

PART TWO

Better to reign in hell than serve in heav'n.

JOHN MILTON

Kill then, and bliss me
But first come kiss me.

ANONYMOUS
16TH CENTURY

CHAPTER EIGHTEEN

THE FAMILIAR ROCKING MOTION soothed Lucy. It was like being suspended in the womb of some giant, but gentle, beast whose only intention was to protect her from harm. She'd learned its rhythms before she'd been old enough to express the comfort she found in them. Before she'd been old enough to dream she was being cradled in the arms of a mother she would never know.

Hazy light filtered through her eyelids. She eased them open. Gerard's dear, familiar features, taut with concern, drifted into focus.

Memory returned in fragments, jagged but complete. A cloud of joy enveloped her.

Gerard hadn't abandoned her after all. He'd somehow heeded her strangled cry and rushed to her rescue as he'd done so many times before. He could never leave her, nor could he deny his feelings for her. They were written all over his face, as plainly as the nameless dread that darkened his eyes to smoky topaz.

She lifted a hand to his face, longing to banish his foreboding with the reassurance of her touch.

Her hand stopped halfway to his unshaven cheek.

She frowned as confusion buffeted her. If Gerard had rescued her from Doom's perfidy, why was her bed creaking like the deck of a ship at full sail? Why was his face hardening even as she watched, its boyish planes sketched in ruthless lines, as if by an artist who would deny his subject was capable of tenderness, mercy, or even the most basic human kindness?

Her outstretched hand began to tremble.

She lowered her eyes to shield them from his predatory scrutiny. He knew, she realized. He knew with inhuman instinct the second she started to doubt.

Her hand shot out with a will of its own. He didn't flinch or make any move to protect himself. She could have struck him full in the face and he wouldn't have so much as blinked.

She clawed at his white shirt like a desperate lover, ignoring the rending protest of its seams. How long had it been since she had sought to bare his chest for her caress? A lifetime ago? She jerked the crisp linen back and down, stripping his right shoulder.

The flawless melding of muscle and sinew was marred by a single narrow scar. She touched her fingertips to it, exploring its uneven border with dumb shock.

Gerard caught her wrist, his grip both gentle and implacable. She slowly lifted her eyes to meet his, already dreading what she would find.

"Gerard Claremont," he said, his eyes sparkling with grim humor. "My friends call me Gerard, but my enemies call me Captain Doom."

Lucy flinched as reality fractured around her just as her father's hourglass had. The blood drained from her face. An icy sweat broke out on her brow. Her ears roared as if flanked by twin conch shells. The soothing fog of unconsciousness drifted toward her, promising respite from a truth she could neither change nor endure.

Before she could succumb, bitter nausea curled through her belly. For one humiliating moment, she thought she was going to be ill all over Gerard's striking jackboots and half wished she would.

Then he was there as he had always been, his competent hands supporting her shoulders, bathing her bloodless lips with a damp rag.

"Stop it!" she spat, batting them away. She couldn't bear his touch. It was a mockery. An abomination.

He at least had the grace to withdraw a few feet from the bed. She threaded her fingers through her hair and pressed her palms to her temples, waiting for both her rioting emotions and stomach to subside.

"The champagne and the *somnorifera* were an unfortunate combination," he said quietly. "When I stole it from the stables, I never intended to use it on you. I'm sorry."

Lucy remembered the smothering softness pressed over her face. She could still taste the sickly-sweet bitterness of poppy on her tongue, scent it in her nostrils.

"Sorry?" She glared up at him through a tangled strand of hair. "Correct me if I'm wrong, but I believe *somnorifera* is *intended* to subdue horses for gelding."

She savored every ounce of menace in the last word. Gerard's lips tensed as if he would have liked to smile, but didn't dare.

He folded his arms over his chest. "Which is exactly why it would have worked to subdue Smythe had he disturbed me. He's the only man I know who sleeps less than I do."

"Was it your *intention* to abduct me or was that an unfortunate accident of fate as well?"

He drew a step nearer to the bed. The silkiness of his voice didn't soften its sting. "Had it been my intention to abduct you, I would have done so long ago. God knows, you offered me ample opportunity."

As their eyes met, Lucy recalled all the other things she'd offered him. Her trust. Her heart. Her innocence. Waves of humiliation and self-loathing washed over her as she realized she'd been nothing more to him than the means to an end. A hapless pawn in some enigmatic game.

Tears sprang to her eyes, but she furiously blinked them back, refusing to debase herself further before this man. If he had the sheer gall to offer her a handkerchief, she might very well lunge for his throat.

"What a mewling goose you must have thought me! How you must have laughed at my calf-eyed adoration, my absurd defense of Captain Doom!"

His impassive silence was as damning as a confession.

She choked a single word past the raw magnitude of his betrayal. "Why?"

He paced away from her, his deliberate distance pounding the wedge between them that much deeper. Outside of a Royal Navy flagship, Lucy had never seen a great cabin of such generous proportions. There was even a window at starboard, a large, rounded porthole that provided a glimpse of a bleak dawn unfurling over a gray sea.

Not even the spacious cabin could confine its master's restless energy. He didn't so much pace as prowl.

When he pivoted on his heel, the man she had known as Gerard Claremont was gone. His usurper was the predatory stranger who had stalked her in this very cabin on the most frightening, exhilarating night of her life. The essence of command was limned in every roll of his sailor's swagger. This was a man who did not feel it necessary to hide his pistol beneath a coat, but wore it jammed boldly into the waistband of a pair of black breeches that clung to his lean flanks like a second skin.

Lucy fought the same breathless fear she had felt when watching the *Retribution* emerge from the night. It was as if she faced some elemental creature of awesome power whose very existence threatened her own. As he approached, she hugged her knees to her chest, knowing them a precarious barrier at best. He had already breached them once.

"Contrary to what you may think," he said, "piracy wasn't always my chosen vocation."

"A pity. You seem to excel at it." Her words sounded as brittle as she felt.

He slanted her a dark look, then resumed his pacing. She supposed she was entitled to her sarcasm. God knows he'd left her little else.

"I went to sea when I was twelve. By the time I was nineteen, I was serving as master of my own merchant vessel."

No small accomplishment, that, but Lucy would have bitten off her own tongue before praising his initiative. "If you've a quill and some paper, I'd be more than happy to take notes for your memoirs."

"Or my eulogy?" he ventured. "After the Spanish switched their allegiance to France, there was a fortune to be made for any captain willing to challenge their combined Mediterranean blockades."

"I'm well aware of Spain's betrayal. It almost cost my father his leg. It did cost him his career."

"I can promise you that it didn't cost him nearly as much as it cost me." Gerard's silky tone flogged her raw nerves. She was thankful when he continued his clipped recitation. "I returned from a voyage to Gibraltar, after inadvertently dismasting a Spanish frigate carrying gunpowder to the French, to find myself something of a hero."

"A role I'm sure you relished."

A rueful smile curved his lips. "It had its charms. I was presented at court and wooed by the Royal Navy. There were very few salons in London that weren't open to me."

Very few beds either, Lucy deduced. It was only too easy to imagine the handsome young captain soaking up the simpering admiration of the *ton*'s beauties. A pang of jealousy disturbed her. How plain and unsophisticated a lowly knight's daughter must have seemed to him!

She hid her discomfiture behind a venomous smile. "So how did this idyllic interlude come to an end?"

"With the appearance of a stranger at a masked ball. A stranger claiming to represent a high-ranking naval official who could grant me the one thing fame and fortune couldn't buy me. I'd already been offered a chance to take the lieutenancy exam, but this man promised me command of my own ship." His voice softened with remembered longing. "A captaincy in the Royal Navy." As if already regretting that he'd revealed too much, he paced away from her, tension coiled in every step.

"Go on," she whispered, aching with bleak suspense.

"I'm sure you're aware of the thin line that separates privateering and piracy during times of war. I was offered a chance to tread the lawful side of that line. To sail to the Caribbean, capture and board French and Spanish frigates, and return one-fifth of their booty to His Majesty to fund the war effort. My crew and I were to split the balance. My anonymous benefactor would commission a ship and the Lord High Admiral would issue a letter of marque to legalize my activities and keep the French from hanging me should I be captured."

His lips twisted, but this time his contempt was only for himself. "Such a scheme couldn't help but strike the patriotic fancy of a brash young man who'd spent his life dreaming of serving his king. The intrigue alone was irresistible. I met my benefactor's representative at masked routs, in shadowed alleys, priest's confessionals. I never saw his face or knew his name. I wasn't to understand the reason why until it was too late."

"You were captured," Lucy said with dread certainty.

"I was betrayed!"

She recoiled from his damning shout. She had exasperated him, infuriated him, possibly even enraged him during his weeks at Ionia, but he had never raised his voice to her with such violence. Her gaze dropped to his clenched fists. She'd seen firsthand the damage they could do when their threat was unleashed. For the first time, she entertained the painful possibility that she might have more to fear from this man than heartbreak.

Following the direction of her gaze, Gerard slowly uncurled his fingers and released a deep breath. "I was *captured*," he conceded, "off the coast of San Juan. Two days before, a Spanish merchant vessel had surrendered without a fight. I boarded her, showed the captain my letter of marque, and proceeded to divest her of her cargo." His eyes sharpened at the memory. "Three thousand pieces of gold, silver bars, spices, cotton, indigo, silk, cinnamon. A treasure to warm the moldering heart of Captain Kidd himself."

"And the heart of His Majesty, I'm sure."

"I was never to know. We were captured by a French warship and taken to a fortress in Santo Domingo. Even when the guards were clapping me in irons, I laughed in their faces because I knew they hadn't the evidence to convict us of piracy. I still had the Lord High Admiral's letter of marque in my possession *and* I'd had the foresight to stash our prize in San Juan."

"Buried treasure. How romantic." Her droll tone implied the opposite.

"My benefactor's henchman came calling the next day. It had been agreed upon that he would be waiting in the islands to defend me in the event of such a situation. All he required was the letter of marque and the location of our cache."

For a stunned moment, Lucy lost the threads of her sarcasm. "And you told him?"

Wheeling on his heel, Gerard shot her a scathing look. "You'll have to forgive me my naïveté. That was back when I still had faith in mankind."

Lucy met his gaze and said softly, "I seem to remember suffering from just such a grave condition myself."

He was the first to look away. "That was the last I saw of the wretch. Without the letter of marque, I had no way to prove myself a privateer and not a pirate." His face darkened. "They hanged my crew the following day, all the way down to the sailmaster's nine-year-old apprentice. They would have hanged me, but my earlier boasts had planted enough doubt in their minds that they feared reprisal from the British government." He added with chilling gentleness, "Do you know what it is for a captain to outlive his crew, Lucy?"

Lucy recalled standing on the misty deck of the *Tiberius,* imagining the ghostly strains of betrayed sailors vowing vengeance. The notion didn't seem quite so fanciful anymore.

She shivered. "I'm sorry."

"I don't want your pity," he snapped.

"Then what do you want?" she cried. She could no longer bear his enigmatic baiting. It was like being batted about by the elegant, but deadly, paws of a leopard.

He swaggered toward the bed. It took every fiber of her will to keep from shrinking back into the pillows. "Would you care to know the name of the ship my benefactor provided me? The recommissioned beauty the French gutted and sank off the coast of Santo Domingo?"

"Not really," she whispered, her mouth going dry.

He ignored her. "The *Annemarie*."

Lucy blanched. A sick feeling blossomed in her belly. "Annemarie was my mother's name. I've never heard of such a ship."

Gerard arched one eyebrow. "My benefactor always did have a droll sense of humor. It was his idea to give me the alias Captain Doom." Her heartbeat quickened as he leaned over the bed, flexing his hands on the headboard behind her to imprison her between his muscular arms. "So you see, my dear, you can't blame me for being a villain, because after all, I'm only what your father made me."

CHAPTER NINETEEN

"YOU'RE LYING!"

With that impassioned cry, Lucy ducked beneath Gerard's arm and sprang out of the bed, desperate to escape his taunting presence. A moment earlier she might have judged herself too weak with shock to stand without foundering, but now outrage fortified her as she took her turn at pacing the immense cabin.

"You're lying," she repeated, turning on Gerard like a mother tigress defending her cubs. "My father is a good man. He's dedicated his life to serving his country and king."

"He's dedicated his life to serving himself!" Gerard snarled.

He was looking at her as if he hated her as much as he hated her father. Refusing to be distracted by the sharp pain in the region of her heart, Lucy retreated behind the cool veil of logic.

She faced him, her hands linked before her with contemptuous calm. "Upon what evidence do you base your absurd accusation?"

Amusement at her bravado glimmered briefly in his eyes, jarring her more than his antipathy. "Your father had the perfect motives. Jealousy of a young, healthy naval hero with a bright career ahead of him. Greed. Desperation."

Lucy gave an unladylike snort. "My father is a wealthy man. He wasn't born so, but the King rewarded him handsomely for his years of loyal service."

"I don't dispute that. What I do dispute is his rather careless method of disposing of his wealth."

"That's ridiculous. The Admiral is a most frugal man. We've always lived comfortably, but never beyond our rather modest means."

Gerard laughed, a hearty rumble that mocked her stilted defense. "Your father is a bloated wastrel who's spent every night since long before you were born at the gambling hells in Pall Mall and St. James. When White's and Brook's tired of his unreliable credit, he fled to the less reputable establishments in Covent Garden. By the time of his accident, he'd not only managed to piddle away his annual income at the gaming tables, but his pension and the roof over your pretty little head as well."

Lucy drew in an unsteady breath, thankful her hands were linked to hide their sudden tremor. Her world was shifting around her again and she feared one more lurch might destroy her fragile balance for good.

She met Gerard's gaze squarely. "You once accused me of concocting elaborate fictions to justify my actions. I must now accuse you of the same. My father would no more resort to reckless wagering than he would to drunkenness or slothfulness or—or . . ."

"Or piracy?" Gerard provided. "Not even with creditors banging down his door? Not even when facing bankruptcy and scandal?" His slanted smile took on a bitter twist. "We all know how your father loathes scandal, don't we?"

Lucy forced herself to ignore his well-placed jab. She had been taught to respect logic above all else, but she was beginning to despise Gerard's grasp of it.

She began to pace again, charting a wide course around his unavoidable presence. "If what you're saying is true, how could you be so bold as to just stroll into our lives?" She paused as a disturbing possibility occurred to her. "Is Gerard Claremont even your name?" she asked softly, already dreading his answer.

"It is now. Richard Montjoy, the man Lucien Snow gulled, died in that fortress by the sea. Gerard Claremont survived."

Lucy inexplicably felt as if she'd been robbed of something precious. "What if someone in London had recognized you? My father? His alleged henchman? One of Lord Howell's guests?"

"Your father was already lamed when he hatched his plot. I have reason to believe he never saw me, except from a distance. My appearance has also changed drastically since my brief tenure of fame. I sported a beard for one thing."

Lucy lowered her gaze, remembering his beard only too well, the teasing prickle of it against her cheek when the man calling himself Captain Doom had taunted her with his carnality.

"My hair was long then," he continued, "worn in a Hessian tail, and much lighter than it is now." His cocked eyebrow belied the gravity of his words. "After all, I hadn't spent five years out of the sun, chained to a stone wall in a French fortress, watching my youth and vitality waste away."

Lucy was shaken. His crew's grim fate must have, in some ways, been more tolerable than his own. This time she was wise enough to bite back her pity. He'd made it clear he had no use for it.

Besides, she thought, studying him from beneath her lashes, there was nothing wasted about this man. He exuded raw power. It was a tribute to his consummate skill as an actor that he'd kept it leashed long enough to appear the most exemplary of servants while in her father's employ.

She was forced to scramble for the threads of her unraveling argument. "What did you hope to find in the Admiral's library? Do you think he would have been foolish enough to retain evidence that could convict him of plotting such a ruthless scheme?"

"Not foolish. Arrogant, perhaps, but never foolish. When the truth comes to light, as I can promise you it soon will, that letter of marque will be the only thing standing between your pompous papa and the gallows. As long as he has it in his possession, he can be convicted of swindling and fraud, but not piracy."

"That doesn't explain why he would hire someone to protect me."

"Did he? Or was he protecting himself? When he read in the newspapers of my untimely resurrection, he wisely chose not to travel by sea. But it obviously never occurred to him that Doom might abduct you. Perhaps he feared the man would try to make contact with you again. Would tell you the truth just as I'm doing now. The authorities might not believe a convicted pirate, but what if the Admiral's own daughter denounced him?"

Against her will, Lucy remembered the Admiral's grueling interrogation after her rescue by the *Argonaut,* his suspicious, sidelong glances. The words tore from her raw throat, as if saying them with enough fervor could somehow make them true. "That's utter nonsense. He hired you because he cares for me. I'm all he has. He needs me."

"You're bloody well right he needs you. So he can savor his role as martyred cuckold. So he can punish you, every hour of every day, for your mother's indiscretions. She had the sheer audacity to die on him, but she left you in her place to pay for her sins. Quite the doting papa, isn't he?"

At Gerard's brutal words, the fierce pain of his betrayal struck her anew. She swayed on her feet. He reached for her.

She recoiled from him, infused with strength by the desperate need to avoid his touch. She couldn't afford to forget that his tenderness, his consideration for her well-being, were nothing more than the tools of a coldly calculated ruse. His eyes darkened at her withdrawal, but he didn't press.

She had to escape him. She knew better than anyone that there was nowhere to flee on a ship, but blind panic sent her striding toward the cabin's door. "This is an outrage. I won't stand for it. I demand to be released at the nearest port or I swear I shall—"

Gerard stepped neatly into her path, blocking any hope of flight. Lucy's breath caught in her nostrils, deceived by the comforting scent of him—tobacco, the spice of bayberry, now mated with the wild and salty tang of the sea.

Tension tingled between them like lightning before a summer storm, but he didn't lay a hand on her. There was no need to. The unspoken threat crackled in the air. As Lucy's gaze shifted to his unyielding features, she was forced to acknowledge that this man, who had once vowed to hold her life as dear as his own, was now her mortal enemy.

"If you've any thoughts of escape, *Miss Snow*"—he lingered over her name as if to deliberately destroy any intimacy they'd once shared—"you'd best think twice. My men are a dangerous lot. Utterly ruthless. Trust me. You don't want to fall into their hands."

So they were back to that, were they? Lucy thought. Well, he wasn't the only one who could read a cue. She tilted her head back, daring a mutinous glare. "You'll forgive me, sir, if I find it difficult to trust you. Tell me, Mr. Clare—*Captain,*" she amended, each syllable laced with contempt, "was your time at Ionia worthwhile? Did you find the prize you were seeking in my father's library?"

His gaze raked her, but Lucy found it impossible to decipher the peculiar blend of emotions in his expression. Amusement? Desperation? Regret?

His gaze returned to her face. "Oh, I found a hell of a prize. I just haven't decided what to do with it yet."

As he swung open the door to depart, Lucy didn't know whether to be alarmed at being abandoned to her fears or relieved to escape his company. She could not resist a parting shot.

"Captain?"

"Yes?" he replied with scorching patience.

"You can blame my father for your villainy if it soothes your battered scruples, but you should never forget that every man is master of his own fate."

He shut the door in her face, his gentle rejection underscored by the rattle of a key and the thud of a wooden bolt being slammed into place.

Lucy sank against the door, betrayed by her quivering knees. Perhaps the only skill she'd inherited from her father was her ability to bluff, for as long as Gerard Claremont was captain of this vessel, he was also master of her fate.

♥　♥　♥

Gerard clenched the forward rail and braced his legs against the swell of the waves, savoring the sensation of once again being master of all he surveyed. After weeks of meekly taking orders from a man he loathed, it was a heady feeling, intoxicating and almost as potent as the temptation to abuse that mastery.

Undaunted by the winter chill and the ponderous gloom of gray seas meeting pewter-tinted skies, he sucked a breath deep into his lungs, hoping it might purge him of the remorse marring his reunion with the only mistress he had ever loved. She baptized him in her invigorating spray and pressed her salty kiss against his lips. His years of captivity, spent buried in stone, yet taunted by the nearby chant of the sea, had only sharpened his craving for her open arms.

Every man is master of his own fate.

Gerard's knuckles whitened with anger at the echo of Lucy's grave rebuke. The prim and pampered Miss Snow had a lot of bloody nerve denouncing him. She'd never had her fate snatched from her hands and given into the hands of others. Cruel hands. Merciless hands. Hands that quenched the light and left him chained in filth and darkness for months on end.

When Lucy had strode toward the cabin door to so gallantly defy him, he had thought to put his hands on her, but hadn't trusted himself to do so. Hadn't trusted himself to test the boundaries of the dangerous shift of power that had occurred in their relationship. He had feared his hunger for her and his thirst for revenge might somehow meld, creating a violent maelstrom that could destroy them both. He knew instinctively that if he ever crossed that line, there'd be no turning back.

Unbeknownst to her, she'd already saved her father's life once. Until he'd learned of her existence, Gerard had fully intended to wring his revenge from Lucien Snow's treacherous throat. It was her gentle prodding of his slumbering scruples at their first meeting that had tempered his desire for vengeance with a craving for justice and birthed his mad scheme to infiltrate his enemy's camp.

He wondered if some residual insanity had prompted him to bring her aboard the *Retribution*. His physical scars were fading, but the deeper mental scars of his imprisonment remained, carved when madness had gnawed like rats in the dark at the frayed edges of his reason.

It would have been far simpler to leave her unconscious on the floor of the Admiral's library, no more aware of his true identity than she had ever been. She might have harbored her own suspicions about her bodyguard's abrupt departure, but they would have been just that—suspicions with no proof to uphold them.

But when she had whispered his alias and slumped in his arms, her soft, boneless weight becoming his own, he'd been seized by a fierce surge of possessiveness, a primitive masculine response more suited to a cave dweller than a ship's captain. He simply could not bear to relinquish her to his enemy.

So he had carried her off to his waiting ship, adding kidnapping to his growing list of transgressions. He knew the Admiral couldn't afford to keep silent this time. Soon the London press *and* the Royal Navy would know the name he'd been born with, his description, and possibly some distorted version of his history. A version in which Lucien Snow would doubtless emerge as the most valiant of heroes.

His smoldering eyes searched the mist-shrouded horizon, but not even the tempestuous charms of the distant billows could soothe his raw temper. Too soon, that horizon would be studded with a fleet of Royal Navy ships, their rows of cannons trained on the *Retribution*.

He'd risked his ship, his crew, and his life, all for nothing more than the opportunity to make Lucinda Snow despise him.

He didn't turn around when Apollo padded out of the shadows beneath the fo'c'sle like the ghost of his conscience. "The first time I brought her aboard, I did not know she was a woman. Can you say the same, my friend?"

His quartermaster's melodious voice was underscored by the rhythm of the islands and lightly accented with the French of his former masters. Gerard knew he was worried. You didn't spend five years chained next to a man without learning his moods, even a man as private as Apollo.

Gerard shot him a dark look. "I might have had more time to consider the consequences of my actions had my crew not threatened to sail without me."

The natural serenity of Apollo's features was disturbed by a faint wince. "Not by choice, Captain. We'd thought to lie low in the shallows for another week, but after that unfortunate incident with the earl's wife, we thought it best to sail before the duel. That's why I sent Kevin to the fancy house to inform you of our need for haste."

"Damn his lascivious hide! I ought to call him out myself." Gerard gave his cheek an irate rub, abrading his palm on the fresh stubble of what he hoped would soon be a thriving beard. One of the things he had detested most about Ionia was having to shave twice a day. "He hasn't a repentant bone in his body. I should never have left him in command." He stabbed a menacing finger at Apollo's freshly oiled chest. "If you'd have only agreed to do it . . ."

At six feet, Gerard was nearly a foot shorter than his quartermaster, but that didn't stop Apollo from taking a hasty step backward. "I like being second in command, sir. It spares me the difficult decisions."

Gerard wedged a hand through his hair, his own doubts tempering his frustration. "Such as what I'm going to do with *her*?"

One of the qualities that made Apollo such an invaluable sailor was his instinctive knowledge of when to retreat. "Tell me, Captain," he asked, revealing the blinding white of his teeth, "was your junket worth the trouble?"

"You're the second person to ask me that today." A bitter smile slanted Gerard's lips as he bent to retrieve the Admiral's splintered strongbox from where he had tossed it. "No letter of marque. No mention of the officer who might have acted as Lucien Snow's agent." He held up yellowed sheafs of paper, letting the gusty wind ruffle them. "Just old newspaper articles immortalizing the Admiral's venerable career." He freed the clippings to scatter across the water, then turned up a velvet-bound ledger, mildewed with age. "And a dead woman's diary."

At first Gerard had thought to read Annemarie Snow's diary, but something in her lilting, girlish handwriting, the very antithesis of her daughter's precise script, had stopped him. He had no right to Lucy's past. He'd invaded enough of her life with his presence—her home, her privacy . . . her body. He closed his eyes briefly, battered by the memory of her melting surrender to his questing fingers.

When he opened them, Apollo was regarding him with the same curious mixture of amusement and empathy he'd shown on the night he'd discovered his captain nursing a stab wound only inches from his heart.

Gerard tossed the diary and the box back to the deck, dismissing sentimentality with deliberate callousness. "You needn't gloat. I might not have accomplished what I set out to do, but I can promise you that my next confrontation with Lucien Snow will occur on my terms."

"You're certain of that?"

Gerard narrowed his eyes as he scanned the far horizon. "Dead certain. Because we're playing my game now and I'm the one holding the high trump."

He only prayed he could summon the ruthlessness to use that precious, but fragile, card to his full advantage.

♥   ♥   ♥

Lucy found little solace in solitude. Captivity maddened her. She paced the great cabin like a bird beating helplessly against the bars of its cage, shying away from the towering specter of the bed and all of its dark implications.

She struggled to keep her mind a careful blank, but as the hours wore on, the effort made her head ache with unshed tears. The vengeful demons of her doubts snapped at her heels. She hastened her steps, knowing she should be thankful she wasn't chained to the wall.

Or the bed.

Lucy swung around to glare at the teak and mahogany monstrosity that dominated the cabin. What sort of libertine would flaunt such an excess of luxury in the impractical confines of a ship? Its very presence offended her innate practicality and sense of decency. They'd probably had to knock out the walls to get the bed in, she thought unkindly, or perhaps they'd simply built the ship around it.

Its carved and fluted splendor was as far removed from the humble bedstead in Ionia's gatehouse as the complex masculine creature who had abducted her was from the simple, common man she had believed her bodyguard to be.

A pang of grief seized her heart as she realized that man was lost to her forever. Worse yet, he had never existed at all except in her gullible imagination.

Yet his voice continued to haunt her. *If I had a woman such as you at my mercy, I'd never let her go.*

Lucy hugged back a shiver, forced to acknowledge the more sinister implications of Gerard's vow by the inescapable decadence of that bed.

She turned to the window, preferring to think of anything else, even Gerard's accusations against her father.

She'd been twelve years old when her father had suffered the wound that ended his career. He had allowed only Smythe to attend him, yet she remembered those dark days well—the Admiral's bitter roars for attention; the frightened whispers of the servants; strangers coming to the house at all hours, banging on the front door and demanding entrance. Might some of them have been creditors, preying on her father's weakness to try and collect their debts?

The unbroken vista of sea and sky blurred before her weary eyes as other childhood memories intruded —her father bidding her a stilted farewell on his way to another of his interminable meetings at the Admiralty Court; the long, lonely evenings with nothing but her sketchpad and her gloxinia for company; footsteps shambling past her room in the wee hours of morning.

For the first time, Lucy thought to wonder if her mother's life with the Admiral had been as desolate as her own.

A tightness swelled in her chest, squeezing the breath out of her. She pressed a hand to her throat, fearing she might smother before she could identify the unfamiliar emotion scorching the tears from her eyes.

Don't gobble your food, Lucinda.

Knees together, Lucinda.

Stop slumping, Lucinda.

The barked rebukes taunted her. What if Gerard was right? What if her father's pious reputation was a carefully crafted ruse? What if he had spent a lifetime indulging his various vices, all the while taking poorly concealed delight in chiding her for the moral failings of a dead woman?

Her hand dropped to her heart as if to shield it from an unbearable truth. She realized with no little alarm that her fear and grief were rapidly being displaced by rage. A rage she'd been meekly swallowing for nineteen years. It seemed that every man in her life had betrayed her. Gerard. The Admiral. All but Smythe. And even his innate reserve had stayed his hand from reaching out to her as he might have done.

A shriek of pure fury erupted from between her clenched teeth. Lucy clapped a hand over her mouth, shocked at the primitive sound.

Even more shocking was the slightly hysterical giggle that followed, a giggle elicited by the gleeful surge of independence coursing through her veins.

There was no one left whose approval she cared for. She could slump and gobble her food and sit with her knees apart if she wanted to. She no longer had to live up to anyone's impossible standards. She no longer had to be the Admiral's good little girl.

Stymied by the irony of it all, she sank to her knees on the cabin floor and buried her face in her hands. It seemed she had lost everything she held dear only to gain herself.

CHAPTER TWENTY

GERARD'S FIRST THOUGHT UPON ENTER-
ing his cabin late that afternoon was that he had blundered into a colossal spiderweb. He batted it away
only to have a damp stocking swing back to smack him
in the mouth. He gave the familiar pink toe of the
disembodied garment a curious tug, recognizing it as
Lucy's. Lantern light filtered through the gauzy silk,
displaying its sheerness to its most shocking advantage.

He cocked a speculative eyebrow, overcome briefly
by his more lascivious instincts. If Lucy's undergarments were draped over the ceiling beams to dry, he
wondered, then what was Lucy wearing? If anything.
Gesturing for Apollo to hang behind, he proceeded in
stealth, sweeping the sodden lace of a petticoat out of
his path to reveal the wreckage of his cabin.

His jaw dropped in mute shock. In a matter of
hours, Lucy had reduced his masculine sanctuary to
utter chaos. Every drawer and door of his wardrobe
sagged open with its contents spilling out. Unfurled
maps and nautical charts were scattered across his

desk. An empty cracker tin was overturned on the table, surrounded by crumbs as if besieged by some overgrown rat. Not a rat, Gerard wryly corrected himself. A pink-eared, gray-eyed mouse.

He bit back a growl of dismay as he saw his beloved first edition of Defoe's *Captain Singleton* sprawled on the cabin floor, spine up. Only the bed remained free of Lucy's ravages, its burgundy counterpane a sea of undisturbed tranquility amid a storm of disarray.

He'd found her untidiness charming at Ionia, but having it stamped so possessively over his own well-ordered domain was as disturbing as the tart hint of lemon verbena wending its way to his nostrils through the aged musk of leather and tobacco.

A peevish mutter reached his ears. He discovered Lucy on her knees in the far corner, scavenging through an ancient sea chest. His heart doubled its pace when he saw she had commandeered a pair of his own discarded pantaloons. The faded doeskin cupped her gently rounded backside and clung to the provocative hollow between her thighs. All it took was a brief mental inventory of the garments strung above the iron coal stove for Gerard to realize there was nothing separating the worn fabric from her bare skin. The image both warmed and provoked him.

He beckoned Apollo forward, thankful for the man's stalwart presence.

"Looking for this?" he asked loudly, drawing the Admiral's ivory-handled letter opener from his pocket.

Lucy started, bumping her head on the chest's lid. She swung around to glare at him, rubbing her brow, then offered him an acidly sweet smile. "I shouldn't be needing it. I didn't have time to leave a forwarding address."

As Lucy climbed warily to her feet, Gerard's image wavered like a chimera before her eyes. She wished she could reconcile her conflicting perceptions of him. When she had seen that familiar sparkle of mischief in his eyes, her first instinct had been to hurl herself into his arms and burst into tears. She squared her shoulders, bracing herself to resist all such futile urges.

Her newfound poise deserted her as Gerard's towering companion emerged from behind the curtain of her petticoat. Lucy had seen only two dark-skinned men in her lifetime, one a small boy the Duchess of Emmons boasted slept curled like a lapdog on a cushion at the foot of her bed, the other an elderly footman, his dignity oddly unspoiled by the powdered periwig and satin livery his master insisted he wear.

She knew she was being hopelessly rude, but she couldn't stop gaping. The man's skin absorbed the light like the richest of coffees unmarred by even a swirl of cream. His bald scalp glistened with oil. A colorful patchwork vest hung open over his chest to reveal massive slabs of muscle. Scarlet leggings clung to the imposing length of his legs, tapering down to bare ankles banded with thick rings of scar tissue. Those scars, raw and ugly, held Lucy transfixed.

"Put Miss Snow's tray on the table, Apollo," Gerard commanded smoothly.

Lucy's heart plummeted to her stomach. Why should she have expected any more of him? Wasn't he a pirate? A brigand? A notorious scoundrel who would give no more thought to trading in human lives than he would to robbing a Royal Treasury ship? Or abducting the woman he'd been hired to protect? She could hardly expect him to suffer from pangs of conscience when he had none.

All of those rational reminders didn't stop her from wondering miserably if anyone had ever died of disillusionment.

She flung Gerard a look of pure contempt and fixed

her nose at its most sanctimonious angle. "You'd best obey your master, Mr. Apollo. I'd hate for him to stripe your back for some imagined hesitation. After all, we're both little more than his chattel, aren't we?"

Gerard sighed and rolled his eyes.

Apollo set the tray on the table and drew out a chair with a graceful flourish. "No man has been my master for nigh on eleven years, missie. I am a freeman."

"Miss Snow, I'd like you to meet my second-in-command—my quartermaster."

Lucy didn't know which was more mortifying—Apollo's gentle rebuke or Gerard's superior smirk. She rather wished she could crawl *under* the chair.

"I believe we've met," she said softly. "I never forget a voice.

If Apollo felt any chagrin at being recognized as her original abductor, he hid it behind an angelic smile.

Which only made Gerard's lazily folded arms and arched eyebrow appear more devilish. "We *have* made the acquaintance of several white slavers during our voyages, haven't we, Apollo? Do you think the Pasha is still seeking haughty young English misses for his harem?"

Lucy's cheeks ignited as Gerard's gaze roamed her masculine attire with insulting thoroughness, but she refused to drop her defiant glare. "Tell me, Captain, while you were at Ionia, was he the one cavorting about the Channel, stripping naval officers down to their drawers and playing faro with Royal Treasury gold?"

Gerard exchanged a cryptic glance with his quartermaster, but declined to answer.

Apollo cleared his throat with a bass rumble. "I'd best see to the watch, sir."

Sir, Lucy thought. A term of respect, deference even, but not of subservience. Had she not been foolishly blinded by the hue of Apollo's skin, she would have realized immediately that these men shared equal footing.

"Stay." Gerard's barked command surprised her. If it surprised Apollo, he didn't show it, but simply stepped back to linger on the fringes of the lantern light.

Lucy blinked innocently and spread her arms as if inviting Gerard to search her. "I'm unarmed, Captain. You've no need of a bodyguard."

But *you* might, Gerard thought, surveying Lucy through narrowed eyes. There was something different about her. Something that ran deeper than the linen shirt knotted carelessly at her waist or the insolent fall of her hair, unfettered by ribbons or combs. Something indefinable, yet undeniably appealing. He made a mental note to obtain some proper clothes for her. She was too damned alluring in his.

He gestured tersely to the table. "Eat. And if you've any childish ideas of starving yourself to gain my sympathy . . ."

He was forced to swallow the rest of his threat as Lucy straddled the chair and began shoveling food into her mouth. Her unabashed enjoyment of the simple fare was jarring. Gerard was thankful Tam had purchased fresh stores in London. He doubted she would have shown such enthusiasm over the wormy oatmeal and weevil-infested biscuits they were frequently reduced to eating after long weeks at sea.

She polished off a plateful of beans and half a loaf of brown bread, then washed it all down with a healthy swallow of milk. Gerard was gratified. He had confiscated the precious beverage from Pudge's private stores. It was almost worth enduring Pudge's whining to see Lucy's aristocratic upper lip painted with a milk mustache. He had the absurd desire to bend down and lap it away.

She rescued him from that temptation only to present an even more beguiling one as her pink tongue swept away the creamy froth with the sensual languor of a cat preening its whiskers.

Biting back a groan, he sank heavily into the chair opposite her and indicated the chaos surrounding them. "I'm glad to see you kept yourself amused while I was away."

Lucy shrugged, unwilling to admit she'd been searching for some clue to his capricious character. She refused to give him the satisfaction of knowing she was still that intrigued by him. And not even under threat of torture would she reveal that she was coming to believe his accusations against her father.

"I'm easily bored," she said airily.

"Ah, yes, and a productive life is a happy life, isn't it, Miss Snow?"

His mockery goaded her. "Pirates must have their own schedule of wicked deeds to complete in the course of an average day. Plundering ships. Terrorizing innocent people."

Gerard's capable hands toyed with the Admiral's letter opener, almost as if he'd forgotten he still held it. "Don't forget drinking the blood of newborns and weaving necklaces of human ears." He shot her a look from beneath his luxuriant lashes, testing the blade against the pad of his thumb. "Have I ever told you what pretty little ears you have?"

Fresh humiliation stung her as she recalled reciting those ludicrous Captain Doom myths. How he must have laughed at her! Her embarrassment coalesced into surging anger.

She tipped her head back, boldly exposing the delicate appendages in question. "Don't cheat your reputation, Captain. You've left off turning your victims to stone with a glance and ravishing ten virgins in a single night."

"Before midnight," he shot back. "Although I suppose ravishing one virgin ten times would suffice. What time is it, Apollo?"

Lucy shrank back in her chair, conceding the effectiveness of his parry. She had foolishly forgotten the risk in baiting him.

"Time for me to see to the watch, sir," Apollo replied smoothly.

"Very well, then. Go," Gerard snapped.

As Apollo took his leave, casting his captain an unreadable look, Lucy shifted her weight, trying not to squirm. She might not have been so hasty to taunt Gerard had she realized she was to be abandoned so soon to the whims of his temper.

She was not comforted when he pocketed the letter opener. She knew better than anyone that he had other, more subtle, weapons at his disposal. The silent specter of the untouched bed loomed behind him.

He eyed her, massaging the hint of golden stubble along his jaw. Lucy wished he was still wearing the spectacles, if only to protect her from his inscrutable eyes. Not even her father's bullying had so tempted her to blather all of her secrets. Secrets that could only disgrace and humiliate her further.

When he finally spoke, his voice was as brisk and formal as the Admiral's. "I didn't come here to spar with you. I came to lay down the law. I thought a civilized discussion would be simpler and far less time-consuming than carving the pirate articles on your"— he fought a brief battle with himself and lost; his gaze flicked down to the faded linen cupping her breasts— "chest."

"Whose law are you laying down? Not the Crown's certainly."

He rose to circle the table and Lucy was reminded of their first meeting. Not being blindfolded gave her no advantage. Now she *knew* how dangerous he was. She wondered how he had managed to suppress his natural arrogance for all those weeks. The air of command was stamped on him as bluntly as his features.

He clasped his hands at the small of his back. "The only law that matters as long as you're aboard this vessel. Mine." She started as he leaned over her shoulder in that disconcerting manner of his. The smoky cadence of his voice caressed her ear. "I strongly suggest obedience. As captain of this ship, I'm afraid the task of"—he savored the word with alarming relish—"*discipline* naturally falls to me."

"Naturally." She swallowed audibly.

He straightened. "Laws are made to protect those who obey them. I ask only one thing of you. You're not to leave this cabin for any reason. Due to its very nature, the *Retribution* is crewed by some of the most vicious cutthroats in all of England. I've managed to keep your presence on board a secret thus far from all but Apollo, but should you escape this cabin and fall into the hands of my crew . . ." His pause was fraught with both warning and regret. "I won't be responsible for what happens."

"Of course not," Lucy whispered, fighting back a shiver of pure misery.

He'd abdicated all responsibility for her the moment he'd nabbed her in the library. She could only guess what was coming next—a generous offer of his *protection* coupled with a thinly veiled threat of tossing her to his crew if she refused.

The last tiny ray of faith in her heart flickered in anticipation of dying. Her brief surge of bravado melted away, leaving her defenseless and dangerously near to tears.

She would not beg him, she vowed. No matter what he did to her. No matter what he forced her to do. He was nothing more than a ruthless stranger who had masqueraded as a man she could love.

"Lucy?"

The gentle query startled her. It was like hearing the ghost of a dead loved one speak. It was even more startling to have the fog clear from her eyes to discover Gerard kneeling in front of her, his expression softened with concern.

"Are you feeling ill again? You may still be suffering from the effects of the *somnorifera*."

He reached to touch her brow, but she shied away. "I'm fine, thank you. Unlike you, I suffer from neither perplexing bouts of blindness nor seasickness."

He straightened, accepting her rebuff with an ounce less grace than before. How could she tell him she was suffering from an affliction far more devastating—a broken heart?

"What do you intend to do with me, Captain? Sell me to white slavers or hold me for ransom? Are you prepared to barter me to the highest bidder?"

"The Admiral can choke on his ill-gotten wealth for all I care. All I want is that letter of marque and a full confession of his complicity in the scheme to defraud me."

The cynicism in Lucy's laugh failed to smooth its edge of despair. "You'll get neither. His reputation would be destroyed. He'd be utterly ruined."

"Then he has a choice to make, doesn't he?" His unspoken threat chilled her. "Get some rest," he commanded gruffly. "There'll be no need for you to rise at daybreak. You'll find my demands on your time far less stringent than your father's."

Lucy watched, stunned, as he turned to go, shoving her petticoat out of his path. She opened her mouth to blurt out his name, then snapped it shut. What was she going to do? Call him back to impugn her honor?

The door slammed.

The key turned.

The bolt slammed into place.

"Why, that miserable wretch!" She sprang out of the chair, giving the leather-bound book sprawled on the cabin floor a malicious kick.

Lucy knew she was being absurd. She'd been terrified he would ravish her, yet now her pride was wounded because he hadn't even tried.

She paced to the window to watch the shadows of dusk creep across the sky. Was Gerard just biding his time as he'd proven so skilled at doing or was he playing the gentleman with her once again? She had literally thrown herself into his lap at Ionia and he had resisted her.

She closed her eyes, bombarded with unwanted memories: Gerard's fingers gently cupping her breasts, stroking the moist, throbbing heart of her womanhood, capturing her helpless cry of ecstasy. The forbidden visions evoked a poignant mixture of longing and shame.

Did he find her repugnant because she was the daughter of a man he despised, or did he find her personally distasteful? As loath as she was to admit it, she found the latter prospect by far the more dismal one.

Her father had been right about one thing. Emotions played havoc with logic. Weary of battling her conflicting feelings, Lucy slumped against the bulkhead and gazed at the enormous bed. It didn't seem as threatening now as it did desolate. Sighing, she extinguished the lantern. Taking great care not to muss the elegant counterpane, she crawled into the captain's bed and surrendered to exhaustion.

♥   ♥   ♥

A slender spar of moonlight fell across Lucy's face. Gerard stood over her, watching her sleep. It had been enough of a challenge keeping his distance at Ionia, but having her aboard the *Retribution*—beneath his command, in his bed—was more temptation than any man could be expected to resist.

She'd curled herself into a wary ball in the precise center of the bed, somehow managing to leave the satin counterpane unruffled. The cabin was cool, the coal embers in the stove waning, yet she'd spurned both blankets and pillows as if to accept their comfort would expose her to the enemy. To him.

Her defensive posture in slumber and the thin veneer of bravado the masculine garments lent her only made her seem more vulnerable. More defenseless and in need of protection. Gerard reached for a strand of the ashen hair fanned across the counterpane, then drew his hand back, reminding himself harshly that it was no longer his job to protect her.

The moonlight illuminated her pallor and the smudges of exhaustion beneath her eyes. He'd had no choice but to confine her to quarters. His first responsibility was to his crew. And to his family. But he dreaded the thought of her languishing belowdeck, fading like one of her fragile gloxinia blooms deprived of sunlight and fresh air. He knew better than anyone how damning to the soul it was to be robbed of freedom. It made him pause to count the steep cost of his vendetta.

With a will of its own, his hand once again sought her hair. He sifted the moon-gilded silk through his fingers, luxuriating in its texture. She had recoiled from his every attempt to touch her, loathing plain in her eyes. What had he expected? That upon learning the truth, she would denounce her father and throw herself into his arms, vowing her undying loyalty? He certainly hadn't earned it. He had betrayed her no less than the Admiral had.

His hand fisted in her hair. She already believed the worst of him. What was to stop him from proving her right? From leaning forward to nibble her slightly parted lips into unwitting surrender. From capturing her wrists and imprisoning her slight body beneath the weight of his own. But he doubted even his powers of seduction, once honed to perfection on some of the most beautiful women in London, were enough to overwhelm her fierce sense of betrayal. As soon as she shook off the fog of sleep and realized what was happening to her, she would fight him.

Then they would both learn just how much of the dark still lingered in his soul.

He let her hair slip through his fingers, some savage, selfish part of him despising his own damnable reluctance to hurt her any more than he already had. What was it about this slight girl that never failed to stir his dormant conscience?

"You're a bloody disgrace to the pirate profession, Doom," he muttered, drawing a corner of the counterpane over her.

She snuggled into it, burrowing deep. As he leaned over her, Gerard ruefully reminded himself to give the cabin's key to Apollo with strict instructions *not* to give it back.

CHAPTER TWENTY-ONE

LUCY AWOKE THE NEXT MORNING TO THE unlikely sound of singing—a charming French *chanson* set to a sprightly island tempo.

She opened her eyes to discover the *Retribution*'s behemoth of a quartermaster depositing a steaming tray on the table. "Breakfast?" she muttered, knuckling her eyes.

"Lunch, missie," he gently corrected. "The bells rang noon over an hour ago."

Noon! Scandalized by her sloth, Lucy sprang out of the bed before remembering she had no schedule to adhere to, no one to displease with her laziness. She fell back on the feather mattress, indulging herself with a languorous stretch and a feline yawn. Apollo disappeared out the door, whistling now instead of singing.

Lucy paused, mid-yawn, shaken by a half-remembered dream. A dream where Gerard, *her* Gerard, had tenderly tucked a blanket around her and brushed her lips with the beguiling warmth of his own. She glanced

down, realizing she *had* been wrapped in the counterpane when she awoke.

Derided by her logical mind, she shook off the fanciful notion. She had simply drawn the counterpane
over her when she became chilled and concocted the
dream from hopeless wishes. But all the logic in the
world couldn't banish the wistful ache in her heart.

Apollo reappeared, lugging a brass-banded trunk
with negligible effort. "The Captain sent these for
you."

Lucy sat up, her heart beating faster. Not Gerard,
but "the Captain." The omnipotent creature of command who wielded ultimate power over her future and
her fate.

She crept out of the bed and sidled toward the
trunk, trying to feign indifference, but failing miserably. "What is it? The severed heads of his former
captives?"

She'd already determined that Apollo was a man of
few words, but he shot her a chiding look before
reaching into the trunk for a bundle of cloth. He unfurled it over his chest, shaking out the most stunning
gown Lucy had ever seen.

She gasped with pleasure. She would have sworn
herself devoid of feminine vanity, but in that instant
she was beset by a primitive covetousness, a yearning
to feel that exquisite mesh of turquoise satin and
cream lace against her skin. Its richly jeweled hues
spoke of another, more passionate era, and bleached
the chaste white of all her Grecian-styled gowns to
insignificance.

"Oh, my," she breathed in awe. "It's certainly fine,
isn't it?"

Apollo smiled, encouraging her to run a reverent
hand over the miniature pearl buttons studding the
puffed sleeves.

"May I?" she shyly asked.

He relinquished the gown to her loving hands. Giving in to her instinctive urge, she held it up to see how it would fit.

Her delight faded as rapidly as it had come. Her feet and another six inches of cabin floor were swallowed by the voluminous hem. The gown had obviously been tailored for a woman much taller than she. And given the yawning cavity of the bodice, much more shapely.

I've heard Doom's tastes run to women with a little more meat on their bones.

Gerard's own scathing denouncement mocked her. What had she been thinking? That prior to her abduction, he had gone to the effort and expense of having a wardrobe tailored for her? She cast the overflowing trunk a disparaging glance. These were obviously the castoffs of other women he'd *entertained* aboard ship. If they were any indication of the voluptuous creatures ordinarily at his beck and call, he must find her unappealing indeed.

She gazed down at herself, feeling particularly gawkish and angular in the masculine attire.

Lifting her chin, she let the glorious gown fall into a heap at her feet. "You may tell your captain that my own gown will suffice. I've no interest in the attire of his former whores."

Apollo looked so crestfallen that Lucy felt a twinge of guilt. He opened his mouth, then snapped it shut as if dire consequences might result if he spoke.

Injured pride fueled her disdain. "You may also tell him that if he thinks to buy my cooperation with a trunkful of pretty baubles, he'd best think again. Contrary to what he may believe, I'm not some timid mouse to be bribed with a hunk of cheese."

As if suddenly remembering he'd forgotten to set

the sails or some other such essential task, Apollo wadded up the gown he'd previously handled with such care and tossed it in the trunk.

He slammed the lid and hefted it to his shoulder. "Very well, missie. I shall deliver your message to the Captain."

"Thank you, sir," Lucy replied. She felt a little ridiculous curtsying in a pair of breeches, but believed she'd retained enough of her dignity to afford to be gracious.

Apollo fled the cabin at a dead lope. Lucy knew a brief moment of hope that he might forget to secure the door, but the twist of the key and the thud of the bolt sliding into place was unmistakable.

Abandoning one's self to one's emotions certainly made one hungry, she thought, going to the table. Besides, she was going to need all of her strength and cunning to cross wits with *Captain* Claremont.

She drew the napkin from the tray. A squeak of impotent rage escaped her, for sitting on the earthenware tray was a tall, foamy mug of milk and a beautifully sliced chunk of cheese.

♥   ♥   ♥

Gerard's demands on her time did indeed prove to be less stringent than the Admiral's. If not for the terse inquiries into her well-being delivered by Apollo each morning, she might have suspected he'd forgotten her existence altogether.

She found herself wildly bored with her own company, forced to endure the monotony of days at sea trapped in a cabin that seemed to shrink with each passing hour. She continued to sleep curled all alone in the middle of the immense bed.

Her restless study of the horizon revealed no landmarks and no hint of pursuit. Or rescue. No opportunities for escape presented themselves, each of

Apollo's departures underscored by that same damning slam, click, and thud. Her temper grew shorter, but she quickly found that being rude to Apollo had no effect. Her cross words simply rolled off his well-oiled hide like water. She thought in a fit of pique that he and Smythe ought to have been brothers.

On the third day, she was reduced by tedium to correcting the havoc she'd made of the cabin. She scooped a book off the floor only to hesitate, beset by curiosity as to what sort of book might hold the interest of a man like Gerard Claremont.

She ran her fingertips over the title tooled in the morocco-bound cover, beguiled by its rich texture— *Captain Singleton* by Daniel Defoe. It took only the briefest perusal to determine the book was a novel thinly disguised as the autobiography of an infamous pirate.

Her lip curled in a delicate sneer. The Admiral had taken singular delight in deriding novels, insisting that something that had never really happened couldn't possibly be of any import. Her scorn faded at the memory. The Admiral had taken delight in deriding a great many things—including his daughter. Pricked by a spirit of defiance, she plopped down cross-legged on the floor and began to read.

She was still in the same position four hours later when Apollo brought her lunch. She ate absently, nibbling on dry biscuits and salted beef while turning pages with her other hand. She had unwittingly found what she'd been seeking between the unlikely pages of a book—escape. The hours melted away as she was transported to exotic climes by the thrilling adventures of the rogue captain.

She finished the novel the following morning, turning the last page with a wistful, but satisfied, sigh. She gently returned it to its rightful place on the bookshelf, then pawed through Gerard's bound atlases and charts until she discovered two more Defoe novels.

She devoured the first and was lying on her stomach on the bed halfway through the second when Apollo entered with supper. She laid the book aside, careful not to ruffle its fragile pages. She'd already noticed the disturbing tendency of Defoe's tarnished heroes to take on Gerard's likeness in her imagination, but the most recent incarnation of Gerard as the noble cast-away Robinson Crusoe and Apollo as his loyal Friday was too much for her to digest on an empty stomach.

She watched Apollo arrange her supper tray with sharpened curiosity. The rich histories of Defoe's characters had given her pause, made her wonder what drove men to the paths they took. As always, Apollo's big-boned feet were bare and her gaze was drawn to the ugly scars ringing his ankles.

He turned to go. She bounced to her feet. "Stay!" Realizing how peremptory the command must have sounded, she twined her hands together and offered him a tremulous smile. "Stay, please? Share supper with me. I'm . . . lonely." Until she said the words aloud, Lucy didn't realize how true they were. Gerard's defection had left her with no one.

Apollo hesitated, then surprised her with a graceful bow. "I am honored to accept the missie's gracious invitation."

As he folded his large frame into a chair, she took meticulous care dividing her supper in half. She could imagine how shocked her father would be to see her breaking bread with a man he would consider little more than a savage. She smiled, inordinately pleased by the thought.

Apollo was dazzled by his hostess's impish grin, the first he'd seen from the girl since her rejection of the captain's trunk. He had delivered her scathing message as instructed that day. Gerard had laughed until he'd been forced to swipe tears of mirth from his eyes.

"Where are you from, Apollo?"

Lucy's innocuous question caught him off guard. Thus far, she had shown no interest in anything but her own churlish complaints. Perhaps she only longed for the comfort of a human voice. Apollo knew how damning protracted silence could be.

"I come from the Zulu clan," he replied, breaking off a dry chunk of biscuit and dipping it in the thin paste of water and flour that passed for gravy. "I was taken from my home in my nineteenth summer and carried to Santo Domingo where a French plantation owner purchased me."

Apollo's voice was melodic, eloquent, the voice of a natural-born storyteller. His precise diction proved him to be a man who loved the English language more for having come to it late. Food forgotten, Lucy propped her chin on her hands to listen.

"My master was a good man, an enlightened man. Instead of sending me to the fields, he educated me— taught me to read and write in French, Latin, and English, taught me the manners of a gentleman's gentleman, spent hours discussing the arts and philosophy with me." Apollo chuckled. "Rousseau and Christ were his undoing. 'Man is born free; and everywhere he is in chains.'"

Apollo's rendering of the noble words that had unwittingly sown the seeds of the French Revolution sent a shiver down Lucy's spine.

"If this Christ, whom he was so eager for me to embrace, had died to set men free, then why was I not free? I finally forced him to concede my point." Apollo's face clouded. "His resolve came too late. Before he could petition the governor for my freedom, the slaves revolted. He was murdered by a neighbor's field hands. He died in my arms."

Lucy found herself perched on the edge of her chair. "What was left for you to do? Join the rebellion?"

Apollo shook his head. "If I learned only one lesson at my master's feet, it was that violence can only beget violence."

An odd philosophy for a pirate, Lucy thought, but chose to keep her own counsel.

"The rebellion was squelched. I was arrested and imprisoned. The authorities were afraid of me—some of my size, others of my education. The slaves revered me for the same reasons. The governor would have had me hanged along with the other captured slaves, but he feared making a martyr of me would only incite another rebellion, bloodier than the first. So they locked me away and waited for the outside world to forget about me."

"Did it?" Lucy asked softly.

He nodded, his dark eyes devoid of self-pity. "Until he came."

Lucy did not have to ask who *he* was. Her leaping heart told her. She didn't want to hear any more. Didn't want to risk any blows to her contempt for her captor. But it was too late.

A bittersweet smile played around Apollo's lips. "His was the first laughter I'd heard in over five years. It was like music—a balm to the soul."

Lucy pushed her plate away, remembering the first time she'd heard that same irresistible laughter. The echo of it still haunted her dreams. "So you liked him right off, did you?" she asked glumly.

Apollo rumbled with laughter. "I hated the son of a bitch!"

She leaned forward, shocked. "You did?"

"My bitterness had been festering for five years. He was a white man just like the men who had locked me away. Not only a white man, but a white man who chattered with every breath. I told him to shut up and leave me the hell alone or I'd strangle him with my chains while he slept."

Lucy shook her head, recalling all the times she'd been tempted to do the same. She was in complete commiseration with Apollo's dilemma. "It didn't work, did it?"

"No. He just kept on, prodding and teasing and poking until I finally started talking just to drown out the sound of his infernal voice. His hunger to learn was even greater than my own. He'd had no formal education. Oh, he could read atlases and cargo lists, and could scribble well enough to keep a decent log, but beyond that, nothing. He had such a gift for languages that within months, he was prattling away both in French and in the dialect of my tribe."

A ponderous sadness claimed Apollo's eyes. "He tried so hard to keep talking. To keep laughing. It was a long time before they took his voice away from him."

Lucy despised her empathy. "I suppose he planned a miraculous escape. Something daring and resourceful. An earthquake, the trumpets of angels blaring from the clouds, or some other such nonsense."

Apollo shook his head. "Our rescue was an act of less than divine intervention." His enigmatic smile warned her that pressing for details would be to no avail.

Lucy studied him curiously. She could understand why two men of such diverse backgrounds might have bonded when forced into captivity together, but that still didn't explain why this imposing giant with his pacific leanings and his fondness for French *philosophes* was serving aboard a pirate ship.

"There must be few places in the world for a man of your"—she faltered, embarrassed by her own tactlessness—"education. I suppose you had no choice but to take up with Mr. Claremont."

Apollo's brow furrowed as if her statement puzzled him. "He is my captain. I would follow him anywhere."

Lucy lowered her gaze, shamed by his eloquent simplicity and troubled by the irrefutable evidence of such loyalty. She longed to explore what had inspired it, but found to her chagrin that her throat was too tight to ask.

♥   ♥   ♥

Lucy keenly regretted sharing Apollo's confidences in the unbearably long hours of the days to come.

Mr. Defoe's novels no longer engaged her. Her mind wandered, haunted by images of Gerard chained like an animal to a stone wall, his sunny smile fading to bitter resignation, his bright eyes dimmed by hopelessness and despair. His pointed physical absence from her life only intensified his constant presence. In her thoughts. In her heart. In her sleep.

He came to her one night in a dream, his face shadowed and elusive, one minute dark and scowling, the next alight with that heartbreaking grin of his. She awakened to find her cheeks damp with tears, her arms wrapped around herself in a travesty of an embrace that offered no relief from her yearning desolation.

She spent the remainder of the night tossing and turning in the tangled counterpane, her desperation growing. She had to escape before she could no longer smother her lingering feelings beneath layers of anger and wounded pride.

She awoke from fitful sleep the next morning to find milky sunlight spilling into the cabin and a narrow finger of land visible on the far horizon.

When Apollo entered with her breakfast, she was standing by the wardrobe, smiling innocently, her hands clasped demurely behind her. "Good morning, Apollo."

"Good morning, missie."

Turning his glistening back to her, he pushed aside a weighty atlas and arranged the tray on the table. Lucy tiptoed toward him, slowly lifting the neck of the bottle clenched in her shaking hands. Her heart thudded with nervous terror and premature remorse.

Without turning around, Apollo said gently, "I'd rather you didn't do that, missie. It's the captain's favorite brandy."

Lucy sheepishly lowered the makeshift weapon, oddly relieved at being spared the unpleasant task of bashing it over the quartermaster's head.

Lucy's second escape attempt was even more inauspicious. Devoid of inspiration, she simply waited until Apollo opened the door and made a mad dash for the hold. She made it as far as the threshold before he caught the hem of her gown and reeled her back in. She brooded the rest of the day, but he remained unaffected.

She allowed Apollo a respite the following morning, hoping he'd lower his formidable guard. Nightfall found her perched on a chair behind the door. When it swung open, she dropped her petticoat over Apollo's unsuspecting head. As he clawed at the clinging material, she scampered between his legs and fled silently out the door.

Resigned to knowing it would only be a matter of minutes before Apollo caught up with her, Lucy darted down the nearest passageway, resisting the temptation to check over her shoulder for signs of pursuit. She hadn't thought much past simply escaping the cabin, but she was determined to make the most of her time. Perhaps she could locate the powder magazine, an ideal location for a standoff should such an opportunity arise again.

She'd never seen a ship's hold designed in such a haphazard fashion. It had more peculiar twists and turns than Lord Howell's topiary maze. Too late, she realized she'd chosen a passage that led deep into the belly of the schooner. The low-burning lanterns hanging at each intersection were her only salvation. She shuddered to imagine being trapped in this splintery web of wood, smothered by encroaching darkness and the stench of bilge water.

She paused to catch her breath and press a hand over her pounding heart. There were still no sounds of chase, only the eerie creak of the ship fighting the relentless swell and pitch of the sea.

A solitary iron-banded door lured her to the opposite side of the corridor. She knew escape was unlikely, but perhaps she could barricade herself somewhere until Captain Claremont demonstrated a willingness to bargain. Her fingers tingled as they brushed the chill handle. She jerked them back, remembering against her will Gerard's dire warnings about his crew.

"Don't be ridiculous," she chided herself. "He was just trying to spook you."

She almost hoped the door would be locked, but a halfhearted push eased it open. The cabin within was as dark as sealing pitch, which only made the intrusion of the lantern light from the hold more startling.

An involuntary shriek caught in Lucy's throat. The shadowy chamber was an Inquisitor's dream, appointed with a handsome torture rack, a barbed cat-o'-nine-tails, three pairs of rusty manacles bolted to the wall, and several other ominous meldings of metal and wood. Lucy's imagination, freshly fertilized by Mr. Defoe, had little difficulty assigning them sinister purposes. An iron maiden reigned over the grim tableau, her features frozen in a sneer of malevolent grace.

As Lucy watched, she would have almost sworn its hinged door began to creak open, inch by inch.

"Missie!" Apollo's voice cracked like thunder.

Lucy slammed the door shut and spun around, throwing herself across it. Apollo towered over her, looking worse than forbidding in the scant light.

She injected a note of false gaiety into her voice. "What's wrong, Apollo? Has the Captain some skeletons in his cupboard?"

"You might say that."

Without preamble, he heaved a weary sigh, bent at the knees, and matter-of-factly tossed her over his shoulder. Her unbound hair blinded her, but as Apollo turned to carry her back to the cabin, a bolt of tension arced through his muscles.

The greeting was deceptively gentle. "Good evening, Apollo."

"Good evening . . . Captain."

CHAPTER TWENTY-TWO

LUCY SQUEEZED HER EYES SHUT IN MUTE misery. She had entertained visions of confronting Gerard with her dignity intact, not draped over Apollo's shoulder in limp defeat.

"Going somewhere, Miss Snow?" The edge had returned to his voice.

She tried not to squirm, only too aware that he was addressing her rump. "It appears not, Captain."

Pleasantries completed, the awkward silence stretched until Gerard's clipped words ended it. "How many times has our guest sought to leave us?"

It was Apollo's turn to squirm. Lucy could almost feel the chagrin seeping from his oversized pores.

"Put me down," she demanded, refusing to let him bear the brunt of the blame. After all, what did she have to lose by brazening it out?

Apollo dutifully obeyed. Lucy swept her hair out of her eyes, then half wished she hadn't. The unreliable lantern light cut swaths of darkness across Gerard's face, reminding her of her disturbing dreams. For the first time, she allowed herself to wonder what manner of man would equip a chamber of horrors like the one she'd just discovered.

Her fear of him infuriated her. She tossed her head with deliberate insolence. "I believe this is my third unsuccessful bid for freedom. What do you intend to do about it?" She offered him her upturned wrists. "Clap me in irons?"

He tilted his head as if to consider the merits of the offer. "A tempting proposition."

Lucy withdrew her hands, not sure how far she could afford to push him.

"Bring her," he commanded Apollo, pivoting on his heel with humiliating disregard.

Lucy marched between the two men like a condemned felon sentenced to the gallows. She might go meekly to her fate, but she refused to go quietly.

"Do forgive my impudence, Captain, but I thought it best to maintain our professional relationship. You, sir, are the pirate. I am the captive. Therefore, as the captive, I feel it my sacred obligation to routinely attempt escape if only to discharge my duty as the previously aforementioned—"

Lucy flinched as a door slammed directly behind her. It seemed that Apollo had abandoned her, leaving her alone in the great cabin with a powerful man she'd just taken great pains to enrage.

Lucy braced herself as he faced her, but nothing could have prepared her for the changes a week had wrought in his appearance. His skin was darker, intensifying the brilliant hazel of his eyes. His hair was lighter and already curling in unruly tendrils at his nape. She squelched a treacherous desire to curl her fingers through them. A beard darkened his jaw, shading its boyish angles with devastating maturity.

A raw edge clung to him, as if he'd spent one too

many sleepless nights. For the first time, Lucy thought to wonder where he'd been sleeping while she slept in his bed, dreaming of him. Oddly enough, the faint air of dissipation only enhanced his rugged charm.

Her bodyguard had been a handsome man. This man was irresistible.

If she'd been unprepared for his altered appearance, she was doubly unprepared for the melting sensation in her midsection, the hazardous yearning in her heart.

"Take off your gown."

His words struck Lucy like a dash of cold salt water. Her bravado withered beneath his resolute stare. "I'm sorry," she blurted out. "I won't try to escape again."

"Damn right you won't. Give me the gown."

He stood before her, six feet of pure male determination. Lucy took a step backward without realizing it. Her misconceptions about her father had proved her a poor judge of character, but was it possible she had misjudged this man so badly as well?

"You can't blame me for trying to escape. You'd do the same if you were in my position." Lucy wished she could have bitten back the words. He'd been in a position far more intolerable than hers. For five long years. "If this is your twisted idea of discipline . . ."

He took a menacing step toward her. "Don't make me strip you, Lucy. I'm well aware that's your only gown."

"Oh, please, I—" Remembering her earlier vow not to beg, Lucy clenched her chattering teeth over her pleas. Gerard's image wavered through a sheen of unspilled tears as she fought to salvage her dignity. "I don't deserve this."

Her softly spoken rebuke had no discernible effect on him. She gathered her skirt, then hesitated, remembering that she wasn't even wearing a petticoat to shield her from his probing eyes. Perhaps that was to be her punishment for dropping it on his quartermaster's head.

She dragged the gown off and stood stiffly before him, trying not to shiver in nothing but her thin chemise, silk drawers and tattered pride. Her fingers bit into the balled-up gown, but she refused to do herself the indignity of covering herself with her hands.

His eyes raked her once, twice, before he came striding toward her. Lucy closed her eyes, dreading the moment when he would lay his hands on her. When he would rob her of her innocence with nothing more than his unrelenting grip as he steered her toward the bed.

He stopped so near to her that she could feel his breath stir the hair at her temple, feel the inescapable heat of his body scorching the vulnerable skin bared by her scant attire. She drew in a shaky breath, then wished she hadn't. He smelled of wind and sea and salt—the aroma of freedom. After days spent locked in the stuffy cabin, the seductive fragrance intoxicated her. Currents swirled between them, more violent than anything the sea had to offer.

Sensing that she was the one in danger of being sucked into their depths, Lucy no longer dared even to breathe.

Without warning, the gown was torn from her clenched fist. Her eyes flew open. To her shock, Gerard had left her to stride to the door. He sent it crashing into the opposite wall, then hurled her gown into the passageway.

She watched, dumb with amazement, as he emptied the wardrobe and sea chest of his own clothes with similar savagery, slamming drawers and muttering beneath his breath the entire time. He ruthlessly whisked both blankets and sheets from the bed, leaving the feather tick bare of all but pillows. Within minutes, he'd fed every scrap of cloth in the cabin, except what they were both wearing, to the voracious mouth of the hold.

He slammed the lid of the empty chest with deafening force before wheeling to face her. "Maybe you'll think twice about escaping the trap now, Miss Mouse. One look at you in that—that"—he swallowed hard—"frivolous creation and my men will tear you apart." His voice lowered to a growl. "By the time they're finished, there won't be enough left of you to feed to the sharks."

It was a creditable impersonation of a leering pirate, but Lucy was not quite convinced. Gerard was glaring at a spot just over her right shoulder. His powerful hands were fisted. In threat or to hide their own unsteadiness? she wondered with dizzying insight.

His unexpected vulnerability emboldened her. Gave her the first clue that she might hold her own weapons in this duel of wits he'd forced upon her. Perhaps she could win back her clothes by less than conventional means.

Shaking back her hair, she forced herself to stroll over to the bed as if she were accustomed to parading about in her drawers before fully dressed men. "That wasn't very sporting of you, Captain. As I'm sure you know, the nights are quite chilly at sea."

For a stunned moment, Gerard couldn't have said whether Lucy Snow was trying to shame or seduce him. Her glance was reproving, but her faint pout hinted at sultry promise. He struggled to cling to his anger. Rational anger at her foolish escape attempt. Irrational anger that she believed him capable of committing the most heinous of crimes against her, even though he'd given her no reason to believe otherwise.

The lantern light worked its revealing magic through her sheer undergarments, distracting him.

It would have been wiser to have Apollo remove her clothes, but there were some things a captain could not ask his quartermaster to do, not even when he trusted him implicitly.

"So you think me a poor host, do you?" he asked.

Her lashes, so dark and striking in one so fair, swept down to veil her eyes. "Would you blame me? You've kept me locked away for days."

"For your own protection."

"So you say. But I won't be of much use to you in your dealings with my father if I take an ague and die of exposure."

She sank down on the edge of the bed, the subtle arch of her back accentuating the provocative thrust of her small breasts against the flimsy silk. Gerard's palms tingled at the memory of their flawless weight in his hands, their incredible responsiveness to his touch. His gaze followed the curve of her lazily swinging calf. Had her legs always been so long? So delectable?

He tried to swallow again, but his throat had gone dry. What had prompted this unnerving display of audacity? he wondered. He would have been lying if he said he was entirely displeased with it. Perhaps it was time to call her bluff.

As Gerard approached the bed, his fleet steps unaffected by the rhythmic cant of the planking floor, Lucy fought to hide the unsettling effect of his nearness.

It became impossible when he reached down and slid his hand beneath her hair. His broad palm cupped her throat. His fingertips pressed against her nape with beguiling tenderness. It was the first time she'd allowed him to touch her since coming aboard, but she could hardly scorn his touch when she'd as much as invited it with her reckless posturing. Too late, she realized she'd challenged a master at his own game.

"Why, you're shivering, Miss Snow!" he exclaimed, his brow knit with profound concern. "Might you already be taking a chill?"

As Lucy gazed into the hypnotic hazel of his eyes, she didn't feel chilled. She felt hot, palsied, possessed by a primitive fever spreading outward from his touch to warm every inch of her sun-deprived body. It melted through her veins like hot butter, drenching her in want.

Her intended whisper came out as a croak. "I think not, sir. My health has always been robust."

Sliding to his knees on the bed beside her, he shook his head sadly. "You mustn't delude yourself, dear. Just look at you." He brushed her hair back from her brow. "You're flushed. Hoarse." His mouth descended on hers; his voice lowered to a husky whisper. "Short of breath."

What meager breath she did have was stolen by the alluring pressure of his lips against hers. As he shaped her mouth to fit the heated contours of his own, he gathered her into his arms, sliding one hand beneath her chemise to claim the bare skin of her back. Lucy had braced herself for his brutality, but this gentle assault on her senses undid her completely. His kiss was tender and rife with promises of pleasure only he could fulfill.

Her lips flowered beneath his, coaxing his tongue to flick the sensitive interior of her mouth to melting acquiescence. He delved deeper, testing the honeyed waters with maddening restraint. Lucy clung to him, enchanted by the tickle of the unfamiliar mustache, the prickle of his beard, the taste of salt and sea and male, the provocative rub of his narrow hips against her own.

His hands slid downward, slipping into the waist of her drawers to knead the softness of her bare buttocks. He deftly tilted her until the rigid length straining against the front seam of his breeches was positioned perfectly at the vulnerable cleft between her thighs. Lucy gasped, believing for a breathless moment that he might actually breach the fragile skein of fabric to possess her.

Instead, he kissed her to the brink of surrender, then drew back, leaving her tingling, limp, and panting for fulfillment.

His eyes sparkled with dark mischief, but his unsteady breathing proved he wasn't as unaffected as he pretended to be. " 'Tis worse than I feared. Your eyes are glazed, your muscles have lost all their vigor." He cast a naughty glance over her shoulder. "Why, even your toes are curled! I don't believe you're suffering from an ague at all, but from a classic case of malaise."

Lucy stiffened and withdrew from his arms. She met his eyes with bitter candor and said softly, "A pity there's no cure for it. I fear it will be the death of me."

For the briefest of instants, she thought she saw remorse flicker through his eyes, but then it was gone, banished by the predatory scrutiny she'd come to expect from Captain Doom.

He caught her chin between two fingers, his grip more possessive than even his kiss had been. "You needn't fret about catching a chill, dear. Where we're going, the nights are much hotter."

As he rose to go, Lucy was besieged by images of swaying palms, shell-strewn beaches, naked bodies glistening with sweat. Her heart thundered to the rhythm of native drums.

Humbled by her own wretched weakness, she called after him, "If I give you my word I won't try to escape, may I have my gown back?"

He paused at the door. "I fear, Miss Snow, that your word means no more to me than your father's."

He closed the door behind him, twisted the key in the lock, and slid the bolt home with a care bordering on tenderness.

Choking out an impotent cry of frustration, Lucy hurled a pillow at the door, then collapsed on the bed in near despair. One more encounter such as that one and there would be no need to sell her to white slavers. Gerard could just keep her locked in his cabin, half clothed and half out of her wits, until she was begging to do his sensual bidding.

Groaning, she curled up on her side on the bare tick, possessed by a raging fever that had nothing to do with ague.

♥   ♥   ♥

Lucy awakened as she had awakened each morning aboard the *Retribution*—to the sound of Apollo's singing. If his majestic bass held a note of false cheer as he approached the cabin, he disguised it beneath the soaring melody of an island hymn.

Unable to bear his undaunted spirits, Lucy wished for a blanket to pull over her head. It felt muzzy and full, as if she'd once again spent her tears in the privacy of sleep.

She heard the key turn, the bolt slide back, the door swing open. The song swelled. She decided to simply lie with her eyes squinched shut until Apollo and his damnable optimism went away.

She was jarred from her self-pity by a crash that seemed to shake the entire ship. An ominous silence followed.

"Apollo?" she whispered.

When her timid query received no answer, she sat bolt upright in the bed. Apollo was stretched facedown on the floor, a giant felled by nothing more than the delicate brocade pillow she had hurled at the door the night before.

The Admiral's voice boomed through her conscience for the first time since she'd learned of his betrayal. *How many times have I told that stupid girl not to scatter things about on the floor? Won't be satisfied till I break my bloody neck.*

"Good God, I've killed him!" she cried, tumbling from the bed. "Gerard will never forgive me for this."

Too distraught to examine why Gerard's forgiveness should matter to her, she rushed toward Apollo's prostrate form, already dreading what she would find.

Her trembling hand sought his throat. His skin was warm, the pulse beneath pounding with the reassuring cadence of a kettledrum.

A sigh of relief gusted from Lucy's lungs. From where she crouched, she could see the faint smile curving Apollo's lips, almost as if he were dreaming of something agreeable.

"Thank you, Lord," she murmured, rolling her eyes heavenward.

The Lord rewarded her prayer with a startling view of the cabin door, which stood gaping open in invitation.

Lucy looked at Apollo. Lucy looked at the door. After all of her botched escape attempts, surely it couldn't be that easy, could it? she thought. Her heart skittered in her breast. She glanced down at her sleep-rumpled chemise and drawers, dismayed by the overwhelming expanse of pink skin they revealed. Gerard's warnings about his crew echoed in her ears. Did she dare?

She scrambled to her feet, knowing she had to take the chance. Last night had proved one thing to her—there wasn't a man aboard this vessel more dangerous to her than its captain, for despite his treachery, she was powerless to resist him.

"Pleasant dreams, Apollo," she whispered, relishing her turn to close the door, twist the key, and drive the heavy bolt home.

♥ ♥ ♥

Determined not to repeat the mistakes of her earlier debacle, Lucy charged in the opposite direction. She had little chance of escaping undetected in a launch. Her only hope lay in assuming the Royal Navy was in pursuit. If she could somehow disable the ship or reach the lower gundeck and send up a signal to alert them to the *Retribution*'s whereabouts, rescue might be imminent.

If Gerard didn't shoot her first.

She brushed aside that glum thought to continue her maddening trek. Lucy had learned her way around a massive seventy-four-gun ship-of-the-line almost before she'd learned to walk, but the design of this modest schooner confounded her almost as badly as its captain did.

She tripped twice, stumbling over steps painted in contrasting colors, the exact opposite of how steps ought to be painted. An upward-slanting ramp led to nowhere while a promising quirk in the passageway brought her in a complete circle. Her heart nearly burst from her chest when she came face-to-face with her own reflection in a perversely placed mirror.

The precious moments ticked away, each sounding a knell of doom to her freedom. Her resolve weakened, but it was too late to return to the great cabin and nurse the lump on Apollo's brow. She couldn't find her way back if she tried.

She collapsed against the bulkhead, tempted to plop down in the middle of the passageway and wait for Gerard to find her. He'd already betrayed her trust, broken her heart, and stripped her to near nakedness. What more could he do to her?

Plenty.

That unvarnished truth spurred her feet forward. Ghostly shades of the *Retribution*'s crew leered at her out of the shadows, their imagined visages growing more dastardly with each frantic footfall. Her flawless recall provided her with a tidy catalogue of the tortures Mr. Defoe claimed pirates delighted in inflicting on their more rebellious captives: tying them to the windlass and pelting them with glass bottles; forcing rum down their throats until they stumbled overboard and drowned; filling their mouths with flammable oakum and setting it afire.

And those were only the atrocities they committed against their own sex.

A hoarse sob of frustration was wrenched from her as she once again came face-to-face with her fear-bleached countenance in the mirror. She slammed a fist into its mocking surface.

Lucy jumped back in shock as the mirror dropped to reveal a ladder recessed into the bulkhead behind it.

Hardly daring to believe her good fortune, she squinted upward into the forbidding shadows. Surely no one would have gone to such lengths to disguise a ladder that led to nowhere.

With fortified resolve, Lucy scaled the ladder and pressed her hands against the planking above. Her nimble fingers quickly located a narrow seam invisible to the naked eye. She bit back a triumphant crow, finally feeling as if she deserved to wear, if not the mantle, at least the gloves of some bold Gothic heroine.

The moment of truth was at hand. She coiled herself as high as the ladder would allow and braced her sweaty palms against the trapdoor, hoping to maintain an element of surprise should her exit be witnessed by one of Gerard's crew.

With one fluid lunge, she gave the trapdoor a tremendous heave and sprang out of the gloom of the hold like a jack-in-the-box.

Sunlight seared her pupils, blinding her. Even more astounding than the light was the warmth. Moist and cloying, it enveloped her in a smothering blanket, forcing her to gasp for her next breath and wonder where the frigid English winter had gone.

She had reason to be thankful for that hard-won breath, for when her vision finally adjusted to the wealth of light, she found herself standing nose to nose with the leering gargoyle of her darkest fears.

Lucy screamed.

The gargoyle screamed louder. The horror staining his freckled features mirrored her own.

Lucy clapped her hands over her ears, fearful his shrill keening would pierce them. Too late, she realized she'd burst not onto the lower gundeck as she'd hoped, but onto the quarterdeck, the most visible of the upper decks. Through a haze of terror, she was vaguely aware of a pale blur behind the gargoyle and other figures perched on the fo'c'sle and in the rigging, frozen to a state of shock by the unfolding drama. The startling ebony of the sails flapped like a mourning canopy over their heads.

Instead of leaping at her, brandishing a cutlass as she expected him to do, the squealing brigand stumbled backward, landing hard on his rump. The impact mercifully cut off his scream, but restored his voice, an all but unintelligible Irish brogue.

"Saints preserve us, Pudge. 'Tis a banshee for sure." His grimy finger signed a clumsy cross on his breast.

The bespectacled man behind him edged toward the rail, his pasty rolls of flesh quivering like an undercooked crossbun. He gazed at her in awestruck wonder. "Not a banshee, Tam, but a Valkyrie come to escort us to the halls of Valhalla. By George, we're doomed!"

Their nonsensical gibbering preyed on Lucy's nerves, melting her fright to confusion. Noticing the familiar butt of a pistol protruding from the Irishman's breeches, she advanced on him.

He scuttled backward like a threatened crab. "Don't desert me now, Pudge! We've been through too much together."

His snuffling companion inched nearer to the rail.

Heartened by their blatant cowardice, Lucy snatched the pistol from the lad's breeches. His eyes rolled back in a blend of terror and near religious ecstasy. "Sweet heaven, deliver me, she intends to have her way with me!"

Pudge hooked one plump leg over the rail. "A succubus! I knew it!"

"Aye," the Irishman wailed. "Beautiful and terrible she is!"

A cool voice, shaded with amusement, sliced through the escalating hysteria. "An apt description, Tam. A pity I didn't think of it myself."

Startled, Lucy swung the weapon around, pointing it straight at their captain's treacherous heart.

CHAPTER TWENTY-THREE

GERARD LEANED LAZILY AGAINST THE mainmast, an infuriating study in nautical elegance. His black breeches clung to his lean legs, tapering down into a pair of dashing jackboots. His white shirt gaped open at the throat and was covered by a dark blue jacket, probably confiscated at gunpoint from some hapless Royal Navy officer. Its shiny brass buttons reflected the sunlight, dazzling Lucy almost as much as his mocking grin.

"Good morning, Miss Snow," he said, as if she weren't brandishing a weapon that could permanently wipe the smirk off his face. "The air below getting a little stale for your refined tastes?"

Tam's shout nearly startled her into dropping the pistol. "Save yerself, Cap'n! She ain't human. She's a succubus with a taste for male flesh. Don't stray too close! She might try to have her way with you."

Gerard's eyes twinkled with mirth. "I should be so fortunate."

Lucy had almost forgotten the man straddling the

rail. "Perhaps not a s-succubus after all, sir," he offered timidly. "A s-s-siren. If she opens her mouth you'd best cover your ears, for her voice is so beautiful, it will drive you mad with longing."

"Oh, for God's sake, stop it!" Her dubious patience at an end, Lucy gave them all cause to wish they'd covered their ears. "Stop it, I say! I won't tolerate another minute of this rubbish! Do you hear me? *Just stop it!*"

Her tone of command froze them all. If Lucien Snow had taught her one thing, it was how to bellow an order. For a moment there was no sound at all but the eerie whisper of those bizarre black sails.

Lucy Snow had had enough. Enough of shifting loyalties. Enough of being the butt of jokes she didn't even understand. Enough of being bullied by men. Her gaze darted wildly between the three men nearest to her.

She turned the pistol on the Irishman. "Get up! Get up this instant and stop groveling. What's the matter with you? Haven't you any pride?"

As he climbed sheepishly to his feet, a buried memory threatened to surface. A nervous snuffle drew her attention away from it.

She waved the pistol at the man clinging to the starboard rail. "And you! Climb down from there right now. And stop sniveling," she barked, "or I'll give you something to snivel about."

He obeyed, still looking as if he'd like to burst into tears.

She swung the gun back around on Gerard. While she'd been distracted, he'd glided a foot nearer to her without appearing to have moved at all. Just like the phantom he was purported to be.

Her voice dropped to a dead calm. "Don't take another step, Captain, or it may very well be your last."

Gerard nodded toward the pistol. "That thing's a bit more lethal than a letter opener. You won't have quite the margin for error."

It wasn't the gun or even the threat of death that captured Gerard's attention. It was Lucy herself. She was too incensed to be conscious of her scant attire, but the wind was taking great delight in molding the delicate chemise and drawers to her taut curves. Pudge, with his abiding love of mythology, had been closest to the truth. With her bare, shapely legs braced against the swell of the deck and her long, blond hair whipping in the wind, she looked every inch a wronged Norse goddess gunning for vengeance.

Her gray eyes flared with murderous emotion. Her generous mouth had tightened in a sneer. Gerard thought she'd never looked more magnificent. He wished the Admiral could see all the spirit and spunk he'd fought so hard to repress come boiling to the fore. Being held hostage to her whims in front of his men should have infuriated him, but his frustration was tempered with fierce pride.

"Did it ever occur to you that the gun might not be loaded?" he ventured. "Do you really think I'd let a muzzy-headed lad like Tam ram a loaded pistol down his breeches?"

Lucy's confidence wavered, but she remembered only too well how convincing Gerard could be when it suited his selfish purposes. "If it's not loaded, then you won't mind if I pull the trigger, will you?"

Gerard's rueful smile conceded her victory. The wary gazes of his men bored into her.

"If you value your captain's life, gentlemen, then I suggest you shorten the sails and drop anchor. We're going to sit right here and wait for a Royal Navy ship to happen by." When they made no move to obey, Lucy steadied her arm against the dragging weight of the pistol. "Do it or I'll put a ball of lead right through his miserable heart! I admit it's a poor target, but it will have to do."

The men glanced uncertainly between her and Gerard. All it took was the faintest shake of his head. Not one of them so much as twitched another muscle.

"I'm sorry, Lucy. I'm afraid my men obey only my orders." Gerard's kindness was even less tolerable than his mockery.

"Then *you* tell them to do it."

He folded his arms over his chest, his expression almost pitying.

Lucy's trigger finger jerked as Apollo stumbled into sight, holding a dripping rag to his head. "*You* mustn't blame the little missie, sir. It's all due to my own clumsiness. I'd still be out cold on the cabin floor if Kev—"

Gerard's eyes narrowed in warning, giving him time to realize it was not the little missie in jeopardy, but his captain. Apollo's great liquid eyes darkened as if Lucy had somehow disappointed him. He moved to stand behind Gerard, a reproving sentinel.

Their united front intensified Lucy's desperation. Perhaps if she chose one of his weaker men . . .

"You!" she said, cornering the man who'd tried to jump ship. "You're the sailmaster, aren't you?" she asked, recognizing the leather apron stretched over his distended belly. "*You* shorten the sails."

He shuffled his feet and tucked his head like a shy pouter pigeon, declining to answer. There was something familiar about his quaint, steel-framed spectacles, something that made her heart contract with nostalgia.

"All right then, you!" she exclaimed, pointing toward the muzzy-headed young Irishman. "You'll be the one to . . ." Her command faded as she studied the dirt rings around his freckled neck. "You," she echoed softly. "You're the one who applied for the position as my bodyguard. The one Smythe booted down the front stairs." The pistol wavered as she studied the familiar faces of the men around her. She pointed an accusing finger at a lithe Oriental man. "You're the one who broke Captain Cook! And you— you're the fellow who pilfered the silver." A hysterical laugh escaped her. "Where were you that day, Apollo? I'm sure I would have remembered you."

"My penmanship is legendary," he admitted modestly. "I forged the Captain's references. Oh," he added, flexing his mighty hands. "And I *detained* the genuine applicants until he was hired."

The legends were true, Lucy thought. The *Retribution* was crewed by ghosts. Resurrected ghosts their captain had used to worm his way into her life. How could the Admiral have resisted the self-assured Mr. Claremont after being besieged by such bumbling applicants?

Tam appeared nearly as shocked as she to recognize her. "Why, miss, I never would have known you. The last time I saw you, you was—"

"Dressed?" Lucy provided.

His freckles melted into a flush. "Aye, that too. Of course, I was a bit flustered, what with you beatin' me brains out with that wee umbreller of yers."

"Tam!" Gerard barked an instant too late.

Lucy took a long, hard look at the lad, realizing that he was indeed the masked assailant who had tried to nab her reticule outside the mercer's shop. Her discovery led her to another, far more chilling, conclusion.

Time tumbled backward to the fireless room of an inn, the tapping of frozen rain on the windows, the beguiling warmth of Gerard's arms around her as he pressed his lips to her bruised throat in a kiss that might very well have been his most bitter betrayal of all.

Blinking through a scalding veil of tears, she lifted her gaze to Gerard's face, utterly helpless to disguise the pain flaying her heart. He took a reckless step toward her, already shaking his head in denial.

She dragged back the hammer of the pistol.

"Captain . . . ?" Apollo whispered on a bass note of warning.

Tears spilled from Lucy's eyes and streamed down her cheeks. These men weren't going to do her bidding. They were nothing but a heartless bunch of bullies. Just like her father. Just like the three men who had thought to rob and rape her in that dank, cold London alleyway. Just like the man who had hired them.

All the pain Gerard had caused her welled up from her aching heart in the nearest thing to hatred she'd ever felt toward him.

He took another careless step. "I know what you're thinking, Lucy, but those men weren't mine. I swear it."

"Why should I believe you? You'd already proved you'd do anything to protect your position." *Even feign an affection he did not feel.*

He spread his upturned palms in a gesture of appeal, offering her an unguarded target. "I've no proof to offer you beyond my word. You'll just have to trust me."

His request was so ludicrous that Lucy started to laugh, the gulping exhalations tearing at her like sobs. She brought the muzzle of the pistol to bear on his heart only to discover that she was even less capable of doing him harm than when she'd stood on this very deck one windy, moonlit night that had changed her life forever.

She swung the pistol straight up and fired into the air. Gerard didn't even flinch.

Her arm fell limp at her side. The pistol clunked to the deck, leaving as the only mementos of her pathetic rebellion the echo of the report, the stench of gunpowder, and a slice of azure sky visible through the grim elegance of the fore topsail.

Lucy sank to a sitting position on a coil of rope, her tear-streaked face a study in defeat. Gerard found he could take little pleasure in his victory. He dropped his jacket over her shoulders, shielding her from his crew's curious stares and glances of grudging respect. A mutiny such as the one she had dared to stage would have earned them a flogging or an even more dreaded abandonment on the nearest deserted island with nothing but a pistol to shoot themselves with before they perished of thirst.

He snapped off a volley of orders that had them wisely scurrying in all directions. Not all of his men were as superstitious about women aboard ship as Tam and Pudge. Tam slunk away with the rest, sheepishly retrieving his fallen pistol, but with uncharacteristic boldness, Pudge hesitated.

He sponged the sweat from his palm with a scarlet kerchief before shyly offering his hand to Lucy. "I—I —I'm sorry, miss. I shouldn't have c-c-called you those names. 'Tweren't very gentlemanly of me."

Shaking off her daze, Lucy found herself looking up into a familiar pair of temple spectacles. A fresh pain lanced her heart, but the brown eyes behind the lenses blinked with such sincerity that she couldn't help giving his hand a comforting squeeze. "All is forgiven, sir. I shouldn't have startled you."

"See to the sail, Pudge." Gerard gave him a gentle nudge toward the block and tackle.

"Aye, sir." He gave his captain a doting salute and limped off to do his bidding.

"Pudge is more skittish than most when it comes to

women," Gerard said quietly. "His wife used to beat him. After she smashed his knee with a poker while he slept, he ran away to sea."

Not wanting to hear these things, not wanting to care, Lucy escaped to the rail, hugging Gerard's jacket tight around her. Sunlight rippled across the scattered whitecaps. A balmy breeze stirred her hair, disconcerting when she'd expected nothing but bitter winter winds. It was her first taste of freedom in days, yet her heart felt as if it were bound in iron chains.

Gerard moved to stand beside her. She childishly edged her elbow away to keep it from touching his. "They were his spectacles, weren't they?" she asked, already knowing the answer.

He nodded. "Damn things gave me the very devil of a headache."

"And Tam?"

"When the *Retribution* sailed, he stayed behind in London, knowing I might have need of him. When you threatened to have me dismissed . . ." Gerard trailed off, before offering matter-of-factly, "Tam's life-long ambition was to be a priest. Only he could never quite master his vow of celibacy. When they caught him in bed with two of the blushing young novices—"

" 'Some of the most vicious cutthroats in all of England.' " Lucy tossed his own words back at him with dull accuracy. " 'A dangerous lot . . . utterly ruthless.' An excommunicated priest? An amateur philosopher who doesn't believe in violence? A sailmaster terrified of his own shadow? These are your devil's minions?"

His unrepentant shrug brought their forearms back into contact. "You haven't met Fidget yet. He murdered his mother-in-law. Of course, they say there never was born a witch more deserving of it."

"You should have introduced him to Pudge's wife," she muttered.

"I'm sorry if their lack of villainy disappoints you. Despite what you may have read, most pirates are and always have been ordinary seaman. Men who prefer freedom to the taste of the lash. Men who prefer a command system based on merit, rather than on the fickle fortunes of birth. We've our share of deserters from your father's precious navy."

She cut him a mocking glance. "Does that make you the only practicing villain aboard?"

His hazel eyes captured hers, their wary heat belying the cold set of his jaw. "Hardly. After all, any man is capable of villainy when confronted with a temptation he can't resist."

Spotting Apollo by the main mast, Lucy tore her gaze away. "If you'll excuse me, Captain, I shall see if your quartermaster would be kind enough to escort me back to my . . . cell."

"Lucy?" The husky query stopped her. Not *Miss Snow* with its sharp, mocking edge, but *Lucy*—tender, bewitching, and fraught with memories. "Now that you're not pointing a gun at my heart, you can believe what you like. But I didn't hire those men. And I'll regret to my dying day leaving you alone in that alley."

She inclined her head, aching to believe him, but fearing he'd once again think her a deluded fool if she did.

Gerard watched her silent battle, wishing its outcome weren't so vital to him.

When Lucy finally tilted her grimy face to him, her eyes were sparkling with a haughty impertinence he had feared was lost forever. "I can't say that I believe you, sir, but I have no proof to the contrary. If I did, Pudge would be sewing up you instead of your topsail."

With that dubious absolution, she marched across the deck and captured his quartermaster. Gerard met Apollo's gaze over her head, offering him a gesture and a faint nod. His mate's stoic face briefly registered surprise, but he saluted his captain to signal his unquestioning obedience.

Lucy had been generous enough to gift him with a fragment of her trust. Even if it cost him his tenuous peace of mind, Gerard could afford to do no less.

♥   ♥   ♥

The hold didn't seem nearly as confusing when navigated by Apollo's confident strides. Lucy was forced to trot to keep up.

"Does your head ache frightfully, Apollo? I'm very sorry about your accident. I shan't throw a pillow at the door again."

He rubbed the lump ruining the symmetry of his sleek pate. "I didn't mind the pillow, missie, but I do wish you'd stop threatening to shoot the Captain."

"I'll consider it," she muttered, refusing to make any promises.

He escorted her inside the great cabin, then turned to go. She poked her head out the open door. "Apollo?"

"Aye, missie?"

"Aren't you forgetting something?"

He frowned as if deeply puzzled, then broke into a broad grin. "Your lunch! I'll fetch it right away."

Lucy was surprised to realize she was ravenous. She would never have suspected that attempted mutiny was such a stimulant to the appetite. "Not lunch. The door. You forgot to lock the door."

He continued on his way, calling back over his shoulder. "No need. The Captain has given you the run of the ship."

Lucy sank against the doorframe, her knees weakened by a long denied hunger sharper than that for food. Apollo might not realize it, but the Captain had given her something infinitely more precious than just the run of his ship.

♥   ♥   ♥

Gerard's breeches and shirt had been a poor fit, but with a few artful nips and tucks by Pudge, Tam's cast-offs fit Lucy as if they'd been tailored for her. Her slender, boyishly clad figure became a familiar sight on the *Retribution*'s decks in the days to come.

Once Tam lost his fear that she was going to whip out a parasol and whack him across his freckled nose, he became a most amiable companion, escorting her about the ship with the vastly superior tolerance of an elder cousin. Lucy suspected he didn't often get the opportunity to lord his knowledge over someone less informed than he.

The ship itself seemed to have been designed by a maniacal genius with a perverse sense of humor. Its decks and hold were riddled with secret companion-ways. Lucy lived in fear of dropping through a hidden trapdoor, triggered by nothing more than the innocent action of brushing against the mizzenmast or peeping through a gunport.

Although its taciturn captain remained an enigma to her, the ship was not so reluctant to surrender its secrets.

A pirate vessel's only salvation lay in being faster, sneakier, and meaner than her opponents. The *Retribution* excelled in all three. Every bit of visible wood on the boat had been stained dark. Gerard had replaced the traditional canvas sails with black double silk, an extravagant but effective method of masking the ship's path through the indigo waters of night. An oversized replica of a galley stove squatted in the stern, equipped to belch out clouds of steam to confuse pursuers.

A false deck had been built into the bulwark, thus explaining the ship's deserted appearance on the night Lucy had first sighted her. The shell could be rolled over the fo'c'sle, quarterdeck, and aftercastle in the event of attack, leaving the crew free to manipulate the ship from below, using an elaborate combination of pulleys, mirrors, and curved spying glasses. The flush false deck also gave them the advantages of speed and agility under sail.

All of those clever modifications allowed Gerard to run the ship with a crew of ninety men, only half of what he should have required. Pudge doubled as both sailmaker and sailmaster. Apollo labored as quartermaster and kept Gerard's logs in his flawless, elegant hand. Only the navigator had one job, his sole task keeping them on whatever mysterious course Gerard had charted.

As Tam hastened to explain, the schooner had been designed for rapid attack and quick retreat, but her most formidable weapon lay in the reputation of her captain. The whispered name of Captain Doom alone could coax most merchant ships, awkward, undergunned, and pregnant with heavy cargo, to surrender without a fight.

A lingering twinge of navy pride forced Lucy to stiffly retaliate with, "That doesn't make him any match for one of His Majesty's warships. A well-placed broadside could reduce this floating circus to so much flotsam."

Tam's green eyes shone with admiration. "That's where ye're wrong, Miss Lucy. Cap'n's the very best. He studied navy strategy in his younger days. It's almost as if he knows what they're thinkin' afore they do."

Lucy was discomfited by the reminder of what Gerard might have accomplished had her father not robbed him of his career. And his freedom.

It was impossible for Lucy not to think of freedom beneath the banner of azure blue that unfurled from horizon to horizon each dawn. Impossible not to think of it while leaning over the forward rail with the wind tossing her hair, the sun warming her back, the cool salt spray peppering her cheeks. How was it possible that as Gerard's defenseless captive, she had never felt so free?

Free to read the morning away on deck or simply drowse in the sun. Free to watch the men at their tasks or badger Apollo for tales of his native Africa.

The spontaneity of life aboard the *Retribution* was irresistible. Except for the bells tolling the changing of the watch, time might have ceased to exist. Unlike the worker ants toiling beneath her father's command, there was nothing regimented about Gerard's crew except for their common and unspoken desire to run the sleek schooner to the best of their abilities.

These men laughed whenever they wanted, frequently burst into song, and paused in trimming the sails to swig rum from a jug or dance a merry jig. They censored neither their jokes or opinions, engaging in good-natured fisticuffs if the occasion warranted, but never forgetting that if any one of them dared to draw steel, he would suffer the traditional penalty of forty stripes.

Lucy's chief amazement stemmed from their treatment of her. A drawing room full of the most impeccably mannered gentlemen in London couldn't have treated her with any more deference. Some, like Pudge, were shy. Others, like Tam, bold enough to court her favor. Even the murderous Fidget, with his pronounced facial tic, inclined his bushy head to kiss her hand upon being introduced to her one sunny afternoon.

"My, my," she whispered to Tam as the friendly little killer went back to waxing a bolt of sail thread. "They must have heard of my father's reputation. If any harm comes to me, the consequences will be quite grave."

Tam snorted. "Not any graver than gettin' their nostrils sliced. That's what the Cap'n's promised to any one of 'em fool eno' to so much as wink at his woman."

The Captain's woman. A treacherous tingle passed through Lucy. "But I'm not . . ." She hesitated. Perhaps it wouldn't be wise to refute such a fable. What if Gerard had only concocted it to keep his men at bay?

She couldn't imagine why the crew would believe such an outrageous claim. Their captain had managed to avoid her presence at every turn, no easy task aboard a three-masted schooner.

The glint of sunlight on brass drew her gaze to the lookout nest at foretop. A man stood within its confines, the breadth of his shoulders and the arrogant grace of his bearing unmistakable. Instead of searching the horizon for enemy ships, he had shamelessly trained his spyglass on her.

Lucy's breath caught in an odd mingling of outrage and gratification. "The nerve of that man," she muttered, but Tam was already out of earshot, scaling the rigging with the lithe skill of a monkey.

Regardless of what they'd been told, Gerard's crew seemed to sense that their truce was an armed one. They had a tendency to vanish when he appeared, as if fearing to stray once again into their line of fire.

At Ionia Lucy had jerked her draperies shut against Gerard's prying eyes. Here she was free to indulge the childish, but far more satisfying, urge to poke her tongue out at him and practice an insolent hand gesture taught to her by Digby, one of his own grizzled gunners. She wasn't quite clear on its meaning but she suspected Gerard would be.

She was correct.

"Wouldn't I love to?" Gerard murmured, lowering the spyglass with a rueful chuckle. He could also think of several more compelling uses for that saucy little tongue of hers.

He watched her scamper after Tam, holding his breath until she reached a safe perch. He didn't really need the spyglass. Every detail of Lucy's appearance was etched in his memory with merciless clarity.

He would have thought it impossible, but the sun had bleached her hair an ethereal shade paler. Her fair skin was kissed by an apricot glow and her features had lost the pinched look that had plagued them at Ionia. He didn't know what had done the most for her —the fresh, salty air or escaping the smothering weight of the Admiral's thumb.

He wondered again at the wisdom of granting her so much independence. He'd locked her in the cabin originally to keep her out of his reach. Now he had to severely restrict his own movements just to keep from tripping over her.

She was everywhere he turned: the two braids she'd taken to wearing inclined over a sail as Pudge taught her a difficult stitch; reading aloud from one of Defoe's novels, his men gathered around her like children around their mother's skirts; leaning against the forward rail at twilight, gazing pensively across the billows as the damson-tinted sea doused the flaming ball of the sun.

He was disturbed by the ease with which the dour Miss Snow had enchanted his crew. He knew they were hungry for feminine company in all of its guises, but he was the one starving for lack of it. Her unadorned beauty swept through him like a bracing blast of salt spray. Her chiming laugh tormented him until he began to regret his own charity with a violence that alarmed him.

He snapped the spyglass shut, knowing there was only one place to take a temper this grim. As he swung down from the foretop, he didn't see the gamin face that peeked out from behind the capstan to follow his progress.

♥　♥　♥

Lucy tiptoed through the shadowy hold toward the iron-banded door, recalling her last inauspicious attempt to breach the mysterious chamber. Gerard had disappeared into it less than five minutes before and it had taken her that long to muster her courage to follow.

Why should she be afraid? she asked herself. After all, he'd expressly forbidden her no area of the schooner, so he could hardly berate her for snooping. She swallowed a squeak of doubt. Could he?

She pressed her ear to the door. Much to her relief, she didn't hear any screams of agony or desperate voices pleading for mercy. She *did* hear the cadences of male voices, raised slightly as if in anger.

Gerard's clipped words were muffled by the thick oak, the answering drawl even more pronounced than his own. Lucy frowned. She didn't recognize Apollo's bass rumble, Tam's brogue, or Pudge's timid murmur. She concentrated harder, deciphering snatches of conversation between each pause in the heated dialogue.

Gerard was saying, ". . . no one to blame but yourself . . . still be safely tucked in her own bed if it weren't for your little indiscretion."

Lucy's mouth fell open. As far as she knew, she was the only *her* within a thousand knots.

Her fascination with herself as a topic of Gerard's conversation enabled her to translate an entire retort from his companion. "Ah, yes, but would she be alone? And as I recall, you seduced more than a few bored noblemens' wives in your heyday."

Gerard's reply was succinct to the point of obscenity. Lucy recoiled. His master gunner, Digby, spoke profanity as if it were a second language, but even he hadn't taught her that particular phrase.

Gerard's companion seemed to be more amused than alarmed by the anatomically impossible suggestion. His reply floated toward the door on wings of sarcasm. ". . . locked me up for my protection or hers?"

Rapid footsteps approached the door. Lucy barely had time to dart around the corner before it flew open. She crouched in the shadows as Gerard emerged. He didn't look nearly as angry as she'd feared, but perhaps, she thought grimly, she was the only one capable of inciting him to a truly murderous rage.

Her heart sank as he locked the door behind him and pocketed a brass key. She huddled in the dark long after he'd passed, shaken by the realization that she wasn't the only prisoner aboard the *Retribution*.

♥　♥　♥

Late that night, Lucy lay alone on the aftercastle, a discarded pile of sail her pillow and a vast sprinkling of stars her only blanket. The Admiral had taught her to think in rigid shades of black and white, but now she found herself wandering in a gray netherworld, unable to separate shadow from substance and no closer to solving the mystery of Captain Doom than when she'd begun.

Was he the man who had vowed to guard her life as his own—tender, patient, fiercely protective? Or was he a man hell-bent on vengeance—embittered, ruthless, cynical, and quick-tempered? For the first time, her bewildered heart was forced to entertain the notion that those two diverse men might be one and the same.

His men seemed to both revere and genuinely like him. He maintained discipline with an iron fist and ready wit, yet rarely impinged upon the freedoms they held so dear. While the Admiral's fierce reputation had been measured by the number of stripes he'd inflicted on his crew's backs, Gerard's threats of reprisal for infractions of the *Retribution*'s code of law were just that—threats. His men respected him too much to test the limits of his patience. They seemed to value his praise more than they feared his punishment.

They were men who did not give their loyalty lightly, yet Lucy had discovered in the past few days that there wasn't a man aboard who wouldn't consider it an honor to lay down his life if their captain required it.

Do you know what it is for a captain to outlive his crew, Lucy?

She was the only one who knew it was the one sacrifice he would never ask of them.

Exhausted from battling the present, Lucy closed her eyes to float in a haze of memory. Gerard puffed a smoke ring at her nose, his eyes sparkling with mischief behind Pudge's homely spectacles. He dusted a sprinkling of cinnamon from her lower lip with his little finger. He twirled her in the dizzying arms of a waltz, his powerful hand encompassing the small of her back.

She was so beguiled by her visions that she didn't even start in surprise when her eyes drifted open to find Gerard leaning over her. Her dreaming hunger for him was such that she couldn't stop herself from reaching up to trace his beardless jaw with her finger-tips.

She blinked, lost in a mist of confusion. A dream indeed, for this was a different Gerard. A Gerard unscarred by time and disillusionment. A Gerard whose bright eyes were unshadowed by cynicism. Her own guilt must have led her to conjure up this creature. This was the Gerard who might have been had it not been for her father's treachery.

She had neither the strength nor the will to resist as his beautifully carved mouth descended on hers. Her lips parted without coaxing for a kiss that was dazzling, deft, and provocative.

And totally wrong.

It was bestowed with the skill of an artist who'd spent countless hours of practice perfecting his technique, but it lacked the elusive spice of maturity. It was a mild spring shower over the English countryside instead of a wild and perilous storm at sea, and it left her curiously, but completely, unmoved.

Lucy's eyes popped open in shock as an acerbic, and all too familiar, voice rang out.

"I had thought to introduce you to my brother someday, Lucy, but I can see the two of you have already met."

CHAPTER TWENTY-FOUR

LUCY'S ASTOUNDED GAZE TRAVELED BE-tween the two men.

Gerard was leaning against the aft rail, his casual stance belied by the dangerous tension coiled in his folded arms. The other man loomed over her, his unrepentant grin slashing a devilish dimple in his left cheek.

Horrified anew, she pounded his shoulder with her fist. "Get off me, you lecher! How dare you take such liberties?"

"Don't be so hasty, Lucy," Gerard chided. "You did appear to be enjoying yourself."

"But that's because I thought—" Lucy bit her traitorous tongue. What she'd thought was even more damning than kissing a stranger. She wasn't about to gratify Gerard's infuriating smugness by confessing that she'd been dreaming about kissing him.

His brother gracefully disengaged himself from her supine form. She sat up and tucked her knees beneath her, trying vainly to rearrange her disheveled hair.

"I'm fully prepared to shoulder the blame, brother," he offered gallantly. "I never could resist a pretty girl in the moonlight."

Gerard's eyes narrowed. "You never could resist any girl in any light. Do I have to remind you that this particular beauty can now identify you to the authorities as Captain Doom's temporary replacement? Why do you think I locked the door of the dungeon when I left?"

"You know as well as I that they haven't invented a lock I couldn't pick. If they had, you'd still be rotting away in Santo Domingo."

"And some jealous husband would have shot you dead by now," Gerard retorted.

Their verbal sparring suggested a contest of long standing. Lucy's gaze bounced between the two men, still trying to absorb the shock of her discovery.

Now that they were both on their feet, the differences between them became far more evident. Gerard's strength was of the compact variety while his taller brother reminded her of a lanky, loose-limbed colt. His hair was a shade lighter than Gerard's and his eyes more green than hazel. From the absence of crinkles around them, she judged him to be nearly a decade younger than his brother.

"Does he have a name?" she interjected when they both paused for breath.

Gerard turned his excoriating sarcasm on her. "You might have thought to ask that *before* you swooned so blissfully in his arms."

Before she could retort, her hand was snatched up and pressed to a pair of eager lips. "Kevin . . ." He hesitated, shooting his brother a panicked glance.

"Doom?" Lucy offered dryly.

"Claremont," Gerard barked.

"Kevin Claremont, my love, at your undying service."

Lucy might have been flattered had she not suspected he greeted every female with the same fervent ardor. Behind him, she could see Gerard mouthing her reply with uncanny accuracy. "Lucinda Snow. My friends call me Lucy, but you may call me . . ." Seized by inspiration, she bestowed a dazzling smile on the younger Mr. Claremont before crooning, "Lucy."

Gerard glared at her over Kevin's shoulder, his gaze sharp enough to cut diamonds.

Kevin's lush lips tightened to a pout. "Damned unsporting of you to sneak this beauty aboard after you were so cruel as to kick off my actress friend in Dover that time."

"She wasn't an actress. She was a prostitute," Gerard shot back. "You didn't honestly expect me to believe she was your cabin boy, did you?"

Lucy climbed to her feet, peering curiously at the sandy hair caught in a queue at Kevin's nape. "It's very odd, sir, but I feel as if I know you."

Gerard snorted. "As well you should. You clipped his absurd feats of derring-do from the papers the entire time I was stuck at Ionia. I'm damned lucky I had a ship to come back to."

"Cap'n Doom!" Lucy exclaimed. "You're the one from the Howells' masquerade. The one with the atrocious costume."

Kevin clapped a hand over his heart. "You wound me, fair lady. I thought I was quite dashing."

"Subtlety has never been my little brother's strong suit. Equipping my ship with a fully functional torture chamber was his idea too."

Before Lucy could object, Kevin linked an arm through hers and drew her close to his side. "Hospitality has never been my *elder* brother's strong suit. I hear he's been woefully neglecting you." He cast his brother a reproachful look. "Sometimes it's difficult for those who are rapidly leaving behind the pleasures of youth to remember how easily bored we are."

Gerard opened his mouth, then snapped it shut. He clenched his teeth in an acidic smile. "If you'll excuse me, I tire easily in my dotage. I believe I'll leave you children to your"—his gaze dropped briefly to Lucy's lips, which still felt moist and swollen from his brother's uninvited kiss—"pleasures." His shoulders set at a painfully rigid angle, he melted into the shadows.

Lucy wiggled in Kevin's grasp, intent on going after him. "Let me go. I—"

"Don't," Kevin whispered sharply. "He never took me seriously until I stopped trotting at his heels. The crew gives him enough adoration. He needs something entirely different from you and me."

Lucy ceased her squirming, startled by the wry note in her captor's voice. As she met his sparkling green eyes, she had the distinct impression that she'd just found a long-lost friend she'd never known was missing.

♥   ♥   ♥

The foretop lookout was no longer a safe refuge for Gerard. Watching Lucy cavort about the ship alone had been a vicarious torment. Watching her cavort about the ship with his brother filled him with a nameless agony. To see their fair heads together. To hear their carefree laughter ringing on the wind as if they shared a joke incomprehensible to the rest of the world.

He'd never been so conscious of his thirty-one years or so keenly regretted the time that had been lost to him. Not lost, he reminded himself bitterly. Stolen. During that time, the plump, awkward, worshipful little brother he'd left behind had shed his baby fat and honed his skills as a reprobate. Using the money Gerard had so painstakingly stashed away for his education, he drank, gambled, and cajoled his way into the company of some of the richest and most notorious rakes in London. With his uncanny knack for numbers and his flawless memory for cards, Kevin had fleeced the more reckless of them of their fortunes, just waiting for the night when destiny would place him across the table from some drunken braggart who might know the fate of his older brother.

After three years of living in such debauchery, destiny had delivered Lucien Snow into his hands. It hadn't taken the sharp-eared Kevin long to make the connection between his missing brother and the man's boasts about swindling "Captain Doom" out of a veritable king's ransom.

Gerard knew Kevin had been tempted to call Snow out on the spot, but he feared the Admiral had the power to have Gerard moved to another prison or killed if he scented a rescue attempt. So he'd simply excused himself, gathered his winnings, and sailed off to Santo Domingo to find his brother.

Gerard had little memory of those first dark days after the rescue. He remembered Kevin's gentle but relentless hands pouring water down his throat, his brother's voice, familiar, but much deeper than it should have been, coaxing him to open his mouth so a spoonful of broth could be dribbled inside. Kevin had forced the wasted wreck of a man that he'd become to survive until Gerard's consuming desire for revenge gave him a reason to live.

Which made it doubly difficult to go strolling on the quarterdeck late one evening to find Lucy holding court with his brother as her crown prince.

All lanterns were to be extinguished after eight, but

a misty orb of a moon bathed the deck in a silvery glow. Lucy sat in a circle of men, flanked by Kevin and Tam, their laughter and teasing underscored by the sporadic clatter of dice.

Gerard approached with the fleet grace for which he was notorious, pausing in the shadows just outside their circle of merriment. It had been bad enough to feel excluded from Lucy's life in London, but on his own ship, the sensation was almost unbearable. It quickened his temper to the point of danger. Made him want to grab her by those ridiculous braids, drag her back to his cabin, and remind her in the most potent way possible just who was master of this ship.

"Here, Lucy," Tam called out, passing her a battered mug, "p'raps a bit of rumfustian will change yer luck."

Lucy took an obedient sip. Her grimace elicited a burst of laughter from Digby and Fidget. "Good heavens, Tam. What's in this stuff? Hemlock?"

Tam ticked off the ingredients on his fingers. "Gin. Sherry. Rum. Spices . . ."

"D-d-don't forget the raw eggs," Pudge shyly offered.

Lucy coughed and sputtered. "Not much chance of that."

When the laughter had subsided, Kevin leaned over and folded the dice into her palm. "Sixes are the main. A kiss for luck, darling."

Gerard's hands clenched into fists. He held his breath, fearing what he would do should Lucy tilt her lips to Kevin's handsome face for a kiss. In twenty-two years, he'd never lifted a hand to his brother in anger; now he wanted to fasten them both around the tanned column of Kevin's throat and strangle him.

His captive breath escaped as Lucy brought her cupped hand to her lips and gently bestowed a kiss upon its contents. Even that innocent gesture made the blood pool, hot and heavy, in Gerard's loins.

He stepped forward, no longer content to hover in the shadows. "What a charming pet you've made of our little hostage. I've heard of vessels keeping a trained dog to amuse them. Or even a pig. But never an admiral's daughter."

Gerard's unexpected broadside jolted Lucy to the core. Her fingers went icy, then numb. The dice tumbled from her hand, rewarding her clumsiness with two sixes. After an instant of stunned silence, the men sent up a halfhearted cheer.

Their captain's slow, sarcastic applause silenced them. His mood had been less than predictable lately. "Cursed with the devil's own luck, isn't she? Or perhaps just her father's."

Lucy's nerves had been stretched taut by the effort of forcing a gaiety she did not feel. At the unprovoked attack, she sprang to her feet to face him.

Tam's hand snaked to his breeches to check the security of his pistol. Pudge inched backward. Fidget's cheek twitched and Digby began to swear softly, but fluently, beneath his breath. Kevin gazed at the fallen dice as if able to divine the future in their inscrutable dots.

"You've a lot of nerve condemning my father for gambling, Captain," Lucy said, stabbing a finger at Gerard's chest. "What do you think you're doing? Isn't there any risk in sailing in circles just waiting for the Royal Navy to find you? Isn't there any hazard in trying to outwit ships with bigger guns, bigger crews, and more brilliant strategists than you could ever hope to be? Why, you're more of a gambler than my father ever was! Only you gamble for keeps. You gamble with these men as your dice. Their lives and their futures are all your stakes and you don't give a damn about any of them as long as you win in the end."

He gazed down at her for a long moment, his unassailable dignity more infuriating than any outburst. "Perhaps we should reconsider getting that pig," he said quietly before turning on his heel and leaving her to mop up her own mess.

The men crept off, one by one, refusing to look at her. She turned her burning eyes on Kevin, expecting him to cheer her show of spirit. His expression was oddly reproving. She sank down and rested her cheek on her folded knees. She'd be damned if she was going to cry again, she thought sullenly. She'd shed enough tears for Gerard Claremont to replenish the sea.

When it finally came, Kevin's rebuke was all the more potent for its gentleness. "Curse him for his stubbornness, Lucy. Damn him for his ambition to succeed, no matter what the cost. But don't undermine his competence in front of his men."

Lucy sniffed, despising the telltale thickness of her voice. "I should have known you'd defend him. The wretch *is* your brother."

"And the only father I'm ever likely to know. He brought me into this world and buried our ma when the job was done. Instead of abandoning me when he went to sea, he found a captain with a wife who would raise me as her own. They hadn't much money, but they had a comfortable cottage in the country—much more than he'd ever had. He might have left me then and not looked back, but he didn't. He was gone for months at a time, but he never returned without some exotic present for his baby brother. Until the day came when he didn't return at all."

Lucy turned her face away, but Kevin squatted in front of her, ruthless in his quest to make her understand. "Gerard's father had the grace to marry our mother before he was lost at sea. She took to the streets after that. My own father could have been any one of a dozen men. I'm a bastard, Lucy, but whatever Gerard's name might be at any given moment, he always shares it with me."

Lucy lifted her head. The breeze snatched at the bitter tears she had vowed not to cry. "Then you should consider yourself fortunate, for that's more than he'll ever share with me."

♥   ♥   ♥

It took Lucy until noon the next day to screw up the humility to apologize. Gerard was standing at the bow, a grim figurehead glaring at the horizon as if he could conjure up a navy warship with the sheer force of his will.

Lucy joined him in his vigil. "Perhaps he's not coming," she said softly. "Didn't it ever occur to you that he might be glad to be rid of me?"

He shot her a crooked glance. "Hourly."

Before she could so much as sputter a retort, he was gone, dropping down into the main companionway without a sound.

Lucy was not the only one to feel the lash of the captain's tongue that day. His brooding mood darkened by the hour, enveloping the *Retribution* in a cloud more inescapable than the billowing sails blocking out the sunlight. He was a man known for his cool head and even temper, yet he barked orders with the poorly restrained ferocity of an Irish wolfhound. His crew scurried to do his bidding, afraid any delay might result in yet another stripe inflicted by his merciless tongue.

When a relieved Apollo reported that the Captain had retired to his dayroom to review the week's logs, Lucy came up with the idea of drawing caricatures of the men to diffuse the tension. She was using Kevin's back as a desk and putting the finishing touches on an enormous pair of spectacles for a delighted Pudge when the drawing was snatched from her hand.

Lucy stared dumbly at the muscled smoothness of Kevin's back. Her heart thudded a belated warning. A lethal quiet descended around them like the tense peace of the sea before an explosion of cannons. She straightened to find Gerard holding the coarse paper to the light. His knuckles were stark white, yet he took care not to smudge so much as a line of the drawing.

"A brilliant likeness, don't you think, Pudge?" he inquired gently.

Pudge shuffled his feet. "Y-y-yes, sir."

"It'll look simply smashing posted on the wall at Newgate."

He handed Pudge his prize and focused his lethal attention on Tam. Tam tried to shove his own sketch down the front of his breeches, but Gerard held out his hand before he could succeed. He sheepishly surrendered the likeness. Gerard frowned. All of them, including Lucy, held their breath. Only Kevin seemed unconcerned. He was watching his brother with an odd mixture of wariness and amusement.

"Far too many freckles, I fear," Gerard finally pronounced. "I'd hate for the magistrates to have trouble recognizing you."

The Captain lifted his tawny head, studying each of his men's faces in turn. Only Lucy was spared his scrutiny, but somehow the omission did not hearten her.

"Fidget," he said, choosing his next victim with deliberate care. "Didn't I see you showing Miss Snow how the steam furnace works earlier in the week?"

Fidget's cheek twitched in staccato rhythm. "Aye, sir, she was . . . curious."

"And you, Digby. Was it my imagination or were

you demonstrating how the powder monkey handed you shot during an attack?"

The elderly gunner scratched his balding head. " 'Twas the damnedest thing, Cap'n. She just happened by and . . . aw, shit, I can't deny it."

Gerard shook his head, his voice so fraught with patience that it sent a shiver down Lucy's spine. "Even you, Apollo. You were the one considerate enough to teach Miss Snow the workings of the false deck."

His quartermaster stood at stiff attention. "Aye, sir. That would have been me."

Gerard paced between their ranks, his hands locked at the small of his back. When the storm finally broke, it did so with a mighty roar. "Why didn't the bloody lot of you just get together and provide her with a diagram of the ship? *My* ship! She could have wrapped it in ribbon and presented it to the Lord High Admiral of the Royal Navy with her own dainty little hand!"

The men gaped at him. They'd never seen their levelheaded captain in such a state.

His eyes blazed with fury. "Have you all lost your minds? You're wanted criminals, for God's sake. Fugitives! Has she got you so besotted that it never occurred to you that it might be dangerous to let her reproduce your likenesses? You won't be quite so charmed by her talents when these sketches pop up in the pages of the *Times* right alongside a healthy reward for your thick skulls!"

Lucy could not allow them to endure a punishment that was rightfully hers. "Captain?" she said, hating the timid sound of her plea. "It really wasn't their fault. They were just trying to amuse—"

"You!" Gerard wheeled on his heel and stabbed a finger in her direction. "You meddlesome little . . ."

Lucy backed away, his inevitable approach effectively separating her from the others. He backed her toward the starboard rail with ruthless efficiency, his powerful body coiled to pounce. Not since the night she'd stabbed him with the letter opener had Lucy seen him in such a murderous rage. But he hadn't killed her then, she reminded herself breathlessly. He had kissed her. Twice.

Her tongue darted out to moisten her lips. For some reason, she didn't feel afraid, but exhilarated. Her back came up against the rail. There was nowhere left to flee.

She met his gaze boldly. "Why don't you go ahead and throw me overboard? After all, it wouldn't be the first time, would it, *Captain Doom*?"

He snatched her up by the shoulders. "I ought to. You're quite an effective little spy, aren't you?" His gaze searched her face, darting wildly from her eyes to her lips, which had parted in unconscious invitation. "All you have to do is bat those silky eyelashes over those big, innocent eyes of yours and twitch that pretty rump and my men spill all their secrets."

"I know too much," Lucy agreed, blinking solemnly. "You can hardly afford to let me live."

He jerked her against him, more of desperation than violence in his grip. Her back was arched against the rail, the softness of her breasts pressed to the tense wall of his chest. The butt of his pistol dug into her belly.

His lips were a scant inch from hers when he gave her a shake harsh enough to dislodge strands of hair from her braids. "Damn you! If you think I'm going to let myself fall under the spell of some prim, underfed brat of a virgin, you've overestimated your charms. Hell, I probably wouldn't even want you so badly if I hadn't been without a woman for six bloody years!"

His words echoed without mercy in the stunned silence. Swearing with Digby's curt fluency, he released her and marched away, stabbing a furious hand through his hair. Lucy collapsed against the rail, the loosened strands of her hair tumbling forward to veil her face.

The men crept around her. Pudge's plump fingers stroked her arm. "Don't cry, Miss Lucy. Oh, p-please, don't cry. I'm sure he didn't mean to be so unkind."

They had to strain to hear Lucy's voice. "Apollo, whose clothes were in that trunk the Captain sent me?"

It was Kevin who answered, his tone matter-of-fact. "They belonged to the prosti—"—he paused to clear his throat of a damning obstruction—"um—my actress friend." His roguish shrug conveyed volumes. "She barely had time to dress before Gerard put her ashore."

When Lucy lifted her head, her eyes weren't shining with tears as they'd feared, but with hope. Her joyous laughter rippled through their jaded hearts like song.

She folded the sailmaster's hand in her own. "Have you ever worked as a dressmaker, Pudge?"

♥ ♥ ♥

Gerard stared sightlessly at the leather-bound logs spread open on the table before him. Something thumped on the ceiling of the dayroom; his eyes shifted upward. Given his erratic behavior since bringing Lucy aboard, his crew was probably abovedeck plotting mutiny. *Captain Lucy,* he thought wryly. He had to admit it had an intriguing ring to it. Pudge could use his talents to fashion a new flag—a pastel pink one, perhaps, with a likeness of a woman's delicate hand squeezing a heart. A fool's heart.

He tossed back a swallow of brandy, wishing his own ban on open flame aboard ship didn't preclude indulging in a cheroot. The liquor's smoky tang only intensified the hollow ache spreading through his body. Lucy had coaxed him into making a royal ass of himself in front of his men and all he could think of was how good it had felt to have her back in his arms.

As he reached for the brandy bottle, a mildewed ledger caught his eye. He drew it toward him. He had picked up Annemarie Snow's diary a dozen times in the past week, thinking to read it, but each time something had stopped him. Some reluctance to disturb the shades of the past. He had enough ghosts in his life clamoring for justice without adding one more.

His weary fingers caressed the moth-eaten velvet. Perhaps he should give it to Lucy. It might keep her out of his hair . . . for at least ten minutes.

Apollo appeared in the doorway, contorting his towering frame into a formal bow.

Gerard regarded him quizzically. "I've never seen you wear a shirt when it wasn't snowing. What's the occasion? Are we being boarded by His Majesty?"

Maintaining his aloof silence, Apollo handed him a scrap of paper etched in the quartermaster's own unmistakable calligraphy.

Miss Snow requests the honor of your presence for supper.

Gerard disguised a flare of raw emotion behind the flippant cynicism he'd had five long years to perfect. "Has she found a more efficient way to finish me off? Poison, perhaps?"

"I don't believe hemlock was on the menu, sir."

Gerard hesitated, poised to decline, then slammed the nearest log shut. "What the hell. I haven't any more promising invitations tonight. My men all think I'm a lunatic."

As he made his way down the passageway, his strides much longer than his present temper, Apollo discreetly vanished.

Gerard paused before the door of his cabin, resisting the urge to straighten his shirt and smooth his
hair. He gave the door a curt knock, then entered
without bothering to wait for an answer. After all, a
captain should hardly have to beg for an invitation into
his own quarters.

He'd expected to find the cabin an unholy mess and
Lucy waiting to pounce on him in her sleek masculine
garments. What he did not expect was to find the
cabin in perfect order, even the morocco spines of his
cherished Defoe novels aligned with loving precision
on the shelves. Before he could absorb the shock of
that, a girl glided out of the shadows.

Not a girl, but a woman, he realized. A woman he
hardly recognized. Lucy had abandoned both Tam's
breeches and the chaste white of her Grecian gown for
a glorious concoction of ribbons and lace. The glimmering turquoise satin was overlaid with a gossamer
web of cream lace. The gently belled skirt fell to a
scalloped hem that just covered her toes.

The antiquated gown might have been scoffed at in
current circles, but its rich hues perfectly comple-
mented Lucy's porcelain complexion and the silvery
tint in her upswept hair. Gerard felt as if he'd stepped
back in time. As if he were twenty-four years old again,
facing one of those exquisite London belles who had
given of themselves so generously to make him a man.

The lacy décolletage of the gown was both less revealing and more enticing than the present fashion,
allowing Gerard to use his vivid imagination to envision the pale, flawless breasts that lay beneath.

A harsh edge of longing closed his throat. Apparently, Lucy didn't plan to kill him off quickly, but to
make him suffer a slow, lingering death for want of
her.

"Thank you for accepting my supper invitation," she said in her clear, cool voice.

Gerard wanted to hear it roughened with passion, hoarse with need, begging him to finish her as he'd done that night in the gatehouse. "I'm not hungry," he said, beyond caring if he was rude. "I don't care for the odds in dice and I'm not interested in having my portrait done."

Her gaze was faintly challenging. "Then why did you come?"

"For this," he said, striding past her prettily laid supper table to take her into his arms.

Lucy had expected Gerard's lust to be inflamed by the elegant gown. She had not expected it to rage out of control, threatening to engulf everything in its path, including her will to resist him. For a trembling moment, he held her wrapped as tightly against him as his arms would allow, his restraint more provocative than any attempt at seduction. Lucy clung to his shirtfront, torn between surrender and shoving him away before he could hurt her again.

"Isn't this why you invited me here?" he murmured into her hair.

The spicy, familiar scent of him flooded her nostrils, making her breath come in shaky gasps. "I don't know. I thought if we could just talk without shouting . . . ?"

He blazed an openmouthed trail of fire down the naked column of her throat. "I'm not shouting now, am I?"

If he had been, Lucy couldn't have heard him over the thundering of her pulse beneath his artful lips. With a will of their own, her fingers delved into the open collar of his shirt, seeking from memory the warmth of his smooth muscles beneath their crisp whorls of hair.

Gerard groaned at her shy touch. He raked his fingers through her hair, freeing it from its loose chignon to tumble around her shoulders. He cupped her face in his hands as if it were infinitely precious to him and lowered his mouth to meld it with hers. He nibbled her lips, laving their supple curves with painstaking care. His kiss held no mockery, no teasing this time, only the hungry reverence of a man who had been born adoring women.

If only he adored her, Lucy thought bleakly. He had as much as admitted that after six years of enforced celibacy, any woman would do to slake his thwarted passions. Even his enemy's daughter.

She still couldn't stop herself from drinking of his bittersweet draught. From welcoming the intoxicating thrust of his tongue against hers. He tasted of stolen brandy and forbidden temptation just as he had that autumn night so long ago. The night when she'd been in danger of surrendering not only her body, but her soul, to Captain Doom.

As if the mere thought of the name had summoned the past to haunt them, a fist pounded on the door.

They both froze as Apollo's disembodied voice floated to their ears. "Seventy-four-gunner approaching, Captain. Flagship *Argonaut*."

CHAPTER TWENTY-FIVE

LUCY HAD NEVER BEEN A GIRL GIVEN TO tantrums, but she wanted to stamp her feet and wail at her father's perverse timing. Her eyes met Gerard's, reading in them a flicker of regret, too quickly engulfed by a blaze of raw excitement.

She reached for him, but he was already striding toward the door, anticipation coiled in every step. "Don't leave this cabin unless I summon you. It might not be safe."

"Gerard?"

It took him a minute to turn, almost as if he dreaded looking her in the eye. He ducked his head like a small boy caught playing Navy in the bath, making her chest tighten with love. "Yes?"

She rubbed her arms, chilled by his abrupt defection. "Take care. He's a dangerous adversary."

A ruthless smile touched his handsome lips. "So am I."

"Don't I know?" Lucy whispered after he'd gone, gazing blindly at the ruined supper Tam had so painstakingly prepared. It seemed the game was on again and she'd lost before it had even begun.

♥　♥　♥

The *Argonaut* was silhouetted against the night sky like the bloated carcass of a mighty dragon. Skeletal fingers of mist caressed her bow, as if the cloying fog of the North Sea had stalked her even to this unlikely place.

Gerard gripped the rail in primitive excitement, his nostrils flaring at the unmistakable scent of his enemy. Lucien Snow was out there somewhere and this time Gerard had no intention of letting him slip through his fingers. He'd bided his time long enough. The moment had come for all the Admiral's debts to be paid, including the ones he'd incurred against his daughter's resilient spirit.

A disturbing pall of silence hung over his crew. They were only too aware that at close range, the imposing pride of His Majesty's fleet would dwarf their lithe schooner, that the man-of-war's seventy-four cannons were backed by a crew of six hundred and protected by an unsinkable fortress of oak.

Yet his crew's confidence in him was a palpable thing. Even Pudge's doughy features were resolute with determination. The timid sailmaster might cringe in terror from the sensual threat of a lovely girl garbed only in her chemise, but Gerard had never known him to flinch in the face of impending battle.

A chill finger of doubt caressed his spine. Hadn't the crew of the *Annemarie* believed in him as well? Gerard scowled. There was something sinister about the lone ship crouched motionless against the horizon. In some perverse way, he would have almost preferred to face an entire fleet of warships backed by the supreme moral authority of His Majesty himself.

"Dawn," he said decisively. "I'll take a launch over at dawn and deliver our demands."

Kevin and Apollo protested in unison, but Digby drowned out both of them. The gunner had a tendency to bellow, a habit developed from decades of shouting orders over the thunder of cannons.

"Hell, Cap'n, not meanin' to offend you, but that's the damnedest bit o' nonsense I ever heard." Digby scratched his balding head with fingers permanently blackened with gunpowder. "I ain't no genius, sir, but from what I can figger, ye're ever bit as important to that Snow bastard as the young miss. If he takes ye hostage, what are we to do? Sit here and scratch our arses?"

"He's right," Kevin said. "You shouldn't be the one to go."

Gerard looked around at their expectant faces, recognizing that Kevin wasn't the only brother he had aboard the *Retribution*. "This is my fight. I won't drag any of you into it any more than I have to."

"Let me go, sir," Apollo said. "As your second-in-command."

Digby bit off an expressive oath. Rudely elbowing the African giant aside, he came to stand before Gerard, drawing his withered frame to its full height. "I'm sixty-five years old, Cap'n. I've been a gunner since I was twelve, trapped belowdeck with nothin' but powder and shot for company. How many chances for glory do ye think I'll have?"

Gerard gazed down into the old man's rheumy eyes, brightened now with youthful ambition. He locked his hands at the small of his back. "Are you volunteering yourself, Mr. Digby?"

"I am."

"Very well. I'll expect you on deck at dawn."

Digby beamed, revealing a mouthful of broken

teeth. As Fidget and Tam slapped him on the back with subdued congratulations, Gerard returned to the rail, wishing he could shake off his chill of foreboding and salvage his waning lust for battle. One by one, his men joined him in his silent vigil, their hollow eyes reflecting the grimmest of his own doubts as they pondered the unspoken question foremost in all their minds.

Was there any ransom, on heaven or earth, of more value than their captain's precious prize?

♥　♥　♥

Lucy paced the great cabin in an agony of suspense, the rustle of her elegant satin skirts mocking her every step. The anchored ship hung in listless stillness, barely rocked by the tide, but its malaise only drove her to pace faster. She pressed her hands to her ears, but could not seem to stop the relentless ticking of the chronometer in her brain. The hourglass was tilting again and she was standing dwarfed beneath it, helpless to shield herself from the smothering rain of glass and sand.

She paused in her flight to nowhere to grip the back of a chair, the wild tumble of her hair mirroring the tumult of her thoughts. Was this how the Admiral had made her mother feel? Battered by a bewildering jumble of facts and emotions? Was Annemarie Snow's alleged hysteria rooted in her inability to reconcile what she knew to be true and what she felt in her heart?

Lucy blew a wisp of hair out of her eyes, struggling to review the facts with a trace of her old logic. The Admiral had lied to her. Gerard had lied to her. Truth be told, she shouldn't give one whit if they blew each other out of the water.

So why couldn't she seem to stop loving either of them? Her fingers bit into the chair back. Despite his perfidy, the Admiral was still her father. Not even the weight of his betrayal could completely squelch a lifetime of blind adoration.

And Gerard? *Oh, Gerard,* her heart echoed. The image of any physical harm coming to him made her racing heart feel as if it were being ripped whole from her chest.

Braced by determination, she straightened, freeing the chair. Despite what the Admiral had raised her to believe, she was not powerless against the machinations of men. If Gerard had taught her one thing, it was that women possessed their own weapons, aside from pistols and cannon shot. Weapons of tenderness. Weapons of grace. Weapons of forgiveness.

She would stop this disaster before it occurred. Before one of the men she loved was maimed, or even killed, she would lay herself down as a sacrifice between them. Surely her love was strong enough to conquer Gerard's hatred. She would soothe his temper with her tenderness and allow him to slake his desire for vengeance on her willing body.

With trembling hands, she reknotted her chignon and smoothed her skirts, preparing to go to the Captain of the *Retribution* and offer him both her innocence and her love.

♥　♥　♥

Lucy approached the Captain's dayroom, the nervous thud of her heart drowning out the murmur of her stocking feet against the planking. Despite her trepidation, she did not regret her impetuous decision. She knew somehow that Gerard would appreciate and honor the inestimable worth of the gift she would offer him. A gift she had once thought to bestow only upon her husband.

A yearning regret touched her, not for that faceless man, but because Gerard was not that man. He would never slip a ring on her waiting finger. Would never give her ginger-haired, hazel-eyed babies with her high-handed temper and his penchant for mischief. Smiling, she brushed an unexpected tear from her cheek. Perhaps it was just as well. Not even the indefatigable Smythe could handle such a saucy brood.

Lantern light spilled into the passageway from the half-open door of the dayroom. Lucy hesitated at the fringes of its revealing arc, the rich cadences of Gerard's voice as mesmerizing as they'd been the first time she had heard them. She could not see Gerard from her vantage point, but Apollo hunched over the cabin's sole table, the graceful scratch of his quill across a sheet of vellum punctuating Gerard's frequent pauses.

He was dictating, Lucy realized. And pacing. Just as she had been doing earlier. His shadow crossed a hammock strung in the corner and she knew where he'd been sleeping since giving her his spacious quarters. The tiny room was more a cell than a cabin and she shuddered, wondering how he had endured it. He must have kept the lantern burning around the clock.

Her empathy faltered as his crisp voice assailed her ears. ". . . have learned only too well how to play your diabolical games, Admiral Snow. Thus far, your precious daughter has remained untouched, but if my demands are not met by sunset tomorrow, *I will ruin her.*"

At the terrible finality of his words, Lucy's hand flew to her throat. Had her innocence been nothing more to him all along than a bargaining tool—the highest trump in a high-stakes game?

He stepped into view, rubbing a hand over the determined set of his jaw. Lucy could only stare at him, at the predator's grace of his lean body, the sensual threat of his sculpted lips, willing herself to believe he wasn't the man she feared him to be.

"What will your beloved London society think of you then, sir," he continued, each sardonic word lacerating Lucy's sore heart, "upon discovering you've allowed your only daughter to become the whore of the notorious Captain Doom?"

Lucy's worst fears were confirmed. Gerard was only too willing to take by force what she would have given him freely in love. She clamped a hand over her mouth, but it was too late to muffle her small cry of anguish.

Gerard jerked his head up. Their gazes locked, his eyes reflecting surprise, regret, then a naked pain that mirrored her own. But he did not try to defend himself. The shards of her broken trust littered the cabin floor between them, making trespass impossible.

With a strangled sob, Lucy gathered her skirts and fled, knowing instinctively that he would not follow.

CHAPTER
TWENTY-SIX

THE SUN HAD YET TO TINGE THE HORIZON with pink the next morning when Gerard found himself standing outside the door of Lucy's cabin. Odd how he'd come to think of the cabin as hers, he thought. How would he bear reclaiming it when she had returned to her safe, tidy life in London? Would a hint of lemon verbena still cling to his counterpane and haunt his barren dreams?

He rubbed his beard with a weary hand, contemplating the door. He'd spent a sleepless night on deck, gazing at the winking lanterns of the *Argonaut,* but seeing only the wounded betrayal in Lucy's eyes, hearing only her muffled sob of anguish in the moment she had turned away from him.

Gerard had known when he had dictated those terrible threats that he'd never be forced to carry them out. The Admiral might care less for Lucy's well-being than she was willing to admit, but the man's sterling reputation was of paramount importance to him. He would not allow it to be tarnished by the scandalous downfall of his daughter.

Gerard knew only too well that society, in all of its perverse hypocrisy, would condemn Lucy, citing some inherent sensual weakness in her character that might provoke a pirate to ravish her. After all, they'd been blaming Eve ever since the spineless Adam had partaken of the apple she offered him.

By nightfall Lucy would be safely aboard the *Argonaut,* cradled once again in the blustering bosom of her father. A pain seized his heart, fierce and unexpected, but he willed it away with the same resolve that had enabled him to spend five years in darkness without going mad.

It wasn't as if he had any choice in the matter. Regardless of how hardily she'd adapted since her kidnapping, a girl of Lucy's delicate sensibilities could never be suited to life aboard a pirate ship. Snow's confession and letter of marque might acquit him of past crimes, but they lacked the power to absolve him of present sins. He had nothing to offer Lucy beyond the vagabond life of an outlaw, always one fleet-footed step ahead of the hangman.

He gave the door a gentle rap, then waited, glancing ruefully at the ledger in his hand. He doubted that he'd fare any better with a bouquet of roses or a foil-wrapped box of chocolates. Lucy was not a woman to be charmed by vain and sentimental gestures.

When there was no response to his knock, he opened the door and eased his way into the unwelcoming silence. As he'd expected, the bed was empty, the blankets undisturbed as if its occupant had risen early or never retired at all.

Lucy stood at the porthole, her lithe figure once again garbed in Tam's castoffs, her silky hair caught in two precise braids. Her gaze was riveted on the stark specter of the motionless *Argonaut*. There was no sign of the beautiful gown, no hint of the enchanting woman who had welcomed him with such warmth only last night. Gerard's breath caught with an aching sense of loss.

He cleared his throat with more difficulty than he would have admitted. "I'll have to confine you to quarters today. For your own well-being, of course."

He might have been addressing a statue. Or an ice sculpture, he amended, fighting an unreasonable flare of irritation.

He tossed her mother's diary on the table with less care than he'd shown since finding it. "I thought this might help you pass the hours. I found it in your father's strongbox. I haven't read it," he added, knowing she probably wouldn't believe him.

Her glacial contempt showed no sign of thawing. Gerard could almost feel his toes beginning to tingle with frostbite. He could not resist snapping off a mock salute at her unyielding back. "Good day, Miss Snow."

He was almost to the door when her soft reply came. "And a good day to you . . . Captain."

As he secured the bolt that would once again make Lucy his unwilling captive, Gerard only hoped he could bluff the Admiral half as well as he had bluffed the man's daughter.

♥　♥　♥

Lucy kept her weary body propped at the porthole long after Gerard had gone. She watched in numb misery as dawn unfurled its glimmering thread on the horizon, despising its seductive beauty.

The sea at dawn is a cathedral, Lucy.

The smoky warmth of Gerard's words stirred memories best left buried.

"Hypocrite," she muttered.

If the sea were a cathedral, Gerard was only too

eager to sacrifice her on its altar. Her traitorous heart lurched as a launch drifted into sight at the corner of her vision. Surely Gerard wouldn't be fool enough to deliver that damning missive himself.

Her heart steadied. With each rhythmic stroke of the oars, the newborn rays of the sun glinted off Digby's balding pate. He swiveled to give the *Retribution* a jaunty wave and a gap-toothed grin. Lucy found herself half wishing she was abovedeck to cheer him on. The elderly gunner's wiry arms propelled the sturdy craft with surprising strength, sending it cutting through the deepening blue of the water in a direct path to the *Argonaut*. A gull danced and dipped above his head, startling Lucy with the realization of just how near they must be to land.

When the tiny craft drew alongside the massive man-of-war to be engulfed by its shadow, Lucy turned away from the window, hugging back a frisson of dread.

The velvet-bound ledger on the table caught her restless eye. She hesitated, reluctant to approach Gerard's offering with anything resembling enthusiasm. The book had landed where he'd tossed it with a resounding thump, dislodging several of its yellowed pages. If he'd found it in her father's strongbox, it was probably nothing more than detailed notes on the Admiral's career or perhaps an impromptu collection of newspaper clippings immortalizing his military victories. A rush of contempt for her father's unrelenting vanity surprised her.

Her innate curiosity got the best of her. She brushed her fingers across the ledger's mildewed cover. A faint tingle passed from her fingertips to lift the tiny hairs at her nape. She drew the nearest scattered page toward her. The date inscribed at the top of the page read 26 May 1780. Lucy frowned, intrigued by the unabashed femininity of the flowing script, so unlike her own.

" 'I write this in English,' " she read aloud, " 'for it pleases him and pleasing him has become my one desire, my only yearning, the sole obsession of my poor, besotted heart.' "

The quaint words echoed in the deserted cabin. Once Lucy might have dismissed them as the trivial ramblings of a sentimental fool. But with her own heart so tender from its recent bruising, they resonated with the timelessness of truth, made all the more genuine by their girlish ardor.

She read on. " 'He is a hero, they tell me, a valiant warrior in his country's navy. I care nothing for that, but only for those grave, gentle smiles he bestows on me with such rarity.' "

Lucy's stomach twisted into a dull knot. She sank into a chair, thinking how ironic it was that she might have once written those very words herself. Her hands trembled with suppressed emotion as she gathered the delicate pages into a semblance of order, finally understanding that they were her last fragile link to the woman who had given her life, then left her to face it all alone.

♥ ♥ ♥

The noon sun boiled down on the *Retribution*'s deck, its relentless heat undiluted by even the whisper of a breeze. The glassy surface of the sea hung in eerie calm, just one more irritant to Gerard's frazzled temper. He paced the length of the quarterdeck for what seemed like the hundredth time, swiping away the sweat tickling his nape. His crew wisely stayed out of his path, knowing it wasn't anger provoking his savage mood, but apprehension.

His explosion of wrath came as predictably as the

toll of the bell ringing the next watch. "I should have never let him go. I should have gone myself."

Gerard knew Tam would alert them from the lookout at foretop the instant the launch was sighted, but he couldn't stop himself from snatching the spyglass from Kevin's hand. Patience had never been a particular virtue of his and it was even less so after losing five years of his life to Snow's treachery. He scowled at the undisturbed tranquility of the water between the *Argonaut* and the *Retribution*. There wasn't so much as a whitecap in sight.

"You gave him until sunset, sir," Apollo cautiously reminded him from his perch on the fo'c'sle.

Kevin's face had lost all traces of its puckish humor. His narrowed green eyes reflected a bitterness beyond his years. "I've played with him before, remember? He's bluffing, is all. Letting us stew in our own sweat. He'll come around, I'll wager. He hasn't any choice if he wants his daughter."

Gerard slowly lowered the spyglass. Kevin's words only colored his urgency with despair. Snow couldn't possibly want Lucy any more than he did, yet he'd be the one forced to surrender her when Digby returned with the Admiral's reply.

If Digby returned . . .

Not even the pounding heat could alleviate a shiver of pure dread at the grim prospect of sending another of his trusting crew to their death. Gerard returned the spyglass to his brother, still nagged by the one question that had haunted him ever since the *Argonaut* had sailed into view and dropped anchor.

A man of Snow's authority should have had the entire Channel Fleet at his disposal for a quest as exalted as rescuing his only daughter from a notorious criminal like Captain Doom. So why had the Admiral brought only one lone ship to their rendezvous?

Gerard steadied his sweating palms on the rail, praying his answer to that question wouldn't come too late.

♥   ♥   ♥

Admiral Sir Lucien Snow belched delicately, then dabbed at his lips with a linen napkin. "I do so hate to sup early. It wreaks havoc on my poor digestion."

As an apple-cheeked young yeoman whisked away the Admiral's plate, Smythe traversed the length of the shadowy galley to approach the table. He fought to keep his gaze from straying to the sheet of vellum shoved carelessly aside to make room for a decanter of the Admiral's favorite sherry.

"Permission to speak, sir?" he requested, the familiar setting stirring to life all of his dormant military instincts.

The Admiral looked mildly amused. "Permission granted."

Smythe shot a glance toward the far end of the galley, where Claremont's improbable messenger was being held at gunpoint by two bored lieutenants. The wiry little man's dour bravado was betrayed by the constant shifting of his feet and the nervous dart of his beady eyes.

Smythe braced his palms on the table, leaning forward to ensure the privacy of their conversation. "Sir, need I remind you that the sun is beginning to set? Every moment you delay places Miss Lucy in graver danger."

The Admiral took up a small silver knife and began to pick at his teeth. "And need I remind you, Smythe, that you've no one to blame for this debacle but yourself. After all, you're the one who led my solicitors on a merry chase while the man was working right beneath our noses. It's still beyond me how you failed to recognize the wretch!"

Smythe kept his face deliberately bland, knowing his employer would delight in using his own anguish and guilt as a weapon against him. "I'm not a young man anymore, sir. My eyesight isn't what it used to be."

"A pity, isn't it?" Snow tossed down the knife and pushed his bulk away from the table, his expression so calculating that Smythe regretted rousing him to any action at all.

He was painfully aware of the drowsy curiosity of the men scattered at ease throughout the galley. Officers handpicked by the Admiral for both their unquestioning loyalty and their discretion. Just as he had been.

As his commander circled him, Smythe could not resist snapping to attention. Old habits seldom died a bloodless death.

The Admiral lowered his voice to the compelling velvet of acting-Captain-as-God. Disagreement would be tantamount to mutiny. Or blasphemy. "What would you have me do, Smythe? Claremont cares nothing for gold and you know better than anyone that I have no letter of marque to give him."

Smythe kept his own voice just as low. "Perhaps a written confession, sir. If carefully worded and balanced against your many noble accomplishments, it might not do irreparable damage to your good name in the press."

"Ah, my reputation for Lucy's? Is that what you're proposing?"

Smythe's boundless patience began to fray. "Your reputation for Lucy's life," he snapped. "*That's* what I'm proposing."

The Admiral smiled as if gratified by his impassioned response. "Claremont won't kill her right away. If she's half as eager to please in bed as her mother was, he'll keep her alive. At least until he tires of her clever little tricks."

Smythe stared at him, stunned by his crass words. His hands balled into fists. Fists he longed to smash into the Admiral's smug face. But his own guilt paralyzed him. After all, it had been he and not the Admiral who had allowed his beloved Lucy to fall into Claremont's vengeful hands.

With a gesture of chilling finality, the Admiral crumpled the sheet of vellum outlining the pirate's demands. "I'm afraid there's only one course left open to me. You read the newspapers before we sailed—the veiled slurs, the sly innuendos. Our little Lucy has spent three weeks at the mercy of rapacious pirates. Her reputation is already in shreds." Smythe's horror mounted along with the wistful regret in the Admiral's expression. "Surely any woman who's endured what she has at Doom's debauched hands would choose a noble end over the disgrace of surviving such an ordeal."

Smythe's fist lashed out of its own accord, striking Snow across the mouth. "You heartless bastard!"

The Admiral staggered backward, knuckling blood from the corner of his mouth. Smythe lunged at him, but found himself restrained by a covey of Snow's minions, aghast that he had dared to strike their commander.

The Admiral's voice crackled with vicious satisfaction. "Take Mr. Smythe below and put him in chains. He seems to be suffering from some sort of brain fever, irreversible, I fear."

Smythe struggled wildly against the arms and legs that bound him. As if from a great distance, he saw the Admiral pick up the silver knife and test its blade against his thumb, heard his jovial voice call out,

"Come forward, Mr. Digby. I've a message for you to convey to your captain."

Smythe's howl of warning was cut off by the butt of a pistol striking his temple. Blossoms of light exploded behind his eyelids. His last coherent thought as they dragged him away was *I'm sorry, Annemarie. So bloody sorry.* Then softer than a sigh of regret escaping his weary lungs—*Lucy.*

CHAPTER
TWENTY-SEVEN

"CAP'N! CAP'N! THE LAUNCH! SAINTS BE praised, there she be!"

Tam's jubilant cry sent every hand aboard the *Retribution* rushing as one man to the starboard rail. With a resigned sigh, Kevin surrendered his spyglass to his brother, preferring its loss to the loss of his fingers.

Gerard squinted into the miniature telescope, brushing a ruffled lock of hair from his eyes. The wind had risen as the sun began its lazy descent into the sea, loosening the grip of the heat to a bearable embrace.

He didn't know whether to celebrate his triumph or mourn his coming loss. He'd never allowed himself to dream beyond this moment, which was just as well, for without Lucy, the future loomed as nothing but a bleak haze, as gray and frigid as the North Sea in winter. She would doubtlessly spend the rest of her life hating him, believing him so mercenary as to have sold her to her own father for thirty pieces of silver and a worthless scrap of paper. A bittersweet victory indeed.

A rousing cheer went up as the delinquent craft

drifted into view. It faded to pensive silence as the men, born sailors every one of them, detected something odd about the launch's course. Instead of slicing purposefully toward the *Retribution,* it bobbed aimlessly among the rising swells, tossed this way and that by the whims of the mounting wind. The lowest edge of the sun crimped along the horizon, staining the sea a bloody orange.

"She looks to be empty, sir! No sign of Digby."

Even before Tam's bewildered voice had sounded the alarm, Gerard had lowered the spyglass and given Apollo a cryptic signal. He watched with a sickening sense of dread as Fidget and Apollo lowered a second longboat into the choppy water. They threw their powerful backs into rowing, straining to catch the launch before the current could drag it farther out to sea. Tam swung down from the rigging to add his silent hopes to their vigil.

The second craft seemed to dwindle in size as it skirted the *Argonaut*'s shadow. His men's vulnerability beneath the hungry mouths of the warship's cannons chilled Gerard, but he was bitterly confident that the Admiral's vanity would insist his handiwork be appreciated before it was destroyed. Apollo held the longboat steady while Fidget snagged the smaller boat with expert skill, dragging it back toward the haven of its mother ship.

Something was lying in the bottom of the launch. From a distance, it looked to be nothing more than a bloody bundle of rags, but Gerard knew better.

He closed his eyes against a wave of numbing grief, opening them only when he heard Apollo's footfalls on the deck. His quartermaster stood before him, Digby's pale, limp body draped across his arms like a sacrificial offering. The naughty twinkle in the gunner's eyes had been permanently extinguished.

Pudge drew off his spectacles to swipe the fog from them with a scarlet kerchief. Tam snatched off his cap, mumbling a paternoster. Kevin bit off an oath that would have done the cantankerous old gunner proud. Only their captain remained utterly still, as soulless in that moment as the lifeless husk in his quartermaster's arms.

"A knife to the belly," Gerard said coolly, eyeing the protruding silver hilt. "Neither a quick death, nor a painless one."

Without so much as a flinch, he reached down and ripped away the paper secured by the blade. His men hovered nearer, but Gerard did not satisfy their curiosity by reading the words aloud. They were intended only for him.

All my life I have taken great pride in refusing to negotiate with men of your ilk. Nor will I begin now.

As Gerard crumpled the paper in his fist, the Admiral's priggish sneer rose before him. *Men of your ilk.* It should have been laughably absurd that the man insisted on clinging to his charade of righteousness. But Gerard Claremont had just lost his sense of humor.

As the sea extinguished the rays of the sun, eerie fingers of twilight swirled around him. He no longer dreaded the dark, but welcomed it, eager to surrender to its seductive embrace. With infinite gentleness, he reached over and closed Digby's sightless eyes for the last time, remembering when he'd done the same for his mother. What was one more death on a soul as damned as his?

When Gerard lifted his head, his crew recoiled involuntarily from his stark expression. "Perhaps the time has come to show the morally upstanding Snow just what a man of my ilk is capable of."

Impatient to ease their feelings of helplessness at Digby's death, his crew muttered agreement and exchanged eager nods. But instead of giving the command for battle as they expected, their captain started for the companionway, his swagger laced with the unbreachable authority of his position.

Kevin was the only one who dared to step into his path.

The brothers faced each other, both their similarities and their differences enhanced by their defensive postures.

"Don't do this," Gerard said softly. "She's not worth it."

Kevin's jaw jutted out much the way it had when he'd been five years old and refused to repent for peeking up the milkmaid's skirts. "I happen to think she is."

Gerard contemplated his baby brother through narrowed eyes. He'd never struck him and had no intention of doing so now. "Out of my way, mister," he barked. "That's an order."

The impersonal words cut deeper than any blow. Kevin recoiled as if he'd been slapped. "Aye, Captain," he spat with pure contempt, stepping aside to stand at rigid attention.

Gerard dropped through the companionway into the hold to find himself no longer pursued by shadows, but in glorious accord with them.

♥   ♥   ♥

Upon reaching the great cabin, Gerard didn't trouble himself with keys or bolts. He simply lifted his leg and shattered bolt and lock with one well-aimed kick.

Lucy looked up from her chair at the table, blinking as if she were too dazed to be alarmed by his peculiar method of entry. She had been reading by the lingering lavender of twilight, so caught up by the past unfolding between the pages of her mother's diary that she'd been completely oblivious to the drama occurring right outside the porthole.

Her big, gray eyes were luminous with recent tears. Gerard steeled himself against their damp-lashed beauty. His pity had died with Digby.

His violence spent for the moment, he eased the door shut on its battered hinges, affording them a measure of privacy. Lucy rose to face him, clutching her mother's diary to her chest. A thrill of satisfaction shot through him. This was no craven bully who hid behind nameless emissaries and took childish glee in browbeating women and gutting old men. This was a woman who boldly defied him each time he deserved it, whether for blowing smoke rings at her nose or for blindfolding her and kissing her insensible. Here at last was an opponent worthy of his mettle!

Lucy's chin had come up, her spine stiffened. Her eyes glittered with mute challenge. Gerard adored her reckless courage, had adored it from that moment in this very cabin when she had dared to engage him in a verbal duel of wits with her body and his soul as the spoils of battle.

As Gerard approached like a stranger from the shadows, the diary slid from Lucy's numb fingers to the floor. She stood her ground, refusing to be on anything less than equal footing with this man. An involuntary gasp escaped her as his face loomed out of the darkness. Its compelling planes had moved beyond mere handsomeness into an irresistible promise of satanic beauty, stripped of compassion and utterly devoid of conscience.

He cupped her cheeks in his palms, his fraudulent tenderness making her shiver with perverse yearning. "One scream would probably bring my entire crew charging to defend your virtue. Wouldn't that gratify you?"

"I remember a time not so long ago when one scream brought *you* charging to defend my virtue."

Her absolution for the one sin he had not committed came too late. His thumbs pressed lightly against her lips, warning her that he would tolerate no reminders of his days as her knight-errant. "It seems the Admiral doesn't care how I get my pound of flesh. Or from whom."

Lucy had expected no less. She bowed her head, but the Admiral's betrayal had lost its power to inflict mortal damage. She felt only a brief sting, a wistful grief for all the time spent dreaming dreams that would never come true. She'd been held in bondage just as Gerard had—for nineteen long years. Held hostage to the Admiral's whims, his vanity, his selfish determination to make her life a sacrifice for her mother's sins.

Well, Lucy Snow was done with sacrifices. What she did from this moment on, she did for herself. And for her future. She tipped her head back, giving Gerard the full effect of her haughty stare. "Have you come to ruin me then, sir?"

His hands dropped from her face as if scorched by her bluntness. She sauntered just out of his reach, knowing she'd been granted a brief reprieve, not a full pardon.

"I've never been debauched by a pirate before," she said, pressing her advantage. "How would you prefer to proceed? Shall I drop to my knees and plead prettily for my virtue?"

His gaze strayed to her moist lips. They tingled beneath his invisible caress. "That should do . . . as a start."

Lucy pressed the back of her limp hand to her brow. "Or shall I fall on the bed in a graceful swoon" —she shot him a naughty glance from beneath her lashes—"waking only after you've had your way with me, of course?"

He nodded thoughtfully. "An excellent suggestion. Although I'd prefer you to awaken *while* I was having my way with you."

His evocative drawl sent tendrils of heat curling through her veins, giving her the courage she needed to stride directly toward him, her arm drawn back as if to deliver a stinging slap. He caught her hand perfectly on cue, just as she had known he would, his grip un-yielding but without a trace of brutality.

She blinked up at him in guileless surprise. "I do hope I haven't offended you. I thought you might en-joy a show of spirit. A flailing about of the limbs, if you will, to give you an excuse to overpower me and dem-onstrate your superior strength."

Triumph surged through Lucy as Gerard's eyes darkened with grim bewilderment. Using her captive hand as a lever, he snatched her against him, wrapping his other arm around her waist. "What in the bloody hell are you trying to do, woman? Provoke me to mur-der?"

Lucy shook a loose tendril of hair out of her eyes. "Why should I have to provoke you? After all, you're the scourge of the North Sea, the enemy of all that is noble and good in humankind. Why, the very whisper of your name terrifies the hardiest of sea captains and chills virgins' blood to ice. I'm only asking you to prove your mettle, sir. To show me what caliber of villain you are."

Lucy's sharp, mocking words were at direct odds with her posture. Instead of recoiling from the hard, ruthless planes of his body, she melted against him, rubbing the softness of her breasts against his heaving chest with the gentle insistence of an affection-starved kitten. She canted her hips to cradle his own, almost faltering at the inescapable evidence of both his power and his need.

She had accused him of being a gambler, but she was about to issue the riskiest challenge of her life. She tipped her head back until her lips were only a breathless whisper from his. "Do your worst, Captain Doom."

His reaction was not what she'd expected. His hazel eyes flamed with jealousy. A frisson of lingering fear shot down Lucy's spine. Had she summoned a dangerous creature of darkness into her arms simply by saying his name?

His fingers bit into the worn cambric sheathing her back. "Is that who you want, Lucy? Your darling phantom? Captain Doom?"

She shook her head helplessly, reaching to touch his bearded jaw, but he caught her hand, blocking her caress with even more desperation than he had blocked her blow. "Who's going to make love to you tonight, Lucy? Me? Or Doom?"

Her voice trembled. "You."

"Who am I?" he whispered fiercely, as if her answer would determine the absolute truth.

She searched his face, knowing it capable of reflecting both cruelty and tenderness, cynicism and hope, the basest of hatreds and the purest of loves. He could call himself whatever name he chose, but she would never again see him as two separate entities. He was simply the man she adored, with all of the complicated strengths and flaws inherent to his character.

Her fingers curled gently around his own, softening his grip. She brought their linked hands to his cheek, rubbing the back of her hand against the beguiling prickle of his beard.

"Gerard," she confirmed. Then more softly, as if

the incantation could somehow banish all the harm they'd unwittingly done each other. "Oh, Gerard."

Gerard was paralyzed by the tenderness in Lucy's eyes. The loving acceptance of all he had been, all he was, all he would ever be. He felt as if she'd given him back something he had lost in those dark, dank years in that French prison by the sea. Something more elusive than just his name or his pride or even his freedom. She had told him at their first meeting that the soul was eternal, but he'd never really believed her. Until now.

He turned her hand, bringing it to his mouth to kiss each delicate knuckle in turn. Her eyes misted with emotion as he slowly lowered his lips to hers. He'd come to her seeking damnation only to taste salvation in the intoxicating nectar of her kiss. He drank of it deeply, its flavor made all the more potent by the risk she'd taken in offering it to him.

As soon as Gerard's lips touched hers, Lucy knew what had been absent from Kevin's stolen kiss. Tenderness. Longing. A passion so strong it made Gerard's powerful masculine body quake with want. Lucy remembered the exquisite care he had taken with her in the gatehouse, the selfless restraint that had given everything, but asked nothing in return.

She wrapped her arms around his lean waist and buried her face against his shirtfront, needing privacy for what she would say. "You don't have to take the time to . . . to seduce me. I know you've waited six years for this."

He cupped her jaw and gently tilted her face to his. His solemn gaze searched her features. "I've waited thirty-one years for this. For you."

For you, Lucy silently echoed. Not for some deft, buxom beauty who could ease his grudging celibacy with the elusive skills taught only by experience. But for her. Shy, awkward, inexperienced Lucy. His revelation endowed her with confidence, making her heart sing to the remembered melody of a Viennese waltz.

"Are you certain?"

His crooked grin laid her heart bare. "I've waited six years. I'll be damned if I'm going to rush you now."

As if to prove his words, he moved away from her to light the lantern. The sight of him enveloped in its tawny haze made Lucy's throat tighten with yearning.

For once, Gerard wasn't afraid of the dark, but entranced by the promise of the light. He wanted to bathe every curve and hollow of Lucy's luscious body in its revealing flame. He no longer wanted to come to her as a faceless phantom in the darkness, but to watch each nuance of pleasure flicker across her delicate features as she cried out his name in a plea for sweet release.

As Gerard began to disrobe Lucy, she stood utterly still, afraid to even breathe for fear of shattering the magic of his hands on her. His warm lips soothed her temple as he raked his fingers through her hair, scattering the taut braids. He slid each button of Tam's shirt through its mooring as if it were a ribbon of lace gliding through a silk chemise.

His hands drifted downward to the waistband of her breeches. His throaty words vibrated against her ear. "I liked you better in *my* breeches. I loved the thought of the fabric caressing you everywhere I couldn't." He reached around to cup one of her buttocks in his palm, giving it a provocative squeeze. "Here." He nuzzled two fingers of his other hand into the hollow between her legs. "And here." The coarse fabric abraded her, making her even more sensitive to his touch. She clung to him, gasping with raw pleasure.

Gerard's hands drifted over her once more, his

skills so refined that her clothing melted into nothingness. The cool air struck her fevered flesh, pebbling her nipples into throbbing buds that ached to be soothed by his tongue.

As the sham of Lucy's masculine garments fell away, Gerard had cause to regret his rash promise to woo her. He might have endured the pouting beauty of her pink-tipped breasts. Might have withstood the temptation of her narrow waist and gently flared hips. But when Tam's breeches slid down her slender legs to pool at her feet, his flesh surged against the constraints of his own breeches with a violence that made him groan.

Lucy Snow was blond.

Everywhere.

Not even in the vibrant fantasies that had sustained him through his sleepless nights at Ionia had he imagined such pale, flaxen perfection. He wanted to bury himself to the hilt in those ethereal curls. He dropped to his knees, burying his burning face instead against her beautiful breasts.

Lucy was alarmed by the ferocity of Gerard's grasp, his heartfelt groan. She sifted the unruly hair at his nape through her fingers, intrigued by its unfamiliar texture. "Are you all right? Have I hurt you?"

He strangled out a laugh. "Mortally, I fear." She shivered at the provocative scrape of his beard against the sensitive skin of her belly, the underside of her breast. "But I don't mind as long as I can die in your arms."

Her arms welcomed him as his heated lips drifted over the swell of her breasts. Had she honestly been fool enough to believe his tongue would soothe her? He wielded it with diabolical skill against her throbbing flesh, flicking and teasing until her nipples tingled and ached beneath his sweet torment. When they were both rigid and glistening with the balm of his ministrations, he claimed first one, then the other, suckling her fiercely until her thighs clenched in an ineffectual effort to douse the answering tongues of fire licking between them.

He stroked the backs of her knees and she collapsed against him, straddling his lap. Gerard wrapped his arms around her, unable to suppress a rumble of pure joy. "A naked, blushing, oh-so-proper Miss Lucinda Snow dumped in my unworthy lap. Have you checked the calendar? It must be Christmas."

"You don't deserve any gifts. You've been a very bad boy this year," Lucy mumbled into his throat, pressing against him to hide as much of her nudity as she could. Her shyness worked to her disadvantage. The contrasting textures of his clothing tantalized her bare flesh, making her writhe in frustration.

"Ah, but you've been a very good girl, haven't you? So there's no point in both of us suffering on my account."

With that devilish observation, he swept her into his arms and carried her to the bed. Without him, its opulent splendor had seemed lonely and forbidding. With him, its sensual promise of luxury was fulfilled. As they sank as one into its feathered depths, Lucy tugged Gerard's shirt from his shoulders, hungry for a taste of his golden skin.

Her open mouth glided down his throat to his collarbone, coming to rest against the circular ridge of scar tissue carved by her own hand. She pressed her lips to it with a soft sound of dismay.

"Don't," Gerard whispered, drawing her head up. "I deserved far worse. Let's just be thankful you have such dreadful aim."

"Oh, I've excellent aim," she confessed. "I just couldn't bear to stab you in the heart."

He pressed her palm to the beguiling warmth of his chest. She could feel his heart thudding against it. "You would have come up empty for you'd already stolen it."

As his lips leisurely caressed hers, Lucy's nimble fingers danced down the remaining buttons of his shirt, freeing him from its restraints. He rubbed his chest against the inviting softness of her breasts, his crisp whorls of hair both tickling and torturing her sensitive nipples. His husky groan mirrored her own breathless delight.

He sucked in a bracing breath as her adoring hands drifted lower as if to sculpt the flat, muscular planes of his abdomen, his lean flanks, hesitating only when they reached the waistband of his breeches. She might have let her curiosity overrule her bashfulness had he not captured both of her wrists in his panicked grip.

"Not yet, angel, or all my noble intentions will be for nothing. Let's not test my restraint, shall we?"

Gerard had no such similar qualms about testing *her* restraint. If she had thought the scrape of his beard against her belly beguiling, the prickle of it skating down the silk of her inner thighs maddened her to distraction.

She tugged helplessly at his hair, torn between delicious anticipation and mortification. "Please don't. You mustn't do such a wicked thing."

His warm hands splayed against her thighs, coaxing them apart. "Oh, but I must. Wasn't it you who so boldly invited me to 'do my worst'?"

His worst proved to be her sensual undoing. All of her inhibitions melted beneath the scorching heat of his mouth. His clever tongue taunted her, whipping her into a frenzy of indescribable pleasure. Her deep-throated moans seemed to be coming from the mouth of a wanton stranger. She arched off the bed in mute plea, and as reward, his blunt, graceful fingers joined the dance, stroking hard and deep the moist, throbbing places his tongue couldn't reach.

Lucy's entire body shuddered, caught in a delirium of ecstasy. When she finally collapsed from its throes, Gerard was there to catch her, to cradle her breathless, trembling body in his arms and kiss tears she could not remember crying from her flushed cheeks.

His eyes gleamed with fierce hunger as he laid her beneath him and eased his breeches from his hips. When she would have indulged her curiosity with a nervous peek, he cupped her face and kissed her deeply, giving her a tantalizing taste of her own fulfillment.

Gerard was afraid it would take little more than the caress of Lucy's eyes to finish him. It had taken every ounce of his control to come this far, and he was too near the edge to make any more reckless promises. He hadn't lied to her. For him, this wasn't like the first time in six years. This was like the first time ever, with all of its callow eagerness, its clumsy, self-seeking hunger.

Her eyes misted with blind need as he reached down to test her readiness for him. He'd hurt her enough in their brief acquaintance. He had no desire to compound his crimes with another, even more unpardonable, betrayal of her trust. His fears were unfounded. He'd never touched a woman as ready for him as she was. She fairly dripped with want. He groaned, rubbing his throbbing length in her luscious bounty as a precursor to his possession.

Her eyes widened with mingled shock and delight as he let her feel in remarkable detail what he had refused to let her see.

Biting back a smile at the charm of her innocence, he braced his palms against the bed and rose above her. He tried, but simply could not resist a glance downward to watch himself breach those damp, flaxen curls one exquisite inch at a time.

Lucy gasped with unexpected pain as her untried body strained to accommodate Gerard's persistence. She felt him hesitate, poised on the brink of paradise.

"It's all right," she assured him shakily. "Really it is. It's quite pleasant. I . . . l-like it."

He glowered down at her, his frown mocked by the pleasure-glazed sparkle of his eyes. "You're lying, you deceitful mouse. You don't like it at all. But you will," he vowed.

For the first time in their acquaintance, Gerard was as good as his word.

He withdrew slightly, surprising Lucy. She had expected to feel relief in his wake, but instead felt only a hollow emptiness that ached to be filled. She wrapped her legs around his hips, urging him deeper. He obliged her, then drew back again, making her whimper with disappointment.

"Oh, please," she whispered.

She could not find it in her heart to begrudge him his triumphant grin. "As you wish, Miss Snow. I live to serve you."

Serve her he did, using the copious nectar of her body to bury himself deep inside of her.

"Better?" he whispered, his own voice cracking under the strain.

Lucy's dreamy smile was all the encouragement Gerard needed. From the beginning he had sensed the passion boiling beneath her icy veneer and she did not disappoint him. As he rocked against her, she arched off the bed to meet him, the provocative motion of her hips enticing him to abandon his exalted plan to treat her virgin body with the tender care it deserved.

He threw back his head, clenching his teeth against a premature wave of ecstasy. "God, Lucy, do you know what you're doing to me?"

Lucy could feel something else seething beneath Gerard's patience—a violence born not of brutality, but of deprivation. Its intensity frightened her, but she was determined to give him a gift even greater than that of her innocence. Her permission to lose control, to slake all of his selfish desires on her willing body.

She had learned more of his character than he had wished her to in the past few weeks. He took care of his crew. He took care of his brother. And even if he would not admit it, he had taken care of her more often than not. The time had come for someone to take care of him.

She caught his face in her hands and said fiercely, "Don't hold back. Not with me. Never with me. I want everything you can give me."

To Gerard, it was as if Lucy's tender invitation opened up a sluice of tangled emotions. Lust seized him, so dark and primitive it was almost bestial. He ceased to think, becoming a creature driven by its basest instincts, instincts denied for so long that it took only Lucy's generous coaxing to send them raging beyond his control. He gazed at her as Adam must have first looked upon Eve, as if she had been created solely to indulge his desires.

And indulge himself he intended to do. But with his last shred of rational thought, he angled his hips so that each of his deep, hungry strokes would rub against the pleasure-sensitive nub sheltered by those entrancing curls.

Lucy pressed her eyes shut, giving herself over to his pounding rhythm as Gerard gave her everything he had. And more. He drove her back against the headboard, then kept coming, giving no quarter, taking no prisoners. When she thought her body had reached its endurance of pleasure, he cupped her backside and lifted her, embedding himself so deeply within her that she could feel his heart beat as if it were her own. A soft, broken wail escaped her, a herald of the exquisite outpouring of ecstasy to come.

Lucy's release was Gerard's downfall. He had no time to ponder the irony before his own body surged with long-denied rapture. As he'd feared, the end had come too quickly, but it seemed to roar on for a sweet eternity, their joined bodies shuddering in magnificent accord, Lucy's bewitching spasms milking him of every precious drop of pent-up pleasure.

His boneless body collapsed against hers. "Did I hurt you?" he murmured into her silky hair, awareness of their awkward position slowly dawning.

Her arms tightened around him, her gentle hands stroking and soothing his cramped muscles. "Mortally, I fear. But I don't mind as long as I can die in your arms."

Lucy tried to wiggle herself to a more tenable position; Gerard held her fast. "Oh, no, you don't. I'm not through with you yet." For once, his boyish grin was untainted by cynicism. "Hell, I haven't even started."

His lips lowered to hers for a kiss rife with all the tenderness she had forced him to forgo in their lovemaking. Lucy moaned at the fresh miracle of his body stirring deep within hers.

His heated lips strayed to her earlobe. She frowned. "Did you hear that, Gerard? It's thundering."

"Nonsense," he murmured, nipping the sensitive appendage. "It's just the pounding of my heart."

Lucy gasped with pleasure as his tongue plundered the inner shell of her ear. She closed her eyes only to be startled by a starburst of light behind her lids. "I do believe it's lightning as well."

"You flatter me, darling. Why don't we see if I can evoke a fanfare of celestial trumpets?"

His foray across the tender skin of her throat might have done just that had not the entire hold shuddered as if pounded by a mighty fist. The ship lurched, tossing them, blankets and all, to the floor of the cabin.

"Son of a bitch!" Gerard jumped to his feet, jerked his breeches up over his hips, and ran to the porthole.

Another clap came, sharper and more sinister than thunder. The mouths of the *Argonaut*'s cannons erupted in gouts of orange fire. The *Retribution* pitched to starboard, forcing Gerard to catch hold of the wall or fall.

"That son of a bitch," he breathed, the oath taking on a far more personal nature. "What sort of monster would fire on his own daughter? What manner of father is he?"

A sound even more unlikely than the rumble of cannons captured Gerard's attention. He turned slowly, disbelievingly. Lucy had cupped a hand over her mouth, but her high-pitched giggle escaped through her fingers. She looked so enchanting with her hair tumbled around her face, her skin still rosy from his robust loving, that it was inconceivable to him that her teasing offer to die in his arms might prove prophetic.

"I'm terribly sorry," she said, struggling to catch her breath. "I can't imagine what's come over me. I'm not usually so emotional."

Gerard's fear of losing her deprived him of any patience he might have summoned. He dropped to his knees and caught her by the shoulders. "Don't you understand what's happening? That miserable son of a—" He grappled for control, clenching his teeth against a wave of raw panic. "*Your father* is firing on us."

To his shock, she tossed back her head with a fresh burst of laughter, her beautiful eyes luminous with tears. "Ah, but there's the rub, you see, for that 'miserable son of a bitch' is not my father!"

CHAPTER
TWENTY-EIGHT

LUCY HAD IMAGINED A MYRIAD OF REACtions to her revelation, but the stark horror reflected in Gerard's eyes was not among them. He sank back on his heels, gazing at her in mute shock.

She supposed it was a bit late for modesty, but she drew the counterpane over her shoulders just the same and swiped a bothersome tear from her cheek. The attack had come too soon after their loving, leaving her with no defenses.

She forced a watery smile through her chattering teeth. "It seems Kevin and I have more in common than you thought. We're both bastards."

"How do you know that?"

"It's all in my mother's diary." Lucy sniffed, dabbing at her nose with the back of her hand. "The really tragic part is that she loved the Admiral just as much as I once did. But she finally had to accept that he would never return to her bed, that his interest in her had been nothing more than a brief infatuation, another conquest of the French. That's when she turned to other men. We should be celebrating, you know. I'm not the daughter of your enemy after all." She disguised the pain of the words with a flippant shrug. "I'm not anyone's daughter."

Lucy had thought herself privy to the most potent tenderness Gerard could offer, but his hands cupped her face with such reverence it was as if he could absorb her pain through his fingertips. A rumbling salvo of cannonfire rocked them.

His eyes darkened with dawning agony. "Dear God, what have I done?"

Then he was gone, snatching his shirt and leaving her shivering in the heap of blankets that still smelled of the spice of his skin and the musk of their coupling.

Wracked by chills, Lucy hugged the counterpane around her and stumbled to the porthole. The *Argonaut,* nearly obscured by smoke, belched another round of fire. Was the Admiral pacing the freshly swabbed deck, she wondered, bellowing orders in his stentorian voice? Orders that would reduce the *Retribution* and the woman he had given his name and raised as his daughter to splinters of wood and bone.

Anger surged through her veins, warming her. She had always believed that if she could only be good enough, her father would love her. But now that Gerard had given her an intoxicating taste of true love, she realized the Admiral was nothing but a petty tyrant, incapable of loving anyone but himself.

Lucy narrowed her eyes as the smoke cleared, its ugly columns dispersed by the rising wind. A full moon bathed the *Argonaut* in unholy light. The seventy-four-gunner sat motionless, poised to pounce on its helpless prey, the abrupt silence of its guns more ominous than a fresh barrage of cannonfire.

A terrible suspicion flickered to life in Lucy's mind. "No," she whispered. Then more loudly, "No!"

She dropped the blanket and snatched up Tam's shirt. The hem fell to her knees so she wasted no time wriggling into the breeches. She raced for the door, praying she wasn't already too late.

♥   ♥   ♥

This time the twists and turns of the *Retribution*'s hold failed to confound Lucy. Most of the lanterns had been extinguished by the ship's uneven pitching, but she plunged through the darkness with blind confidence, her love for the vessel's captain the only light she needed.

Within seconds she'd reached the mirror hiding the secret companionway. She pounded on it, but it refused to budge. Its hidden latch had been wedged shut by one of the *Argonaut*'s blows. Lucy collapsed against the cool glass, fighting her first impulse to weep with frustration. Instead, she shoved back the hair straggling over her eyes and glanced frantically around, finally locating a fallen timber small enough for her to lift. Without an ounce of remorse, she drew it back and smashed her reflection into a thousand fragments.

Heedless of its sharp edges, she swept the glass aside and scrambled up the ladder. She heaved open the trapdoor only to be engulfed in roiling smoke. She batted at it, coughing to clear her lungs. A pile of crippled sail dangled to her left, extinguished, but still smoldering.

She fanned the smoke from her stinging eyes only to have them fill with tears.

She was too late.

The flag of surrender rippled against the pallid circle of the moon, its grace a stark contrast to the charred destruction surrounding it. It was a measure of his men's faith in him that even as Gerard prepared to surrender their beloved vessel, not one of them protested. They stood silently on the battered deck, their heads bowed, but their shoulders unbent.

Lucy passed among them like a pale wraith. She knew she should be embarrassed by her flimsy attire, her tangled hair, the scandalous signs of Gerard's possession, but she had found among their ranks all the things the Admiral had taken such perverse pleasure in withholding—acceptance without judgment, affection without reproach, a nobility born not of birth or military stature, but of behavior.

She stopped in front of Gerard. Her low voice trembled with emotion. "You can't do this. Do you hear me? I won't allow it."

He stared right through her, as if he'd been struck both blind and deaf by the enormity of his actions. Seeing no help there, Lucy turned to Tam. His freckled face was stark white.

"You mustn't let him do this, Tam. I forbid it!"

The young Irishman gazed at the distant horizon, his hands fumbling with a battered string of rosary beads.

Lucy ran to Pudge. Her heart lurched to discover a fat crack running through the right lens of his spectacles. Somehow that was the worst affront of all. "Please, Pudge. Try to talk to him. Tell him he's making a terrible mistake." Pudge only shook his head sadly. "Is this what you ran away for? So that wretched wife of yours could watch you hang at Newgate?"

Dashing her tears away before they could blind her, she turned to Apollo. An ugly gash marred his temple. She clutched at his arm. "Oh, Apollo, dear Apollo, if anyone can stop him, you can! My father won't bring him to trial. He'll kill him. Now. Tonight. And he'll see the rest of you hanged or jailed. Is that what you want? To spend the remainder of your life in chains?" The former slave stood unmoved by her pleas, his features carved in stark ebony.

A lone man slouched against the quarterdeck rail. Lucy seized upon him with desperate hope, fighting hysteria. "Kevin! He's your brother! Surely you can make him see reason. Even if we surrender, the Admiral will find a way to silence me. He's realized that I know about his privateering scheme. I can discredit him. Destroy his precious reputation!" A thread of blood trickled from Kevin's fair hair. She brushed it from his brow with trembling fingers.

Kevin gently pushed her hand away, his wry, pitying gaze so like his brother's that it chilled her to the bone.

She pivoted on the deck, turning her beseeching gaze on each man in turn. Once she had stood in that very spot and demanded they betray their captain; now she would entreat them to spare his life. The wind whipped at her hair, tore the tears from her cheeks.

"Don't you see? He'll find a way to silence all of you. Why do you think he only brought one ship? Because he didn't want any bloody witnesses!"

She nearly collapsed with relief when a warm pair of hands closed over her upper arms from behind. At last, someone to help her make their captain see reason! But the voice in her ear *was* Gerard's, its rich cadences deepened by regret.

"I can't risk battle with you aboard. At least this way you'll have a chance. If the Admiral blows us out of the water, you'll have no chance at all. These men chose this life and, by consequence, this death. Even Digby had a hand in his own fate." He steered her to port, showing her not out of cruelty, but out of love, the grim, canvas-wrapped bundle lying limp on the fo'c'sle.

Lucy's knees faltered, but Gerard was there to support her as he had always been.

Grief roughened his grip as he drew her against him, shielding her from the wind. "You're not like them, Lucy. I dragged you away from your safe, orderly life and carried you aboard this vessel by force. You had no choice."

Lucy pulled away from the refuge of his grasp to face him. Determination banished her hysteria; her voice was as crisp as a bell ringing across the waves. "I'm choosing now. Don't do this. I'm not worth it."

Gerard threw back his head with a despairing laugh. His eyes shone with admiration and another, far more fragile, emotion, that robbed Lucy of her breath. "Oh, God, but you are, angel. You're positively priceless."

Hope flared in her heart. She fisted her hands in his shirt and shook him, her voice rising to a shout to combat the wind, the flapping of that terrible flag, and loudest of all, the smug silence from the *Argonaut*. "Then don't let him win, by God! Fight! *Fight for me!*"

CHAPTER TWENTY-NINE

GERARD GAZED DOWN AT THE DELICATE, but determined, fists tangled in his shirtfront. It seemed Lucy was no longer content to be the Admiral's puppet, but was willing to seize all of her hopes and dreams and shake them until they surrendered. She'd finally chosen him over the man she'd spent a lifetime believing to be her father. His enemy had become her enemy.

She'd proven herself willing to beg for him. Willing to fight for him. Willing to die for him. Could he offer her any less?

When he lifted his head, the familiar glint of resolve in his eyes caused a hopeful stir among his men. He called out, "What say you, gentlemen? Are we going to let this bold lady prove us all to be craven cowards?"

A rousing cheer went up from his crew.

"I'd say not, Cap'n," Tam yelled, his freckled face split in a wide grin. "If she's armed, we're all done for anyway!"

Squealing with joy, Lucy threw her arms around

Gerard's neck. He spun her around, lifting her clear off her feet.

Pudge whipped off a salute, his broken spectacles only adding to his roguish air. "Shall I withdraw the flag, sir?"

Gerard's gaze flicked to the rippling symbol of their capitulation. A wicked smile slanted his lips. "Not . . . just . . . yet."

Lucy recoiled in mock horror. "Why, Mr. Claremont, you wouldn't!"

He leered down at her. "I'm a villain, remember. I don't fight fair."

"Neither does he."

His smile faded at the somber reminder of all they were risking—his ship, these devoted men, that precious, tenuous emotion binding them in common accord. As he brushed his lips against hers, savoring her taste, his men each found a task to occupy their hands, some vital preparation for the battle to come.

His mouth hovered above hers, reluctant to break contact. "You're to go below and stay there. Don't come up no matter what you may hear."

"Is that an order, Captain?"

"Damn right, it is. And I expect to be obeyed."

Lucy took a step backward and snapped off a salute that would have made Smythe beam with pride. "Aye, aye, sir. I live to please."

Gerard chuckled, raking an appreciative gaze over her unconventional uniform. "That you do."

Lucy flew back into his arms for a final embrace. Her lips devoured his as if her kiss alone could infuse him with the strength he needed to face down the Admiral. Gerard rubbed her slender back, absorbing the essence of her right through his bones.

When she drew away to obey his order, his arms had never felt quite so empty.

♥　♥　♥

Lucy made it as far as the lower gundeck, where she found several gunners preparing for battle, and five powder monkeys, most still in their teens, arguing over who should be promoted to gunner now that their master was dead.

A willowy lad, his cheeks cratered with the scars of smallpox, stabbed a bony finger at the other boy's chest. "I'll be eighteen next month. The job needs a man, not some pimple-faced boy."

His companion's voice cracked with dismay. "You may be older, but I come aboard first. I been with the Cap'n since 'is maiden voyage."

As the others chimed in, the argument quickly disintegrated into a shouting match with each of them casting aspersions not only on the others' manhood, but on the marital status and temperaments of their respective mothers, a futile exercise since the majority of them were orphaned at birth.

"Gentlemen!" Lucy's unladylike bellow startled them into silence. "We haven't much time. Is this squabbling necessary?"

They gazed at her nervously, knowing the Captain's woman, though slight in appearance, was a force to be reckoned with.

Lucy softened her voice to the cajoling tones she'd frequently used on Sylvie's younger brothers when she needed them to fetch her shawl or some lemonade. "I'm sure Mr. Digby would have wanted you to settle this dispute in a reasonable manner."

They exchanged a baffled glance. *Reason* wasn't a word they'd associated with the cantankerous "Mr." Digby.

Lucy sighed. "Very well, then." She pointed to the only gunner who hadn't threatened to resort to fisticuffs to solve the dilemma. "You, sir, are promoted to gunner."

While his companions muttered in timid protest, the soft-spoken youth scratched his head. "Aye, but that'll leave us one monkey short. Who'll carry me shot?"

Eyeing the kegs of gunpowder and the eighteen-pound iron shot stacked like dragon eggs in the womb of the long, narrow gallery, Lucy smiled wanly.

♥ ♥ ♥

Jeremiah Digby might have treated the world at large with loquacious contempt, but he had showered affection on his beloved cannons. Their ebony barrels gleamed in the checkered moonlight streaming through the gunports as if polished by a lover's caress. Lucy had learned enough about the subtleties of piracy at Tam's feet to know that only in the most dire of circumstances, when all attempts at subterfuge had failed, would the captain actually give the command to fire them.

As she crouched beneath a gunport, watching the *Argonaut* plough through the inky billows in a direct course for their bow in preparation for boarding them, she was hard-pressed to imagine a circumstance more dire. The warship painted a silvery wake against the canvas of night, a shimmering highway to heaven. Or hell.

"Wot the bloody 'ell is 'e waitin' for?" one of the gunners muttered. "An invitation?"

Lucy might have echoed his sentiments had she been able to squeeze a word past the icy lump of dread in her throat.

Her stomach knotted in kind as the seventy-four-gunner swelled to monstrous proportions, blocking the moonlight, blocking the sky. The gundeck was swallowed by darkness, its sputtering lanterns casting more shadows than light.

"Do something," she whispered. "Anything."

As if to fulfill her reckless wish, the narrow oak gallery listed to port with a grinding creak, sending them all careening across the sand-sprinkled floor. Lucy caught the barrel of a cannon before it could swing around and smack her insensible. Groping for handholds, she staggered back to the starboard gunport, dropping to her knees to compensate for her lost equilibrium.

Her foresight cheered her. Now she would have far less distance to fall when she collapsed in her death throes. For it seemed that Gerard had unfurled every remaining scrap of sail and set them on a collision course with the *Argonaut*.

"Christ, the Cap'n's gone balmy," a scrawny boy breathed, suddenly looking more the fifteen he was than the seventeen he'd claimed to be to gain a coveted berth aboard the *Retribution*.

Lucy threw one arm over the nearest cannon to brace herself for impact. She longed to close her eyes, but couldn't drag them away from their imminent destruction. A curious exhilaration seized her, tempering her terror. At least Gerard would die not at the whim of others, but standing proudly at the helm of his ship, master of his own fate. Tears of pride burned her eyes, fierce and hot.

They sliced through the indigo water toward the massive warship, so close she could see the tiny figures scrambling in panic on its deck. It was too late for the *Argonaut* to negotiate a retreat or even a turn. Its sail pattern was too complex, its lumbering weight too awkward. Its very might damned it to ruin.

But not so the *Retribution*. Just prior to impact, just before that fatal instant when the scream building in

Lucy's throat would have erupted in blind terror, the sleek, graceful schooner swung about, raking down the *Argonaut*'s hull with a hideous scrape that made Lucy want to clap her hands over her ears. The risky maneuver was not without cost. Somewhere abovedeck, a mast snapped with the macabre crack of splintering bone.

Like a bellow of pain at the needless destruction of something precious came a mighty roar. *"Fire!"*

Lucy gaped at her new compatriots, wondering if her own expression was as comical as theirs. Realization dawned in a flash of gunpowder. Gerard's brilliant, if dangerous, maneuver had enabled the smaller, lighter ship to come in *under* the warship's guns, rendering the pride of the King's fleet as helpless as a kitten without its claws. Gerard might be risking damage to his own vessel by firing at such chilling range, but it was a risk carefully calculated and weighed against the odds.

They might have stood frozen that way forever were it not for the booming eruption of a quarterdeck cannon and an exasperated shout Lucy recognized only too well. "Halloo! Is everybody asleep down there?"

The gunners and monkeys scrambled as one to begin the steps of the complicated minuet that would start their cannons firing in synch.

As he touched the hissing match to the first fuse, one of the gunners gave a jubilant crow. "This one's for Digby, ye bloody bastard!"

The cannon roared in response. Lucy rather thought Mr. Digby would approve of the tribute.

Time stumbled to a halt in the narrow gallery, reduced to the stench of burning gunpowder, the deafening thunder of the cannons, and the protesting shudders of the *Retribution* at being caught too near to her prey. Lucy lost count of the number of times she staggered back and forth across the pitching floor, her arms aching beneath the weight of an iron cannonball or a keg of gunpowder.

Smoke burned her eyes; heat scorched her fingers; powder blackened her arms and hands. Yet still she pressed on, driven by the sheer exhilaration of battle. After a life wasted on surrender, she'd finally discovered someone worth fighting for.

Like David pounding Goliath with nothing more than a slingshot and a rock, they pumped shot after shot into the *Argonaut*'s hull. Lucy was hefting another ball and stumbling blindly toward the gunports when one of the gunners caught her by the arm.

His lips moved with dizzying haste. Lucy frowned up at him, both dazed and baffled. Her ears crackled with an annoying whine, but she couldn't decipher a single word he was saying. Realizing her dilemma, he pried the cannonball from her cramped fingers and gently led her to a gunport.

The *Argonaut* was retreating with nary a shot fired from her massive cannons.

The gunners and powder monkeys leaped around like young colts, slapping each other on the back in congratulations. Lucy would have loved to join in their celebration, but she suddenly discovered she was so exhausted she could barely remain on her feet. Smothering an enormous yawn, she crawled over to collapse against the bulkhead, using her folded hands as a pillow.

That was precisely where Gerard found her over six hours later.

It had taken him until dawn to bring his crippled ship limping into the balmy bay of an uncharted island off the coast of Tenerife. Turning command over to Apollo, he had dragged his weary body to the great cabin, his exhaustion lightening at the cozy image of

Lucy curled up in his bed, tousled by sleep and eager for his touch.

Finding the cabin abandoned and the rumpled bed-clothes on the floor exactly as he'd left them, he'd combed the ship from bow to stern, growing sicker with worry each passing moment.

When he finally strode onto the lower gundeck to discover the limp bundle crumpled against the bulk-head, his heart stopped.

Alarmed by the sudden drain of color from his captain's face, one of the powder monkeys rushed forward, still clutching the bottle of whiskey that had kept him company after his mates had passed out from a surfeit of rumfustian and excitement.

"She's wore out, sir. And well she should be. She did a capital job last night." The lad's bleary eyes gleamed with admiration. "Done ye right proud, she did."

Gerard's heart resumed its rhythm, if at a slightly brisker pace than before from trying to absorb the shock. The man Lucy had believed to be her father for nineteen years had just tried to murder her, but instead of collapsing in hysteria, she had plunged eagerly into the fray, fighting at Gerard's side as surely as if she'd been leaping about the quarterdeck with a cutlass between her pearly teeth.

He sank to his knees beside her, counting each precious rise and fall of her chest beneath the tattered shirt. He smoothed back her tangled hair. At the sight of her grimy little face, blissfully serene beneath its mask of gunpowder, tenderness seized him, intensified by a damning wave of guilt at the jeopardy his selfish vendetta had placed her in.

She had taught him how to smile again with that odd combination of haughty dignity and childlike innocence his jaded heart found so endearing. She had banished his fear of the dark with her reckless courage. She had reminded him, against his stubborn will, that there was something in this corrupt world of more value than vengeance.

And how had he repaid her? By rejecting her, betraying her, purchasing a one-way passage to certain doom and dragging her along for the voyage. Going out of his way to make her feel he wanted nothing more from her than her lithe, supple body to warm his bed. He wondered bitterly which one of them he'd been trying to convince.

He touched his finger to the tip of her nose. It came back smudged with grit. She didn't belong in the dank hold of a pirate ship, he thought despairingly. She belonged in some elegant London drawing room, serving tea to a bevy of wealthy admirers. His gaze traveled to her cracked and blackened fingernails, her scorched knuckles. Before he'd invaded her life, her delicate hands had been sheathed in immaculate gloves, her milky complexion shielded from the sun by a lacy parasol, her cheeks tinted by rice powder, not gunpowder.

What in God's name had he done?

Her eyes fluttered open, softening to misty welcome at the sight of him.

Gerard's relief was so acute that he wanted to choke her. He clasped her to his breast, burying his lips in her smoke-scented hair. "You bloody little fool! What possessed you to stage such a lunatic stunt?"

Still half asleep, she snuggled against his chest as if rooting for truffles. Her complacency only increased his frustration.

He held her away from him until her limp head fell back. "When I asked you to go below, I didn't mean to the bloody lower gundeck."

She blinked up at him. "Huh?"

"Don't play the innocent with me. You knew exactly what I meant."

"What?"

"And stop shouting! If you think you can distract me with your bellowing, wench, you've got another think coming."

Humbled by how close he had come to losing her and saddened by the grim knowledge that he would lose her anyway, Gerard drew her to him in a fierce hug, determined to cherish her warmth, her solidity for as long as he dared. He showered kisses on her face, not caring that she tasted of gunpowder and sweat.

Since she couldn't understand a word he said, Lucy should have been alarmed by Gerard's bizarre behavior. She'd never seen his face quite that shade of scarlet. But as far as she was concerned, he could go on scolding her forever as long as he kept punctuating his harangue with such tender embraces and delightful kisses.

She sighed with drowsy contentment as he swept her into his arms and carried her from the hold. His exhausted, exhilarated crew wisely hid their furtive smiles and knowing winks at the spectacle they made. Gerard's lips never stopped working, not even when he plunged into the shallow waters of the bay, still cradling her in his arms.

He marched through the water, ignoring the rosy dawn blushing the sky, until they reached a narrow inlet, sheltered from view of the ship by a throng of swaying palms. Only then did he set her on her feet.

The hem of Tam's shirt ballooned on the surface of the water. Lucy stood in dumb confusion as Gerard alternated between smothering her brow with kisses and shaking her by the nape as one would chastise a disobedient spaniel. She peered intently at his beauti-

fully chiseled lips. He seemed to be repeating the same
thing over and over.

She was shaking her head to indicate she didn't understand when her ears cleared with a resounding pop.

"—love you, dammit!"

She flinched at the volume of his desperate bellow.

Disbelieving wonder flooded her, warmer even than
the gentle swells that cradled them. Her toes curled
into the sandy ocean floor. "You do?"

Her tentative whisper seemed to jolt him back to
sanity. His brow crumpled, his expression suddenly so
vulnerable, so inexplicably miserable, that Lucy had
the absurd desire to comfort him, to reassure him that
it was all an unpleasant dream or a tropical fever. His
love for her was nothing that couldn't be cured by a
piping hot cup of coffee and a strong dose of cinchona
bark.

"For God's sake, stop looking at me like that!" he
shouted. "You're exhausted. You need food, drink,
and rest. But if you keep looking at me like that, I'm
going to make love to you again. Thoroughly," he
barked in afterthought.

Lucy's hearing had been restored with such acuity
that she could hear the surf whispering against the
shore, the warbling cry of some exotic bird, the desperate cadences of Gerard's breathing.

"I know what I need more than any of those
things," she said softly.

"Some common sense?" he offered.

She slipped the first button of Tam's shirt from its
mooring. "A bath."

Even a less rational man than Gerard could find no
argument with that. He groaned as the shirt slipped
from her shoulders to reveal her rose-tipped breasts,
their pale perfection even more beguiling in contrast to
the sooty streaks marring her arms and throat.

He staggered toward her, drunk with desire. His first urge was to seize her into his arms, but instead, he scooped water into his cupped hands and dribbled it over her gently rounded shoulders. It trickled between her breasts in lazy rivulets, beaded into molten diamonds on her nipples, tempting him to lean down and flick them away with his tongue. Her hands clutched at his hair; her head fell back, ceding her body and her heart to his tender dominion.

As the sky melted from misty pink to gold to a crisp, dazzling blue, they bathed each other's battle-weary bodies in shimmering cascades of warm water, shivering with want when their open palms and questing fingers lingered in some sweet, forbidden place.

Gerard had told Lucy that the nights were hotter where they were going, but he'd failed to warn her about the mornings. When his fingers delved beneath the water, sliding in and out of her in a sinuous promise of delights to come, her body ignited in a fever hotter than the fiery ball of the sun ascending in the sky. Her legs drifted upward, wrapping around his lean hips in languid invitation.

This time Gerard was determined to prolong their pleasure, to woo her luscious body, still tender from his eager possession of the previous night, with every erotic skill at his jaded disposal. Water streamed from their melded bodies as he carried her ashore, laying her on a sugary bed of sand. He stood back, dragging off the clinging remainder of his clothing with impatient hands, his hungry gaze locked on Lucy's parted lips. Her dewy skin was the same ethereal pink as the inner curves of the broken shells scattered around his feet.

Lucy's mouth went dry at the sight of Gerard's sun-gilded body. The first time they'd made love, he had denied her the pleasures of exploration, but the uncompromising morning light made it possible for her to appreciate him with an artist's eye for sheer masculine beauty. In her innocence, she had once thought that sunlight showed him to his best advantage, but she'd never dreamed just how spectacular that advantage was.

She cried out in involuntary empathy as he peeled off his stockings to reveal ankles banded by thick rings of scar tissue. Their gazes met, hers questioning, his faintly defiant, as if expecting her to recoil in distaste. She realized that while Apollo might display his scars as badges of honor, Gerard still considered them emblems of shame. His chains might be broken, but he'd yet to be freed from their shadow.

She rose to her knees, gently bathing the sand from his scars with the dripping tendrils of her hair. She continued her tender ministrations, gliding her hands up the back of his calves to muscular thighs, lightly dusted with hair. A broken sound escaped his throat, half gasp, half groan, emboldening her to pursue her rapt exploration. When both of her hands failed to encompass the steel-sheathed-in-velvet perfection that throbbed so exquisitely to her caress, she touched her tongue shyly to its tip.

Pleased beyond rational speech at her unspoken acceptance of his imperfections, her beguiling boldness, Gerard seized her by the hair, tilting her head back. Her eyes were luminous; that naughty, elusive dimple had reappeared in her right cheek.

"Miss Snow," he choked out, "if you don't learn to curb that inquisitive tongue of yours, this may be over for you before it's begun."

Laying her back on the altar of sand, Gerard worshipped her body in kind with exquisite patience, its creamy folds and vulnerable hollows his own private temple of delights. His deft hands nuzzled and stroked her, drizzling her melting core with its own succulent honey until she was ripe and quivering for his possession.

Lucy moaned in anticipation as Gerard's shadow blocked the sun. Not even his painstaking anointing could prepare her for the delectable shock of his rigid length sliding into her, filling her to the brim with each hard thrust. As if that wasn't sensual torment enough, he reached between them and rubbed his thumb against her damp curls until thick, pulsing throbs of ecstasy enveloped her, not once, not twice, but three breathless, magical times.

As Lucy cried out his name in a bewitching incantation, Gerard's own release came with a bittersweet force that shuddered him to the soul.

They drowsed in the sun for an eternity, their bodies entwined, their hearts slowing to some semblance of normal rhythm.

"I loved you from the first moment I met you," she whispered.

"What romantic balderdash!" he mumbled into her shoulder. "You detested me. I was an insufferable boor. On both occasions, I might add."

She combed her fingers through his tousled hair. "You still are. But I don't love you any less."

His arms tightened around her. The urgency in his embrace chilled her despite the heat. She shook off her foreboding. Perhaps at last her patience was to be rewarded by a tender declaration of love, a promise of undying devotion.

"God, I'm ravenous. I can't remember the last time I ate." Gerard sat up, briskly brushing away the sand that clung to his sweat-dampened skin like flecks of gold sugar.

Lucy frowned, feeling rather bereft as he tossed her his own shirt and tugged on his breeches, refusing to meet her eyes. As she fastened the shirt over her nakedness, Gerard moved to stand at the edge of the foaming surf, staring out to sea with his hands on his hips. Lucy wondered if he was thinking of his ship, scorched and lamed just beyond those palms.

The balmy wind toyed with her hair. She hugged her knees, besieged by wistfulness. "I wish we could stay here forever."

"Romping naked in the waves like Adam and Eve?" At first, Lucy thought he was making sport of her, but when he turned, his eyes were dark, devoid of amusement. "Even in Paradise, there was a serpent."

"The Admiral." It was a statement, not a question.

He nodded. "Tenerife isn't quite the haven for pirates that it was a hundred years ago. It's only a matter of time before he returns with more ships, more men, more guns. Before, I was only guilty of thievery and a bit of mischief, but by forcing me to fire on a British naval flagship, he's ensured I'll be branded a traitor and hunted down as a dangerous fugitive. They won't stop this time until I'm dead."

His grim resignation brought her to her feet. "Then we'll go somewhere else. Somewhere safe. To the ends of the earth if we have to."

He shook his head sadly. "Columbus proved the earth is round, dear. No matter how far you sail, you always end up right back where you started from."

"Oh, God," she whispered. "You're taking me back, aren't you?"

His silence was answer enough.

Blinking back a treacherous rush of tears, she threw her hands up in the air. "That's bloody rich, isn't it? What a capital idea! You can deliver me right to my father's doorstep. I just can't help but wonder how long it'll be before I succumb to a nasty tumble down the stairs or a bad bit of kipper."

"I'm not taking you to your father. I'm taking you to Smythe. He'll know what needs to be done to protect you. He's a man who can be trusted."

Lucy averted her face, afraid he was astute enough to read her bleak suspicions. She was rapidly losing her battle with the tears. They trickled, hot and bittersweet, down her cheeks, prompting her to dash them away before she faced him again.

"That's just fine, Gerard Claremont, you take me back. Not every man in the Royal Navy is as corrupt as my fa—"—she faltered, closing her eyes briefly to compose herself—"as corrupt as Lucien Snow. There must be good men among their ranks. Men who will listen to reason. I'll find them and I'll clear your name, by God, if I have to go to the bloody Lord High Admiral himself!"

Gerard crossed the sand, catching her roughly by the shoulders. His face was taut with helpless pain. "You'll do nothing of the sort! Unless you want to get your pretty little ass tossed in Newgate for aiding and abetting a wanted criminal and for suspicion of treason against the British government. Do you know what they do to women of your ilk in a place like that? Of course, if the Admiral gets wind of your inquiries before the authorities do, you won't have to worry about it. He's already proved to what lengths he'll go to silence you."

"What the bloody hell am I supposed to do then?" she yelled, belatedly thankful to the dearly departed Mr. Digby for providing her the vocabulary to have this absurd conversation. "Sit around on my pretty little ass knitting stockings until you come back for me?"

All traces of anger fled his face, banished by poignant regret, imbuing Lucy with a knowledge more painful than anything she might have imagined. His face blurred before her eyes. Her knees crumpled. Instead of catching her, he gently lowered her to a kneeling position in the sand, brushing his hand lightly over her hair, his touch rife with pity for both of them.

Had Lucy been able to make herself believe, even for the space of a heartbeat, that he didn't love her, that he had only used her, then cast her aside after his sensual curiosity was satisfied, she might have begged right there on her knees, might have fought for a future with him.

But she knew better. Gerard Claremont was one of those rare men capable of doing the job that had to be done, regardless of the cost. So all she could do was watch him turn his back on her and walk away down the deserted beach, his gaze riveted on the sea he loved as if seeking solace in her azure arms.

CHAPTER
THIRTY

AN ICY BLAST OF WIND SKATED ACROSS the frothy whitecaps, stirring the cauldron of the North Atlantic into a forbidding witch's brew. It sliced through the coarse wool of Lucy's peacoat, but she didn't even shiver. She'd grown accustomed to its bitter caress, preferring its bleak honesty to the warm, cozy deceit of a cabin that promised shelter, but left her heart exposed until it was raw and bleeding.

A thin layer of ice coated the forward rail where her bloodless fingers rested. She wished for nothing more than a commensurate numbness, but perversely enough, she seemed to have lost her ability to blunt her emotions. She hurt all the time now, a dull, hollow ache in the pit of her stomach. Yet since that day on the beach at Tenerife, she had failed to shed a single tear except for those whipped from her eyes by the relentless wind.

After the sunny skies and azure seas of the Canary Isles, she found the gray skies and leaden billows of the North Atlantic soothing to her raw senses. She stood stiffly at the rail as daylight faded into twilight, measuring the seamless passage of another day.

Gerard was determined to return her to London before the Admiral had time to sic his sea dogs on them. Laboring beneath his curt instructions, it had taken the crew of the *Retribution* less than three days to make their mistress seaworthy for the voyage. To chop and fit a new foremast, to swab her decks of the charred consequences of battle, to repair the shredded black gown of her sails. To bury her salty-tongued master gunner in the sandy soil that had welcomed so many of his kindred seafarers.

In those three days and in the two and a half weeks that had followed, Gerard had kept himself aloof from her. If they happened to meet on some narrow stretch of deck or brush past each other in the shadowy belly of the hold, he would inquire gently as to her well-being, then excuse himself, averting his eyes as if fearing they might confess what his lips could not.

The crew had taken their cue from him, growing even more subdued as they neared the mouth of the Channel. Tam's youthful exuberance and Kevin's rakish charm were muted by a pall of dejection. Apollo's lilting island melodies were supplanted by wistful spirituals that sang of a home never to be reached in this pilgrim lifetime. Lucy supposed they would miss their funny little "pet" when she was gone, but after a while they would forget her. Perhaps their captain would get them a pig.

She was still standing at the rail, bathed by the pale globe of the moon, when the *Retribution*'s sleek bow ploughed into the choppy waters of the Channel, her lanterns extinguished at her captain's command for silent running.

The miasma of gloom hanging over the ship was disturbed by a commotion at port. Lucy tried not to care, but the ship had truly seemed a ghost ship in the past few days and any sign of life was a diversion.

She ducked beneath the foreboom to discover Apollo and Gerard standing at the port rail and Kevin lounging against the foremast shrouds as if they were a hammock. Her heart quickened at the sight of Gerard's broad shoulders silhouetted against the night.

"Thought you might want a look at this, Captain," Apollo said, handing him a spyglass.

Lucy had no need of a spyglass to see a flash of orange fire in the distance, vivid and shocking against the murky canvas of the night.

"As far as I can tell," Apollo offered as Gerard surveyed the scene, "it appears to be a Royal Navy frigate, under fire from two French privateers."

"Pirates, you mean," Lucy said grimly, joining them at the rail. "We haven't been at war with France since the Peace of Amiens was negotiated. They're probably Napoleon's minions, masquerading as common thieves."

Gerard maintained his enigmatic silence.

"I vote we throw in with the French," Kevin suggested brightly. "When has His Majesty's navy ever done us any favors?"

Without a word, Gerard handed the spyglass to Lucy. Their eyes met briefly as their fingers brushed, the most intimate contact they had enjoyed since that day on the beach in Tenerife. Lucy brought the tiny telescope to her eye, granting him his wordless request.

The hapless frigate was taking a brutal pounding beneath the guns of the twin square-riggers. As Lucy watched, a spectacular broadside tore a jagged rip in the fabric of her stern. The roiling smoke cleared; another blaze of cannonfire illuminated the modest man-of-war's familiar figurehead. Lucy gasped in dismay.

"What is it?" Gerard murmured.

She lowered the spyglass, turning her frightened gaze on him. "The *Courageous*. Lord Howell's ship. He requested command of her after his victories at Copenhagen. He wanted to patrol the Channel so he could spend time writing his memoirs and getting to know his children again."

Apollo bowed his head.

Dread seized her, its icy grip tightened by images of Sylvie throwing her slender arms around her papa's neck; little Gilligan riding him like a pony, his plump, jam-smeared hands curled in the Earl's graying hair; Lord Howell lining up his boisterous sons to teach them to knot their cravats. Now that Lucy had no father of her own, the prospect of losing such a splendid one was too tragic to contemplate.

"His children," she echoed, oblivious to the effect of her imploring words on Gerard.

He pried the spyglass from her tense fingers. "Cannons?" he snapped.

She shrugged helplessly, not seeing how the armament of the doomed ship could possibly matter. "Twenty? Twenty-five?"

"Crew?"

"Over a hundred."

Kevin sprang out of his comfortable seat as if someone had touched a lit fuse to the impeccably polished toes of his boots. "Not another word, sweeting. Don't encourage his lunacy. Can't you see what he intends to do?"

As Lucy met Gerard's wry gaze, she knew exactly what he intended to do. And what it might cost him.

She clenched the rail as her desperate gaze shot to the distant battle. Even from this distance, she could see the *Courageous* was faltering. It would be only a matter of minutes before the French boarded her, stripping her of booty before she sank without a trace into the icy arms of the sea.

Every man is master of his own fate.

Her own words haunted her. This might be Gerard's last chance to fulfill his dream of serving country and king. A dream he had cynically forsaken after it had been tarnished by the corruption of men who served only their own greed.

She knew deep in her heart that she would never be able to divert him from his course and she wasn't about to lower herself in his eyes by trying. If he was the sort of man who could sail blithely past the *Courageous,* ignoring her distress, he wouldn't be the man she loved.

Warned by the fierce glint of pride in Lucy's eyes, Kevin staggered back against the rigging, swearing in defeat.

Lucy clicked her heels together and lifted a hand to her brow in a formal salute. "Powder Mouse Snow, sir, reporting for duty."

♥   ♥   ♥

The phantom ship melted out of the night in eerie silence, her silk sails billowing like the raven wings of an avenging angel. Tendrils of mist enveloped her deserted decks on a night when there was no mist. Her graceful rigging glistened silver in the moonlight, a deadly web of destruction.

At her inevitable approach, a handful of French unfortunates threw themselves overboard, preferring certain death to the specter of the unknown.

Later, many of the more superstitious French sailors would swear to their skeptical, but intrigued, First Consul that it was not a single ship, but an entire fleet of demon ships, spawned from the docks of hell by a Satan jealous of Napoleon's ambitions to conquer what had been promised to him—the world. Their suspicions were reinforced by the terrible swiftness with which the sleek raptor swept down upon them and the chaos that ensued.

Their British prey forgotten, the square-riggers reeled in a desperate attempt to escape the inescapable. They careened through the waves, trapped in a vortex of their own terror. The relentless ghost ship sliced between them with only inches to spare, gliding so swiftly and so soundlessly that by the time a panicked gunner could get off a shot, it had vanished from sight.

The errant cannonball smashed into the rigging of its sister ship, shredding her topsail. The ships collided, shattering the abrupt silence with the protesting wail of splintering oak.

Before the phantom ship could rematerialize, and heedless of the further damage they did to their vessels in their haste, they disentangled themselves and made for the far horizon and France without so much as a backward glance.

To the Englishmen aboard the rapidly sinking *Courageous,* who had already been making peace with whatever God they served, the reappearance of the phantom schooner was received with mixed emotions of delight and dread. The shadow of her bow fell over them, followed by a grim creaking, as if the rusty gates of heaven were being thrown open to receive repentant sinners.

They stood knee-deep and shivering in the frigid water, wondering if they would live to tell their grandchildren of the *Retribution*'s miraculous intervention. Did she represent salvation or damnation for their battle-weary souls?

As if in answer, a rope ladder unfurled from the heavens, smacking into their upturned faces. They snatched at it with grateful hands, not caring for the moment whether they were climbing to meet a loving or a vengeful God.

♥ ♥ ♥

"I can't believe you're doing this. Have you lost your bloody mind?" Kevin muttered out of the corner of his mouth, his jaw rigid with disapproval.

"I haven't much choice," Gerard hissed in reply, watching from the fo'c'sle as the pale, sodden sailors filed aboard a deck already crowded with the somber members of his own crew. "After taking such pains to rescue them from the French, it would have been a bit ill-mannered to let them drown, don't you think?"

Kevin returned a sulky shrug, but Gerard knew his brother wasn't as bloodthirsty as he appeared to be. He was just half out of his mind with worry. For him.

Gerard was seized by a similar insanity as Lucy emerged from the hold. He had expressly forbidden her the lower gundeck, fearing it might come into use, but from the smudge of grime on her nose and her guilty expression, it appeared she had managed to wiggle her way into some sort of mischief after all.

He started toward her, desperate to shield her from the wildly curious stares of their new passengers, but a jubilant cry stopped him in his tracks.

"Lucy! Lucy, my girl, is that you?"

Like the exceptional commander he was, Lord Howell had chosen to be the last man to abandon his foundering vessel. As a consequence, he was soaked all the way to the trailing ends of his gray hair. As his men half assisted, half dragged him over the starboard rail by the braid of his uniform, he sneezed heartily, then shoved their clinging hands away to stagger across the deck to Lucy.

Lucy quaked at the blunt shock of emerging from the hold only to be enveloped in Lord Howell's soggy, familiar embrace. He couldn't have greeted his own daughter with any more heartfelt enthusiasm. His generosity tore open her fresh wounds, letting in the air they needed to heal. She crumpled into his arms, allowing herself the long-denied luxury of crying on a shoulder broad enough to absorb her tears.

"There, there, girl," he murmured when the tumultuous shaking of her shoulders had eased. "Stand back, why don't you? Let me have a look at you."

She obeyed unthinkingly, dabbing at her nose with the back of her hand. Lord Howell surveyed her masculine garments with a curious eye, then beamed at her with genuine affection. "None the worse for your adventures, I see. Your poor father has been going out of his mind with worry. Almost got his silly self courtmartialed by absconding with one of the King's warships without waiting for His Majesty's approval. Of course, His Majesty, being a father himself, took pity on him when he returned, half mad with grief at failing to retrieve you."

Mad indeed, Lucy thought bitterly. Probably foaming at the mouth with rage.

She was spared fabricating a suitable reply by the abrupt shift of Lord Howell's attention to the fo'c'sle behind her.

The Earl's mouth fell open in disbelief. "Claremont? Is that you, fellow? I thought you'd skulked off in shame after the abduction. Good God, I hadn't realized Lucien had hired you to rescue his little girl. What a splendid job you've done! You're quite the hero, aren't you?"

Lucy held her breath, afraid to even blink for fear her expression would betray her. A wild hope thundered in her breast as she realized the Admiral, in his desperation to conceal his own misdeeds, still hadn't made Gerard's identity public. Please, God, she silently prayed, turning to watch him descend from the fo'c'sle with her heart in her throat, please let him brazen it out.

Brazen it out he did, swaggering across the quarterdeck with a dazzling bravado that made her mouth go dry with yearning. "Spare me your accolades, sir," he drawled. "They might impress Gerard Claremont, but I can assure you Captain Doom hasn't the vaguest interest in them."

CHAPTER THIRTY-ONE

LUCY CLAPPED A HAND OVER HER MOUTH to smother a moan of horror.

To Lord Howell's credit, he looked genuinely aggrieved, not the least bit elated at the prospect of hooking such a remarkable catch. "I say, Claremont, are you trying to tell me that *you're* Captain Doom?"

Kevin plunged down from the fo'c'sle. "Balderdash! He's nothing but a craven impostor. *I'm* Captain Doom!"

Without even looking, Gerard swung his fist back and smashed it into his brother's face. Kevin went down like a stone.

Gerard's merry grin was unrepentant. "*I'm* Captain Doom. *He's* unconscious."

When Lucy came rushing at him, Gerard sighed, reluctant to dispose of her in like manner. One look at her frantic face and Lord Howell would clap them both in irons. Feinting to make it appear her motion was his, he seized her around the shoulders, whipped his pistol from his breeches, and pressed it to her temple.

"Unless you'd like our next dance together to be the gallows hornpipe," he muttered into her ear, "I suggest we make this convincing."

Lucy had no trouble making it convincing. She was furious. Gerard was proving to be no less a tyrant than the Admiral, always making high-handed decisions about her future without consulting her.

"Why did you confess, you idiot?" she bit off beneath her breath, squirming wildly in his less than tender embrace.

"He's a smart man," Gerard replied through clenched teeth, wincing as her ruthless heel ground his toes into pulp. "It wouldn't have taken him long to figure it out for himself. Dammit, listen to me! We haven't much time. When we get to London, I want you to go straight to Smythe."

"And you, sir, can go straight to Hades," she snarled.

If Lucy had reverted to addressing him formally, Gerard knew he was in dire straits. Afraid she was going to incriminate herself out of sheer spite, he raked back the hammer of the gun.

Lucy went limp with shock, wondering if he might actually shoot her for smashing his toes. She suppressed a hysterical giggle, finding it utterly absurd that even while he was holding the balance of her life in his unscrupulous hands, she could take such perverse pleasure in the warmth of his arms around her.

The deck threatened to erupt into anarchy, the crew of the *Courageous* drawing steel to compensate for their waterlogged pistols, their reluctant hosts bristling at the threat to their captain. Apollo stepped forward, using nothing but his imposing size to coax one whey-faced lad into sheathing his sword. The *Retribution*'s crew might be outnumbered, but they weren't out-manned.

Gerard's voice rang with authority, stilling them all. "I have only one condition for surrender, Lord Howell."

The Earl's worried gaze flitted across Lucy's face. "What might that be, sir?"

"That my crew's valiant and self-sacrificing actions in coming to the aid of the *Courageous* be duly noted and amnesty considered for each and every one of them."

Lord Howell nodded somberly. "I shall note it in my log with all due gravity. But what of yourself, son? Have you no plea to make on your own behalf? For leniency, perhaps? A more merciful execution by shooting? A promise not to display your body for the amusement of the masses?"

Gerard felt Lucy's flinch all the way to his bones. Not even Lord Howell could grant him the one thing he wanted—time. Time to stand before a minister of God and vow to cherish this woman for the rest of her life. Time to watch her slender body ripen with his child. Time to romp in the autumn leaves with their grandchildren. But most precious of all, time to explain to her that he was tired of running. That without her by his side, there was nowhere left to run.

"I'll tell you what I want, sir. To be rid of this spoiled little bitch." Gerard gave Lucy a shove, praying it would be hard enough to remove her from harm's way for good. She stumbled to her knees at Lord Howell's feet. Tossing her hair out of her eyes with a jerk of her head, she glared at him disbelievingly, her gray eyes smoky with hurt. He sneered down at her with all the contempt he could muster. "There ain't no ransom worth having a woman like her aboard my ship."

Laying a hand on Lucy's shoulder, Lord Howell said gently, "I'm afraid it's no longer your ship, sir. Seize him."

Lucy watched in fierce misery as the crew of the *Retribution* was stripped of their weapons and directed to the lower fo'c'sle for interrogation. Gerard vanished into the shadows of the hold, flanked by two burly sailors.

Lord Howell tugged at her elbow, helping her to her feet. "Don't worry, child. The rascal will soon be in irons where he belongs." Attributing her bleak shudder to the cold, he draped an arm over her shoulder to block the frigid wind. "I can't even imagine how overjoyed your father will be to see you."

Lucy averted her grim face from his kindly gaze. "Neither can I, sir. Neither can I."

♥   ♥   ♥

Over a century earlier, the body of Captain William Kidd, preserved by tar and bound in a metal harness, had been left to swing from a gibbet over the choppy waters off Tilbury Point. Some claimed that on windy nights his chains could still be heard dancing in the wind, their eerie creaking a reminder to honest seafaring men everywhere that the path to hell was paved with noble intentions.

As the *Retribution* cut through the water of the Thames toward Greenwich, crowds of curious onlookers gathered on the banks to pay tribute to a man who had failed to heed that warning.

Rumors flew up and down the river on wings of excitement at the odd spectacle of a pirate schooner boasting the rippling splendor of the King's own standard. Six years before, London had welcomed the man now calling himself Gerard Claremont as a conquering hero. A city that loved its sinners with no less ardor than its saints, it prepared to embrace Captain Doom with equal enthusiasm, its delighted denizens thronging the dock where he was to disembark hours before his arrival.

Ignoring the grumbling of the sailors and dockhands trying to carry out their duties, they milled in pleasant chaos, both the poor, starved for a taste of romance in an existence consumed with daily survival, and the wealthy, thirsting for a thrill to flavor their jaded lives. Many of those were content to watch from the open doors of their luxuriant carriages rather than risk offending their delicate nostrils with the salty stench of rotting fish and the earthy taint of the merchants, prostitutes, and costermongers peddling their wares on the narrow planking walks.

Shortly before noon, the ship was finally spotted by a small boy who had honed his vision with expectation. A pall of speechless wonder fell over the crowd. Even the reporters paused in making their notes, their imaginations captured by the forbidden majesty of the outlaw schooner, her grim beauty unscathed by the winter sunshine. An approving roar went up from the crowd, infusing the scribes with purpose. Their pencils flew over their pads in a desperate attempt to describe a legend with only the fickle vagaries of the written word.

The crowd's excitement surged as the schooner was brought to heel and a ramp laid in place. Both sailors and rogues spilled out with utmost haste, as if eager to escape the vessel's cramped confines and the displeasure of each other's company. Even the most casual of observers would have wagered that the short journey had not been an uneventful one.

A freckled lad in civilian garb sported two black eyes, presumably earned by defending his captain's honor. His plump companion, wearing a pair of cracked spectacles and a scarlet kerchief, leered at a bouquet of well-dressed ladies huddled beneath pastel parasols, eliciting a trill of delighted giggles and at least one convincing swoon. The woman was revived by the fluttering attentions of her companions only to faint dead away as a towering behemoth, his skin the rich hue of ebony, strode past in stoic silence.

Anticipation mounted as the ramp cleared. The throng craned their necks for a glimpse of a breed of rebel whose era had come and gone, leaving their mundane world safer, but duller, for its passing. They barely noticed a diminutive figure hovering on deck, her hair smoothed into a neat chignon beneath the hood of a navy cloak.

Their patience was rewarded by the emergence of a man, flanked by four armed guards, at the top of the ramp. His disheveled appearance did nothing to detract from his striking good looks or his air of authority. Even shackled, his step was laced with the fleet grace of a man born to reign on the high seas.

Gerard blinked, blinded by the pale sunshine, deafened by the unexpected roar of adulation. Fearing his presence might incite mutiny, Lord Howell had kept him chained belowdeck for the brief duration of the voyage. The seething mass of humanity on the docks jolted his drowsy senses to life.

Prodded by the muzzle of a musket against the small of his back, he started down the ramp. One of the guards muttered a curt warning as his brother elbowed his way to his side.

Kevin's voice carried beneath the roar of the crowd. "Would you listen to that? And they haven't even heard of your daring rescue of the crew of the *Courageous* yet! Why, I'll wager you're destined to become a popular hero."

"Sort of a seafaring Robin Hood, eh?" Gerard

snorted in bleak bemusement. "They're a fickle lot. They'll cheer just as loudly when I'm convicted."

"As should I after that nasty poke you gave me." Kevin pinched the bridge of his nose, reducing his rich baritone to a nasal tenor. "I think you broke it."

"It'll do you good, brother. Now maybe you'll be able to find a wench prettier than you are."

"I wasn't lying, you know. I *was* Captain Doom. For two brief, glorious months."

Gerard didn't care to remember how *he'd* spent those brief, glorious months. For a man with no future, dwelling on the past was an exercise in futility. But as they reached the bottom of the ramp, he could not stop himself from murmuring, "How is she?"

The determined thread of cheer in Kevin's voice unraveled. "Holding up. Bravely struggling to maintain this charade you've forced upon her. But I'm afraid it's only a matter of time before she cracks—"

"Father!"

The joyous ripple of sound jerked both their heads around. Lucy flew past them in a rush of fresh, lemon-scented air, her arms thrown wide as if to embrace all of London. Fascinated by this new drama, the crowd parted to let her through. Her hood fell back as she flung herself into the arms of a regal figure garbed in the blue and gold braid of an Admiral of the Fleet. Only the most astute observer would have noted the infinitesimal heartbeat of hesitation before he welcomed her into his arms.

"—beneath the strain," Kevin finished lamely.

Gerard sucked in a breath through clenched teeth, stunned by the force of his unjust anger. "Quite convincing, isn't she?"

Crippled with irrational jealousy, he watched the Admiral bend his snowy head to his daughter's sunny one, earning the crooning approval of the charmed crowd. The Admiral could not resist angling a glance of gloating triumph in Gerard's direction.

A musket prodded him between the shoulder blades. "March, Doom. You've a rendezvous with the hangman."

Gerard wheeled around with such ferocity that the man recoiled as if the chains binding him were nothing more than silk ribbons. He curled his lip in an icy sneer. "Don't fret. The bastard won't start without me."

Gerard's last sight as they ushered him into the cart that would bear him to his dark, cramped cell at Newgate was Lucy's coolly averted profile framed by the gilded window of her father's carriage.

♥　♥　♥

Lucy sat stiffly in the carriage seat opposite her father, her hands folded in her lap. She wished for a muff to hide their betraying tremor and tried not to think of the many times she had shared this vehicle with her bodyguard.

She stole a glance at the Admiral from beneath her lashes, reminding herself that he was no longer her father. His formidable presence made that reality more difficult to remember. She studied him with a newly critical eye, wondering how she could have been so blind to the debauched corpulence weighting his features, the spidery webs of dissipation around his eyes.

It seemed she had never stopped seeing him through the adoring eyes of an affection-starved child. She didn't know whether to feel pity or contempt for that poor deluded creature.

The Admiral gazed out the window, watching the scenery unfold with blunt indifference. He was biding his time, she knew, like a hawk waiting to swoop down on a helpless mouse. She only prayed that by the time he realized she'd sharpened her teeth on a predator far more worthy of her efforts, it would be too late to spit her out.

He turned his penetrating gaze on her. "Are you well, daughter?"

So that was how it was to be, eh? They were to fall right back into their roles of overbearing father and dutiful daughter. What did he expect of her? That she rush home and resume work on his memoirs as if he hadn't tried to murder her in cold blood? The scope of the man's vanity was astounding. All she had to do was twist it to her advantage.

She forced a smile, hoping to inject just the right note of wry bitterness into her voice. "Quite well, Father. Our devoted Mr. Claremont was nothing if not shrewd when it came to his own profits. He knew he'd get little reward for returning damaged goods. I rather think he enjoyed playing the gallant with me. For those not born to it, it must be a challenging diversion."

"Harrumph."

Lucy had almost forgotten how infuriating his snorts of disapproval could be. Perhaps he wasn't a hawk after all, but a bellicose moose, pawing at the ground, preparing to charge. She smothered an ill-timed giggle behind a delicate cough.

His cold gaze raked her, chilling her everywhere it lingered. "It might still be wise to have my physician examine you. You may have suffered an injury you're not aware of."

Lucy suppressed a shudder at the memory of the doctor's icy, invading hands. This time, she might not pass his impersonal examination. She wondered how the Admiral would react if he inadvertently discovered she was carrying Gerard's child. Not even her dread of the consequences could entirely squelch a primitive thrill at the possibility.

She met his heavy-lidded stare coolly. "Whatever you think best, Father."

Ego soothed, he settled back in his seat. The squabs groaned beneath his weight. "I suppose the rogue kept you entertained with tales of your depraved father's villainy."

Whatever reaction the Admiral might have expected, it was not Lucy's chiming laughter. "I had never heard such fantastic fables. Royal commissions that vanished into thin air. Buried treasure. Noble men imprisoned unjustly. Why, I thought I'd stumbled into one of those absurd fiction novels you'd always warned me against! I half expected to return and find you'd taken to the high seas with a patch over your eye and a jug of rum in your hand." She swiped at her streaming eyes. "Can you believe he thought me harebrained enough to accept such ridiculous accusations without even a shred of proof? The man is clearly unbalanced, driven by his own delusions to these desperate acts."

The Admiral favored her with an indulgent smile she would have gladly given her life to receive only a few short weeks ago. "The man obviously forgot whose daughter he was trying to dupe."

And just whose daughter would that be?

His ruddy face clouded and, for an instant, Lucy feared her expression had revealed too much. "I must confess that I've been deeply troubled by a certain unresolved matter between us."

"What is it, Father? It aggrieves me to see you so distressed."

"Men who are given great authority are often required to make great sacrifices. Such was the grave position I found myself in at Tenerife." His sigh was so heavy, it ruffled her hair. "I could not afford to concede to the miscreant's demands, nor could I allow him to slip from my grasp to continue his reign of tyranny over the seas. I had no choice but to fire upon his vessel despite your presence. I only hope you can find it in your heart to forgive me."

Had playing cards with Kevin not taught her the strategic value of a bland countenance, Lucy would surely have betrayed herself with a skeptical snort to rival any moose's. "There's nothing to forgive. If anyone understands what you've sacrificed in the pursuit of your duty, it would be me. No harm was done, Papa, so let us speak of it no more."

For a moment, Lucy thought she'd overplayed her hand. She'd never called him *Papa* in her life.

But to her surprise, he reached over and patted her folded hands. "You're a good girl, Lucy. A fine daughter."

His praise, delivered too late and for all the wrong reasons, nearly choked her with rancor.

♥ ♥ ♥

As they descended from the carriage to the paved cobbles of Ionia's drive, Lucy's step was lightened by a nervous expectancy so acute she was afraid she was going to float away if it wasn't soon relieved. She took the Admiral's proffered arm purely to anchor herself. It might have been her overwrought imagination, but he seemed to be leaning on her more than his cane.

Guided by Fenster's gnarled but capable hands, the carriage rolled on to the stables as they marched up the walk to the front stairs, their identical postures so rigid they might have been leading a formal processional.

The front door creaked open. Lucy's heart danced in her chest to the seductive song of hope.

The music came to a discordant halt as a cadaverous figure in satin livery and powdered tie wig appeared in the doorway. "Good afternoon, sir," he intoned, his ponderous voice lacking the crisp snap of Smythe's. "And this must be your lovely daughter."

Lucy's step faltered. "I don't understand. Where . . . ?" For the first time, her courage deserted her, scattered by the unthinkable nature of the question.

The Admiral shook his head sadly. "I didn't want to mar your homecoming, my dear, but I'm afraid there's something you should know."

CHAPTER

THIRTY-TWO

LUCY WAS RELIEVED TO FIND THE WARDS of the Greenwich Hospital for Seamen spacious and sunny. In the two weeks it had taken her to escape the Admiral's watchful eye, she had envisioned a wealth of horrors, most of them inspired by once listening to Sylvie give a colorful, if exaggerated, lecture on the monstrosities committed against the helpless inmates at the Bethlem Hospital for Lunatics in Moorfields.

"Aye, we takes pride in our lads, we do," Mrs. Bedelia Teasley proclaimed as she bustled ahead of Lucy down the broad corridor lined with drowsing old men. "We give 'em mutton on weekdays and beef on Sundays with a pint o' porter to wash it all down. It's the porter they love best. Ain't it, Willie?"

The blind seaman she chucked under the chin gave her a toothless grin, his face wizened beneath an old-fashioned tricorne hat.

She stopped in front of a heavy door to fish a key from her voluminous apron. "Of course, there ain't no charity provided for your Mr. Smith. He's to have only the best of everything. The finest linens. The freshest rations. The best grade o' laudanum." She inserted the key in the lock and gave it an expert twist. " 'Spare no expense to make him comfortable,' the Admiral says. He's a fine chap, your father, lookin' after his own that way."

"Yes, he is," Lucy murmured absently, swallowing her dread as the door swung open.

The cell was spacious and clean, its walls white-washed, its wooden floor freshly swept. Sunlight filtered through the iron bars at the window, casting a hazy glow around the shrunken figure huddled in a wheelchair below its sill. A white bandage circled his brow.

Lucy took an involuntary step toward him, besieged by a wave of helpless love.

Mrs. Teasley's voice dropped to a doleful whisper. "He may not know you, dear. He just sits like that, hour after hour, starin' at nothin'. He don't sleep much neither. I hear him thrashin' about at all hours, callin' out a woman's name. Sometimes it's Anne. Sometimes Marie." She shook her head sadly. "We get a lot like him here. They usually don't last through the winter."

"May I have a few moments alone with him?"

The woman threw a guilty glance into the corridor. "It's against the Admiral's orders. He don't want him fatigued." Her broad face crinkled in a conspiratory wink. "But I don't see how a few minutes alone with a pretty girl could do him harm."

Mrs. Teasley departed, but Lucy stood rooted to the floor. The kindhearted woman had no way of knowing how much harm she'd already done him. After all, her hands might have passed the cannonball that had put him in this place.

Drawing in a shaky breath, she crept toward the wheelchair. Smythe's hair, grayer than she remembered, was slightly tousled by the bandage. He wouldn't like that, she thought, reaching to correct an errant strand with her fingertips. He wore a silk dressing gown she recognized as a faded castoff of the Admiral's. A blanket had been tucked around his legs to protect him from the chill. His hands lay limp in his lap. It was only after noting all of those irrelevant details that Lucy allowed herself to look at his face.

His expression was bland, the twinkling intelligence in his eyes replaced by a vacant stare.

"Oh, Smythe." Overwhelmed by a sense of loss, not only for this man she loved so dearly, but for all of her hopes and dreams, she sank to her knees in the folds of her cloak. She gathered his cool, dry hands in her own, warming them against her cheeks, bathing them in her tears.

Lucy.

The croaked whisper was so faint she might have imagined it.

She slowly lifted her head. Smythe's unfocused gaze had drifted downward. Sadness weighted the corners of his mouth. "So sorry, Lucy. So many mistakes."

He sighed, threatening to slip back into that netherworld of consciousness, dismissing her as a dream or a ghost. Yet instead of closing his eyes, he gazed directly into the brilliant sunshine, his tiny pupils almost swallowed in murky pools of brown.

He's to have only the best of everything . . . the finest linens . . . the best grade o' laudanum . . . he's a fine chap, your father, lookin' after his own that way.

Lucy flew to her feet. She snatched at the cotton bandage wrapped around Smythe's brow, unwinding it with careless haste. She pushed back the lank hair falling over his temple to discover a gash that had probably been nasty at its inception, but was now scabbed over and healing well. His skull bore no indentation. She pressed the back of her hand to his brow. It was cool and dry with no sign of the dreaded brain fever the Admiral had admitted him for.

She caught his shoulders, giving him a fierce shake. "Smythe! Look at me! It's Lucy! I'm here, Smythe. I'm really here. *Look at me!*"

At first she thought her pleas had been in vain. Then his gaze shifted, almost imperceptibly, to her face. She rewarded him with a tender smile. He lifted his trembling hand. It drifted over her hair, its touch as intangible as a breath of hope.

"Thought you were dead," he mumbled. "Thought I'd killed you."

"No, Smythe. I've alive and well. Listen to me. The Admiral is keeping you drugged. He wants you out of the way until after they execute Gerard. Do you understand me?" She curled her fingers in the lapels of his dressing gown, desperate to communicate her urgency. "They've locked him up, Smythe. In chains. In the dark. They're going to hang him if we can't provide proof of his innocence. You have to help me!"

Smythe's eyes fluttered shut. That was when Lucy realized his withdrawal ran deeper than battle fatigue or even a forced addiction to the laudanum. He was suffering from a sickness of the soul, giving in to the temptation to retreat to some safe, becalmed waters where his regrets could not follow. Lucy was frantic, the prospect of coming so far only to fail utterly unbearable.

If her entreaty couldn't shake him out of his complacency, perhaps her wrath could. Ruthlessly tamping down her compassion, she sharpened her tone until it could have flayed his fragile, papery skin from his slack bones.

"Stop being such a coward! I know it was you. You were the one who betrayed him. You acted as my father's agent and robbed him of everything he was, everything he could have been. You owe him, dammit!"

Smythe turned his head from side to side in a vain attempt to escape the searing light of truth. Lucy had to strain to hear his broken words. "Had no choice. Admiral threatened to tell you he wasn't your father . . . to cast you out in the streets. You were only a child . . . couldn't bear it."

With an effort that agonized her, Lucy kept her voice chilly with rebuke. "So you duped an innocent man?"

Smythe opened his eyes. For the first time, they seemed to focus on something beyond his own pain. "A good man. Young. Gifted. Eager to serve his country. His whole life before him."

"Is that why you didn't expose him when he came to Ionia?"

Smythe nodded. He moistened his parched lips, his speech flowing easier with each halting word. "Always believed in second chances. My hands were tied, but I thought he'd be clever enough to rout the Admiral. Never dreamed he was the sort of man to take you . . . hurt you . . ."

Lucy gave his hands a fierce squeeze. "He didn't hurt me. He couldn't hurt me if he tried." Only too aware that her face was drawn with strain, her eyes shadowed from lack of sleep, she added, "Not intentionally anyway. Your instincts were sound. He's a good man. An honorable man. But the Admiral plans to testify against him. To see him convicted not only for his current crimes, but for acts of piracy committed six years ago. Without that letter of marque, he'll hang for sure."

Smythe's head fell back. "S'gone," he mumbled. "Destroyed it."

Lucy's heart plummeted. She sank back on her heels, her gaze going as bleak and unfocused as Smythe's had been only moments before.

A wracking cough shook Smythe's spare frame. Lucy's concern turned to shock when that cough turned into a feeble chuckle. "He thought I was fool enough to destroy it. Arrogant bastard always underestimated me. It was my only leverage if he threatened to cast you out again."

Smythe crooked a finger to beckon her nearer. She moved her ear next to his mouth, listening intently to what he had to say, then nodded her understanding with dawning joy.

She straightened, longing to give him a gift of equal value in return, but knowing that was impossible. She reached into her cloak, drew out a ledger, and laid it in his lap. His hands shook as they enveloped the dog-eared diary of Annemarie Snow.

Lucy peered into his face, gathering her courage to ask the most difficult question of all. "Are you my father, Smythe?"

The regret on his face was so keen that she knew the answer even before he spoke. "Would to God that I were. I was your mother's friend, her only confidant, but never her lover."

Lucy's disappointment burned her throat like acid. "Then it's true. She didn't even know who my father was."

"Nor did she care." At the bitter cast of Lucy's features, Smythe swallowed, gathering all the eloquence he could summon in his muddled state. "All she cared for was you. The Admiral quit her bed shortly after they were married, yet she was determined to have a child. She knew Lucien would never divorce her. That he would always provide for her and the child for fear of scandal. I thought it a mad scheme from the start, but I could deny her nothing."

Perhaps she needed something to nurture. Gerard's words, so perceptive, so compassionate, so like him, echoed through Lucy's mind. God, how she missed him!

Smythe reached out to stroke her cheek, his tender gaze riveted on her face. "Don't judge her too harshly, my dear. She loved you. She risked everything to have you, even her life. I'll never forget the joy in her eyes when I placed you in her arms."

Lucy bowed her head, humbled by his generosity. He had given her a gift more incomparable than any he had bestowed upon her before—her mother's love, an emotion so sweet and fierce that it transcended even the barriers of time and death.

She threw her arms around his neck. He returned her embrace, the strength in his hands increasing with each whispered word. "You don't know how many times I longed to gather you into my arms. But I was afraid the Admiral would send me away. So I was forced to stand idly by while he browbeat your sweet spirit into submission."

At the harsh reminder of the Admiral's cruelty, Lucy was beset by a fresh sense of urgency. She drew back to gaze into Smythe's eyes, finding in their depths a ghost of a familiar spark. "Pretend to take your medicine, but don't swallow it. It's best we let the staff of the hospital believe your condition unchanged for now. I'll be back for you. I swear it."

He seized her hand, squeezing it tightly. "Take care, my love. He's not one to concede defeat gracefully."

Lucy's face hardened. "Then perhaps I'm more like him than either of us would care to admit."

♥ ♥ ♥

On the day Gerard Claremont, alias Captain Doom, was to be tried for multiple acts of piracy spanning six years, the abduction of one Miss Lucinda Snow, and high treason against His Majesty the King, Lucien Snow awoke in a frightful snit.

His temper worsened when breakfast was served late, his kippers were cold, and the medals he had chosen to display on his favorite uniform when he made his testimony that afternoon had yet to be polished.

Damn Smythe anyway! he thought, slamming the lid back on the serving tray. The blasted traitor had done the work of ten servants. The man's defection had carved an enormous hole in his beloved routine.

Perhaps after Claremont was dead, he mused, he would invite his butler back into the household. By then, the man should be docile enough. Not only would he have the questionable fate of his insipid Lucy to fret about, but the Admiral could parcel out just enough laudanum to ensure his loyalty. Perhaps he would even look into procuring some opium.

Cheered by the image of a bright and orderly future, the Admiral dressed himself, not wanting that ridiculous fop he'd hired as a valet hovering about on such a momentous occasion. When he was satisfied with his appearance, he went to the wardrobe and removed his dress pistol. The weight of the weapon fit comfortably into his hand.

Today justice would be served, if not by the court, than by him. He'd already offered a substantial bribe to two of Newgate's guards. If the jury showed signs of delivering a less than satisfactory verdict, a dramatic escape attempt would ensue.

Slipping the pistol into his sash, he admired his reflection in the floor-to-ceiling pier glass.

When Claremont broke free of his chains and raced for freedom, he would have no choice but to gun him down cold. After all, what else was a hero to do?

CHAPTER THIRTY-THREE

KEVIN CLAREMONT HAD PROVED HIMSELF an excellent judge of human nature.

On the afternoon of his brother's trial, the benches and galleries of the Old Bailey were filled to overflowing with a seething mass of supporters, a surprising number of them women. There wasn't a newspaper in London or any of its outlying counties that hadn't published a dramatic account of Gerard Claremont's daring rescue of the crew of the *Courageous* and his noble sacrifice of freedom for country and king. It was the stuff of irresistible romance and Captain Doom was being hailed as a hero from Surrey to Suffolk.

"There he is!"

"Gawd, 'e's a 'andsome fellow, ain't 'e?"

One woman waved a sketch of his profile she had purchased for a hard-earned ha'penny. "Ye can carry me off, Cap'n Doom. Won't have to worry 'bout me defendin' my virtue, 'cause I ain't got any!"

The crowd roared with bawdy laughter as Gerard was led through the ranks of his admirers by two armed guards. His own grasp of human nature was even keener than his brother's. He knew that by noon tomorrow, these same zealous souls would be thronging the courtyard at Newgate with baskets of food and bottles of gin to watch him hang.

He acknowledged their raucous cheers with a gracious nod, playing his role of doomed hero to the hilt. Someone might as well get some enjoyment out of this farce, he thought, and it damned sure wasn't going to be him.

A roar of approval from an upper gallery brought a genuine smile to his lips. His crew had chosen their seats as the ideal spot from which to heckle the proceedings.

"Give 'em hell, Cap'n," Tam shouted.

"Likewise, sir." Pudge waved his kerchief in a jaunty salute.

Their familiar faces gave Gerard a pang of bittersweet satisfaction. This time he would go to his fate without dragging his crew along with him. As he'd requested, the King had granted them an unconditional pardon due to their valiant actions in the *Courageous* incident, provided they vowed to never again turn their talents to piracy. His Majesty was obviously hoping such benevolence would appease a populace already resigned to Gerard's impending martyrdom.

Only Apollo was absent. Gerard's request that the imposing African be allowed to represent him had been met with pitying contempt. The magistrates didn't believe the dark-skinned "savage" capable of speech, much less eloquence. He'd been banned from the courtroom for fear his startling appearance and unpredictable temperament might cause a riot. They'd proceeded to assign Gerard a mousy serjeant whose wig had faded to yellow and whose breath reeked of gin.

Gerard doubted it would make much difference, for neither he nor his lawyer would be allowed to question or cross-examine any of the witnesses. His trial was to be little more than a formality. A diverting prelude to his execution.

At his brief pause, one of the guards gave the shackles at his wrists a sharp jerk. Gerard didn't even flinch. They had no way of knowing their chains couldn't hurt him; he'd been toughened to their bite long ago.

As he sank onto the bench, he discovered his brother had wrangled a seat behind his, all the better to offer irrelevant commentary, a particular talent of Kevin's. "I never dreamed being a condemned felon was such an enticement to the ladies," he whispered. "Why, they're all but tossing their drawers at you."

"Don't rush it. I'm not condemned yet."

But as the doors at the back of the court flew open and Admiral Sir Lucien Snow swept in, medals gleaming and the fringe of his epaulettes starched to crisp perfection, Gerard knew it was only a matter of time. The Admiral's passage to his seat was greeted by a gratifying chorus of boos and hisses from the gallery. The crowd stamped their feet, eager for any excuse to cause a commotion.

The judge pounded his gavel on the bench. "Silence now! I won't stand for chaos in the King's court!"

It wasn't the tiny man's querulous demands for order that silenced the boisterous mob, but the unexpected arrival of a second figure. With a collective gasp of excitement, the crowd craned their necks for a look at the most elusive object of their curiosity. Even the jurors could not resist a shy peek.

Lucinda Snow stood framed in the doorway, garbed in magnificent white from the soles of her dainty kid slippers to the ribbon of ivory satin crowning her elegant chignon. A woolen pelisse was draped over her slender shoulders and a matching reticule dangled from her gloved hands. At the sight of her, Gerard's mouth went dry with yearning.

To his acute relief, no rude catcalls, whistles, or ribald jibes accompanied her graceful promenade to the seat next to the Admiral. The Admiral did not look pleased to see her, but when had he ever?

"The press?" Gerard murmured to his brother, unable to tear his eyes away from her. "Have they treated her unkindly?"

Ignoring the warning glares of the guards, Kevin leaned over Gerard's shoulder so his words would not be overheard. "At first they were eager to paint her as a ruined woman, but her carefully calculated public appearances at soirées, the theater, and the like has convinced them otherwise. As you can see for yourself, she's behaving like a lady with nothing to hide and they're damned impressed." He couldn't resist a mocking leer. "They're speculating that she spurned your wicked advances, even at risk to her own life. She's being hailed as an inspiration to maidens everywhere, a veritable bastion of chastity, a guardian of—"

"Oh, shut up," Gerard growled. "I get the point."

Its irony failed to amuse him. While Lucy had been promoting her moral purity in salons all over London, he'd been surviving the darkness of confinement only by dreaming of her luscious body sugared with sand on the beach at Tenerife. The echo of her voice, hoarse with passion and love, had been the only thing powerful enough to drown out the inescapable clink of his chains.

There was no trace of that passionate creature in the courtroom today. Lucy looked cool and beautiful and . . . eager to see him hang.

He scowled. Perhaps the reality of having her own

swanlike neck stretched on the gallows had finally penetrated. He ought to be delighted. He'd gotten exactly what he wanted—Lucy safe from harm and protected from scandal, free to build a future with some decent, law-abiding man who had a life expectancy over twelve hours. So why did he want to wring her fickle little neck?

"If you don't stop glowering at her like that," Kevin whispered, "you're going to damage her reputation beyond repair."

Gerard jerked his gaze away from her, rubbing a tense hand over his beard. He suppressed a groan as the Admiral was called to testify. He wasn't sure he could endure the man's bombastic tirade without even a drop of Smythe's coffee to keep him awake.

It was worse than he feared. Two hours later, he was still fighting to keep his face impassive as the man discredited him, painting him as an avaricious monster who thought his scheme to defraud an Admiral of the Fleet a fine joke upon Navy and Crown. The mood of the crowd was beginning to waver. The jurors started casting him covert, but condemning, glances.

"Easily swayed, aren't they?" Kevin muttered. For the first time, Gerard heard the frustrated fear in his voice. It was one of the things he hated most about this nightmare. That Kevin would have to learn in such a harsh way that his big brother wasn't immortal after all.

He kept his own tone deliberately playful. "Don't say I didn't warn you. By the time he's through, they'll probably want to lynch me themselves."

Lucy sat silently through her father's damning testimony, never once glancing his way. Kevin poked him. He was glowering again.

Gerard breathed a sigh of relief when the Admiral finished his diatribe with a rousing call for justice, then limped back to his seat, leaning heavily on his cane for dramatic effect. Gerard was tempted to applaud the performance. As Lucy bestowed a tender smile upon the wretch, he stirred restlessly, rattling his chains.

The prosecuting attorney made a great show of examining a sheaf of papers through his quizzing glass. His nasal voice rang out. "I should like to call as an informer to the prosecution"—he paused to clear his scrawny throat—"Miss Lucinda Snow."

CHAPTER

THIRTY-FOUR

GERARD SANK BACK ON THE BENCH AS IF he'd been struck a mortal blow. Christ, he thought, even hanging would be preferable to this. Not even his brother's bracing hand on his shoulder could ease his anguish.

"My compliments," Kevin offered as way of condolence. "When you set out to make a woman hate you, you do a capital job."

The crowd's initial furor subsided into rapt silence as Lucy took the stand. She perched on the edge of the crude wooden chair as if it were a throne and she a princess determined to see a common knave punished for daring to touch the hem of her gown. Her gloved hands were folded demurely over her reticule. Gerard shot a furious glance at the Admiral, expecting to find him purple with triumph. The man looked as shocked as he felt.

Of course he would, Gerard realized. The Admiral would never approve of his daughter making a public spectacle of herself this way. Lucy must have con-

cocted this petty little revenge all by herself. He shook
his head ruefully, amazed that even as she was squeezing the last drop of blood from his heart, it could still
surge with admiration for her.

"Miss Snow," the prosecutor began, "could you
please identify the man who applied for employment
as your bodyguard"—the word drew a few ugly snick-
ers from the crowd—"this past October?"

"Certainly." She pointed a gloved finger straight at
Gerard, her composed face betraying not so much as a
flicker of emotion. He met her gaze squarely, lounging
back on the bench with deliberate arrogance.

"You are respected as a woman of superior intellect," the prosecutor continued. "I must deduce that
this blackguard gave you cause to be suspicious of his
sinister motives from the very beginning."

"No, sir, he did not." Lucy's voice was so soft that
the crowd had to strain to hear her. Strain they did.
Not so much as an indrawn breath or rustle of move-
ment profaned the tense silence. "Mr. Claremont was
quite chivalrous. He vowed to hold my life as dear as
his own."

Gerard's bewilderment grew, but he knew he
couldn't have looked half as dumbfounded as the
prosecutor. These were obviously not the answers
they'd rehearsed in his chambers.

The hall was drafty and chill, yet a trickle of sweat
eased from beneath the man's wig. "Well, ahem . . .
I hesitate to offend you, miss, but the court can only
assume the rogue was making sport of you."

Lucy's doe-eyed gaze reproached him. "Oh, no, sir.
Mr. Claremont showed nothing but the most tender
regard for my feelings, protecting me from attack on at
least two separate occasions."

Gerard realized then that something was terribly
amiss. The Admiral was unnaturally still, his waxen

features frozen in a sneer he should never have allowed the public to witness.

The flustered prosecutor drew a handkerchief from his robes and mopped his brow. He scowled at Lucy as if she were a dull-witted child, a tactic that elicited a rumble of disapproval from the crowd. "Perhaps he was only trying to gain your trust, Miss Snow. To make it easier to carry you off."

Lucy looked directly at Gerard then, her big, gray eyes softened with such tenderness that Gerard thought he would die right there and save the Crown the expense of hanging him. Was she truly so vindictive? he wondered wildly. What sort of diabolical punishment was this?

Then with a flash of horror, he realized what she was going to do. He leaped to his feet, straining against his fetters. His guards gave them a vicious tug, binding him in place. "Don't do it, Lucy! Dammit, I'm not worth it!"

Almost in the same breath, the Admiral barked, "Lucinda! Not another word! Silence yourself this instant!"

A small, secret smile played around her beautiful lips. She drew in a breath, plainly aware that every soul in that courtroom was hanging on her every sigh.

"Mr. Claremont didn't carry me off," she lied. "I accompanied him willingly. We were lovers, you see, even when we were living beneath my father's roof."

The court erupted in a frenzy of shock. Before the judge could restore any semblance of order, Lucy drew a faded oilcloth package from her reticule and waved it in the air.

Her voice rang with the conviction of truth. "The document is a bit worn from being hidden in the bottom of a gloxinia plant for six years, but I also have in my possession the letter of marque that will prove Mr.

Claremont began his career as an honorable merchant named Richard Montjoy. It was only the greed and villainy of Lucien Snow that forced him into a life of exile as the pirate we've all come to know as Captain Doom."

"You lying little whore!" The Admiral jumped to his feet, drawing something from his sash.

For Gerard, time ceased to exist, each set of impressions blurred, yet distinct enough to be forever imprinted on his memory. The gleaming muzzle of the pistol pointed at the snowy target of Lucy's breast. The triumphant flush bleaching from her face as she realized what was happening. Tam's shout of warning. The prosecutor diving behind the bench for cover. Kevin's desperate dash for the Admiral.

Kevin wasn't going to make it. The click of the pistol's hammer being drawn back cracked like thunder in Gerard's roaring ears.

The guards weren't prepared for his supernatural surge of strength. He tore from their grip, ripping both chains and bloody furrows of skin from their palms. Had his hands and feet not been fettered, he might have been able to knock Lucy out of the way. As it was, he could only lunge across the distance separating them, throwing his body across hers as a shield.

Fire exploded in his chest. He staggered, his chains suddenly too heavy to bear. Lucy threw her slight body beneath him to break his fall. Odd, he thought, as they collapsed to the floor in a tangle of arms and legs, that such a ridiculous tumble would finally put him back where he wanted to spend the rest of his life. In Lucy's arms.

She cradled him across her lap, her gloved hands frantically trying to staunch his bleeding. Scalding tears trickled from her chin to wet his cooling brow. Her soft, moist lips brushed his cheek, his hair, his mouth, limning his lips with the salty taste of the sea he loved.

"Damn you, Gerard Claremont," she said savagely, "you are the most stubborn man!"

He was surprised to discover the pain was already fading, retreating into the gray mist that had obscured the rest of the courtroom, obscured everything but Lucy's beautiful face.

He caught her wrists in his weakening grip, not wanting her to ruin her pretty gloves for the likes of him. He smiled tenderly up at her, wishing for the strength to brush her tears away, to smooth the crumpled lines of pain from her cheeks.

"No lectures, please, Miss Snow," he whispered hoarsely. "I was just . . . doing . . . my . . . job."

His trembling fingertips arched toward her face just as a veil of unconsciousness descended between them, mercifully sparing him her piercing wail of agony.

CHAPTER THIRTY-FIVE

THE GULL'S SHRILL CRY PIERCED THE SE-
renity of the rocky cove. The bird wheeled against the
brilliance of the sky, its graceful wings spread wide to
capture the wind, then made for the open sea. Lucy
narrowed her eyes against the sting of the salt-laden
spume, envying its freedom.

The airy sunshine and azure sky were a stark reminder that spring was coming to Cornwall. Lucy
wished she could summon even a small measure of
enthusiasm for the fat, fluffy lambs that would soon be
frisking over the moors, the lush wildflowers that
would sweeten her every breath with their perfume.

The sand felt cool beneath her bare feet as she
strolled along the beach. A stiff breeze tugged at her
broad-brimmed hat. She secured it with one hand, listening to the melancholy whisper of the surf against
the shore. The sea was calm today. As calm as all of
her days had been since fleeing to this haven where she
had spent her childhood summers. And just as lonely.

She conceded defeat in her battle with the mischievous wind and dragged her hat off, swinging it by its
ribbons in lazy rhythm to her stride. Strands of hair

licked at her face. She brushed them away to discover a lone figure had descended from the cliff path at the other end of the beach.

Even hazed by distance, his bearing was so distinct that Lucy's heart started thundering like a kettledrum. His gait, though stiffer than she remembered, had lost none of its confidence, his broad shoulders none of their casual grace. The wind ruffled his shoulder-length hair while the sun lovingly polished its hints of ginger.

Lucy wanted to feel surprise, but somehow she had never stopped believing he would come. She'd never met a man who hated unfinished business as much as Gerard Claremont.

He finally stood before her, his eyes somber and his face devoid of any expression she could interpret. Her toes curled in the sand. She was beset by a terrible shyness.

"Your beard is gone," she blurted out, as if he'd misplaced it somewhere on the journey.

He ruefully rubbed his clean-shaven jaw. "I have you to thank for that. Smythe shaved it off while I was sleeping. I suppose it was your idea to run off and leave me in your butler's fastidious care? Why didn't you just check me into the Admiral's cell at Bedlam to convalesce? If I'd have known you were going to be so vindictive, I would have never called you a spoiled little bitch."

"Smythe wanted to take care of you. To make up for . . ." She trailed off.

"Oh, I know what he did. He confessed all while he was spooning mutton broth down my throat."

Lucy dug a line in the sand with her toe, reluctant to meet his eyes. "And you didn't shoot him?"

"How could I after he'd explained his motives? How did he put it so gracefully? 'I did it' "—Gerard flattened a hand over his heart—" 'all for the love of Lucy.' "

Lucy shot him a suspicious look from beneath her lashes. It was impossible to tell if he was mocking her.

His hand dropped. "What about *your* motives?" he asked, his speech clipped. "Would you care to explain why you abandoned me as soon as the doctors gave you the unfortunate news that I might live?"

Lucy turned to gaze out at the sea. How could she explain how she had felt that grim dawn when they had finally told her that his strength of will was such that not even a pistol ball to the chest could kill him? Her mingled relief and guilt had been so acute that she had thought she might be the one to die from it.

"I was ashamed, I suppose. I was so furious at you for surrendering yourself. I was determined to prove that I could make my own decisions, could exert some control over my own fate." Her fingers knotted nervously in the ribbon of her hat. "But my childish stunt to publicly discredit the Admiral almost cost you your life. I thought you might not want to see me again. That I wouldn't be anything to you but a reminder of past unpleasantness."

"Then why don't we forget the past and begin again?"

Lucy drew in a shaky breath, afraid to hope. "Very well." She turned and offered him her hand, keeping her voice light to belie the risk she was taking. "How do you do, sir? I'm Lucinda Snow. My friends call me Lucy, but you may call me Mrs. Claremont if you like."

He rocked back on his heels and cocked one eyebrow. "Why, Miss Snow, is that a proposal? Shockingly forward of you, isn't it? I should hate to cause a scandal."

Lucy withdrew her hand. It was one thing to publicly confess to being the mistress of a pirate, quite another to actually assume the role. Fighting the repressions of a lifetime, she whispered, "If you'd prefer an indecent proposal . . . ?"

He sobered. His warm fingers found her chin, tilting it upward. He gazed deep into her eyes. "I fear I have only one mistress." He nodded toward the sea. "She's a jealous witch, but I adore her."

The ribbons slipped from Lucy's fingers. Her hat went limp against the sand. She turned her back on both him and the sea, no longer able to bear their beauty. "I read of your pardon," she said stiffly.

"It seems His Majesty decided that the five years I'd already served was punishment enough." Wry amusement threaded his voice. "The Admiralty is eager to help right the wrong done to me by one of their own. They've even offered me a commission. Not a captaincy, of course, but an opportunity to take the lieutenancy exam and a berth aboard one of their finest flagships."

Swallowing her selfish pain, Lucy dashed a tear away and forced a smile into her voice. "How very wonderful for you. Congratulations."

His hands came to rest gently on her shoulders. She trembled with the effort it took not to shrug them away. His pity was intolerable.

His warm breath stirred her hair. "I happen to know a certain Claremont who would benefit from a healthy dose of structure and discipline. Kevin will make a wonderful officer, don't you think? If he can stand all those months at sea with nary a petticoat in sight."

Lucy frowned. "Kevin? What about you?"

His hands caressed her shoulders. "Oh, I had to turn them down." His voice softened, its smoky tenderness sending a shiver down her spine. "After all, there's no place for a wife on board a military ship."

Snatching up her hat, Lucy spun around, her eyes widening. At that moment, a ship rounded the jagged edge of the cliff, slicing through the swells with all the majesty and grace at its command, its billowing sails bleached whiter than snow. Except for the laughing man at her side, it was the most beautiful sight Lucy had ever seen. The crisp sails captured the wind in a breathtaking promise of freedom.

A new name had been carved on the ship's bow—a name that embodied all of Lucy's hopes and dreams for the future.

Redemption.

Her misty gaze shifted to Gerard as she realized with breathless wonder that never again would the two of them be forced to brave uncharted waters alone.

"I have to warn you," he said solemnly, "that being the wife of a common merchant master may not be nearly as thrilling as being the mistress of a pirate."

She threw her arms around his neck and smothered his clean-shaven face with kisses. "Why, Mr. Claremont, you're the most uncommon man I know!"

Gerard swept her into his arms, twirling her in a wide circle. A roar of approval went up from the ship. Lucy's heart surged as she spotted Tam's bright copper head in the lookout nest, Pudge's scarlet kerchief fluttering from the rigging, Apollo's glistening brow. Leaning against the port rail was another man. A man who should have seemed curiously out of place among a crew of recently reformed pirates, yet who rode the swells as if he'd been born to seek adventure on the high seas. As warm tears fogged her vision, he relaxed his rigid butler's posture, tore off his starched cravat, and cast it into the wind in wordless tribute.

Lucy's hat went sailing in reply as she and Gerard fell laughing and kissing into the waves, eager to embark upon the greatest voyage of their lives.

ABOUT THE AUTHOR

A self-professed army brat and only child, TERESA MEDEIROS spent much of her childhood talking to imaginary friends. She's now delighted to have a chance to introduce them to her readers. She wrote her first novel at twenty-one and enjoyed an earlier career as a registered nurse before realizing her dream of writing full-time before the age of thirty. She lives in a log home in Kentucky with her husband Michael, five neurotic cats, and one hyperactive Doberman.